LOVE TO TEMPT YOU

J. SAMAN

Cover Designer: Shanoff Designs

Photography: Wander Aguair

Editing: My Brother's Editor

Proofreading: Danielle Leigh Reads

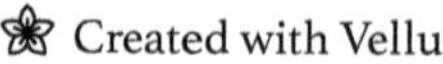 Created with Vellum

I do not typically include trigger warnings in my books. If you've read me then you know I don't hold back and I get emotional. I labored over including this, but given the age of the character and the nature of what is written (I do not get graphic, but it is discussed) I felt it important to warn readers who might already be struggling.
If you need help, talk to someone. Do not suffer in silence because you are never alone!
If you read this book, please read my end of book note for my reasons as to why I wrote this.

I hope you enjoy Keith and Maia. Theirs is a story unlike others I have written before.

PROLOGUE

Keith

Time seems to stand still, suspended above my head like an angry cloud as I stare up into the starless night through the windshield. It's going to storm tomorrow. I can feel it in my bones. If it storms, I won't have football practice. That means I can sit inside all day and jam with the guys. She'll come for that. She always does.

She loves to watch us play.

"Keith," she whispers, and I smile, turning to her in the passenger seat. She's so pretty when she smiles it makes my chest flutter.

I haven't seen her smiles in so long. Not the real ones anyway, which is what this is.

Her smiles haven't touched her eyes in months. Maybe longer. I don't even know anymore. But tonight feels different—it fills me with a burgeoning hope.

She had fun at the party. She laughed and danced with her friends.

Maybe she's finally starting to get better?

I reach out and touch her face, the bones sharp yet fragile beneath my fingers. The hollow dip of her cheek is more pronounced than it was even a few weeks ago. I frown a little at that before I can stop it, a swell of anxiety filling up my gut.

She catches my expression and pulls away, staring straight ahead and out the car window. I take her hand instead, bringing it up to my lips, and press a kiss into her palm. I need to fix the mood I just soured and any time I open my mouth lately, I practically cringe, petrified I'm going to make things worse not better.

"Tonight was fun."

She nods, turning back to me, and her face has more of that glow it had before I touched her cheek. "It was. I'm so glad I came out with you."

"School starts in a week. Senior year."

"And you're leaving for California when that's all done."

I chuckle at her excited yet insistent tone. "If the Crimson Tide and my father don't get their hands on me first."

She shakes her head, her smile light and playful. "No way. You're meant for the stage, Keith Dawson. Bright lights and drumsticks."

"And you'll be there front row."

"No matter what, I'm forever and always your biggest fan."

I stare into her eyes and kiss her palm again. Knowing she loves it when I do that.

"You should get in before your mama comes out here and tans my hide for keeping you out late," I tell her though I hate the idea of her going inside and our perfect night ending.

White teeth sparkle as her smile widens, her pale blue eyes glittering against the sliver of moonlight that somehow manages to seep into the car. "She's asleep. Both of my parents are."

I laugh, bouncing my eyebrows suggestively. "Are you inviting me in then with you, babe?"

Her smile falters. "Not tonight."

There's something in her voice that tears at me a little, and I can't understand what it is. Did I say something wrong? She hasn't let me touch her in so long, and all I want to do is touch her. Show her how much I love her. Always.

None of that other stuff matters to me because I'm here with her to the end.

"Goodnight, Keith. I love you."

I lean across the seat and kiss her lips. She opens for me instantly, her tongue sweeping against mine. Warm. Soft. Wet. "I love you too, babe. See you tomorrow, okay? Breakfast, right? I'll be back early for you."

"'Night." She steps out of the car, and it's like she's gone. Disappeared. Swallowed up by the blackness of night.

Streaks of her platinum blonde hair ghost across my face and I reach out, trying to grasp at the strands only to have them slip through my fingers one by one. My heart starts to pound.

I can't find her.

I can't see her.

I can't feel her.

Now my heart is beating too fast. *Slow down*. But it can't. I try to take a deep breath and a *gasp* ricochets through my skull. *Is that me?* No. It can't be. It was her.

The room is abnormally bright. All the lights are on and it's hurting my eyes. Why are her lights on? Dread clings icily to my skin as I drift toward her bathroom. I call out to her, but she doesn't respond.

Come on, babe. Answer me.

Ring. Ring. Ring. The blaring sound scatters my thoughts, dragging me away from her room. Away from her bathroom.

I'm dreaming. I need to wake up. WAKE UP!

I don't want her to die tonight.

My eyes snap open, my chest heaving in rhythm with the pounding of my heart. Cold sweat covers my body and I shudder, sitting up and blinking as I frantically look around.

Home. I'm home in my bed.

Fuck! I haven't had a nightmare in months.

Startling me out of my dark thoughts, my phone rings on my

nightstand, and I realize that's what interrupted my dream. I'm grateful for it until it dawns on me that it's only a little after two in the morning and this is the second time they've called in as many minutes.

Scrambling quickly across my bed, I grasp my phone, swiping to accept the call when I see it's Gus. "Hey," I answer immediately. "What's wrong?"

Because Gus never calls in the middle of the night. Not like this anyway.

"She's in labor," he announces, and I sag against my headboard in relief at the jubilation in his voice. I rub a hand up and down my face, trying to wipe away the residual heartache and panic of my dream. "Fucking Viola is in labor. Jasper just called. They're headed to the hospital."

I grew up with these boys. My bandmates. My brothers from other mothers.

And because of that, part of me is tempted to tell him about the dream I was just having. Always the same dream. Every damn time I dream about her. No matter what.

Only tonight I never made it into the bathroom.

I mentally shake my head. I don't think telling him would accomplish anything other than making him worry about me. Not to mention, this is clearly not the time for that.

"That's amazing. Wow. Another baby." I sit up a little straighter, the residue of devastation slipping away as I think about the new life that will be born tonight. A life that I already love because it belongs to Jasper and Viola and they belong to me.

He chuckles into the phone. "Did I wake you out of a dead sleep? You sound out of it."

I wince at the description he just used and ask, "Where are you?" instead of answering him because it sounds like he's in the car.

"On my way to the hospital, dude. Naomi went over to Jasper's to stay with Adalyn, so Jasper and Vi didn't have to wake her and drag her along."

Good. That's good. I can't imagine how jarring all of this will be for four-year-old Adalyn, autism or not. Her getting a good night's sleep and then meeting her new baby brother or sister is the way to go.

"I think it's a boy," I tell him.

"I'm still going with another girl and if I win, you owe me a grand and so does Henry."

Speaking of... "Did you call Henry yet?"

Gus snorts into the phone. "He's my next call. Come on. Get out of bed and come meet our new niece or nephew."

Gus disconnects the call and I climb out of bed, ambling into the bathroom as I force myself to shut my thoughts off. To focus on the new baby being born into our lives. I turn the shower on to hot and the tap on the sink to cold. I splash some water on my face and find my haunted eyes in the mirror.

Guilt swarms through my chest like a hive of angry bees. Will this feeling ever go away? Will the nightmares ever stop? Will I ever be whole again?

Gus has Naomi. Jasper has Viola and Adalyn and now his new baby.

Henry is happy living his bachelor existence having sworn off love.

And I have none of that.

Worse yet, I don't see how I ever will. Not when I've already lost everything.

1

Maia

Seven months later

In my mind, fantasies are tangible. I'm not living across the country from where I grew up, dealing with rich assholes who like to grope me while sipping their twenty-dollar martinis. I have enough money to pay off all the debt my father accrued in my name after my mother died and still make it through college without choking on life at the end of it.

But in reality, fantasies are the cruelest form of mockery.

"Maia, get your ass moving," my boss barks though his eyes are aimed directly on my tits as I leave the kitchen, a large tray filled with food and drinks that cost more than I make in a week poised effortlessly in my hands. If I wasn't going to get fired and lose what little I have left in my life, I'd kick him in the nuts.

"Fucking pig," I grumble under my breath.

"What was that?" he snaps back.

I roll my eyes as my friend Alyssa passes me, catching her amused smirk on the way.

"I said the pork looks fantastic."

I don't wait for his reply because I know he won't give one. He's already onto poor Alyssa. Our misogynist boss has no clue that my eyes are brown but knows full well what my cup size is. He doesn't hide the fact that he hires waitresses based on tit to waist ratio. He claims it's so he can order us proper fitting uniforms, which is his way of avoiding a sexual harassment suit, I guess.

This is not how I expected my life to be at the age of twenty. Not even close.

But in truth, things were worse before I came to Los Angeles, so I'm hardly in a position to complain about a job that pays my rent and manages the minimum payments of my debt.

"Here we are," I say to the table full of celebrities from some reality TV show I never cared enough about to watch.

The men are all those polished types with expensively coiffed hair, golden tanned skin, and ultra-white teeth. The women are as blonde and big busted as I am, but theirs comes from a salon and a surgeon whereas mine comes from my father and grandmother, respectively. My mother was pixie small everywhere, and on more than one occasion, I've wished I took after her more than my father's side.

"Are you an actress or a model?" one of the men asks as he takes a sip of his whiskey, his gleaming eyes appreciative as they rake over me.

I stifle a scowl as I finish setting out all the dishes and the second round of drinks, removing the empty first round. "Neither. I'm in college." Or at least I will be starting back this fall if, by some miracle, I can scrounge up the semester tuition.

"Oh. That's fun," one of the girls snarks and the others giggle under their breath, like the idea of an education is such a waste when you can earn huge money doing nothing of significance with your life other than make out with random men while wearing a bikini. I suppose from that perspective, she's right.

But that will never be me.

I straighten after I'm done and meet her with a steadfast gaze and a strong smile. "Is there anything else I can get you for now?"

"No thanks. I think we're all set," the appraising guy answers for her, and I spin on my cheap heels and leave them to it.

They're not the first ones to ask if I'm one of the many who works as a waitress in between acting or modeling jobs. We have a few struggling actors here. But that's not why I came to Los Angeles.

I finish off the rest of my tables, working my tail off until the kitchen closes and the restaurant turns more into a bar, taking in the after-hours action this city is known for. Bruce, the bouncer who works the door, walks me to my car, making sure I get in safely while he chats my ear off about his new baby boy who has colic.

"That'll get better, right? I mean, Kathy says it will, but she's so exhausted all the time and with me working nights, it's hard to help."

I smile and pat his humongous shoulder. I have zero experience with babies, but I don't think he's actually looking for me to supply him with a real answer. He just needs someone to vent to and I'm a good listener.

"Hang in there, Bruce. This phase won't last forever and before you and Kathy know it, he'll be sleeping through the night and then you won't know what to do with yourselves."

Bruce lets out a hearty chuckle, opening the door to my car for me as he always does because he was brought up with manners. I throw him a wink and a thank you for walking me to my car, and then I shut the door. Turning the key to start my car up, I clench my eyes shut, sending up a silent prayer that it starts without issue. Once it does, I blow out a breath, relaxing and leaning back in my seat.

I didn't have a chance to count my tips tonight before leaving and after glancing this way and that, determining that the lot is clear of people, I slip my wad of cash out of my pocket and start counting the bills. One hundred twenty in cash and another one hundred plus that in tips I'll collect on payday next week since it was done through a credit card.

I smile a little to myself, doing some quick mental math. "Getting there," I whisper, tucking the money into my purse and driving out of the back lot of Lavender Bar and Grille.

It's well past midnight, but in this part of town, that hardly matters on a Friday night. The street and sidewalks are littered with expensive cars and beautiful people. Sitting at a red light, I turn on my ancient radio, dialing up the sound on the song that comes on because it's one of my favorites from Wild Minds' new album.

Belting out the lyrics at the top of my lungs, I unabashedly people watch, rocking out and bopping along to the heavy drumbeat. A man in a red Ferrari convertible pulls up beside me, eyeing my car and the fact that I'm blatantly singing and dancing with harsh disdain.

It makes me laugh.

People in this city have no chill in them. Always too concerned with their outward appearance to let loose. Then I laugh a little harder.

When the hell have I ever let loose?

The light turns green and I toss him a wink and a wave, driving through and not sparing him another thought. It doesn't take me more than a few minutes until I'm past the lights and glitz of Hollywood, heading deeper into Los Angeles.

A yawn slips past my lips and I slide the shoe off my aching left foot. I'm exhausted. My job at Lavender is not my only one. I work Monday through Friday as an administrative assistant for a large law firm. Well, I'm actually just a temp through an agency, but I've been there a little more than two months now.

But tomorrow I can sleep in a bit, working a double on Saturdays at Lavender, but not having to arrive until eleven am. Sunday is my one and only day off, and I can't help myself from counting down the hours until the end of my shift tomorrow night.

Pulling up to another red, I search around, not seeing anyone coming, and start to turn right, more than anxious to get home and into bed.

The sudden blaring of a horn startles me to the point where I jump in my seat, both my hands now clutching the wheel.

But it's too late.

I turn my head just in time to catch a truck aiming straight for me, futility attempting to swerve at the last second. "Holy shit, I'm gonna die."

My eyes shutter closed and my breath stalls, my body growing rigid as it anticipates the impact I know is imminent. Half a second later, the sickening crunch of metal on metal and the shattering of glass rips through the air. My car spins and my body is thrown, the ancient seat belt doing nothing to hold me securely in place.

Sprays of glass fly every which way as the car continues its trajectory.

My head collides with the driver's side window, which is mercifully still intact. Unfortunately, that hit is quickly followed by my left forearm smashing into the steering wheel, the full force of my body weight going along with it, and I feel an agonizing *snap*.

My stomach rolls as a howling scream tears from my lips. My right hand comes up instinctively to cradle it, tears burning my eyes and falling helplessly down my cheeks, mixing with something warm and sticky that can only be blood.

Finally, the car stops moving, the front tires smashing against the curb. A few errant hisses and pops break out into the night only to die just as quickly, leaving me suffused in an eerie silence.

I'm half on my right side, pressed against the plastic center console and emergency brake. My seat belt is cinched across my chest and I can already feel the burn from it. A pain that's almost insignificant compared to my arm that doesn't take a doctor to know it's broken.

Righting my body, I cradle my arm closer to my chest, whimpering and wincing and tensing with every move I make. Without thinking, I unclick my seat belt, anxious to get it off me. The click is so loud I wince again while staring bewilderedly out my front windshield.

"I'm facing the wrong way." I shake my head at that. My phone. I need my phone. I need to call… someone.

I don't even know who to call.

I have no one to call.

"Hey," a voice rasps in sync with a sharp knock on my window. "Are you okay? Are you hurt? Can you move?"

Yes, I think, but don't say to his onslaught of rapid-fire questions.

I think I'm okay.

But I'm definitely hurt. Not dead, but most definitely hurt. "Is that why my life didn't flash before my eyes?" I whisper to myself. That would have been more like a horror real than a fond sendoff.

Panic and realization start to flow through my veins in toxic waves. My car is no doubt totaled—a car I cannot afford to replace. My arm is broken, and my head is bleeding. I don't have health insurance. Add to that, I'm so fucking broke and already in so much debt, I have no idea how I'll possibly be able to pay any of the medical bills I know will come with this.

Especially when I won't be able to wait tables with a motherfucking broken arm.

The knock comes against the glass again. Right. The other driver. I think I forgot he was there.

Only instead of sitting here, like I probably should since I'm injured, I unlock the door with my right hand and climb out. I can't stand to be in this car anymore. Not when my life is falling apart on me again. Not when I had finally just hit a good stretch and now a car accident feels like it's derailing everything.

Dammit.

You've survived worse, you'll survive this. It's all you can do. Keep fighting the current and eventually you'll make it upstream.

The man takes a large step back, giving me a wide berth despite him telling me I should stay put and we should call the police and an ambulance since I'm obviously bleeding. I tell him no. I think I do. Maybe I didn't? I don't even know. My head feels like it's on a seesaw. Everything is moving strangely.

My stomach roils and I force myself to swallow the bile as it rises up the back of my throat.

As if that's not enough there's a seriously loud whomping sound through my ears. What is that?

"Hey," the man tries again, this time a bit louder, grasping my shoulder gently as if he's afraid of hurting me but still needs to force my attention in his direction. Somehow his urgency breaks through my fog, clearing my head a little. "You're bleeding." He curses under his breath. "And your arm looks bad."

"You hit me," I reply instead of addressing any of that.

I catch him shaking his head. "No. You went right on red against the light."

"What?" I shake my head in return. That doesn't even make sense. I don't do that. I'm a good driver.

"There's a no right turn on red sign. Right there." He points to something, but I don't turn to look. "You went through it while I had a green arrow. I didn't see you until it was too late."

It's my fault then? That makes this so much worse. He'll sue me. How could I have not noticed that sign? They're all over this city. But not in my neighborhood and not at all where I'm from, so I didn't think about it.

"Can you sit back down in your car or on the sidewalk? I'm going to call an ambulance and the police. I don't like you standing. It's making me nervous."

That's when I start to lose it. When the sobs start coming and my broken body starts trembling. And fuck, that *hurts*. "I can't afford an ambulance."

"Don't worry about any of that now. We just need to make sure you're all right. But my phone is in my car and I don't feel right leaving you standing here like this. So either you're coming with me to my truck so I can make the call or you're going to sit back down in yours."

He has a southern accent. Not much. But it's there. Different from my accent that is more hillbilly and less smooth twang. I like his voice. His accent too. It's comforting somehow. I have no idea why a man with a similar accent is soothing right now but I'll take what I can get.

The man moves directly into my line of sight, pressing something against my forehead and trying to meet my eyes.

"That burns." And it makes my head spin a little faster.

"It's just a shirt. I'm trying to stop the bleeding on your hairline."

"Why are you being nice to me? No one in this city is nice."

He chuckles and goose bumps explode across my body at the sound. I shudder and he steps in closer. Almost protectively. I look up, right into his eyes before I blink and sway and then drop my gaze. His hand meets my hair, touching the long strands. It's a strangely intimate gesture. One I don't understand nor attempt to stop. "What's your name?" he whispers, his voice suddenly thick. Apprehensive almost.

"Maia Alice Angelo." Then I shake myself. Why am I giving him my full name?

Finally, I find him again, curious about the man and his voice with its smooth accent I like so much. He's tall. Like really tall. I mean, I'm tall, but he's a lot taller than I am and I'm five-ten. He towers over me. He has brown hair and light eyes.

Something about this I find almost amusing.

It's the exact opposite of me. I have light hair and dark eyes.

He's also insanely good-looking. And now that really makes me laugh because the fact that this man is hot is the absolute last thing I should be focusing on.

A sharp intake of air whirls past his lips as our eyes meet for a second time, his growing wide as they scavenge around my face. Oh no. I must be worse off than I thought. He steps farther into me again, his hand cupping my jaw and tilting it closer to his for a better look.

His thumb brushes my cheek and I emit a stuttered breath.

"How bad am I?"

He doesn't respond, his eyes growing pensive and cajoling. Almost as if he's waiting for me to say something profound.

But there is something else about him. A recognition that hits me in the most ironic, ridiculous of ways. I stand here, staring up at him, into his eyes and all along his concerned face that's growing darker and fuzzier by the second. "I was just listening to your song. I like it."

I hear him bite out a loud curse just as my legs give out beneath me and my body falls into his. The last thought I have before my world goes black is that this is so much worse than I initially thought. I caused an accident with one of the world's biggest rock stars. And there is no way that can end in anything other than disaster.

2

Maia

Beep. Beep. Beep. Beep. Goddamn, it's like someone is playing tennis in my head. Whap. Whap. Whap. Over and over again. It's incessant and never-ending and it takes me so much longer than it should to realize that sound is likely coming from me. From my heart. From the blood rushing through my ears.

From the sound on a monitor.

As in, I'm in the hospital.

I wonder if he called an ambulance after all despite my protests.

It makes me not want to open my eyes. It makes me want to linger a little while longer on the periphery of oblivion and consciousness.

Because really, what good has consciousness ever done for me?

Half the town I grew up in was addicted to either oxy or meth. That's what poor folk in Appalachia do. Because we're all poor. Even the ones with steady jobs not collecting welfare checks every month are poor. And there is no end in sight to that. All that poverty does is breed an infestation of hopelessness, which leads to drugs, and yeah, you get my schoolhouse special.

But right now, for the first time, I'm starting to understand the desire to feel something other than hopelessness. Other than poverty or despair. Other than pain. So, I keep my eyes closed and try to ignore that goddamn beeping noise as it reverberates through my skull.

Do they have to have it so loud?

It doesn't matter. I'm awake. I can't fall back to sleep the way I'd like. My thoughts are too wired. Too keyed up. Why does life have to suck so bad for so many? I once heard our preacher say God never gives us more than we can take. But I'm really starting to think that was his bullshit attempt at comfort.

Because this is more than I can take!

I had gotten out. I was one of the lucky ones.

And then absolutely everything fell apart on me. Or more like was taken from me. I had no options. No recourse.

A friend told me to go out west. That a girl who looks like me can earn some big money. So Los Angeles is where I ended up. In my 1989 Chevy Monte Carlo. A car that bespoke of exotic riches but lacked all luxury. A car without airbags.

Hence the fucking beep. Beep. Beep. And whap. Whap. Whap.

"I'm not understanding what is taking so long," a strong, somewhat raspy male voice growls. He sounds like what I imagine whiskey to taste like. Smooth with a slight burn on the end that makes you feel nothing but warm on the inside. His tone is pure agitation. Why is he here? "You X-rayed her. You fixed her broken bones and X-rayed her again. You did a CT scan of her head and sewed her up. You've taken blood and given her medicines. So why is she not awake yet when you told me specifically that she would be by now."

Oh boy. It doesn't take a calculator to add up the sum of all those tests.

"Mr. Dawson," a woman starts, her voice not nearly as annoyed as I would be if someone spoke to me that way. Suddenly that beep, beep, beep is turned way down. "Please, do not touch the monitors.

You can see her heart rate just fine without having to listen to it. The noise was disturbing other patients."

Keith is the one who turned it up? Why?

"You didn't answer my question?"

"All of her tests came out clear. But head injuries are precarious and not exact. You just have to be patient." Why is she being so gentle with him? "Give her time to wake up. Her body needs rest to heal and she has a long road ahead of her. I know you're worried about your fiancée. But she really will be fine."

Um. Say whaaaaat? Did she just say *fiancée*?!

"And her arm and fingers?" *Fingers?* "I ask for an orthopedic surgeon to come and evaluate them."

I can practically hear the woman smirking as she responds, "It was a simple and isolated break of her ulna. X-ray confirms this. The bones in her fourth and fifth fingers were reset as well. No further evaluation is required. The break does not need surgery and there is no tendon or ligament damage. She has a good cast on her, but her injuries will take four to six weeks to heal."

Four to six weeks?

It takes everything in me not to open my eyes and scream. But at this point, in the middle of this conversation, that almost feels weird. Like I'm the intruder somehow. I don't know how to reconcile this. It's impossible to have hope that things will get better when they've only ever gotten worse.

"You're telling me the only thing I can do now is *wait*?" Again, he's incredulous.

"Yes, Mr. Dawson. That is *exactly* what I'm telling you."

He huffs out a breath, and I hear a door sliding shut leaving me alone with Keith Dawson. Drummer for the band Wild Minds. That thought elicits an unexpected and ill-timed flutter in my belly.

If I were the type of girl who swooned over rock stars or celebrities, which obviously I am not, I would right now. Because I am a fan. I'm not just talking a small fan at that. I'm talking I used to save up all the money I earned working at the Dairy Queen three towns over to afford tickets to one of their shows, fan.

Katy Fucking Perry "*Teenage Dream*," panties wet, mind crazy, fan.

But like I just said, I'd only do that if I were that type of girl.

Beep. Beep. Beep. Beep.

Crap. Slow the hell down heart! You're giving us away!

"Your eyes are twitching and slightly scrunched. Plus, your heart rate just jumped through the roof. How awake are you and how long have you been like that?"

Dammit. Busted.

"I hope you don't mind that I told them I'm your fiancé. It was the only way they'd let me stay here with you, and there was no way I was going anywhere until I knew you were okay."

I blink my eyes open because there is no point in pretending any longer. It takes me a few seconds to adjust but when I do, I lock in on Keith who is so much closer than I expected him to be.

He's right here, directly beside my bed where my head is resting.

And unfortunately, with him this close to me, I realize he's *way* better looking than I originally thought. Seriously hella hot. Adonis hot. His jawline is sharp and chiseled, and the two days-worth of scruff that line it appears rough and yet soft. The kind of scruff I imagine would feel incredible against my palms or, you know, between my legs. Not that *I* would know from that.

The pale blue of his eyes—eyes that are staring intently into mine—is so beautiful it reminds me of a summer sky right before sunset, with long, dark lashes framing those puppies. With a straight nose and thick chestnut hair that has a hint of a wave to it, he is perfection.

Then there's the rest of him. Tall—that I already knew from earlier—with thick, broad shoulders and large, well-defined arms. He even has a few colorful tattoos that pop out from beneath his tee. I have no doubt the rest of him is just as impressive.

I hit a rock star with my car and he's the closest image to sex on legs I could have ever conjured up in my wildest dreams.

Only this isn't a dream.

It's a fucking nightmare.

"How bad?" And I'm not asking about myself since I just heard the tell-all between him and the nurse. "What's the damage to your car?"

Mine is totaled. I saw that much when I stepped out of it. It would cost more to fix than it's worth which means I'm stuck with taking public transportation to work.

And then I awkwardly laugh. Out loud, I think because his eyebrows knit together in confusion at the random bitter sound. I glance down. My entire left arm from my elbow to the tips of my fingers are covered in white plaster. White. Not even a cool color.

But that's not even close to the larger concern of the moment. Work.

How the hell can I work with a busted arm and hand?

I can't waitress like this. I don't think I can type either, given that the cast covers my entire left hand. Not my dominant hand, but does it matter? I'm a temp. So easily replaced.

"My car is fine. Don't worry about my car."

I shake my head at his gorgeous face. "Just tell me."

"Honestly, I don't know. I didn't look too closely. You passed out in my arms and I didn't think twice about it. I just scooped you up, grabbed your purse and shoes from your car, and drove you here. I called the police and told them about the accident. About what I did with you. Your car was towed to a lot somewhere."

I grimace, looking away, my stomach dropping to the bottom of my toes. I hear him swallow hard and something about that has me reluctantly turning back to him.

"I told the police it was my fault."

I sputter out some sort of deranged noise at that. "What?" I try to sit up, but he quickly pushes me back down, pinning me with an admonishing glare. "Why? Why the hell would you do that?"

"Because you said you couldn't afford it. And I can. My insurance won't drop me or increase my premiums. My insurance will pay for your car to be fixed or more likely just cut you a check for whatever it's worth."

Which is next to nothing, but still.

I blink at him. Stunned out of my goddamn mind. "I can't let you do that."

"You can. It's done. It's on record already. The police came and spoke to me while you were unconscious. Your statement is insignificant now that I've claimed blame."

"No..." I trail off, feeling like I must be hallucinating. No one does that. Especially for someone they don't know. Especially for someone who evidently took an illegal right and caused a major accident.

And why is he staring at me like that?

Like he doesn't want to but can't help it. *That stare.*

I shift my sore, aching body up on the gurney, glancing down as I do, only to discover I'm wearing nothing but a blue and white gown and a flimsy white blanket that barely covers my lower half.

I should be embarrassed to be in this state. I mean, I know my nipples are hard. It's damn cold in here and I can feel them popping out and saying hello. But I'm just too... angry with him to acknowledge just how vulnerable I am.

"I didn't ask you to do that. I'm not a charity case. I can take care of myself."

I know I should be more grateful to him. And I am. I truly am. But him taking blame and paying for everything makes me feel weaker and more pathetic than I already do. But honestly, how could he have known other than the look of my old car that I can't afford to pay for any of this? All I said was that I couldn't afford an ambulance. That was it.

"I don't like being in debt to people," I continue when he doesn't respond. That's an understatement. I downright loathe it.

"You're not in debt to me."

I hiss between my clenched teeth. He's too matter of fact about this. It's only infuriating me further. "But—"

He cuts me off. "There is no but. You, Maia Alice Angelo, were not at fault. You will have no hospital bills to pay. You will be compensated for your car. That's all there is to it."

Tears burn my eyes like someone doused them in acid, but I tamp my emotions down, refusing to lose this last shred of my dignity.

I open my mouth only to close it immediately because there is no way I can speak without sobbing. I'm hurt, half-naked, stuck in a hospital bed with a head injury, a broken arm and fingers, and a wrecked car.

Now this rock star is claiming full responsibility when he is absolutely not at fault. I'm perplexed he would go to these extremes. I'm flabbergasted he would put the blame on himself and pay for everything.

But I'm also leery.

And scared.

I'm really scared about what happens next for me.

By tomorrow—or wait today, I don't even know what day it is—I will be gainfully unemployed. Unhireable for at least four to six weeks as the nurse said for my arm to heal. I can't lift a tray of food. I can't type over ninety words a minute.

I am expendable.

I clear my throat and when I think I have control over my voice, I whisper, "Why?" It's all I've got left. "Why did you do all this for me?"

Something dark and broken flashes across his features before it's just as quickly gone. He sits back, putting distance between us. "Because you needed me to."

He says that like that's really all there is to it. But it can't be that simple. Nothing is. No one does anything for free in this world. Everyone expects something in return. And Keith Dawson is no different, no matter what he says. There has to be something he's after.

3

Maia

"I DON'T FUCK men for money."

He laughs. I don't.

"That's not what I'm after. That's not why I helped you. If I wanted sex, I could get that from a dozen women in this city who don't have stitches in their head and a busted-up arm. Hell, I could go out to the nurses' station and end up laid within ten minutes."

I scowl and he chuckles, smiling wide with perfect white teeth and a dimple I hadn't noticed before in his right cheek. Looking at him now, I believe everything he just said to be true.

"That's super classy. A real turn-on. I can see how you get so many women so easily," I deadpan, letting him know I'm not at all impressed by that.

He hasn't stopped grinning. His eyes haven't left my face. Not once. "I'm not saying this to sound like an arrogant dick. It's a stupid fact of my job, okay? But it is what it is and that's not what I want from you."

And because I'm a lame girl at this moment in time, I frown even deeper. Because I'm totally cute and insanely fuckable. Which makes me feel awful to even think. I'm relieved he isn't propositioning me or thinking I'm that type of girl. I'd smack his sexy mug before spitting in it if he were. I've met those guys in this town. The ones who think women are there for nothing more than to spread their legs and provide an easy, open pussy. And I've met those girls too. The type who will sleep with anyone anytime for their shot, leaving their dignity somewhere in the dust in the name of their 'dream'.

That's not me.

All I want is to go to college, graduate with a degree in psychology so that I can go on to get my master's in school psychology and be a school counselor. It's all I've ever wanted to be.

"So you admit you do want something from me?" I manage, still a bit dazed.

"That's not how I meant it, though you look disappointed that I'm not trying to fuck you."

A ghost of a smile hits my lips for the first time. "And you're insanely arrogant. That's not what my frown was about."

His eyes lock on mine, the raw intensity in them making me want to squirm and look away even as I force myself not to.

"So you admit you are disappointed," he quips, throwing a variation of my words back at me. I blink, taken aback by his suggestive tone. I open my mouth to say... something. I don't even know what, but the way he's looking at me has any retort freezing on my tongue.

His molten eyes sweep over my banged up and broken form. They linger on my lips first before meticulously gliding down my chest, over my erect nipples that salute him through my flimsy gown. They drift down over my belly, and I feel just a bit pathetic.

Bloody and fractured on a hospital bed.

If his eyes weren't gleaming with something extra that speaks directly to my long-forgotten pussy, I would think he was mocking me. His eyes find mine once more and that cocky, take no prisoners smirk re-affixes itself to his lips. "Since you're still not denying it, I'll be honest and say I wouldn't mind it. In fact, I have no doubt I'd enjoy the hell out of every second of it. You're so outrageously beautiful no man stands a chance. But no, I'm not trying to screw you. I'm not helping you so I can hold it over your head later."

"If it's not about sex, then why are you doing this?" I press.

He blusters out an aggravated sigh, but too damn bad. I didn't ask him to stay. I didn't ask him to do any of this for me. So yeah, I think I'm entitled to know the motive behind his actions that up until this point, seem completely altruistic.

Which is just a life fallacy right there. Everyone knows that.

"I already told you, you needed my help and I helped. That's it. I don't take advantage of women. Especially women who are vulnerable. I don't lie either, and everything I've done for you is on the up and up. I do not want anything from you other than for you to get better."

I stare dumbfounded. Blinking. A lot.

"Why are you looking at me like that?"

"Who does something like that for a total stranger? Did you hit your head too?" I question. "Did they check you out? X-ray and CT and whatever the hell else they do?"

"Um, no. My car has airbags—not that they even needed to deploy—and is twice the size and weight of yours. It was a tank hitting a Matchbox car."

Right. What a perfect description of what I endured tonight. That's exactly how it felt.

Still… "I'm confused. How did you know I couldn't afford to pay for any of this?"

"You told me all about it in the car as I drove you here. You were half-conscious and rambling. Non-stop."

"Oh?" It comes out as a question, considering as far as I'm concerned I didn't return to consciousness until just recently.

"Yep. You told me how you're a waitress and temp as an admin for a law firm. You asked if I had heard of them and I said I haven't. I have eaten at Lavender where you work though I'm positive I've never seen you before." A darkness pulls at his features again before he just as quickly clears it away. "You also mentioned how you don't have any health insurance."

Well, shit.

I stare at him blankly. The heat rising up my face and the rapid sounds of my beep, beep, beep, are quickly giving away my embarrassment. Despite that, I soldier on, hoping I didn't give him the tell-all book of my life. "Anything else?"

"You said you couldn't believe it was me. That you're a big fan of the band and our music."

"Oh." This time it comes out in defeat.

Keith clears his throat, looking a tad uncomfortable for the first time, but we're interrupted by the doctor who comes in to give me a final exam and go over home care directions with me. I am to have someone to stay with me for the next twenty-four hours at least. They need to check on me while I'm sleeping and wake me up a few times to make sure I'm doing okay because I have a mild concussion. I am to cover my cast when I shower, and he'll give me the name of some orthopedic doctors who can remove it when it's time and who will set me up with physical therapy.

I listen. I even smile. And when he hands me my discharge paperwork, I take it with a shaky hand. Keith hasn't left and I don't know why. He did his good Samaritan work. And when the doctor leaves, I tell him as much. His only response is to smirk. Again. That seems to be his thing and I can't find it in me to complain about that.

"How are you getting home?"

"A cab or an Uber," I say, though I know I'll be taking the bus.

"Come on. I'm driving you home."

I shake my head. "You really don't need to." And I'd really rather you not see where I live.

"Humor me."

I growl under my breath but follow him as we leave the emergency room. I just don't have any more fight in me. I'm hurting and exhausted and all I want to do right now is go to bed for the next decade.

I tell Keith my address and he punches it into his GPS with a deep frown. While he winds his way out of the hospital and out onto the streets, I shoot off a quick text to my bosses at Lavender, telling them what happened and that I'll have to miss my shift today. Then I send one to my temp agency. It doesn't even take three seconds for the main boss at Lavender, Gerald, to blow up my phone.

I peek in Keith's direction, but his eyes are on the road.

"Hello?" I answer, my heart starting to pound. Gerald has never called. Never once.

"Maia, yes, hi. It's Gerald. I'm so sorry to hear about your accident," he shouts to the point where I practically have to pull my phone away from my ear. Or maybe it's just that my head is pounding, and every sound right now feels piercing.

"Thank you, sir. I'm sorry about my shift today. I'm not sure—"

"Listen, Maia, I'm going to cut to the chase here," he interrupts, and I know what's coming before he even finishes his statement. My stomach sinks. "We can't have you working in the restaurant with a broken arm. Not only can you not waitress like that, but it's a huge liability for us."

"Um. Well, I was thinking that maybe I could hostess."

"Except we have no open positions for a hostess at the moment. How long will your arm take to heal?"

I swallow, my mouth suddenly bone-dry. I glance over at Keith again and though he's still feigning ignoring me, I know he can hear Gerald. "Four to six weeks, sir."

"How about you give us a call then and we'll see if we still have an open waitressing slot for you. We'll mail you your final paycheck. Take care now."

And he disconnects the call.

Just like that.

After over a year of working my ass off for his restaurant. Today was the first day I missed a shift and that's it. Fired.

I knew it was coming. I mean, I suspected it. But to hear it so straight off the bat? So matter of fact? It's gutting. And to make this worse, I doubt the temp agency will be any more accommodating. I transcribe at least a dozen letters or emails a day for the various lawyers in the firm. That's in addition to everything else I do there, but I need to use both hands to type.

They expect things done in seconds, not minutes.

One hand will not do.

Even if they do keep me on, I don't earn enough there to pay for my apartment, food, and make the minimum on my debts. The money I was pulling in at Lavender was everything and now I have nothing.

I don't even have a car.

My phone slips from my fingers onto the seat beside me.

A burgeoning swell of panic rises from within, and I turn toward the window so Keith can't see my agony.

I can't fall apart yet. Not in front of him. Never in front of anyone.

Maybe I can call Carvalo. Call the credit card companies. Work something out with them.

Suddenly the twang of country music fills the car and my head whips around to Keith who is focusing on the road like he's driving home his newborn baby. "Country?"

"I'm from Alabama."

"I know, but I guess..."

"Did you think I'd be playing my music? Do I look that narcissistic to you?"

He has a point, but I think I kind of did expect that. "Maybe I was just expecting more rock or indie. Like your stuff."

"I'm full of surprises, darlin'. Where are you from? You have an accent, but it's different from mine and it's not Texas either."

"Northern Virginia, right on the border of Kentucky and West Virginia. Appalachia country. My hillbilly accent throw you?"

He chuckles, rubbing a hand along his stubbled jaw. "I like it. It's soft and pretty with a bit of a bite to it. Sort of like you."

He cocks an eyebrow, and I grin a little at that before turning back to the window. I like that description of me. A whole lot. Especially him calling me pretty. Something I've been called frequently in my life, but for some reason, it means a little extra coming from him.

Like he means it more.

Which is just insanely stupid. Who gives a shit if he thinks I'm pretty? He's going to drop me off in a few minutes and I'll never see him again. I need to focus on my next steps, not a man.

"Is your car damaged?" I didn't even think to check the front of his truck when we got in.

"No. It looked fine."

That's a relief at least. I'd hate to have caused him more trouble.

"Are you going to be okay?" he asks after a quiet beat, and I wish he hadn't done that. I was hoping the music was his way of saying we didn't have to talk about it. I've been nothing but broken and vulnerable in front of him and it's not a costume I wear all that well around others.

"I'll be fine. I've survived worse."

"You live in a real crap neighborhood."

I laugh, but there isn't much humor to it. He's distracting me and I appreciate that on some level. But right now, I seriously just want to be alone. Being forced to chit-chat about my accent or my shit neighborhood is pushing me to the brink.

"Yes, it is."

He makes an angry noise in the back of his throat. "A woman like you shouldn't be living here. You're barely twenty—"

"How did you know that?" I snap, indignation flaring because it's easier to be angry than anything else.

"You told me in the car. More of your ramblings. Turned twenty last week."

Fantastic. Just freaking wonderful.

"And that is too young to be living here on your own."

I glower at him. "Who said I was on my own."

"An educated guess. Tell me I'm wrong."

I can't, so instead I shrug because even though he helped me out, that doesn't mean he's entitled to my truths. "No one should be living here or living this life," I deflect, panning my hands out the window. "But it's life and it's mine, and you've already done more than enough to help it last night. How about you don't go judging me, rock star, and I won't judge you either."

The streets are littered with homeless people, drunk or high or just sleeping on the sidewalks or in alcoves. Men and women dressed in flagrant gang colors are shooting the shit while covertly conducting business on the street corners. Barely dressed women who look like they've had a hard night are heading who knows where.

I point to a building with chipped away tan stucco and Keith pulls over his huge and expensive truck which garners more than a few glances.

"This is your building?"

"Yes, but I've got the penthouse." I wink at him. He's not amused.

This is not the neighborhood the tour buses come anywhere close to. But it's cheap and I have two deadbolts and most people don't pay me much attention. I keep to myself and they let me.

I twist in my seat to face him. I even take a second to admire him. Every gorgeous feature and perfect inch. In another life, if he weren't him and I weren't me and we had met another way, I could have really crushed on him. Arrogance and all.

I hit him and he turned that around and saved me. I still don't know why.

"Do you have someone to come and stay with you?" he asks, his tone sharp as he gives me an unhappy look that makes me want to smile. "The doctor said you needed to for at least twenty-four hours. Plus, you're gonna need help getting around with that arm."

"Thank you, Keith. I'm so very sorry about the accident I caused last night. But you took me to the hospital, and you stayed with me when you absolutely did not have to. Then you took it upon yourself to go and claim the blame for the police and insurance and even take on my hospital bills. I saw you sign whatever form that registration lady brought you. I don't know how or when I'll repay you, but I fully intend to."

He shakes his head, his jaw clenching. "I don't want you to repay me."

"And I don't want to be in your debt."

He scrubs his hands up and down his face, looking tired and worn out with the girl who keeps trying his patience. And before he can say anything else or do something else crazy, I lean across the large center console and plant a kiss on his cheek.

"Thank you," I whisper this time, trying my best not to inhale his masculine scent. Some kind of expensive aftershave or cologne that smells like heaven and sandalwood and rugged man while making me just a little dizzy with lust.

I grab my purse and hightail it out of his car. I'm two hot seconds away from giving in to this nightmare I see no way out of and bawling my eyes out, and the last thing in the world I want is for Keith Dawson to catch me doing it.

4

Keith

I'M NOT sure I've ever been this mad in my entire life. And I have absolutely no right to be. I don't know this girl. I don't know her at all. She hit my car making an illegal right on red and I should have called the police, an ambulance, my insurance company, and left it at that.

But when she stepped out of her crumpled tin can of a car and looked up at me with those terrified, big brown eyes... fuck, I couldn't breathe. I couldn't think. I just reacted.

And while she was rambling in my car and then unconscious in the emergency room, all I could do was stare. I kept looking at her hair and her adorable upturned nose and her full heart-shaped lips.

Her face.

I sat with her unconscious in the hospital and just continued to stare at her. Out of my mind incredulous. A touch scared shitless. A lot sick. And stared.

I took in every feature and tried to make sense of something that still doesn't feel like it makes a whole lot of sense.

I blow out a silent breath, desperate to get myself back under control when it's nothing short of impossible. This woman. This infuriating, stubborn, stunning woman knocked me for a loop and I'm not even talking about the accident.

I watch as the door to her building closes behind her. She didn't even spare me a backward glance, and I'm grateful for that. I should go. I need sleep and a shower and to put last night behind me. Forget like it ever happened.

So why can't I make myself leave?

I close my eyes and picture Maia, ignoring the ancient ache her face elicits. She's all sass and sharp words. But her cadence is slow, and her voice is sweet. It's different though.

She's different.

She's not her.

I heave in a deep breath and force the thoughts from my mind. Opening my eyes, I'm more than ready to leave. I stare out the window, taking in the neighborhood around me.

"You can't save her," I tell myself even as my gut twists with rage at that. A guilt embedded so deep I no longer know where it ends and the rest of me begins.

My hands scrub up and down my face.

This girl is not my problem and it is not my job to save her.

My hands fall to the smooth leather wheel and I take one last peek over at the front door to her place. She's safe as long as she's up there, but who will help her? She needs someone to check on her. Probably help with basic functions like cooking, showering, dressing. Doing things one-armed isn't easy. I broke my wrist freshman year of school and that was a bitch. But that was nothing compared to her break, and I had my parents and sisters to help me out.

She has no one.

"Fuck," I yell, the butt of my hand slamming repeatedly into the wheel. "Goddammit! She is not my fucking problem!"

I cannot go down this road with this girl.

I have enough of my own life going on and she doesn't want my help. She said so herself. She doesn't want to be indebted to me. She can take care of herself.

My hand hits the gear shift and just as I start to push it into drive, something vibrates on the passenger seat and I stop. Her phone. Her cell phone is sitting forgotten, and just like that, my resolve solidifies before I even have a chance to fight it off.

I lift her phone, and the text window pops up without my even having to unlock it. It must be from her temp agency as they're telling her they'll find someone else to fill her position in the law firm and to call them when her arm is better, and they'll try to find her a new gig.

"Right, then."

Clutching her phone, I turn off my car and hop out of my truck, hitting the clicker until the alarm makes that loud beep sound. It doesn't matter. If someone wants to boost my car, I have no doubt they'll have the skill to do so regardless of my warning.

"I wouldn't leave your truck there, man," a homeless guy says. He's sitting in the alcove of the building next to Maia's, an empty coffee cup in his hands. He looks youngish, maybe mid-thirties, and hasn't seen a bed or a shower in a very long time.

"How long do you think I have? I need to run in and check on someone."

"Miss Maia is a nice girl. She brings me leftovers from her restaurant sometimes."

I hold up her phone. "She left it in my car."

"I can holler out if anyone goes near your ride."

I smile at the man and slip a hundred out of my wallet. I walk over and place it in his empty cup. "Thank you. I'll give you another if it's still here when I come back."

The man's dark eyes light up as he takes in the amount I gave him and nods.

Maia's building has those push buttons to ring for which apartment you need, but there are no names written in any of the slots. Lucky for me someone exits before I can start pressing random buttons and I slip in behind them.

The building is dark and dirty and dank. It also reeks like someone is cooking up drugs. Either meth or crack, the chemical smell is already giving me a headache. I take the stairs up two at a time, going up to the fourth and top floor since she told me she had the penthouse. I hope that wasn't a joke and she really does live on the top floor. Otherwise, I'm going to be banging on a lot of doors.

There are four apartments up here so I knock on the first one on my right. I wait, but there's no answer and I move on to the next. A couple of floors below me a couple appears to be having a pretty heated argument in a language I mercifully cannot understand. I knock on the second door, my insides growing more restless the longer it takes to find her.

Just as I'm about to give up and go on to door number three, I hear someone moving inside. "Hello?"

It's her. That's her voice. "Maia? It's Keith."

She curses under her breath and I can't stop my small grin.

"What do you want, Keith?"

"I have your phone."

"Oh." That got her attention and I hear about five different locks disengaging before she opens the worn door a small crack and sticks her hand out, keeping her face averted behind it. She's got to be kidding me. I give her a look that says as much though I don't think she can see it. "You can just hand it to me and go."

"I need to use your restroom," I lie.

That pulls her up short and the surprise has her slipping back a few inches to glance over her shoulder back into her apartment. I catch sight of her face and it's obvious she's been crying. Her eyes are red-rimmed and puffy, the tip of her nose too. She finds me staring at her and turns away in embarrassment, wiping at the small mascara stain under her eyes. A blush creeps up her cheeks as she starts to worry her bottom lip between her teeth.

"Um. Well. It's really not much of a bathroom." Her eyes refocus themselves on me. "Besides, I'm sure you can hold it until you get home."

"And what if I can't?"

She blusters out an aggravated sigh. "Come on, Keith. What the hell are you doing?"

Good question.

Something I should absolutely not be doing, that's for damn sure.

Without waiting on an invitation, I push forward, forcing her to take a step back. "Hey! I didn't invite you in," she snaps, but she doesn't try to stop me either. Instead I catch the defeat and hopelessness in her eyes as I walk through, handing her phone back to her.

"You have a text from your other job on there. I didn't mean to read it, but the window popped up when I picked it up. I'm sorry," I tell her as I look around.

And the moment I see this place, that's it. If I thought I was resolved in the car when I found her phone and read that message, that shit has nothing on me now.

A creeping fire of fury crawls up my spine and I have to take a deep breath to snuff it out. Her apartment is clean, but that's its only redeeming quality. It's tiny, likely no more than two hundred square feet. Half the size of a regular hotel room. She has a small, closed window despite the insufferable heat and rising stench from downstairs.

Her twin-size mattress sits directly below it with a couple of storage bins acting as her closet. She has a mini-fridge and a hot plate as her kitchen. A toilet, tiny white sink that's affixed to the wall, and an open stall with a hand-held sprayer and a drain in the floor as her bathroom.

I turn on her, my mind going wild, spinning in a hundred directions. And I can't contain it. I can't stop it. She can't live here like this. Not anymore. Not hurt the way she is.

"Pack your stuff," I manage through gritted teeth. "We're leaving. You're going to stay with me."

There's a hard glint to her eyes. "Keith, this is none of your business."

I know it's not. I. Know. It's. Not. But that doesn't change anything for me right now.

"If you don't do it in the next two minutes, I will do it for you."

Anger darkens her features, staining her cheeks red but her anger has nothing on mine. I can go all day over this.

"No, you will not. My home may not be up to your standards, but I will not apologize for it. You may have helped me out last night, but I don't know you. You do not own me, nor are you in any position to dictate where or how I live my life. Now get the fuck out." She points to the door with her good hand.

"I can't do that."

"The hell you can't!" she yells in my face, working up a good head of steam and shoving at me. "I did not invite you into my life. I have enough shit to deal with. I don't need you adding to it. Please go!" she points again at the door, but her voice cracks and her chin trembles.

I soften my approach as I take a small step in her direction. "I'm not here to add to your burden. I'm here to help it. To make it better if I can. That's all I'm trying to do."

She shakes her head, not trusting me for a second. I inch in closer, expecting her to shove at me again, but she remains still, pissed-off and skeptical of my intentions.

I don't blame her.

Men have not treated this woman well. Hell, humans have not treated this woman well. But men especially if I had to guess, considering she automatically assumed I was only helping her for sex. She's young and beautiful and built like a playboy centerfold.

And men can be real pieces of shit sometimes.

"Do you truly want me to leave? To walk out that door and never come back?"

My question stuns her somehow and she spins around, giving me her back as she faces the window.

"Yes," she says after a beat, but she's lying. I can hear it. That's her pride talking, not her heart. She's scared and untrusting.

It's about a hundred degrees in here, the hot late-summer California sun is beaming straight through the glass. The acrid scent of cooking drugs wafts up through the floorboards. No one lives here unless they have no other option, or they want to be off the police radar. This girl has a story. Likely not a good one.

She could be trouble for me. For my very public image.

But right now, in this room that is nothing but the definition of desperate and broke, I don't care about my image. Or even what the guys will say when they see her... and they will have a lot to say when they see her.

She evokes every ounce of caveman-quality, alpha-male protectiveness in me, and I can't do it. I can't go despite my threats. "You deserve so much better than this."

"I don't need you to save me," she whispers, her voice gathering strength. "I appreciate what you're doing and what you've already done but now it's time for you to go."

She turns back around and the sorrow and torment in her eyes drops me to my knees.

I've seen this look before.

My hands come out and before I know what the hell I'm doing, I'm cupping her face, tilting it so she's looking directly into my eyes. I stare back into hers with an intensity I cannot hide, and for a flicker of a second, I get lost in her. My skin tingles and my heart races. If this were any other woman in any other situation, I'd kiss the hell out of her right here and now. Part of me wishes I could just so I could wipe away her misery and replace it with something else.

I smile softly into her eyes. I like that she's tall. I'm six-five and typically I tower over women. Not this one.

"Please do this for me, Maia. Think of it as my repayment for last night if that makes you feel better. But I cannot walk out of here and leave you behind. The thought fucking kills me. It's not the kind of man I am."

Tears cling bravely to her eyes, wetting her lashes, but none fall. "Why?"

There is so much pain and confusion and fear behind that one word. She's not asking why I can't leave her; she's asking why I'm so determined to bring her with me.

I can't answer that without revealing too much and I can't go there.

"All I want to do is help you. That's it. There is nothing sinister going on here. It's not about sex or anything else bad that's going through your pretty head. You need to take this, Maia. Don't let something stupid and insignificant like pride keep you here when I'm offering you something so much better. I have a nice house that doesn't smell like drugs and isn't hotter than the fucking sun."

She smirks a little and relief swims through my chest, releasing some of the tension in my muscles. My hands drop from her face and I take a necessary step back. She doesn't understand that I have to save her. I fucking have to. Please say yes, Maia. Please.

"And where would I be sleeping in your house?"

I grin devilishly because I just said it, didn't I? Men can be real pieces of shit sometimes and she's just about the most gorgeous thing I've ever seen. "You don't want to sleep with me?"

She growls and I chuckle, shaking my head and throwing my hands up in surrender.

"You'll have your own bedroom, Miss Angelo. Own bathroom too with a real shower and a door you can lock if you want. I'll even put you in the guestroom that's farthest from mine."

"Keith—"

"Maia, say yes. Please, say yes."

She puffs out a breath and spins around, indecision warring in her mind. She looks around and then down at her broken arm that's cradled against her chest. Finally, she meets my eyes again. "This is only temporary. Just until I'm back on my feet a bit."

She's warning me now, trying to steal back some of her control. She's a 'no one puts baby in the corner' chick and that's the last place I'd ever want her to be.

"Absolutely," I assure her.

Her eyes bounce back and forth between mine, doing her best to read me. Until dejectedly she whispers, "Okay. I'll pack my things then."

5

Maia

I FEEL like I'm the butt end of a sad country song. All broken down and busted. The second I had stepped out of Keith's car and entered my apartment, closing and locking my door behind me a piece of me died. A piece of me lost hope. Was so absolutely terrified out of my mind that my thoughts were gruesome and incoherent.

That's how close to the edge I just was.

Then Keith knocked on my door and swept into the room the way he did in the hospital. Bold and in control. Like a shining, valiant knight. Girls fall for that without even batting an eye. And with a man like Keith Dawson, drummer for Wild Minds and likely a gazillionaire, I can't blame them. Hell, without all that extra stuff, I can see how easy that would be.

I just refuse to be one of them.

Even if he did save my ass yet again.

I can't speak to him. I can hardly look him in the eye. I should say thank you, again, but I have a weird pride thing going on and the words are lodged in my chest, unable to be expelled. I packed all my clothes and things into the only suitcase I own. Keith carried it downstairs and tossed it effortlessly into the bed of his truck.

That was it.

The only things in that apartment I actually owned are my clothes. Everything else was there when I rented the place.

I'm not moving in with Keith, but I think it's safe to say I will never return to that apartment.

What's the point?

I can no longer afford it and I pay that rent week to week. A text to my landlord and it's done. I officially don't live there anymore.

Where I'll go after Keith's is anyone's guess, but not having the weight of that rent over my head will make losing my income a touch easier. It gives me a bit more freedom too. At least that's how I'm going to force myself to look at it. I will use my meager savings to pay my debt, and as much as it burns me up to even think it, school will have to wait at least another semester.

"Why did you give Isaac that money?"

"Who's Isaac?"

I think he knows exactly who I'm talking about and is stalling. When we left my apartment, he dropped a hundred-dollar bill in Isaac's empty cup and told him thanks. That was it. But there was something behind that. There had to be.

"The homeless man on the doorstep beside my building."

"He watched my car for me. Why did you tell him tomorrow is a better day than today?"

"Because I have to believe it will be. Or what's the point of any of this? When your chips are down and you're out there faltering, if you don't believe it can get better, then you won't survive."

Keith pales instantly, his expression more grim than I've ever seen, and he looks away from me instantly.

"Is that why you said yes to coming with me?"

I can't answer that.

In truth, I'm not sure why I said yes, other than I let a moment of weakness and despair rule my emotions. I was scared and panicked, and he presented a good case at the right moment that was just a bit too powerful for me to say no to.

I mean, what kind of person agrees to packing up their life and moving in with a man they met a few hours ago? A crazy person. A desperate person.

But when you have nothing left to lose, you have nothing left to lose by saying yes.

And I refuse to think any deeper on it because then I'll start second-guessing more than I already am and I am in no place to second-guess anything right now.

"The leg would have been better," I quietly muse, staring woefully down at my arm that is starting to feel more uncomfortable as the seconds tick. Keith's head flies in my direction, his eyebrows pinched. I point at my arm wrapped in ugly white plaster. It throbs like mad, but I'm not going to take the pills the doctor gave me. "Breaking my leg would have been easier than my arm. I could have still typed and done my duties at the law firm. I maybe could have even continued to waitress. It sure as hell would have been easier to dress and undress."

I tried to take off my work shirt once I got home. It didn't go so well. Doing things with one arm sucks.

"I uh. I can help you... with that."

"Oh, I just bet you can."

He grins and shrugs, fighting a laugh as he rubs a hand along his scratchy cheek, turning back to the road. "You will need help," he states matter of fact. "If not me, I can hire someone or ask one of my female friends."

Christ, this was a mistake.

The fierce independent side of me is beyond annoyed and frustrated with this predicament. I don't like having to depend on others. And this guy. This rock star... he makes it too easy with his soft sexy smiles and adorable dimple and smoldering blue eyes that seem to cut past all my defenses.

"You're doing enough. The rest I can manage on my own."

"There's no shame with people helping you. It's when people refuse the help of others that they lose their way."

"Did Jesus tell you that or did you read it on a bumper sticker?"

Keith curses under his breath, and the hand that was rubbing his jaw is now raking through his chestnut hair. I exasperate him. I anger him. I likely annoy him.

The worst part? I think I enjoy riling him up a bit. His reactions are fun and diverting. I can't remember the last time anyone was this focused on me. Probably never.

But still...

I adjust myself in the soft leather seat so I can face him better. Look at him a little closer.

"You're not at all what I expected for a rock star."

"No?" he clips when I wait him out, but I think he's still a touch mad at me. Or maybe he just doesn't like it that I keep calling him a rock star. I get the impression Keith just likes being a regular guy.

"Nope. In fact, you're nothing like any of the celebrities I've met before."

"Are you waiting for me to bite and ask how I'm different?" He angles his head quickly in my direction before going back to the road.

"Not really." I smile at the way he clenches his jaw and grips the wheel. Yeah, he's not very happy with me right now. "I like that you're unexpected. That you're different." I inch a little closer, crawling halfway along the large center console that I'm resting my broken arm on. I watch as he stiffens the closer I get and for some reason, that makes me want to reach out and touch him.

But I don't and I won't.

"I'll try to do better with the asking and accepting of help. Okay?" I whisper because I can't make the words come out any louder. He doesn't know me, but surely he can tell what saying something like that costs me.

His eyes scour my face, dark and severe, and I miss the flirty, easy-going Keith. This version of him makes my skin itch. "Have you ever been to Alabama? Have any family who's from there?"

My eyebrows crease and I slip away from him at the sudden

change in topic and demeanor. I'm stunned speechless, so I just shake my head.

"You're sure?"

"Yes, I'm sure. I was born and raised in Brookside, Virginia as are all my kin whether living or dead. Why?" I ask, suddenly tense and wary.

"It's nothing." He turns to me with a smile that doesn't touch his eyes. "You just... you look similar to someone I knew growing up. That's all."

"Is that why you're helping me?" I bark, suddenly indignant and uncomfortable. "I look like your old girlfriend or something?"

He pales and I must have hit my mark dead on.

Wow. I can't even with that. "Please pull over, Keith. I don't want to do this anymore." I move closer to the door, ready to start jerking on the handle. That's how badly I want to flee this car and this man. I should have known it was something. That his intense need to help me came with a caveat.

A hand on the bicep of my bad arm shocks me back and I turn, trying to pry myself free. We're at a traffic light and if I were ever going to get out of the car and run from this man, this would be the time. But his expression is holding me paralyzed.

His eyes burn a path straight through me. "I didn't mean to upset you. I'm sorry if you took my asking the wrong way. You look similar to my high school girlfriend. At least your hair color and some of your features. But that's not why I'm helping you. She was smart and beautiful and so are you. But you're not her and she wasn't you."

He releases my arm and I hold it over my chest. *Was?* Is she dead? My stomach drops as my body folds in on itself. He can say whatever he wants but if I look like a high school girlfriend who is likely dead...

The light turns green, but he doesn't move. He's giving me the chance to go.

A horn honks behind us, but he just continues to watch me. Waiting. "Last chance," he warns, and I turn, facing forward.

He takes that as my answer and pulls through the light. I wonder if all interactions with him will be this volatile. Even my toenails are vibrating with the tension between us. I don't know what to say and I feel like the longer we sit here in silence, the worse this gets.

Say something.

Only I don't know what to say. I'm not a funny or witty girl. I'm rough and sarcastic. Too serious for my own good, as my mama always told me. *Maybe that's why you've never been laid before.* Probably. Hell, I've only kissed three guys. Got felt up by one. But when nearly fifteen percent of your high school class gets pregnant before their senior year, you stay away from boys. When you know that getting good grades and not going to parties is your only way out of a life you don't want anything to do with, it makes you serious.

I used to watch my parents get high on pills and drunk on their friends' homemade moonshine. The girl who grew up in the trailer next to ours got pregnant when she was sixteen. She dropped out immediately and didn't graduate high school. She's likely still living with her parents.

I promised myself right then and there that would never be my life.

That I wanted more for myself. And now look at me. Homeless, jobless and broke. Relying on a man I just met last night. Irony might just be my least favorite word.

But if I'm going to be living with this man, even for a short while, he should know what he's getting into with me. And for some inexplicable reason, I want him to know.

"My daddy and mama were very into pills and booze. All they could get their hands on. They didn't have much time, love, or patience for the likes of me. When my mama died, she left me a little money," I start, unable to look at him though I know he's listening to me now. "In truth, I think my parents forgot all about that life insurance or they would have spent that money a hundred different ways to Sunday before she died. Anyway, I used it and went to college. Left my small town and my miserable life there and didn't look back. I had almost two perfect semesters until I found out my father took out two credit cards in my name, as well as a hackle of debt with a bookie-slash-mob boss that was known around our parts. My father used me as collateral," I whisper that last admission though my tone is sharper than a blade.

What kind of father does that to their teenage daughter? Sell them off like that?

I wasn't even nineteen yet.

Keith's jaw tics, his hands gripping the wheel again.

It amazes me how we let people who haven't earned the right own a piece of us. My mama didn't know I was around half the time. My daddy stole my education, put my body in peril, and my financial future in jeopardy. And yet I still hurt over them, if for no other reason than how much I hate them.

Their actions have dictated so much of my life.

The fact that they still have that power over me is inherently what's wrong with the human condition.

"Then what happened?" he asks.

"Then I came out here. First of all, I had to leave school because I could no longer afford it and I couldn't get loans because I suddenly had a ton of debt in my name. Second, to get away because I refused to go back home. But third, because it felt like a fresh start, you know? A chance at a new life I was so very desperate for." I twist to face him now, propping myself back on the console the way I was earlier.

"Yeah, I know. That's why everyone comes out here. Myself and my friends included."

I laugh a little at that. "I think it worked out a lot better for you and your friends than it has for me."

His eyes meet mine for a beat before they're forced back to the road. We're climbing up into the hills a bit and the last thing Keith wants is to get into another accident. "What happened with the bookie?"

My fingers glide up the rough texture of my cast. It's so uncomfortable I have no idea how I'm going to survive so long with it on. "I worked out a deal with him. He didn't care about my daddy. He wanted me. It's why he made the deal in the first place and from what I gather, it wasn't his first time doing it. But I told him I wasn't for sale, and eventually, he must have decided that my mouth wasn't worth the hassle of trying to get my body. I'm paying him every month with a boatload of interest."

"Did you ever think about not paying him?"

I shrug, looking back out to the passing Hollywood landscape. "I tried that once. He flew out here to talk to me and made it clear that if I didn't continue with the payments that he'd so generously negotiated that he'd not only kill my father, but he'd also either take me or kill me."

His eyes rove over me until they capture mine and I look away. I can't stand the pity I see in his blue eyes.

"Anyway, that's my sad story. Well, most of it at least. It's also why I don't trust so easily or so well. Especially men. I think you're crazy for taking me with you. I bet you do too. This all just kinda exploded on both of us and now look. You don't know me, and I don't know you. But I'm trying because I'm not sure I have much of a choice right now. I'm used to doing everything myself and the few times I've ever put my faith in anyone other than Jesus, it backfired."

"Jesus?" He chuckles, and I shrug.

"He's as good as anyone. Better than most, actually. He can't hurt me and he's a good listener."

"I really wouldn't know. I haven't been on speaking terms with anyone holier than Jack Daniels in a while. But thank you for telling me all that. If anything, I'm even more relieved that you're here in my truck and staying with me for a while. I do think this is all a bit crazy—"

"A bit?"

He laughs. "Maybe a lot. But I don't regret it, Maia. I don't. And I hope you don't either." He gives me a quick smile, one that lights up his face a bit, making him look less rugged and a little boyish. The type of smile that makes my insides squirm and my belly fill with butterflies.

It's the kind of smile you return automatically, even knowing the danger a smile like that holds. Still... it feels impossible to resist. Sort of like him. Though I'm determined to try.

6

Keith

THE MOMENT we pulled past the gate and drove up my long, winding driveway, my heart started to race. Like the last twelve hours with this girl were something out of an alternate reality or a dream and now reality was setting in.

I brought a strange woman to live with me.

A woman who is broke and jobless and admittedly has so much debt she's basically drowning in it. Add to that a fucking mob boss who threatened to take her and kill her if she didn't pay with money she doesn't have.

In what universe does this make any sense for me to do?

She could rob me blind and run.

Still, it's like I told her. I haven't found an ounce of regret in me.

I've been telling myself I would do this for any woman. That if it had been Viola or Naomi, I wouldn't have hesitated. That I didn't do this simply because she looks like... Amy. But deep down, I know there is something special about her. Something that hits me on a different level. Something I already know I need to lock down and ignore.

She's too young. Too vulnerable. Too... untouchable.

"Have you ever heard the story of Pandora?" she asks as I drive up, her eyes on the trees and the grounds and finally on my house.

"Like Pandora's box?"

"Yes. She is actually the Greek version of Eve. Did you know that?"

I shake my head no.

"Well, Prometheus gave fire to humans, which seriously pissed Zeus off and he decided to take vengeance. He ordered Hephaestus, another god, to create the first human woman out of soil and water. Then Zeus ordered each god to give the woman a gift. Athena gave her wisdom, Aphrodite beauty, Hermes cunning, and so on. In fact, the name Pandora means all gifts in Greek."

She glances over at me as I park in the garage beside my two other cars that she eyes with a bit of awe. She doesn't move to get out, and I can't stop myself from listening. I shift to face her, and she does the same with me.

"But despite these incredible gifts, Zeus made her human and therefore flawed. This was intentional, mind you. Zeus was no fool. He gave Pandora a jar—"

"Jar?" I interrupt. "I thought it was a box."

"That's a common misconception. According to Hesiod, Zeus gave her a large jar. The jar became a box during the Renaissance when the word was mistranslated."

"Huh. Okay."

"Zeus commanded Pandora not to open the jar under any circumstances and sent her to Prometheus's brother, Epimetheus. Prometheus had warned his brother not to accept any gifts from Zeus. However, Epimetheus took one look at Pandora and married her without question. You see, much like Pandora, he was unable to resist the temptation. Of course, shortly thereafter, Pandora opened the jar and released all evils upon the world. Hatred, war, death, hunger, sickness, and any disaster you can conjure up. As always, women are blamed as they are in the bible."

"And why do I get the impression you're equating me to Epi... whatever the fuck his name is?"

She giggles a little and I smile in return. "Epimetheus. And yes, you catch on quickly."

"You're worried I won't be able to resist your temptation?"

Now she laughs. "No. I'm worried by taking me in, you're about to unleash all the evils that come with me on your world simply because you're inherently a good man tempted by an ancient heartache."

Shit, if she didn't just get my number on the first try.

"Pandora, there was no way I could leave you in that box you were living in. Let me be your Atlas and hold up your world for a while. Even if your world is filled with evils."

She blinks at me, a bit stunned, and I toss her a wink, hopping out of my truck and slamming the door behind me.

"Greek mythology is my lady porn," she calls out, and I laugh, coming around to her side of my truck to help her down.

"I'll be sure to remember that," I tell her as I point at the door to the house. I grab her suitcase and follow after her, staring at her ass and trying desperately not to because she might be right about that temptation thing more than she knows.

Especially as I open the door and she cautiously steps in, her gaze wandering and curious.

My house is a little different. It's why I bought it and restored it actually.

It's partially built into the side of a hill. The architecture is modern, open, angled with huge floor-to-ceiling windows that allow light and sun in but are tinted on the outside so no one can see in. The front is partially sustained on stilts and the back has a huge open patio and pool that I do laps in every morning when the weather cooperates.

It's my oasis. My haven. The quiet respite that does not see or entertain the outside world of cameras, fans, or paparazzi.

And now she's here changing the frequency of the air by adding a new pulse and tempo I can't quite pinpoint but feel all the same.

"This is stunning," she compliments softly, almost as if she's speaking to herself and a smile curls up my lips.

"You must be dying for a shower and a nap. I sure as hell am. And some food. I'm starving. Life rule #27: Always eat and eat well whenever your body is hungry."

"I don't know what to focus on with that. The number or the fact that you have life rules to begin with."

I shrug. "Everyone should, don't you think?"

Now it's her turn to shrug. "Number twenty-seven? How many life rules do you have?"

"More than I keep track of." In truth, the numbers are arbitrary at this point. I came up with my life rules when I was a teenager. They're what got me through when I didn't think getting through was possible.

So yeah, I have a lot of life rules. And yeah, they keep me sane.

A lot of them have to do with my past.

With being the things that propels me forward. Food is one of them for reasons I won't be explaining to her right now.

Besides, it's practically midday already. She has to be hungry. Everything is fucked up.

I'm supposed to be at Jasper's in a little more than an hour to work on some tracks, and there is absolutely no way that is going to happen.

"I guess." She lets out a slightly incredulous laugh as she wanders deeper and deeper along the first floor. "In any event, all you mentioned sounds pretty good." She spins on me suddenly, her dark eyes clear and assessing. "Do we need rules?" She waggles her finger back and forth between us.

"Rules?" I parrot, not quite sure what she's getting at or even if she's trying to mock me.

"Yes. Obviously not your life rules. More like co-habituation rules. This is your home. I feel a little like Eliza Doolittle from *My Fair Lady*. It's freaking me out."

I tilt my head in her direction. "Never seen it."

She shakes her head in dismay. "We'll have to change that. I'm a whore for classic films."

Right. Not touching on that one. "I don't exactly have rules for my house. As far as I'm concerned you have free rein of the place. Anything in the kitchen is yours to use or eat. If you have anything specific you like to eat or drink, write it down and my housekeeper, Diane, will get it for you when she comes on Monday."

"You have a housekeeper?" she interrupts, and I nod.

"Yes. She does all my grocery shopping and cooks a couple of meals for me that I eat during the week. She cleans and does my laundry. What? Why are you smiling at me like that?"

"I don't know. You're a single guy."

"I'm also not home a lot. I don't really know how to cook the things she does and going grocery shopping isn't the easiest thing for me to do anymore without being photographed or hounded for autographs. I thought we weren't judging."

She stares at me, baffled. "You're right and I apologize. It's just... wow. I mean, I know who you are, obviously, it's just that feels very foreign from this and all we've been through in the last twelve hours. Like you're a rock star and then you're also this guy." She waves her hand up and down me in front of me. "Sorry. I digress. Continue what you were saying."

I smirk, shaking my head at her. "Thank you for permission." She rolls her eyes at me and I laugh. "Anyway, Diane will get you whatever you like, and no, before you start to argue because I can see it building, you are not paying for any of that. She has a monthly food allowance I never even come close to hitting." She bites into her bottom lip, something I'm learning she does when she's uncomfortable or unhappy with something. "I'll show you how to work the television in the family room and the big screen in the media room—"

"You have a media room?"

"This is going to take a while if you keep interrupting me."

She throws her good arm up. "Sorry, it's just... I'm not used to this.

Grant me an adjustment period, would ya? You saw my apartment and my dorm before it nor my parents' trailer were much better."

"Fine. How about I show you everything later. For now, let me take you to your room." I walk over to her and clasp her hand, her suitcase in my other, guiding her past the kitchen and the never-used dining room, the office and the music room beside it, the family room, and my gym. I walk her up the floating staircase to the second floor, leading her to the bedroom she's going to be sleeping in. I turn on her before opening the door and stare into her eyes in the darkness of the hallway. "I don't have rules. Just be respectful and I'll do the same. And don't touch my drums or anything in my music room without asking first."

She emits a small, shaky breath and then I open the door for her.

"This is your bedroom and bathroom. Mine is down the opposite end of the hall."

I step back and let her enter first, walking behind her and setting her suitcase which isn't all that full or all that heavy considering it holds the contents of her life, down on the bench under the window.

I turn to leave when her voice calling my name stops me in my tracks. I spin back around, noting the blush on her cheeks and the nervous shifting of her eyes and gait. "I um. I need some help."

I want to tease her for finally asking, but this is clearly not the moment for it.

I move back into her, crowding her until she's forced to meet my gaze. Staring into her eyes, I suddenly feel winded. Breathless. I watch as the dusting of pink on her cheeks grows deeper, her breathing quickening, and I think I know exactly what she needs help with.

"Are you going to take a shower first or just rest?"

She swallows thickly. "I'd like to shower first."

"And you need help removing your clothes?"

"Yes," she hums out, her sweet breath fanning across my face and my cock instantly thickens.

I do my best to push away the lust looming in the back of my head. "Are you in pain?"

She looks away, but I cup her jaw, urging her back to me. I like her eyes on me. They're open windows where everything else about her tries to remain shut. "A little," she answers softly. Like it's a weakness she's loathsome to admit. She's fighting every single instinct and gut reaction she has right now. Its weight taxing her to her brink.

"Okay. Why don't you start the water and I'll go get your meds and—"

"No. I don't want those pills. I won't take them," she interjects sharply.

Right. She mentioned her parents popping pills.

"Tylenol then?"

"Tylenol," she agrees.

"I'll get you some of that as well as a bag and tape for your arm."

With quick, purposeful strides I leave the room and go about the things I need to do. I don't think about the fact that in a few minutes, I'm going to have my hands on her body. Removing her clothes. Feeling her heat against my fingers and inhaling the scent of her skin. No. I don't think about any of that. Not yet anyway.

7

Keith

FUCK. I'm a dirty bastard.

"Focus, motherfucker," I bark under my breath as my feet hit the first floor.

Except suddenly I can't.

I brought Maia here to keep her safe and all I can think about is her naked on my bed, her legs splayed wide and her pussy wet. Waiting. Her big tits desperate for my large hands as her chest rises and falls with all the desire she feels for me.

Plastic bag. Tape. Tylenol. Water.

I chant that over and over again until my cock goes from rock-hard to a semi. I scour my downstairs, going through and finding each item she's going to require one by one. But my heart is already beating faster. Anticipation is licking a sweet trail up my spine.

She may be Pandora and I may be that guy with the E name I can't seem to remember, but I will not be another asshole in her story.

I will not take advantage of her. I will not allow myself to be tempted in the wrong direction from why she's here.

Plastic bag. Tape. Tylenol. Water.

Right. My mission.

I continue that chant as I take the stairs back up to her room. The sound of water running and her moving about inside halts my movements. My eyes flutter shut, giving myself a moment to collect my thoughts and get myself in line.

Once that's done, I knock on the door with the hand holding the glass.

"Come in," she calls out, and I suck in a rush of air, holding it deep in my lungs as I enter.

I set the glass of water and the bottle of Tylenol down on the dresser just as she exits the bathroom. Her shoulders are squared, and her eyes are trained on me as she walks with confidence in my direction. She stops in front of me and I see her struggle unfolding before my eyes.

"I can manage my pants myself, but..." And suddenly all that bravado fails her as her words skip. "I'm having trouble with some of the buttons on my shirt and I can't get the sleeve over the cast. It's too tight."

"Right." *Fuck.* "How about you undo the buttons you can, and I'll help with the rest. We'll get your shirt off and then I'll put the plastic bag over your arm and tape it on."

"Aye, aye, Captain Serious. Sounds like a sound plan."

I belt out a laugh along with that stupid breath I was still holding onto as I spoke. "And you're not serious?"

"No. I'm nervous and had to lighten the mood before I passed out. You're the one who looks like he's about to march to his death because I asked for help with a few buttons."

"You're mocking me?"

"I'm completely mocking you."

"That's ridiculously unfair, you know."

Her head tilts. "How do you mean?"

Does she really not know? "I'm trying to keep my mind out of the gutter. Something I'm not exactly known for doing all that well. I'm trying to be a gentleman because I told you my bringing you here was not about sex. I want to be someone you can trust and rely on. But you're beautiful and curvy in all the places I love a woman to be curvy, and you're asking me to undress you."

"Wowzers. Okay then," she murmurs. "That's far more honesty than I was expecting."

Her gaze drops to her chest, her cheeks that bright pink again and I'm guessing she's trying to hide it. She immediately sets to work one-handed on her buttons, her hands trembling making her fingers fumbles and the task more difficult.

"Gonna be honest with you." She laughs nervously. "This is not how I envisioned undressing for the first time in front of a man."

"What?" stumbles past my lips.

Her eyes flash quickly up to mine before returning to her blouse. She doesn't say anything, but she doesn't have to. That meaning along with the expression on her face are as crystal-clear as it gets.

She's a virgin.

Not just a virgin, but completely untouched if she's never been undressed or naked in front of a man before.

Goddamn. I really am the ultimate piece of shit.

I close my eyes instantly, attempting to give her privacy, something I should have been doing all along. She is not here for my voyeuristic enjoyment. I realize now I'm in completely uncharted waters. When the hell was the last time I was with a woman this long who I wasn't about to have sex with other than my friends' wives or my family?

She starts to giggle, likely at my obvious discomfort.

"Gotcha with that one, didn't I? I think you're blushing, Keith. And how cute are you for closing your eyes so you don't see my tits?"

I groan. Does she have to say the words tits like that?

"You're learning all kinds of things about me today, aren't you?"

"Shhh. I'm trying to remember the words to 'Amazing Grace.'"

She laughs louder, nudging into me a little with her shoulder. "Open your eyes. You can't help me blind, and while this is awkward and weird since we seriously only met a few hours ago, I'd like to get this over with so I can clean up and rest my head."

"I'm trying not to look."

"I know. Gesture appreciated. Now undress me already, Keith."

I groan again. Louder this time. "Say my name again."

She smacks my shoulder, and I can't stop my dopy grin. "Only if you promise not to make any jokes about Pandora's box?"

"I'm not going there, or I'll say something about how I want to open it up."

Opening my eyes, I instantly meet hers and then slowly trickle down her body, my heart already a jackhammer in my chest.

"Wouldn't want that, now would we," she quips with narrowed eyes and a half-grin. "Come on. Let's get this over with."

Right. Undressing her.

She got through four buttons but had to skip a couple, and the moment I start to work on them, I understand why. They're small and the shirt is stiff.

Unlatching the buttons from the loop isn't as easy as it should be.

My hands press a little deeper into the dark fabric of her work shirt, and I catch glimpses of black lace and the full swell of creamy skin beneath. I lick my suddenly dry lips and continue down, hoping, praying, she doesn't look down too because she'll see that I'm harder than steel.

I finally manage the last button and she shirks her good arm out of the sleeve while I slowly, gently, work on the other sleeve. It's not so easy to get it over the thick white cast, and there is a lot of maneuvering to do.

She's standing here in that bra I caught a glimpse of; her chest is slightly angled away from me, the black shirt now hanging from her broken arm. She shifts again, attempting to help me, and dear God, does her chest have to be so close to where my hands are working? Do my eyes have to be trained on that very spot for me to be able to help her?

Her tits are... fucking perfect.

Pretty pink nipples peek through the lace, beckoning me, and I'm trying so hard not to look. Not to be that guy. I really, genuinely am. But they're so close and she smells as good as I knew she already did, and *I want her*.

How? Why?

I can't make sense of anything other than I'm so screwed it's not even funny.

Finally, *finally*, I get the shirt off her, and she turns away, giving me her back, but it's not much help. It's *just* enough that I'm no longer teetering on the edge of picking her up and tossing her on the bed.

I take her arm, not looking, not thinking, hardly breathing, and wrap up the cast in the plastic trash bag I brought up, securing it on with tape so it doesn't get wet. Every freaking one of her movements slams against me, and I cannot focus on anything but her. Her. *Her*.

Too young. A virgin. Too vulnerable. A virgin.

"Can you... um..." Deep shaky breath. "Can you undo the clasp of my bra?" Her voice is barely audible, but it's like cymbals crashing through the air.

I freeze.

What was I just thinking? I had deterrent thoughts but suddenly the words bra and undo messed that all up.

"This bra is old, and the clasp is warped, and I... I always need two hands with this bra. I'm sorry. I know this isn't—"

"It's fine." *Just stop talking!*

I stare at her shoulders. The slope of smooth, creamy skin over her delicate bones. The small half-heart shaped birthmark on her right shoulder. That's where my fingers are itching to start. Right on that birthmark before dragging down along the fine lines until I reach her bra.

I bet the straps would slip down so easily, falling gracefully over her narrow shoulders. Her tits would be even more exposed, overflowing all the more as the lace cups lose purchase.

I bite the inside of my cheek so I don't moan, tasting blood when all I want to taste is her. Before I can stop myself, I do exactly what my mind was just envisioning. Despite my inner voice screaming at me not to be a creepy asshole.

But her skin.

It's milk and honey, and I want... no, I *need* to touch it. And when this moment is over and she's in the shower, naked and soapy, I will be in mine, taking my cock in my hand to fantasies of her.

Her skin is everything I knew it would be and more. She shudders beneath my touch and I just about lose it. I bite the inside of my cheek harder, more blood pooling, so I don't tell her all the ways I want to do wicked dirty things to her.

I unclasp her bra. It snaps away quickly like it's just as desperate to be removed from her as I am to remove it. I don't look. I don't fucking dare look.

"Thank you."

"You shouldn't be thanking me," is all I can manage through clenched teeth before I tear myself away from her and out the door, slamming it a little too hard behind me.

I should have left her there in her apartment.

I should have never started any of this.

Because now she's here and I have no idea how I'll keep my hands to themselves.

8

Keith

THERE IS a special ring in hell that I know intimately. I hang out there quite frequently. In fact, you could say I own prime beachfront real estate and spend my summers there as well as every holiday. All my mail is forwarded there too. You get where I'm going with this.

But this special ring in hell, it has a name.

Something like misery or despair or well and truly fucked. The name changes depending on the reason behind my visit there, but right now, I'm going with the latter.

"Selfish. Arrogant. Fool. Asshole. Creep," I grumble to myself as I storm down the hall.

"You're being too hard on yourself," she calls out through her closed door. "No one said dealing with Pandora's box would be simple."

"Stop talking about your box, Pandora," I throw back, and the wicked temptress laughs.

Thank god she could undo her pants herself because if I caught sight of her box, or pussy since euphemisms never did much for me, my stunning little Pandora wouldn't still be so untouched.

She doesn't respond past that laugh. There really is nothing to say, and right now, I'm not to be trusted around her. And that pulls me up short. Because I should be the one she trusts. She has no one else. No one. I brought her here, to my home, with the promise of this not being about sex. Of me not being like every other deviant in her life.

Life Rule #109: Don't start something you don't intend to follow through on fully.

And I live by my motherfucking life rules!

Being denied the things I want is going to be a steep learning curve.

I yank my phone out of my pocket and shoot out a text in our band's group messenger to Jasper, our lead singer, his fraternal twin, Gus, our lead guitarist and back-up vocals, and to Henry, our bassist.

Not going to make it in today. Was in an accident last night. Long story and even longer night. I'm fine. But I need to talk to you guys later about something.

I shut my phone off because I know my bandmates, and they'll be blowing up my phone all morning—afternoon, I correct—long.

Part of me wonders if this has already made it to TMZ or any other rag and then I decide I don't care. What can they say, that I was in an accident? Hardly newsworthy.

Unless my sweet Pandora in there decides to alert the media that she's now living with me, I can't see how any of this will be anything. I don't exactly see her doing that either. She doesn't seem the type.

Then again, I've been wrong before with that. We had a public nightmare on our hands only a few short years ago courtesy of someone we all trusted.

I enter my bedroom, shut and lock my door, strip down and get in my shower. It's ice-cold, but it warms up quickly. My cock hasn't lost an ounce of blood and I grasp it hard, squeezing it tight the same way I envision her pussy squeezing it.

A virgin. Shit. She'll be tighter than this.

I shake my head in anger, pounding my fist into the wall. I can't allow myself to go there.

But my body is anxious for a release with nothing but her on my mind.

Her mouth is around my cock, eagerly sucking me down and fingering herself as she does. She's whimpering and moaning and slurping me up just the way I like it. She tells me nothing she has ever had in her mouth has tasted better and a groan sears past my lips. Her tits are heaving, wet, and soapy.

The prettiest I've ever seen. Everything about her is.

She comes, riding her hand, and I explode like a teenager, lacking finesse, or control, or fucks to give. Already knowing this paltry, fleeting high is nothing compared to what touching her would be like. The fantasy inadequate with the real thing down the hall.

But it sure beats the hell out of blue balls. Pun intended.

And within minutes of leaving my shower, still soaking wet and not even close to satisfied, I collapse onto my bed, naked, angry as all sin with myself, and pass the hell out.

AN INCESSANT RING followed closely by a pounding has me reluctantly opening my eyes. Blinding sunlight streams across my face, and I growl low, flopping over onto my back. Visions of Maia come flickering through my head like a warped movie reel.

The accident. The hospital. Everything after.

I drag my sorry ass out of bed, tugging up a pair of gym shorts as I go.

I don't have to look out the window or pick up my phone to know who is at my door.

"Shut up," I snap as they press the bell. Again. "You have keys, assholes." I wonder why they're not already breathing down my neck. That's what we did to Gus a year ago.

Stumbling down the stairs, I note with some relief Maia's door is still closed. I head across the house, yanking open the front door, taking in the three sets of eyes that are all trained directly on me.

Jasper Diamond. Gus Diamond. Henry Gauthier.

I roll my eyes like a defiant pre-teen. "I said *later* when I texted."

"It is later, dick," Henry starts with unmistakable venom in his tone. "It's three hours later, and you returned none of our calls or texts. So yeah, sorry if we're worried about you."

"Oh."

"Oh?" That's Gus. His right elbow is cocked lazily up against my house, and he's smirking because that's sort of how Gus rolls. I'm not actively bleeding out in front of him, so he knows I'm straight. But he also knows there is more to the story and he wants all the goods. Jasper, the broody, quiet bastard is hanging back as he tends to do, waiting on me to give up the details I'm hesitant to share. "Are you going to give us the Vanity Fair tell-all or do we have to hold you down and beat it out of you the way did in high school?"

I flip him off. "You always lost so I don't know what you're so anxious to fight about." I'm bigger than he is but not as much as I was in high school. "I was in a car accident. I'm fine. My truck is fine."

"Yes. But there's obviously more to this story than that since you said you needed to talk to us later," Jasper interjects, a smug grin on his lips, his green eyes calling me out. "If it weren't important, you would have texted it on our stream or hell, waited until you saw us next."

I blow out a breath, stepping outside and walking over toward my garage because I have no idea if Maia is awake and I need to talk to them without an audience.

My eyes widen as I round the corner. Evidently, I left the bay open which surprises me. Yes, my land isn't so easy to access, and it's gated, but I'm always careful. Always. Then again, I didn't exactly sleep last night, and I had a bit of a distraction beside me.

"A girl took an illegal right on red and I hit her. Her car was totaled, and she smacked her head and broke her left arm and a few fingers." All their faces grow troubled. One by one. "She passed out in my arms and I brought her to the hospital. But on the way there she kept talking, murmuring half-consciously about how she doesn't have health insurance and—"

"And let me guess, you took the blame and paid for everything," Gus interjects.

"And you wouldn't have?"

He shrugs. "Not saying I wouldn't have. Just saying I already know you did because that's how you operate."

I squeeze the back of my neck. "Her car was older than each of us by at least ten years. And she was hurt..."

Gus's hands are in the air. "Again, no judgment. But you're awfully defensive."

"I'm not. I don't need to sell you on her."

Jasper laughs. "True. Yet you're explaining everything you did like we're your parents and you're afraid we're going to ground you."

Shit. Am I doing that?

"Are you married? Is that why you're talking about her like that?"

I flip Henry off. "Don't be a dick."

"So you brought this girl to the hospital and took the blame for it. Why is this front-page news?" he asks.

"Wait," Gus barks out. "Hold that thought. If this story is headed where I think it's headed can we at least come in and sit down? I ran like ten miles this morning and my thighs are burning."

"Awww," Jasper mocks. "Poor baby. So fragile. Should we get you a bag of ice? How about a white wine spritzer to take the edge off?"

"Who the fuck drinks spritzers since the eighties, man? And that comeback was wicked lame. Your A-game needs some serious work."

I shake my head. I can't even with this right now. Any second Maia is going to wake up and though I don't have to explain anything to them, I feel like I do. That's just how we roll. We tell each other everything. No secrets.

"Can you whiny bitches shut up for two minutes and let me finish my goddamn story?"

They all look at me once more with bemused expressions.

"Apologies. Please finish," Jasper declares.

"As I was saying... yeah, I paid for everything and took the blame.

There was no way I couldn't. After she was discharged, I drove her home and she ended up leaving her phone in my car. Her neighborhood, man." I shake my head, propping my hands on my hips. "Anyway, I went to return it and..." I bluster out a breath. "Her apartment. If you can even call it that. It was a shack in a building. A walk-in closet with a non-existent kitchen, a half-baked bathroom, and the scent of cooking drugs seeping in. I couldn't do it. I couldn't leave her there in that place hurt the way she is."

They all nod like they're finally starting to get it.

"Where is she now?" Henry asks like he already knows the answer.

"Sleeping upstairs in the guest room."

Gus hitches up an unconcerned shoulder. "Don't look such a mess about it. We'd all have done the same thing. If it had been Naomi..." He trails off, not needing to finish that. There is nothing Gus wouldn't do for his fiancée.

"So, she's here staying with you or is this just for today?" Jasper questions.

"She's staying with me for a while. I don't know how long."

"Does she know who you are?"

"She does," I tell him. "She knew immediately when she saw me. But that's not what this is. I don't think she cares. I mean, she said she's a fan, but doesn't seem all that interested in that. Not like the groupies or the phishers have been when they realized who we are."

"You sure about that?"

I nod at Jasper, my gaze earnest. Jasper got trashed one night at an after-party and a girl who was looking to get knocked up by a celebrity did exactly that. Nine months later Jasper had a baby girl and six months after that, the woman who gave him Adalyn was gone and dead from an overdose.

Jasper wouldn't change anything. Adalyn is his world. Our world. She's ours.

And now he and his wife Viola have a second baby and Gus is engaged. We're a family. Better or worse. Richer or poorer. Till death do us part. But all that means is we have more to lose and cannot afford to be cavalier.

"She is not Karina. She chewed my ear off every time I tried to help her. She didn't want me to take the blame or pay for the hospital. And she definitely didn't want to come and stay here. I had to talk her into everything."

"And obviously you did."

I glare at Henry. "What was I supposed to do? Leave her like that? You wouldn't have." I point an accusing finger at him.

"No. I wouldn't have. And if you tell me it's not about who you are or the money in your bank account, I believe you. I just want *you* to be sure."

"I'm sure."

"Okay then," Jasper and Gus say together. Then Gus flips to Jasper. "Jinx."

"You haven't jinxed me since we were ten."

"Dude, you can't speak if I jinx you."

"Cut the crap," I bark at them, still exhausted. Still unsettled. Still a goddamn mess.

"Are you already fucking her?" And before I even know what I'm doing, I'm growling like a bear, like a caveman at Henry. His hands fly up and he takes a step back, looking to Gus and Jasper for backup. "I wasn't serious, man. Shit. I'm not used to you like this. What the hell happened last night with her?"

I know he wasn't serious. *I know he wasn't.* "Don't talk about Maia like that, okay? It's not like that with her."

He nods. Then he smirks. "You're already in love with this girl. Like *so* in love." He makes an obnoxious kissy-face with loud, wet lip-smacking sound and everything.

I laugh in spite of myself, flipping Henry off. "I'm not in love with her. I just met her last night. I'm trying to help her out. That's all."

"Uh huh."

"I mean it."

"Okay."

"Shut up, dick."

"You could have texted or called. Why are we here?"

"Good question," I say to him. "I didn't invite you."

"Can we finish this up?" Gus grouses. "Like I said, my thighs are burning here. And really, why can't we talk inside instead of in your driveway like we're a bunch of mob bosses doing business?"

I roll my eyes at him but lick my lips as I lay out the thought I had earlier in the car on the way home. "I'm thinking maybe we could hire her to be our new PA since we fired Sophia." Sophia was our assistant until she betrayed us by paying off members of the media to spread lies about us while we were on tour. She was jealous. Jasper was in love with Viola, the nanny at that time to his daughter Adalyn. We all grew up with Viola, only we hadn't seen her in seven years after she broke up with Gus. She and Gus were high school sweethearts, but in reality, Jasper was always in love with her. And the moment Sophia realized that the feeling was very mutual, she tried to tear our band apart.

Tear them apart.

"Our new PA?" Gus parrots, his eyes casting over to Jasper's as they frequently seem to do when they need to have an unspoken twin conversation that no one else will understand.

"Yeah," I soldier on. "She's young. Just turned twenty, but she's smart. Was in college before life turned shitty for her and she had to leave. Anyway, she's been working two jobs to make ends meet and with her broken arm..." I shrug. What am I doing?

The right thing.

"Anyway, she needs a job, is hardworking, and we need a PA. Especially with us taking on those tour dates. It just seems to work."

That's when three sets of us fly up past my right shoulder toward the window overlooking the driveway. This one is not as tinted as the ones facing the front, and I don't have to look to know Maia's standing there. Their expressions say it all.

Henry gasps. Jasper takes a step back. Gus curses.

"She looks like..."

"But she's not," I tell Henry, who stares in stunned amazement. "She's different. The hair is the same color and her face shape and nose too. But everything else is different. She's tall for one. Curvy, not petite. Her eyes are dark brown, not blue. Her hair is straight, not curly—"

"And for someone you just met last night, you're already cataloging pretty hard all the differences between her and Amy," Jasper cuts me off with a well-placed narrowed glare. "Keith. What the fuck are you doing?"

"She's not her," I spit out defensively. "That's not why I did any of this."

Well, not entirely. Helping her the way I did in the hospital might have started that way. And a lot of my chronic guilt might have spurred me on after that. But by that point it was about her, not how she looks.

He stares me down with troubled eyes. "You can't bring her back. You can't save her. This girl. Are you sure about this girl? I mean, for the right reasons?"

"She's not her," I repeat emphatically because I'm not sure about anything except that.

I want to say that I am. I want to say that I'm positive. That all this rush of blood and adrenaline and desperation are from Maia and nothing else.

And I have to wonder if her hair was brown instead of blonde and her nose was a different shape, would I even consider anything else? All I know is that it wouldn't have changed the outcome. She would still be here, and I would still be helping her.

"This girl pushes my every freaking button. She's feisty and angry and doesn't take my shit. I mean it, I think she'd be a great PA for us," I finish with, refocusing the conversation on where it belongs.

"Does she know she looks like..."

"Amy," I supply for Gus, saying her name out loud for the first time in... I don't know how long. Since that night, maybe.

All their eyes turn wider than saucers at that. Sympathy for me etched all over them. I suffered the way no one ever should after Amy died. I was as haunted as a man could ever be. My pain was savage. It owned me. Still does.

"Yes. I told her she looks like a girl I was once with. Well, she figured it out after a few prying questions, but that's semantics."

"Keith..." My name stretches tragically from Gus's lips, hanging in the air like the foul stench of grief.

"She looks like her," I admit. "Sort of. But they're so different. Everything about them is. I swear y'all would have done exactly what I did. If it had been one of my sisters, or Naomi or Viola..." I let that hang, hoping they get it already and back off a bit on this.

I'm tired of explaining it.

I'm tired of repeating myself.

I have a woman who I don't know staying with me. It doesn't make sense. I paid for her car and her hospital bills. I scooped her up and took her out of her home and brought her to mine. Now I'm trying to give her this job.

I don't know what I'm doing.

All I know is that I don't want to stop, and I don't want to analyze all the finer details that might add up to me being just a bit crazy. Isn't that what Maia said this was? Crazy?

"Is this job coming from your dick, your heart, or your brain?" Henry pushes out. His voice strung between agony and fear.

My brothers are worried about me, and we wouldn't be us if we didn't do this straight up and outright. I throw my hands up helplessly but that has to be good enough for them.

I need them. I need this. And they know it.

They were all there with me after Amy died. They stuck by my side and held me up and my face over the toilet as I lost myself in alcohol, drugs, and faceless women. The women came later, after the drugs and alcohol were no longer enough, and were what put my face over the toilet. It took me years until I could be with one without it making me physically ill.

I still don't look them in the eyes. Not one.

"Okay," Gus states. "I'm in with her then. I'd like to meet her first. Have a conversation. But if you tell me she's our new PA and right for the job then she's our new PA."

Jasper hums in agreement because if I say she's it, he's cool with it. That's how our dynamic works.

Henry is still posturing. "If she works for us, you can't stick your dick in her."

I want to punch him flat out. Right here and now. "I'm not," I grit out in a tone that does not hide my ire.

He grins. Laughs a little. "But you want to."

"Shut up, asshole."

He laughs harder. "Well then. Are you going to finally invite us in to meet our new assistant?"

"I haven't mentioned the job to her yet."

"Actually, you just did," she says from right behind me. I seriously should have seen that one coming.

9

Keith

I TURN AROUND and practically growl out once again. The woman really does make me a caveman. She's wearing a simple black dress, one that drapes loosely over her bra-less breasts before cinching to her narrow waist and then flowing down to her bare feet. Her hair is down, and her face is shiny and beautiful.

But her breasts… her perfect *bra-less* breasts.

I'm assuming she could not put on a bra one-handed but come on.

I whip back around, ready to kill all, but the guys aren't even looking at her chest. None of them are, not even Henry, who is the only other single one of us. I should have known better but when you're met with a woman who resembles the love child of Kate Upton and Brooklyn Decker, her face is just one of the treasures that hold you captive.

She shifts in my direction, her cheeks pinking up as she takes in my chest. The color darkens further as she scrolls down me before her eyes meet the ground. It's only just now I realize I never put a shirt on when I ran down for the bell. Shit. No wonder the guys were teasing me. Making sure this wasn't about sex because it probably looks like that's exactly what we've been doing.

She clears her throat, forcing her gaze back up, most definitely avoiding me.

Sauntering toward us, her broken arm is held up high on her body, her other hand holding it protectively against her. She stops beside me, a world of space between us as a smirk quirks up her full, pink lips.

She glances at each one of the guys, a sparkle in her deep brown eyes.

"Well then. Are you going to introduce me to your friends or are we going to skip over all that and allow me a moment for a proper fan-girl swoon?" All the guys simultaneously blink then blush. "I'm a huge fan, boys. Yours was my first ever concert. I think my last one too," she laughs in a slightly self-conscious way. "Holy hot potatoes, this is insanely surreal. I didn't expect to be this nervous, but I am."

"You weren't nervous when you met me," I challenge.

"I had just been in a major car accident and was not only bleeding from my head but in a lot of pain with a broken arm. Besides, I don't even know them, and I think I already like them better than you."

An incredulous burst of air flies past my lungs. "That's only because they haven't said anything yet."

"Right. Already an improvement to you."

Jesus. This girl. I run a hand through my hair.

"You're gorgeous. Will you go out with me?"

Maia tilts her head at Henry. "You know I'm a virgin and broken beyond repair, right?"

He laughs, a bright smile gleaming across his face as he looks at her. It makes me want to hit him again. "I didn't, actually. But I don't scare as easily as Keith does. That all actually works for me."

"He didn't tell you?" A fresh bloom of rose colors her cheeks.

"Believe it or not, I felt it ungentlemanly to discuss your sexual and personal history."

"Oh," she states, finally staring directly at me. "Right. I guess that makes sense." She shrugs and then laughs, her expression a mix of uncomfortable and mortified.

"But hey, I bet all this heat is why your cheeks are so red. Clearly not because you're embarrassed or anything."

She ignores me completely. "Kindly disregard everything that just happened in the last thirty seconds," she says to the guys.

"Does that include my asking you out?" Henry pushes. He looks crestfallen.

"I wouldn't have a clue what to do with a man like you, Henry. But I'm flattered beyond words."

He points at her while looking at me. "I like her. I approve."

I bark out a laugh. "Maia, these are my bandmates, Jasper, Gus, and Henry. Guys, this is Maia Angelo."

"Like the poet?" Jasper asks.

She gleams at him, nodding. "Only spelled differently. I don't think my parents had any clue when they named me. They weren't exactly known for reading poetry."

She turns back to me, an accusatory brow raised in my direction. "You're not wearing a shirt."

"Do you need me to?" I can't help but tease, hoping she'll blush again.

Her eyes trail over every single inch of my waist, abs, chest, shoulders, and arms. My cock jumps in my track shorts, and without the benefit of briefs beneath to hold me in, I have no doubt all are witnesses to his enthusiasm at her perusal.

"I think I might. As a virgin, six-pack abs and well-defined muscles scare me to death."

"You're fucking with me now?"

She smirks. "Absolutely. But I'd still like you to put on a shirt."

"You sure about that? Because your eyes are telling me something different."

"Yes. I'm sure. And while you're at it find somewhere else to park your ego. It's a bit too crowded out here with it taking up all this space."

"I'm a go on hiring her as well," Gus remarks with a delighted grin. "She doesn't take your shit so that's an automatic win in my book."

"Agreed," Jasper concurs, his smile matching his twin's.

She stares inquisitively at the guys. "It doesn't bother you that your friend brought in a stray and is now trying to pawn me off on all of you? Especially when you know absolutely nothing about me or my qualifications?"

"No," all three of them say in unison.

"Yikes. Okay. Well, since I have no idea what this job actually entails or why Keith believes I'd be so perfect for it, I think I'm going to need more details. And then I'm going to have to think about it because Keith seems to have a problem with trying to be my hero, and while I appreciate all he's done for me, I don't want any more of his charity."

"It's not charity. Nothing I've done has been charity," I growl through clenched teeth.

"Then what would you call it?" she retorts, the fire in her eyes growing.

"Helping someone who needs it."

"Right. Like I just said. Charity. I may talk slow, but that doesn't mean I am."

I run my hands through my hair, gripping the back of my neck so I don't throttle her. "You are the most infuriatingly stubborn, prideful woman I've ever met."

"You say that like it's a bad thing for a woman to be all those things."

I open my mouth to continue arguing with her when Jasper interjects with, "I think we're going to go. Keith clearly has this under control. Or not since it looks like it might be Maia for the win. Despite that, we're just in the way."

"Speak for yourself, dude. I'm about to go pop me some corn and pull up a seat to watch the show."

Jasper and Henry snicker at what Gus said. I don't. This woman drives me crazy. I don't know if I want to strangle her or kiss the hell out of her.

"Come on." Jasper tugs on the back of Gus's shirt propelling him into action. "It was very nice to meet you, Maia. I hope you end up working with us."

"Yeah," Henry continues, gazing at Maia with some combination of awe and appreciation. "What he said. And if you don't work with us, consider that date."

"I'll be sure to do that. At the very least, it was wonderful to meet you guys." She throws them a wave and takes a step back toward the house.

The guys retreat into Jasper's SUV, loaded with car seats, and they leave. Just like that.

Abandoning me with the hellcat.

"I like them," she says after they're gone. "They're... normal. Hot as fuck, but still normal."

"Hot as fuck?" I pivot, crossing my arms over my chest as I gaze down at her.

She purses her lips, her tone unconcerned as she toys with a lock of her hair that hits her chest in the breeze. "I just call 'em like I see 'em."

"What did you expect them to be?"

She twists to face me, staring up into my eyes through her thick lashes. "I don't know. Rock stars?"

"Do you have any idea how much you exasperate me?"

"I think I do. It's not intentional. Well, not fully anyway. Maybe it partially is. I'm not sure anymore." Her contrite, innocent expression quickly morph into something playful. "You're kind of sexy when you're all fired up."

"Kind of?"

She shrugs noncommittally.

"Do you believe people are one-dimensional? That their job dictates they mold to the cliché?"

She shakes her head slowly. "No. I believe we're all multifaceted.

But still, y'all have been larger than life in my head since I was young, so it's all a bit much to take in." She reaches out and places a hand over my bare chest. Over my heart. Her eyes are still on mine, her touch soft and warm and my insides quake. "You're hellbent on saving me, but I need to be the hero of my story. I need to stand on my own two feet or nothing I've done to get myself out and away is worth a damn. I've already taken more from you than I should have."

"You can be your own hero and have one helping in the wings too. That doesn't make you less brave or in control. But if you need me to be a villain in your story, one that's right in front of you that you can touch and hit, one you can spit all your pent-up vitriol at, then fine. I'll be that guy. But really, you need a job and we need an assistant. It's truly as simple as that. This is not some made-up job I'm offering to you out of charity. Our last assistant betrayed us, so we've been gun shy on pulling the trigger to hire another one. But we're working on finishing up our sixth album, and next month we're going on the road for ten days, playing six shows each in different cities. So yeah, we need help. This is not a temporary position either. We're looking for full-time help, but your schedule is flexible unless we're traveling because then we'll need you with us."

"What does a band assistant do exactly?" she asks, her voice soft but strong. Just like the hand that's still pressed against me. That is until she drops it, holding on to her broken arm again. But the sear of her touch on my flesh lingers. Unexpected and unwanted.

"A lot of different things. Basically, whatever we need."

"Elaborate, please. Whatever you need is a very loose and dangerous phrase."

"Making sure we eat when we're working in the studio because if we get really deep into something, we sometimes forget. Arranging our hotel rooms for when we travel. Taking over our social media posts because we're not so great with that. Doing whatever Marco, our manager, needs extra help with. There's a lot more to it but I can't think of everything off the top of my head. A lot of it just sorta comes up organically. Does this sound like something you could manage?"

She swallows thickly and nods. But there is excitement brewing in the back of her eyes. She wants this. "What else?"

A strange cocktail of resolved peace and wild frustration war through me. My pulse jumps and I wish I didn't react to her the way I do. I wish I wasn't as drawn to her as I already seemingly am.

"You'll get a phone, iPad, and typically a car allowance because we need you to have reliable transportation. But since you can't drive with your broken arm, you'll travel with me or the guys until you lose the cast. We also provide full medical coverage as part of your salary. We will require you to sign a non-disclosure agreement as well as some other legal documents, I'm sure."

"I want my living expenses while I stay here taken out of my pay." I shake my head, but she stops me quickly by saying, "That's a non-negotiable term of employment for me."

"Okay. I'll have to talk to Marco about the specifics of your salary because I honestly don't know. I'm guessing around six figures all said and done. Are you saying yes to the job?"

She licks her lips and smiles, her face glowing like the brightest of stars in the night sky. "Yes. I'm saying yes. I'd be a fool not to." Then she laughs, sinking her teeth into her lip like this is all too much. "How can one of the worst nights of my life lead to one of the best days of it?"

She doesn't wait for an answer to her rhetorical question. Instead she spins on her bare feet and heads in the direction of the house.

"Come on, Keith. I'm starving and I'm sure you must be too."

She goes inside, leaving me here to take the minute I find I suddenly need. Talking about Amy got me all spun around. Dealing with Maia seems to have done the same only in the opposite direction. I'm dizzy and disoriented. Unsure how I'll ever be able to right myself and find my way again.

Especially when the woman now living in my house already has me lost in her spell, a place I have no business being.

10

Maia

After we came back inside, Keith heated up a frozen pizza and we ate while chatting about nothing all that important. But his sudden and unexpected change in disposition set me on edge. Something had noticeably shifted in him from when we were in the driveway to that moment only a matter of minutes later.

He was distant. Almost rigid. Not only that, he refused to so much as look at me.

And just like that, doubt instantly began to creep through me.

I spent the rest of the day wondering for about the hundredth time if he regrets all he did for me. If I'm more of a pain in the ass than what he wants to deal with. I haven't been making it easy for him, and it's something I vow to work on.

All he's trying to do is help me. Not take away my independence or keep me as a kept woman. If anything, I'm a burden to *him*. And if I am going to accept this job and his help, I need to learn when to quit.

After our late lunch, he went and did his thing, and I didn't want to be in his way. Not only that, but I also didn't feel comfortable anywhere in the main living spaces, so I spent the rest of the afternoon and evening up in my room.

It feels weird to say that. My room.

Nothing in this big, gorgeous house is mine.

My night was spent tossing and turning. Hurting and sad and feeling so lost and lonely. So out of place in the world. A lone ship in hurricane waters, my chances of making it through unscathed nearly impossible. Or maybe this is the start of something new. Something better.

The sound of water splashing wakes me out of the few hours of sleep I managed, and when I clamor to the window, I find Keith doing laps in his pool like an Olympic athlete. Strong, powerful, broad strokes slice effortlessly through the water. He's impossibly easy on the eyes and impossible to look away from.

But it's the hour that's giving me pause. It's barely seven in the morning.

Is he always this early of a riser or is there something pressing on his mind?

He doesn't quite seem to have the quintessential cliché rock star life. Maybe I'm overreaching here, but I always assumed guys like him had a harem of women clinging to them, wearing bikinis and nothing else while bottles of empty liquor are littered about.

Or maybe I've just seen too many movies.

I dress quickly as best I can in a sports bra—since I can get that on myself—and a flowy coral dress that hits around my mid-thigh. I'm hungry and if Keith is in the pool, now is a good time to go and find myself something to eat. It's strange intentionally trying to avoid him and though on one level, I'm extremely disappointed I feel the need to do that, on another, it suddenly seems like a necessity.

An awkwardness that wasn't there before descended upon us.

Or maybe I'm just reading too much into this and the situation at hand. I don't exactly have a lot of experience with men and certainly not men like Keith Dawson.

Padding barefoot down the stairs, I skid to a halt when I find a man with creamy mocha-colored skin, dark hair, and dark eyes looking at me. He's wearing coral skinny jeans—the same color as my dress—a white shirt that contrasts brilliantly against his gorgeous skin color and a smile. He's sipping his coffee, perched on one of the stools at the breakfast bar in the kitchen, his scrutiny appraising and genuine.

"'Morning," he drawls, his gleaming white smile growing as he eyes his pants and then my dress. He stands, setting his mug down to come and greet me. "I'm Marco Morales and I like you already since we both have fabulous style. I manage Wild Minds. You must be Maia since you're young, beautiful, and the only woman here."

I match his smile, liking him instantly too. I shake his hand with my good one. "The broken arm or cut on my forehead didn't give me away?"

He laughs, ushering me over to one of the stools. "Sweetness, the best thing a man can do in this world is point out a woman's good features, never the bad."

"If only all men were as wise as you."

"Amen. Do you want some coffee? I made a lot and Keith has really good stuff for the home-brewed variety. He's a bit of a snob like that. Be thankful you're not at Gus's. You'd be drinking whatever cat piss he came across when shopping."

"Well when you put it like that, I'd love some coffee. Thank you. How long have you been their manager?"

He throws me a sideways glance as he goes about pulling out a large black mug and filling it with coffee. "Forever. Cream, sugar, sweetener?"

"Just cream. I'm sweet enough." I wink at him, and he grins.

He slides the mug over to me and I graciously accept it, wrapping my hand around the warm porcelain and holding it there even though it isn't cold in the house.

"To answer your question, I've been with them since shortly before they released their third album and it's been love ever since.

But I won't lie and say that the last two years or so since they fired their previous assistant haven't been rough."

I tilt my head as I take a sip of coffee. It is really good. "How so?"

"Well, I manage the band. Their brand and their business. I don't manage them, and that makes a big difference when they don't have a personal assistant who does. Get what I mean?"

"I think so. Keith mentioned a lot of my responsibilities would be looking after them. Making sure they eat when they're working. Making sure their hotel arrangements are in place. That sort of stuff."

"Yes. I can't tell you it's all glamor and Hollywood, because it isn't. On a regular week, it's running a lot of mindless errands and bullshit like that. On a travel week, it's a lot of long hours and dealing with crap. Basically, you're in charge of whatever the guys need and I'm in charge of whatever the band needs. But our relationship is symbiotic, which means I don't tolerate anything less than openness and honesty."

"That all works for me. I think. But since we're going to be open and honest, I have no fucking clue what I'm doing or how to begin. I can make hotel reservations, Marco, but I'm assuming these guys don't stay at the Holiday Inn. I'm assuming they have specific places they like and specific types of rooms and specific things in those rooms that's personal to them. Or have I been watching too many movies over the years?"

He laughs, getting up again and walking over to one of the cabinets, helping himself to a Tupperware container of muffins. He's very comfortable here. Obviously knows his way around the kitchen and something about that sets me a bit more at ease.

"Lucky for you, their last assistant was incredibly organized and proficient. She left detailed spreadsheets and documents in a drive she and I used to share. It's all in there and anything you're curious about, ask me or the guys. They're not assholes. Well..." He holds his hand up. "Jasper can be a bit on the broody side, but since he married Vi and popped out another kid, he's been better. Anyway, they're extremely easy-going and easy to work for as far as artists go. You can trust me on that. You'll also receive a company card to purchase everything so you don't have to worry about expensing anything. Muffin?"

I nod, smirking. "Did Keith ask you to tend to me?"

"He didn't ask. He suggested you need to take it easy as you have a broken arm and a concussion, and since I'm no slouch in the kitchen, I can heat us up a couple of muffins while we talk shop."

"Fair enough. A muffin would be wonderful. What's all this?" I ask, tapping my fingers along a thick red folder.

"Your employment documents including your NDA because we do not fuck around. And just so we're clear and I can get through my bitch speech, that NDA extends to all aspects of anything that has to do with the band. Not just in your role as their PA. Get what I'm saying? That means any of your interactions with the band members as well as their spouses and children at any time is confidential. After the shit Sophia pulled, I take this extremely seriously. If at any point, we feel you're violating that, you're gone on the spot and we reserve the right to sue your ass for any damages."

"I have no problems with that," I tell him, staring him straight in the eyes. I've been betrayed enough by people I thought I could trust. By my own family. It's not something I would ever do to another.

"Good," he replies, relieved. He finishes up the muffins, taking out butter and plates and silverware and even some fruit and setting it all out in front of me like a buffet. We help ourselves, and just as I'm popping a piece of warm muffin into my mouth, he asks, "Now that all that nastiness is out of the way, is all that Jasper told me last night true?"

I swallow the piece in my mouth, washing it down with coffee so I don't choke. "Considering I have no idea what Jasper told you, I can't say."

He gives me a satisfied grin. "Spoken like a true PA. Evasive. But what Jasper told me is that you crashed into Keith and then he proceeded to pay for everything at the hospital and then forced you here to stay because where you were living was something between a crack house and a meth lab."

"That's sort of the abridged version, but I guess it's all true."

Marco blinks at me, his expression suddenly guarded and watchful.

"What?" I ask. "Why are you staring at me like that?"

"So, you're like, staying here, staying here? Like… with Keith?"

I can feel heat starting to crawl up my skin. "Marco, you're making me feel like this is the opening scene of a horror movie and next you're going to tell me all about the family who was murdered in the room I'm sleeping in. It never works out well for the blonde in that situation, so I'd feel better if you'd clue me in on what I'm missing."

"Could you imagine? I would die." Then he covers his mouth with one hand, gripping my shoulder with the other. "Shit. Probably for real. The gay man of color always gets it in horror films, same as the blonde. Anyway, as far as I know, no one has ever died in this house and it's not haunted. But you didn't answer my question."

"And you didn't answer mine." He waits me out with a raised eyebrow that says you tell me yours and I'll tell you mine. I take another sip of my coffee, shifting in my chair to face him. "I guess I'm not sure what you're asking me."

He smirks, his dark eyes sparklingly knowingly. "Oh, I think you do, sweets. Give me the E True Hollywood Story, girlfriend to girlfriend, because in all the years I've known Keith, he has *never* had a woman other than his sisters or his mother stay here. I doubt he's ever even brought a woman back here. He's certainly never had one for more than one night. And before you go on asking how I can know all that, I do. First up, it's my job. But it's also not a secret. We all know this about him, and we all talk about it. Keith Dawson does not date or do repeats."

"Ever?" I bark out incredulously.

"Ever. He has random hookups with random women and then never sees them again. It's a one and done. Usually in public like at a club or something so he doesn't have to take them home or go home with them. He doesn't even have a regular, no strings booty call. So again, dish it."

I shake my head. There is so much in what he just told me that I can hardly wrap my head around it. Keith mentioned his high school girlfriend. The girl I look similar to. The one who is dead if we're going by the way he was speaking about her.

Has he not dated anyone since? Never had more than one night?

Jesus. That's a lot to take in.

"Sorry to burst your gossip bubble, but there is nothing to dish. I'm staying in the guest room. And there is nothing going on between me and him."

Marco deflates, looking crestfallen. "Really?"

"Truly."

"Well, that's shit. I was hoping he was finally sweet on someone. Keith is a flirt and a chronic tease, yes, but he's also as loyal and good as they come. A total grizzly alpha with a heart of gold. I guess I don't have to tell you that." He waves his hand up and down me, and I can't stop my frown. I don't even know where it comes from or why it's sitting on my face.

I'm not special to Keith.

And the sooner I stop myself from thinking I am, the better.

I'm his employee and he doesn't date. Ever. And I'm not really interested in that anyway. I have too much going on. Too many things I have to straighten out about myself and my life before I could even entertain anything considered a romantic entanglement. We also bicker like cats and dogs. Totally incompatible.

Not to mention he and I and the worlds we live in are as different as night and day.

But still… that small flicker of disappointment is there.

One I need to get over right here and now. Liking Keith Dawson is not an option.

I clear my throat. "And the other guys? They date?"

"Well, Jasper is obviously married, and they have two daughters. The first from Jasper's previous relationship. And Gus is engaged to Naomi Kent." I nod. I never spent money on tabloids, and I don't own a television because cable and streaming networks were out of my price range. But I do remember when the media exploded all over Jasper, Gus, and Jasper's now-wife, Viola. You couldn't go to the pharmacy without seeing them spread over every glossy magazine cover. I had also heard little snippets about Gus Diamond and Naomi Kent. I just didn't realize they were engaged.

"And Henry?"

"He dates. Nothing ever serious or longer than a couple of weeks and nothing in a while. Henry is firm he doesn't want what Gus and Jasper have, though he never elaborates on why. But yeah, Keith's the odd man out with that because unlike Henry, he does want what the others have."

I pick a little more at my muffin as Marco finishes going over everything that's in the folder, forcing myself not to feel anything but upbeat and hopeful. I have a bunch of documents to read and sign. A tablet and a sheet of logins for our shared drive as well as a company credit card and cell phone.

Marco stands to leave, and I follow him to the door. "Don't look so stressed, sweets. It seems like a lot, but you'll pick it up quickly. And call me anytime. You and I are in this together now and that makes us besties."

I reach out with my good hand and hug Marco. There is something about him that makes you feel connected. Like he truly is an instant bestie. And since we have this NDA thing going, I feel like I can trust him. As much as I can trust anyone.

I shut the door and flip the latch to lock it.

And before I can talk myself out of it, I head for the back door and the pool where Keith is still doing his laps. I think I need to get to know my new boss a little better.

11

Maia

STEPPING out into the warm morning sun, I make my way over to the steps of the pool. It's long, rectangular, and crystal-clear blue. There's an attached hot tub off to the side, but it's not on at the moment. Keith hasn't slowed his motion, though I bet he saw me the last time he rolled his head for a breath of air.

I sit on the stone edge, dipping my feet into the cool water and sighing. It feels nice, but the mounting tension between us doesn't. He does two more laps with me sitting here before he comes to a stop, shaking his hair out and running a hand over his face to remove the excess water. His toned forearms crisscross on the lip of the pool, his feet kicking out behind him as his stoic gaze hits mine in such a way I instantly have butterflies.

"Everything get settled with Marco?"

Okay, so this is how we're going. Business.

"Yes. He gave me all the paperwork and technology goodies. I have to look through everything and sign on the dotted line."

A sudden heavy silence descends upon us and for the life of me, I have no idea how to fill it.

He looks angry.

I'm not.

His expression makes me want to smirk.

I resist. Poorly I might add.

"How's your arm today?"

Still sore as hell, but I say, "Much better, thank you. Are you typically such an early riser?"

He ignores my questions completely, turning to face me and giving me his undivided attention as he stands up to his full height in the shallow end. Ribbons of water playfully glide over his face, down his neck, across his shoulders, chest, and abs before they get reunited with the pool as it laps gently along his waist.

"Bet you're wishing you could swim. It's hot out here."

I'll say. The man is shredded like lettuce and tastier looking than a filet mignon. He's the salad and the main course, and I bet whatever is hidden beneath those black trunks is most definitely the dessert. I wonder if he's size appropriate considering he's... "Six-three?"

"Five."

Oh. Is there some kind of metric that that correlates—

"You're staring at my junk through the water."

"No, I'm not!" I squeak, my voice so high-pitched a dog off in the distance barks. "I'm just thinking about something. Not related to you of course. Or your... you know." I glance up because I have no other choice but to hold firm (stupid pun in my head) and meet his eyes.

"Dick? Cock? Penis?"

"Right. That. I'm not thinking about that. It was just a weird coincidence that my eyes were there."

"As you were asking how *large* I am? Not to mention you're blushing the reddest I've seen you yet. You're wondering about my dick size. Admit it."

Never.

"If muscular chests and abs scare me, it's ten times as bad for—"

"You can say it. Come on."

Bastard. I never had a problem saying it until it became about *his* dick in particular.

"Dicks. Besides, don't they always say the bigger the ego and cocky attitude, the more the man is compensating for their lack of size and virility?"

He smirks arrogantly, and I hate how easily my face gives me away. My mama used to say it was the Irish side of our blood. That's why her face was always beet red when she drank. For me, it just translates into a built-in lie detector.

"I'd be happy to show you just how wrong that is," he drawls. "At least for me. I can't exactly speak for others. But I think we both know that's not going to happen, is it, sweet darlin'?"

Him calling me sweet darlin' should not have the effect it has on my panties.

It's... demeaning, right? I mean, being called either sweet or darling feels like it should be. But rolling off his smooth tongue while his eyes hungrily take in every inch of me feels nothing short of erotic and splendid. I could roll around in that endearment and feel zero shame for it.

"Nope. Boss."

He cringes a little at that and I smile brightly. If I have no idea what to do with a man like Henry, I have to imagine it's worse with a man like Keith. He just drips sex and experience. And baggage. He drips that too, and I've already got plenty of my own to carry around despite what my pathetic luggage upstairs would suggest.

"If you want my body and you think I'm sexy," I start singing, and he explodes into a loud bark of a laugh. Thank god. There is only so much of his intensity I can take without having a stroke.

"You're too young to know that song."

"So are you." I laugh, reaching in with my good hand and splashing some water his way.

He smiles, the light of it hitting his eyes in all the right places, and he looks so damn hot right now. I wonder if he kisses as well as I imagine he does. His lips are full, almost feminine they're so full. Like soft pillows of marshmallows, which shouldn't be enticing on a man, but it is on him. Would he put his hands through my hair and hold my face to his or press against my lower back, so my body is forced to feel his as he takes my mouth?

"You're staring at my lips now."

Crap. "Am not." I cup more water, flinging it his way, the only diversionary tactic at my disposal.

"No fair splashing me. I can't return the favor. And I may be too young for that song, but I'm a lot older than you."

"Is that a warning, Keith? It sure sounds like one."

I'm taunting him. Why am I taunting him?

He licks his lips, his expression growing austere. He takes a step forward in the water. A step toward me, and I instinctively sit up straight. "Yes."

And just like that, playtime has left the arena. Frazier is down! My daddy used to throw that line out whenever any of his friends would pass out. It's a boxing thing, I think, but he used it enough that it's all kinds of tainted.

But right now, it's my big mouth that got knocked the fuck out.

The problem is, I can't seem to help it. All my life I've played by the rules. Colored inside every line. And it never worked out well for me. This is the first time, other than moving to California, that I've ever taken a risk. Done something that many would consider dangerous or crazy. I'm living with a man I hardly know, accepting a job I have no experience with. It's like my body is taking all that undersexed, repressed, hopelessness and throwing it away along with caution and common sense. If I want my tomorrow to be better, I have to make it so. I can't just sit around and wait for that to happen.

I think that's what I'm trying to do now.

"I like that you're scared of me," I tell him. "It's sorta cute for the big bad man to be afraid of the little blonde riding hood."

Before I know what he's doing, he's splashing through the water in my direction, a determined scowl on his face. I want to get up and run. I stay planted instead, and when reaches me, he shoves my legs open enough for him to step in between them. His hands drop on either side of me, gripping the stone edge of the pool and caging me in.

My dress is already short and like this, I have no doubt my panties are visible.

If he looks.

Which he's not.

His eyes have transfixed themselves totally and completely on mine.

Drops of water launch themselves off his body and onto my dress, but I don't care about the cold or the wet. It's welcome with all the heat radiating off him.

I don't move. Hell, I hardly breathe.

He leans in, his eyes coasting softly down to my lips, sticking there like he can't tear himself away, and he inches in closer. Practically touching mine. Mere inches separating us. And for one agonizingly beautiful moment, I think he's going to kiss me.

And though I know I shouldn't, I would kiss him back.

Which is why I lean in just a tiny amount. Just to see what happens.

Unfortunately, he stops just short of the end mark. His warm breath fans across my lips and I want him to do it.

Just do it. Just kiss me.

But I already know he won't. That's where the determined scowl comes into play.

His fingers drag up, saturated in water, and run along the crest of my cheek. His eyes follow the motion before they're back on mine.

"You're so beautiful, Maia. And I bet when men look at you, that's all they see. Your beauty. It's exquisite. And the fact that you're so much more than just beautiful? It's crippling. Your smart mouth challenges me like no one ever has, and I love it. I'd be lying if I said otherwise. Even when you exacerbate the hell out of me, I can't stop thinking about it." His nose brushes up along mine and I tilt my head so I can get more contact. He pulls away and I know what's coming next. "But the flirting has to stop. The sexy teasing too. You work for me now, and that means I cannot touch you. It means I *won't* touch you."

The unyielding resolve in his voice makes my breath catch. It also makes me frown and I hate that I frown. It gives him power over me.

"Don't look at me like that. You think I don't want to kiss you? That I don't want to do more?"

I shrug, feigning indifference and failing. I already know he's right. I don't even know why I'm acting like this. Maybe it's because, for the first time in my life, a man is turned on by more than just my face and body. It's so goddamn sad, but it's also true. I challenge him and he loves it.

And I don't want that to be over despite the necessity behind it.

"I want you to stay here in my home," he continues. "I want you to feel comfortable like it's yours too. And me acting like a horny jackass is not doing that for you. Me sparring with you like we just were, only turns me on. So, we're going to find a common ground. We're going to be friends while we're in this house. Friends who trust and can talk and be ourselves. And when we're working, we're still friends, but friends who have a mutual work ethic, goal, and respect. And everything else between us, whatever the fuck this fucking chemistry is, will die. It has to."

And with that, he pushes off, climbing the three steps and heading into the house, scooping up his towel and wrapping it around his waist as he goes.

My heart is pounding in my chest, and my stomach is filled with nervous flutters over that man.

But he's unequivocally right.

About everything he said.

And a million things he didn't. When I'm with him, it's so easy to get swept up in our back and forth. I love challenging him as he said. I've never had this with anyone and I'm already positively addicted to it.

But... in my heart, I know it could never, *should never*, go beyond our verbal sparring.

I'm not a one and done type of woman.

That may work for some, and more power to them for being able to accomplish it, but I've given enough of myself over to others without gaining anything in return and I will not do that with my heart or my body.

And Keith doesn't date.

He doesn't do relationships.

He looks at me and sees a dead ex-girlfriend, which in it of itself is a huge red flag. He would plow through me, literally, and then be done in the next second.

Then where the hell would I be?

Yet another cliché I refuse to become.

So I like his boundaries. They're protective. They're smart. They're necessary for survival.

Now I have to figure out how to just be friends with a man who I already like way more than I should.

12

Maia

"Your move," Keith says, and I shift my gaze away from the HUGE screen in his media room, back down to the table in which his Harry Potter Wizard's chess set is in full action.

"Really?" I growl. "You're such a cunt."

He barks a harsh laugh. "A cunt? Women don't use the word cunt."

"Well, I just did because that's exactly what you are. You seriously moved your knight there to fuck with me. We both know you give a rat's ass about that rook. What's your game here, Dawson? What are you playing at?"

"Maybe I just like mowing down the little people on my road to ultimate domination."

I snort. "Wow. That's super sexy. Nothing like a world domineering tyrant. Seriously, my panties are wet."

"Maia," he warns.

"So easy." I roll my eyes at him. "I still can't believe your sister bought you this set, and you never used it before I came here."

"Believe it or not, I never played chess until you brought it out. It was a joke since I thought playing life-size chess like in the book and movie would be cool."

"Oh, I believe it. You have no strategy. I've only played on my phone before and I constantly kick your ass."

He scoffs. "More like I let you win, darlin'."

"Whatever." I shift quickly back to the screen because this is one of my favorite scenes.

"How do you like this stuff? You're twenty, not eighty."

"You're missing it all Keith. We're talking Grace Kelly and Jimmy Stewart. All the suspense. All the clean Hollywood drama that earned its money in the story and clothing and acting. Not in the special effects or over-sexualization of a generation. Hitchcock, for all his faults, and the man had many, was a cinematic, storytelling genius. 'When two people love each other, they come together—WHAM—like two taxis on Broadway.' I quote. I mean, come on. Grace Kelly, who was the embodiment of stunning, says this while wearing a gown for the ages and a flirty smirk for her man. You need to watch this. I mean it. The suspense is just so good."

"Tell me how you got into classic films," he commands instead of following my request, though I've caught him a time or two when it's my move checking out the screen.

I eye the board and discover a bishop he left unsecure when he moved his knight. Rookie mistake and I do mean that with the pun. "In the week I've lived here we've been together practically non-stop and watched almost half a dozen classic films. I'm shocked it's taken you this long to ask."

He cocks an impatient eyebrow.

"Fine," I grouse. "I used to watch them growing up. My mom liked them—one of the only things we had in common—and I got into them because they were beautiful and such a perfect escape. They were free to borrow from the library, so we did that often, and whenever we went, she'd let me check out a book or two because they were also free. That's also how I got into history and Greek mythology. Anyway, I became a film minor in college. My freshman film classes were super cool and all old films that showcased some of the best Hollywood's golden era produced."

"What was your major?"

"Psychology. I wanted to be a school guidance counselor or psychologist."

"Wanted to be? Past tense?"

I shrug. I'm not going there right now. I'll get back to college eventually. My plan for the moment is to save every freaking penny I earn as the assistant to Wild Minds and pay off all the debts. By my calculations that should only take a little more than eight months and that includes me finding another dump to live in. After that, when I'm debt-free, the world is my oyster and I plan on finding all its pearls.

"Is that why you came out to Los Angeles? Searching for Hollywood glory?"

"Noooo." I scrunch up my nose. "Acting is not my passion or my desire. I just like to watch movies. Your move."

"You took my bishop," he complains, eyeing the board with regret.

"You left him unprotected. Pay closer attention next time. If I were smart, I'd have wagered huge dollars on this game."

"Don't discount me, sweet darlin'. I'm unexpected as hell."

Ain't that the truth.

"Are you hungry? I bet you're hungry."

He reaches out, flipping my hair and then covering my eyes with his hand as he moves whatever piece he's moving on the board. I hear a few things clattering around. "Hey." I laugh, trying to pry his unrelenting grip from my eyes. "Why are you covering my eyes?" I finally break free only to find the board wiped clean of all black figures. I meet his, not even remotely close to an apologetic grin. The man is a wolf if ever there was one. "You totally cheated."

"No. I sneezed."

"Oh my god. Are you kidding me? You did not sneeze. And even if you did, the big bad wolf that you are couldn't have come close to this tactical of a blow. No one is that talented with their mouth."

"Maia."

I laugh harder at the warning tone in his voice. "Blow? You're really getting all penis hot over that? You're the one who brought up the analogy."

"Penis hot?"

I shrug, unwilling to take it back.

"I can't even say my penis isn't hot because that's just wrong on so many levels. But we said we weren't going to flirt or use sexual words or innuendos with each other, and since I'm a man of my life rules, that's how this goes for us."

"Oh, but not cheating isn't one of your sacred life rules? Cheater. I'm calling you a cheater. How's that work for you?"

The man is all about his life rules. As far as I've been able to discern, he pops these random rules out at random times, and they all have random, nonsensical or sequential numbers. Like yesterday he said, "Life rule #208, Maia: Always let them hear your battle cry and make sure they know you mean it." We were watching a Yankees, Red Sox game and the fans at Fenway were chanting Yankees suck. Hardly a battle cry, but I didn't argue it.

I also wouldn't exactly call that a life rule either, but he's so full of them that I think he makes up on the spot.

"Let's just call it a draw and eat some dinner while we watch the end of your technicolor film."

I point a stern finger at him."Not a draw. You're a cheater. That's the last time I let you play me, Dawson." I point a stern finger at him.

He stares at it like he wants to suck it into his mouth but mercifully he doesn't. Because we're friends and friends don't suck on friends' fingers. I think I learned that in kindergarten.

But yeah, that's what we are. Friends.

This past week since the hard-on in the pool incident as I silently call it has been filled with Keith being gone a lot during the day as he works on the album the band is trying to finish up. Marco and I spend the majority of that time going over everything I need to learn. But our nights have been spent watching movies and TV, reading and playing chess. Talking and laughing. Basically, my own personal version of heaven.

I always win at chess, but tonight was obviously his breaking point with that.

"I'll remember that, Angelo. So… hungry?"

"I could eat. But only if you sit with me on your big ol' sofa and watch a film with me."

"Will you rub my feet?"

I grin. Because how can I not? This man. This man is just… too many things that I cannot think about or even go near. "Not on your life, pal. Remember, I am one-handed for the next few weeks."

"How could I forget? Okay. Go sit down and pause your flick. I'll be back with some of the things Diane made me for us."

Us. I don't read into that. Not at all.

Diane, his housekeeper extraordinaire cooks very healthy. I'm guessing that's how Keith keeps his body as hot as it is. I mean, obviously he works out hard. The man does a bazillion laps in his pool and then hits his home gym, which is larger than my previous apartment times two.

But food plays a large component, and carbs are scarce while protein and veggies are in abundance. At least with dinners. There are plenty of muffins for breakfast, but I have yet to see him eat one.

Only rich people eat this way.

When I used to bring Isaac, the homeless vet who lived on the neighboring stoop, home leftover meals from the restaurant, he never once mentioned the carb to protein ratio. And the staff meals at the restaurants were usually some form of pasta that all of us waitresses and waiters ate happily because it was free food.

Get where I'm going with this?

Diane cooks protein-rich meals like a dream and again it's food I don't have to hunt/gather, so I'm happy with anything.

Keith returns a few minutes later with two plates loaded with salad, steak—mine is already cut up if you can believe that—and asparagus. It looks and smells divine and my mouth waters.

He sets it down in front of me and leaves instantly only to return with a beer for himself and a water for me. He teases me that I can't have a beer because I'm only twenty. Cue the eye roll, but it doesn't matter because I've never had a drink in my life, and I don't plan on starting now.

I take a bite of my food, chewing slowly as Keith hits play, settling in beside me. Like this is just the most normal thing in the world for him to do on a Friday night. But how can it be? Keith is a gorgeous, wealthy, single man. A celebrity to boot.

Plus, I heard him on the phone earlier with Henry. Henry was trying to get him to go out somewhere and Keith said he wasn't in the mood. That he was just going to stay in and watch a movie with me. It sounded from the one-sided version I heard that Henry was giving him some shit about that too.

Something inside of me stirs uncomfortably.

"What would you be doing tonight if I weren't here? It's Friday night."

He pauses mid-chew, only to continue a second later and swallow. He takes a sip of his beer, almost as if he's stalling, and then glances over at me. "I don't know. Depends."

"On what?" I press as he goes back to his meal like it's the most fascinating thing he's ever seen.

"On what I felt like doing," he says evasively, and I raise an eyebrow, making sure he catches it. He grunts. "I might be here watching a movie or a ballgame. I might be over at Jasper's since that's where we always seem to congregate. I might be out with Henry or another friend at a club or a party. Like I said. It depends."

"You can still do all that, you know. You don't have to stay here and babysit me." He ignores that in favor of his dinner and something about that frustrates me to no end. "I mean it. I'm not so helpless that I can't be by myself or heat my own dinner. I've already ingratiated myself on your life enough. If you want to go out, you should go."

He grins but tries to hide it by taking another sip of his beer. "Are you trying to kick me out of my own house?"

"No. Of course not."

"So you just don't like spending time with me then?"

"God, why are men so aggravating?"

He laughs. "Says the pot to the kettle, darlin'."

"I just mean—"

"I know what you mean," he interrupts, his gaze meeting mine with a hint of something I can't place behind it. "And if I really want to go out, I'll go out. If I didn't want to be here with you, I wouldn't be."

I smile before I can help it only to quickly realize how stupid that is and let it slip from my face. He said he wants us to be friends who can be ourselves with each other and I feel like we are. At least I am with him. So if that's how he wants us to be, I suppose that means I can ask him anything.

"When you go out with Henry or your other friends, do you meet women to have sex with?"

Keith chokes lightly on his bite of food, clearing the obstruction away with a few heavy hacks and then he pins me with a wary stare. "Why would you ask that?"

"Just curious how it all works for you. I mean, I know you don't date any of the women you take to bed—"

"Who told you I don't date?"

Oh. Well, crap. That slipped out, didn't it? I can feel my stupid cheeks heating. "Marco might have innocently mentioned something in passing."

He blows out a frustrated breath, running a hand through his thick dark hair. I bet that feels nice to do. I bet the strands are silky and soft. "Yes. Sometimes when I go out, I meet women and have sex with them. Not as often as you think, but it does happen from time to time. And no," he adds with a finality to his tone. "I don't date those women. I have sex with them and that's it. Is that all you're curious about or is there more you want to know about my private sex life?" His eyes are all over me. Rough and unapologetic.

He's saying don't dish it if you can't take it.

"You know mine."

"Yes, I know all about yours. Believe me, I'm very aware of it.

There's more though, what do you want to know?" He waves an impatient hand in the air, indicating I should just ask and get it over with.

"These women are okay with that? Just sex and nothing more?" I whisper because suddenly my heart is starting to pound in my chest, and I don't even know why I'm nervous. Maybe it's the way he's looking at me. The way he said he's very aware of mine.

"Yes. They are. Most of them are only after that as well. A quick and dirty fuck and nothing more." He's watching me even more intently as he says that, and I have to look away from his scrutinizing gaze. It makes me want to squirm so badly. The way he says dirty fuck like that. "Some of them are looking for more. They want to fuck a rock star. They want the money and fame and notoriety that comes with dating one. They want to be able to brag. But I never slip my cock inside them until they agree it's just one and done and sign the same NDA you did."

Jesus. He's really trying to rattle me.

He's completely succeeding too. My face is a fireball. My chest is heaving. My nipples are hard and tight. This time I can't stop the squirm, my eyes dropping. He's still watching me. I know he is. Even though I can't manage to meet his eyes, I can feel the weight of his.

"Did I answer your questions, sweet darlin'? Is that what you wanted to hear? Or were you looking for specifics as well on how exactly I pleasure them."

"Stop it," I clip tersely. "You're being mean. You didn't have to answer me if you didn't want to." My eyes flash over to his. They're no longer blue. They're black and feral and possibly a bit angry. "You know that's not what I was asking. I was just curious."

He leans in, his fingers sweeping along my cheek as he brushes a lock of my hair behind my ear. My breath hitches as he leaves it there, gliding his thumb back and forth on my lobe before he rights himself, pulling away from me completely.

He returns to his meal like none of that just happened.

And when he speaks again, his voice no longer holds any of the heat it just had. "No, Maia. I don't date any of the women I take to bed. I don't want to date any of them. I don't want relationships or girlfriends. I don't take women out to dinner or to a club. I don't ask for phone numbers and truth be told; I don't really care about their names."

Because they're not her, I want to say but don't.

I've already pushed him farther than I should have. His sex life is none of my business and I shouldn't have asked. It's not something that should have been eating away at me the way it has been. I am his friend and he is my boss—and I feel sick.

I shuffle some of my food around on my plate before I pick up another bite and force it down. I don't waste food. Growing up, I was never sure where my next meal was coming from or when I'd have it. But right now, it's a task even to chew. Maybe it's because I'm young or inexperienced or have watched too many Hollywood movies, but I want to be the one who is different for him.

Stupid, right? Things like that never work out the way you imagine they will.

There is no changing a man like Keith Dawson. Not with his life rules and residual grief that hovers just beneath the surface, only visible at certain times and if you look hard enough.

I don't know what I'm searching for with him or why.

And I need to let it go.

"Do you want to watch *Die Hard*?"

"What?" He laughs, tilting his face in my direction, some of the light I had extinguished with my prying returning to him.

"Die Hard. You know, yippee ki yay, motherfucker."

"Can we have popcorn?"

A gust of relieved air passes my lungs in the form of a bemused laugh. "Popcorn is a must with a movie like that. But I didn't think mister I'll-pass-on-the-carbs-thank-you, ate such things."

"I love the hell out of popcorn. Pull up the flick and I'll get going on that." He stands up, plants a kiss on my forehead, and takes our plates. *Did he just kiss my forehead?* Just a simple innocuously innocent gesture shouldn't make my heart beat like this.

I keep fighting it. I keep pushing back the thoughts. I keep telling myself that it will never happen because he just said it, he doesn't even care about their names. He doesn't want to date them or make them girlfriends.

But the bastard knows my name.

He stays in with me night after night. He watches my movies even though they're not his movies. He cuts up my steak because he knows I can't. He asks me all the questions and listens while I give him all my answers. We play chess and laugh and talk endlessly. And when we're silent, we don't need to fill it because it's not awkward.

It's perfect.

I have no idea what to do or how to stop my ever-growing infatuation with Keith Dawson, but that one stupid, nothing of a kiss just became so much more for me. I just said I need to let it go and that press of his lips derailed me. I should watch a YouTube video or read a self-help book that can guide me back to safer, *friendlier*, no-feelings-involved pastures. All my inexperience is proving dangerous and detrimental to my heart.

He likes the way I look. That does not mean he likes *me*. At least not in that way. Maybe I should ask him for the name of his tattoo artist so I can get that inked on my forehead.

"Hey Keith?" I call out.

"Yeah?" He turns back to me expectantly.

"For what it's worth, I'm glad you've been staying in with me."

He smiles a smile that lights up his whole face, and my heart gallops in my chest in a way it never has before. "Me too."

Dammit, he means it.

As much as that pleases me, it also scares me.

I TURN AWAY, listening as his footfalls grow fainter, and when I'm sure he's good and gone, I plant my hand over my heart, begging it to stop beating for him the way it is. He'll break me, and I'm not sure that's a wound I can recover from this time.

13

Keith

WITH MY AIRPODS in and my eyes closed, I'm listening to the lyrics Jasper laid down along with his acoustic. He evidently wrote this last night and the sick bastard that he is, wants to add this to our album that is so near completion we can taste it.

"What's another song? So our album will be eighteen songs instead of seventeen. Big shit."

That's what he said this morning when he sent it to me to work on, waking me up out of a sound sleep I had just recently fallen into. I haven't slept well since having Maia here. Then freaking Marco came knocking on my door, as he does every weekday morning, bright and shiny early and there was no more rest to be had.

He likes to have 'team meetings' with Maia first thing, which I honestly think is just the two of them gabbing over my coffee and muffins.

And just like every morning he shows up, I go out for a swim.

And just like every morning, I send up a silent prayer to the heavens that the laps and the extra weights I've been lifting will help me get my head back on straight.

That I will somehow be able to stop constantly thinking about my band's stunning new assistant. The one I hired and took cock-blocking responsibility for.

Setting our boundaries straight last week was the only thing I could do.

We have too much sexual tension. Too much chemistry. That's a tough thing to fight and it typically only ends one way. Naked. Not an option for us. So yeah, boundaries. Rules!

And since that morning, I've stuck to them.

I should run from this woman, but instead I spend all my time with her. And when I'm not with her, I'm thinking about her.

I've been good despite her prying questions and pretty brown eyes and alluring take no prisoners smile. We've been friends. Playing games and talking and eating dinner in front of the television. It's been more fun than I thought staying in could ever be. More fun than I can remember having in a very long time.

Even if my mind is filled with nothing but filth when it comes to her.

"Keith," she says with a gentle tap on my shoulder as if she's afraid of breaking into my concentration. On this particular verse, the beat is starting to flow through my head so interrupting me is exactly what she just did.

"I'm working."

"I know," she replies, her tone nonplussed with my shitty attitude. "But as your assistant, I am obliged to inform you that if we don't leave now for the studio, you will be late to meet your band members. Per the schedule I have on my calendar for today, you have eight hours booked starting at ten am."

"Already on the ball, I see."

"It's Monday. Most people are."

I open my eyes and find her farther away than I thought she would be. She changed her dress too. She's still got her flip-flops on, but now instead of the short, lavender halter thing she was wearing this morning, she's in a more demure pale blue tank top dress that flows down to mid-calf. The only problem is she's still wearing a sports bra, so her tits are pushed up and together and revealing enough cleavage to draw the eye. Unfortunately, I know she can't help that and I'm not about to offer to help her put on a different bra since it's obvious she can't do that herself.

It's one thing if she's dressed like this in front of me or Marco, but I hate the idea of her walking into the studio, being around all those people like this.

"How are you getting along with your arm? Do you need help with anything?"

She never asks for help. Never. I either do something for her without asking her first or she finds a way around it. It's not great.

"What do you think I need help with?"

Your bra? "Nothing in particular. I just want to make sure you're not overdoing it." And I even manage to pull that off with a warm smile and not the slightest hint of desire. Go me. Life rule #327: When you make a promise to yourself, commit to it all the way and never break it. This is what we masters of the universe call control, motherfuckers, and clearly I'm slaying it.

"I'm fine for this morning, but I would appreciate it if you'd be willing to do the plastic bag thing later so I can shower. Other than that, I've learned some good tricks in the last ten days."

"Like wearing dresses and flip-flops?"

Her cheeks pink up a little bit, but she nods with a self-satisfied smile. "Like dresses and flip-flops. Something I'm going to purchase a few more of once I get my first paycheck."

"I can—"

"Nope." She holds her hand up stopping me. "Don't even try it. Now come on, we need to leave. I won't tolerate being late on my first official day on the job."

She's spent all last week learning and going over things with Marco, but today is the first day she's coming into the studio. Honestly, I kept her home to make sure her head and concussion were fully healed. But today I'm bringing her along. Not something she really needs to do, but in addition to her probably going stir crazy, I want her to watch us play.

We hop in my truck and I instantly set it up so that Jasper's newest is playing through the sound system. "Tell me what you think of this."

Maia's brown eyes flash to me and then to the dashboard as if she's watching the lyrics unfold before her. I'm tapping on the wheel, still hearing this new beat in my head as I maneuver us through Los Angeles traffic, heading farther east where Turn Records, our label and studio, is located.

Time is a capsule unexplored.
Time is a lie with no detour.
But if time is a lie then you saw my truth.
A switch of fate no one can undo.
So brighten my sky, my darkest day.
Loves a game I no longer know how to play.
Switch. Switch. Switch it for me.
Lost in that memory pushing me out to sea.
Switch. Switch. Switch it that way.
The high I feel in your eyes is here to stay.
Switch. Switch. Switch till it stops bleedin'.
Finding you could be all I needed...

"This is about his wife, right?" she asks softly, and all I can do is give a non-committal half-nod and shrug.

But the more I listen to it, to all the lyrics, the less I'm sure. That's just one verse, but the lyrics of this song are all about the past. They're all about love and loss. They're all about finding something, *someone*, new who can switch up all that heartache for you.

I mean, it's possible that it is about Vi. Jasper wrote our entire first album about her who at the time was dating Gus. All his secret, pent-up love that he hid from everyone, especially from her. And after she broke up with Gus and walked out of our lives, there were more songs about her that followed.

We all pretended like we didn't know. But we did.

And when Viola came back into our lives and she and Jasper

finally got together, there were more songs. More romantic prose all about her, his muse. Plenty about Adalyn and his newest daughter, Cora too.

But this feels different. This song has a darker note to it. A pain interlaced in the lyrics.

Why do I have the sneaking suspicion he wrote this song for me? About me?

Or maybe I'm reading too much into it and extrapolating my own thoughts based on his lyrics. I suppose that's what a great artist does to their listeners and Jasper is the best.

"Well, it's beautiful. I obviously haven't heard the others on the album you're working on, but if they're like this I have to imagine you'll have another hit on your hands. I will be honest; this is quite the trip. I'm speaking metaphorically, of course. Not about the ride to the studio. I mean working as a band assistant. Especially with a band I've always loved and admired as much as I do. It's crazy, right? Surreal. That's the word I constantly flitter back to. Surreal."

"Nervous about something?" I quip.

She flips me off but she's smiling so wide and her enthusiasm is infectious.

"Terrified more like, but really excited. For the first time since I left for college two years ago, I'm excited about something."

That's unbelievably depressing. "You weren't even excited when you moved out here?"

"Nooo. I was running. And needed money, ASAP. That was all that was on my mind. Surviving and not getting in deeper. But this feels like the best of both worlds. Something I can do for me and be good at and use to pay off those debts."

"This is your way of saying thank you, isn't it?"

She giggles with gleeful abandon. "Yes, but I didn't think you'd like me to say it again, so I'm just relaying my supreme joy with my new job in the hopes that you'll understand what it means to me and how grateful I am for the opportunity."

"I'm glad, sweet darlin'. You're fun to watch when you're happy."

And making you happy makes me really happy and I refuse to think too deeply on the darker side of why that is.

A sparkle of mischief hits her eye. "Sweet darlin'? Is that mean to be ironic?"

I laugh, throwing her a quick eye. "You're sweet. I'm sure." I tilt my head, winking at her. "Well, I'm sure you have some sweetness mixed into all that fire you breathe."

"Maybe once. Maybe sometime again. So I'll keep your new nickname for me. I like it."

She shoots me a saucy grin, and as I stare at her lips for the umpteenth time just today, I woefully admit to myself that this sexy blonde is officially my devil. If Amy was my angel, this woman is her opposite. They may share some physical resemblance, enough that I occasionally internally trip a little, but this woman sitting beside me is nothing but trouble.

We pull into the underground lot and I lead my wide-eyed companion through the lobby and over to the elevator. "That was..." She trails off, her breath catching high in her throat. "Oh my god. Keith. Holy taco Tuesday. Was that freaking Gabriel Rose? Like, *the* Gabriel Rose from Blind Tears?"

"Yup."

"But you waved to him. You know him?" she whisper-shrieks. I shrug indifferently, which only seems to fuel her on. "Keith!" She slaps my arm. "You know him?!"

"Yes." I grin as we step onto the elevator and I press the button for the studio floor. "He is Lyric Rose's father and Lyric is not only the CEO of Turn Records, but she's also our main producer."

"Shut the motherfuck up."

Now I can't fight my laugh. Her awestruck, wide-eyed thing is impossible to resist. "Again, you weren't like this when you met me."

"You're kinda okay and all, but that was Gabriel Rose."

"*Kinda okay*?"

She shrugs, twisting to face the elevator doors, effectively dismissing me. "I think I might like Henry better. He's charming in all the ways you're abrasive. And Jasper's lyrics are exquisite poetry I can't resist. Oh, and Gus's—"

I swat her ass before I can stop it. It makes a nice loud *smack* in the quiet din of the elevator. She spins to me, her mouth popped open and her brown eyes incredulous as they lock onto mine.

Shit, I just spanked her.

My new assistant.

In an elevator as we go to work. After I told her we were to be friends and respectful.

I just undid everything I spent the last ten days fighting.

The car starts to slow but neither of us has moved or even uttered a sound. We just continue to stare, both of us shocked with no idea what to do about what I just did. I should say something. I should tell her I'm sorry. That I was unprofessional. That it wasn't intentional and it just kind of happened. But again, no sound comes out.

My palm stings from how hard I hit her so I know her ass must too. That shouldn't turn me on as much as it does, but let's be real here, her ass... if she wasn't standing before me, I'd be biting my knuckles to muzzle my groan. That's how unbelievable her ass is.

I don't move. She doesn't either. She's silent. I can't manage a sound. It's a fucking standoff that has me nervous and far more excited than I have any right to be.

Just before the elevator stops, she steps into me, her hand diving into my hair cupping the back of my head and dragging my face to hers. Her lips press boldly against mine, a startled gasp fleeing her lips, like she's as shocked by her move as I am. That gasp just as quickly turns into a moan and I think that just became my favorite sound ever.

I stand here, dazed for a half-beat, only to close my eyes and kiss her back.

Her lips are warm and soft and so full. Like pillows I want to sink into and get lost in. Her fingers toy with the strands of my hair as she moves her mouth against mine. Slow, light kisses that she intersperses with deeper plunges and slips of her tongue.

Kisses that leave me dizzy and breathless and *aching*.

My hands grasp her face, holding her against me, tilting her head and deepening the connection because I just can't fucking get enough. My tongue goes in for the kill, tasting her, toying with her. Taking no motherfucking prisoners as I consume her mouth like the greedy bastard she makes me. My cock strains against my jeans and I push into her without conscious thought. Hell, conscious thought fled my mind the second her lips touched mine.

I'm dying for her to feel me. *Feel me!* Feel how hard you make me, Maia. Feel how desperate I am for you.

I want this woman.

I want this woman so bad.

And now she knows exactly how much. Her second gasp as I grind against her sweet body tells me there is no mistaking it. No playing it off. It's all for you, I want to say but I'm too busy tasting every inch of her mouth to speak.

All too soon the car glides to a stop and the elevator dings and the doors part and she draws back, a thin trail of saliva going with her and clinging to her bottom lip when it breaks.

Fuck, that's so hot.

Dilated pupils darken her eyes. Her cheeks are the most devastating shade of pink. She smirks, licks her lips taking in that tiny pool of my spit, and says, "I'd say the kiss made us even for the smack on my ass, but I think it's pretty obvious I enjoyed both a little too much for that to have been a punishment for either of us. Oh well, I'll just have to try harder next time."

She saunters out of the elevator, and I quickly press the button to keep the door open, so I don't get shuffled off to the next floor.

I blow out a breath. Then another. Then a discombobulated laugh.

Ho-lee-shit. What the hell was that?

I'm panting and smiling and all I want to do is grab her, haul her ass back in here and do it all over again. Her kiss is like candy. Like a drug. Sweet and addictive and damn.

"Come on, Keith. We're gonna be late."

I grin wider. Even though I shouldn't. Even though I promised both her, myself, the guys, and I think even her pal Jesus once or twice that I wouldn't touch her.

I guess that's kind of fucked now. You know, since I ground my cock against her.

Damn. I probably shouldn't have done that.

"Keith!"

Right. Recording.

"I'm officially mad at you, Maia."

She laughs. I don't. How many life rules did I just break with that one kiss? And how many more will I end up breaking before this is over?

14

Maia

I KISSED HIM. I shouldn't have kissed him. What in the name of Buddy the Elf was I thinking?

Actually, I know exactly what I was thinking.

I was thinking the man smacked me on the ass. That's what I was thinking.

I was thinking that after the smack on the ass, and the strange heat that subsequently flowed through me, that I wanted to kiss him to see if I was the only one feeling it.

Spoiler alert: I wasn't.

Call it experimental. Call it an irresistible temptation. Call it pure freaking insanity.

Whatever the hell it was, it was a one and done thing. Just like how he is with all his women. Because the second he stepped off the elevator, he said just that. "Now that we got that out of our systems, we can't do it again. Not if this is going to work."

Right. He's right. I know he's right. Ugh! So Keith. Strong and in control without even the slightest hint that what happened in the elevator thirty seconds prior was even a factor in his head. I tried not to let it sting, but let's be real here, we all know it did.

The studio setup is pretty nuts. In a very cool way.

I've been sitting in a reclining and massaging leather lounger for the last few hours, listening to the guys work through this new song Jasper decided had to be added at the last minute. Lyric Rose, *the* Lyric Rose, is here too since she's their producer. She's been patiently and expertly walking them through it.

Well... sort of.

"Gus why do you keep changing that chord up?" she asks, speaking into a microphone since the guys are in the booth, all with instruments, all playing together, which she told me is not standard for when they're laying down a track. Then each artist typically plays separately.

"I don't know," I hear him answer since she's not wearing her headphones. She has all the sound pipped through the room so I can hear it too. Very cool and classy move if you ask me since I am no one but the assistant and I'm sure my thoughts and input aren't warranted or appreciate "I don't mean to. It's just where my fingers naturally go on the frets. Where the words are sort of leading me."

"No, I like it," Lyric tells him. "I think it works better than what you had before."

"So, what if we did it like this?" Keith suggests, tapping something out on his drums, and a half-beat later Gus chimes in his with electric guitar only to be quickly followed by Henry on the bass. Jasper is just kind of standing there, staring at Gus, his acoustic hanging around his neck and dangling at his stomach while he listens.

I had no idea this was how music was made.

I guess I never quite gave it much consideration before, but it's such a process to get one line of music down and have it match the lyrics. The main aspect of the song seems to be coming from Keith and Gus. They've been going back and forth with each other, writing things down on paper and toying with different arrangements. Henry seems like an accessory, though he's an insanely talented one. He picks up everything they're doing instantly adding a depth to the sound that really brings it to life.

Jasper is obviously the words and he appears to enjoy stepping back and letting Keith and Gus do their thing. They have a science. A very specific way of crafting their art.

It's astounding and beautiful to watch, especially as a fan.

And before I know what I'm doing, I stand up, take my work phone out of my purse and snap a picture of them. Then I go into their band's Instagram, Facebook, and Twitter accounts and post the pic with the caption: Are you ready? We've got something extra special we're working on for you! #ComingSoon #WildMinds #InTheStudio

This is my first official time posting for them, as them, and I hope this one goes well. I was told nothing personal. No pictures of Jasper's children or Viola. If they want something like that posted, they'll do it themselves. I was told the same with regards to Naomi Kent. Henry and Keith both said they didn't care as long as it wasn't personal or embarrassing.

"Do you know what I hate?" Lyric asks out of nowhere, and it takes me a long couple of seconds to realize she's talking to me.

"What do you hate?" I retort after she swivels in her chair to face me. Lyric is adorable. She's petite, blonde, and perky. Even for a tough as nails record producer and executive. She's also wearing bubblegum pink, so I think that only drives that home further.

"When brilliant artists feel the need to throw on an extra song to their nearly finished album and the new song is so good that I can't even argue putting it off for the next one."

I laugh a little at that, because I agree. I mean, about the brilliant artists and amazing new song. "It's beautiful. I haven't heard the other tracks yet, but I'm really loving this one and it's not even close to done."

"No." She sighs. "It's not. It's going to be a long day. Why did Keith drag you here just to have you sit?"

Good question.

"I don't think he likes leaving me alone for too long. He either thinks I'm going to rob him blind or views me as a helpless damsel in distress." I hold up my broken arm. "I haven't figured out which yet."

"Or maybe he just likes having you around." She wiggles her eyebrows at me and after that kiss in the elevator, I blush. Again. Because that seems to be all I do when it comes to the man. So lame.

"I doubt that. I'm more of a pain in his ass than anything else. But you know, you've all been at this for a while. I'm going to run out and grab a bunch of sandwiches and things. What do you like to eat?"

Isn't that what Keith told me to do? Feed them when they're deep into their work?

"Burritos, girl. Bring in burritos and these boys will work all afternoon and I'll be forever in your debt. There is this yummy place on the corner that I can never remember the name of, but I think it has viva in it. Anyway, here's what they like."

She writes everything down for me and I scurry out, following her directions and quickly finding the restaurant. And as I wait for our order to be ready, I scroll through the band's social media. The post I just created already has over three thousand likes on both Facebook and Instagram respectively as well as a number of excited comments and a bunch of shares.

They have nearly a hundred and twenty million followers—talk about mind blown—but their postings have been sporadic and a bit lackluster. Mostly album covers and tour and release dates. Nothing personal about the band or its members.

I'm hardly on social media myself, and I'll be the first to admit, I'm a novice. But I think I can do better than what they had going.

Fans want to connect with their favorite bands. Not just musically but on a personal level. We like to feel we're connected. Part of the inner sanctum.

Even if we're actually not.

A surge of excitement rushes through me for more than the band I'm working for or the paycheck. I think I could love this job, grunt errands included. Doing this makes me feel real and acknowledged and giddy and freaking out of my mind with... that pulls me up short. Like big time.

Messing around with your boss is a no-go. Like rule one in that playbook. Keith Dawson caliber life rule even.

And yet I kissed him.

And he kissed me back.

But it's not like it's going to happen again. It was an impulse move. Nothing more.

So why does that leave a sour taste in my mouth?

I quickly brush all that away. I need to focus on my new job. I need to focus on healing. I need to focus on paying off all the debt in my name. Eight months till financial freedom.

That's given me a high like nothing else.

An inner grit and fortitude to keep surging forward.

Keith and I talked about how I wanted to return to school, and he said he was all for that. He said he thought it was fantastic, and that if I continued with this job, which he hoped I would if I enjoy it, then the band would make sure I have the time in my schedule for that.

To earn the salary I'm earning and be able to go to school would be a dream.

Which means no distractions.

Entering the studio, I find the guys standing in the lounge area with Lyric. Sweat glistens their foreheads and sticks to their shirts as they wipe themselves down with towels and drop haggardly onto the sofas. "I bring sustenance," I tell them, holding up the bags of food with my good hand.

Keith frowns. "You shouldn't have carried all that back yourself."

I roll my eyes at him. "Slow your roll there, Doc Brown. I have two hands. Obviously." I hold the bags up again right before I set them down on the large square coffee table.

"Did you just Doc Brown me? You do realize he was not a medical doctor?"

"Sort of forgot that part, but I was blanking on film-based doctors at that second. I'll work on my zippy comebacks. How's that?"

He grunts, but I think I catch a hint of a smirk. Or maybe that's just me. Still, it's not awkward or weird between us after what happened in the elevator. We're back to us, which is obviously awesome. Perfect, in fact.

"Why are you smiling?" Henry asks, before turning to look at the other guys. "Right? She's smiling."

I laugh at that, taking a seat and grabbing my own burrito from the bag. The guys must be ravenous because they dig in, mumbling out their thank yous in between large bites. "Why wouldn't I be smiling?" I ask just before taking a bite, grateful that burritos are single-handed food.

"I don't know," Henry murmurs around a mouthful of food. "It's a different smile, I guess. A happy one."

"A different smile?" Jasper questions, looking at me with an inquisitive brow before turning back to Henry. "You studying her smile now, man? Careful not to do it too closely. She works for us."

Jasper says this in jest. In fact, Henry calls him a hypocrite while throwing a balled-up napkin at him and Jasper laughs. But I still catch Keith wincing out of the corner of my eye before it's just as quickly gone. Regret is oozing off him in waves though. We may still be us and it might not be awkward between us, but he hasn't met my eyes since the elevator.

Not once.

It makes me want to provoke him just to get him to look at me.

"Henry is right actually and clearly observant as hell." I wink at him, giving him more of that smile.

"I play bass. It's my job to be observant. Spill it. Why are you smiling such a beaming smile?"

"What dude says beaming smile?"

"What's up your ass, man?" Henry snaps back at Keith. "You've been a twatty bitch since you stepped into the studio."

Keith just grumbles under his breath, going back to his burrito. Yeah, that might be my fault there, Henry. I kissed your bandmate and I don't think he's too happy about it.

"Well," I jump in, wiping my mouth and reaching into my purse. "Check this out." I pull up their Instagram account since that has the most action going. We're up to over two hundred thousand likes and several thousand comments already. I hand it to Henry first since he asked why I'm smiling.

"That's us from this morning?" His brows pinch together. "Damn, that's getting some serious movement."

I nod. "Yup. I also updated the links in your profile so that it has your new album's pre-order at the top."

"And I'm very grateful for that," Lyric chimes in, her hazel eyes glowing as she winks at me. "That was smart thinking."

"For real. I should have you to take over Naomi's social media," Gus states. "She hates that. Like deep in her bones, hates that."

I can understand why after all she's been through. At least what was published publicly.

"I'd honestly be happy to Gus, but this was my first go and I'd hate to not do your girl up proper. Give me a week and if things continue to go well, I'd love nothing more than to help your lady love out."

"And this is why I already love you." He points a finger at me, and I grin.

"I actually ditto that. Not only are you more than likely getting these guys added pre-orders on their album, but you got my burrito order perfect and as they can attest, I'm a picky bitch."

I gleam at her. More of those different smiles Henry noticed super-injected with a healthy dose of happiness.

"Then my job here is done." I give a half bow.

And then it hits me. Why my smile looks different.

No one has ever given me praise before. Not for something I've done at least. Never at home growing up. Not at college either, and definitely not when I was working at Lavender or for the law firm.

That's what's making me happy.

The overwhelming pride I feel.

Henry doesn't know me well enough to know this, but I haven't felt happy like this in a very long time. And before now, it was only once before. When I first left home and went to college. Even now, this feels different. Better.

That happiness was fleeting as it was all ripped away from me.

Like everything else in my life always has been.

Is that what's going to happen now?

I look at each of the guys, laughing and shooting the shit, and then over to Keith who I discover is staring at me with an indiscernible expression. Despite that, his eyes are searching, and while I've been nothing about candid with him since we met, suddenly, I don't want him to read me so well. I don't want him to know how jumbled up my mind is.

How he's a large part of that mess, already, which just seems ludicrous.

The man who only a few nights ago admitted he doesn't even care about the names of the women he fucks. Would I be so meaningless to him? Does it even matter?

No, I decide. It most certainly doesn't because nothing will ever happen between us again. He said so himself.

And I have to guard myself. I have to protect my heart. I have to protect this job.

At all costs.

I can't lose this. This feeling. This second chance. It's everything, and right now, it's all I've got.

15

M aia

"WHO ELSE IS GOING to be there tonight?" I ask as Keith drives us up higher into the Hollywood Hills section of the city.

"Just us."

I throw him an impatient glare I know he doesn't see since his eyes are fixed on the road. "Who is us?"

"Jasper, Viola, Adalyn and Cora. Gus and Naomi. Lyric and her husband Jameson, who I don't think you've met yet. Henry. I think Marco and maybe even Ethan because he's in town."

"Who is Ethan?"

"Another producer, but he's also the COO of Turn Records. He's mostly based in New York now though. You'll love him. Him and Marco like to do shots together and tease the hell out us beefy straight men as they call us."

"He's gay too?"

"Yes." Keith nods.

"Are him and Marco..."

"A couple?" he asks, filling in the blank. "No. Marco is about twenty years older than Ethan, and Marco has been seriously dating someone for the last year."

"That scag," I gasp. "He never told me that. All those breakfasts and he never once mentioned anything about a boyfriend."

"That's because Marco does not talk about him. He says it's a jinx and the guy he's with is very anti-LA, music-industry, or anything celebrity. He's an accountant for an auditing firm."

"I freaking love that. Still, that must make it rough for Marco."

"Yeah, I've only met the guy once or twice, but he seems great," Keith says, grinning quickly in my direction. Then, almost as if he catches himself doing it, quickly shifts back to the road.

We haven't talked about the kiss. Or the ass smack. Or the elevator. Not since he told me it wasn't going to happen again.

No, we're completely immersed in this safe, neutral world where Maia and Keith live in a copacetic existence. It's all superficial without flirting or teasing or easy banter. Basically, it's our boring alter-ego, but right now, a necessary one. One I think we both seem to appreciate because we know the elevator was a moment of recklessness and temptation that can never, under any circumstances, happen again.

"And we're going to be swimming?"

I'm a little, or a lot unhappy about that. I didn't know we were going to be going to Jasper's for a barbeque after being in the studio all day. This was our fifth day in a row there and today felt like the longest yet. I'm gross. I could use a shower and a nap and a change of clothes. Plus, swimming with a cast is a no-no and I don't even have a bathing suit. But Viola called Jasper and told him that Naomi was already there, and they wanted everyone to come for dinner.

And since I really love Viola and Naomi, I readily agreed. Those two have been nothing but warm and sweet with me. They instantly took me into their fold as a friend. Even if the first time I met Viola she looked like she was about to burst into tears at the sight of me. She felt terrible about it afterward.

"I'm sorry for the way I reacted when I first saw you. I should have said this to you earlier, but I'm still a bit... I don't know. Anyway, I'm sorry."

"You knew Amy?"

I didn't even know her name until Henry told me it. He said she died tragically and would not elaborate beyond that because Henry believes it's up to Keith to tell me. Only Keith does not talk about her or what happened. I still don't know anything beyond her name and that she looked like me. When Henry and I talked about it, he swore to me that I am nothing like she was. Night and day were the words he used.

Viola nods, glancing at Naomi who I assume already knows what's going on since these people don't seem to have secrets kept between them. "Yes, I knew Amy. We went to high school together. She and I were friendly simply because I was dating Gus and she was dating Keith. But she and I were never what you'd call close. Though I don't think anyone really was with her."

"What do you mean?" I ask, the words flying out of my mouth without filter.

She glances past me in Keith's direction, lingering there for a long moment and then turning back to me. The grim look in her eyes makes my heart instantly start to pound. "She kept her distance is all. Has Keith talked about her?"

I shake my head no. "I haven't asked either."

"Well, the story needs to come from him. But as far as I know, he hasn't talked about it since it happened."

Since it happened. Not since she died. It's a strange choice of words.

I've tried not to focus on that conversation since. On her reaction to me. On all the questions I have about Amy and how she died and what happened to Keith after.

Still, the fact that she had this sort of reaction in the first place sits all kinds of wrong in my stomach. I don't want to look like Keith's ex. I don't want to remind any of them of a dead girl they all once loved.

I want them to see me, not Amy.

I want Keith to like me not because I look like her.

I never had a moment's insecurity before, but whenever I think about this strange situation, I'm flooded with it. It's not something that fits all that well on my skin or in my heart.

Whatever. It is what it is and again, I've been trying not to focus on it.

Especially as we're pulling into what can only be described as a mega-mansion. This is the second time I've been here, but it still knocks my socks off. "You know, this is what I was expecting your place to be like." I sit up a little straighter, using my stupid cast a microphone and holding it up in front of my mouth. "I'm Maia Angelo, reporting to you live for Lifestyles of the Rich and Famous."

Keith laughs. "I think you're mixing a few things up here, darlin'. Wasn't that some British dude who did that? And wasn't that show in the eighties."

"Oh yeah. It most definitely was." I bounce my eyebrows at him.

He shakes his head at me, still chuckling. "Jas bought it when Adalyn's birth mother, Karina, was pregnant. He keeps talking about moving, but Vi loves it here too much for that to happen. Plus, now that they have Cora, I think they like having the bigger space."

"And you're sure Viola can lend me something?" I ask as he parks in the circular turnabout in front of the house.

He twists to look at me and then down to my chest for a fleeting second and then out the front windshield again. His fists clench the wheel as his jaw tics. "You don't have to wear a bathing suit," he grits out. "I doubt anything Vi has will fit you."

"Worried I'll give your friends a boob shot? Have a nipple slip situation?"

He growls out a curse. Oh, boy. This tense growly Keith is something else.

"Keep your shirt on, literally and metaphorically, and I'll keep mine on. How's that? Still, I wouldn't mind dunking my lower half, so if she's cool with it, I think I will borrow a suit."

He mumbles something I can't discern under his breath before he gets out of the truck, jogging quickly around to help me out. He always does this, and I'd be lying if I said I hated it.

We don't make it to the front door before it flies open and Viola

Diamond is standing there in all her perfection. She really is just a ray of sunshine wrapped in colorful rainbows. She and I have more in common than you'd think considering who she's married to now, but her past is nearly as ugly as mine.

She waves at Keith before quickly wrapping me up in a hug. This is only my second encounter with her, but she never makes you feel like an outsider. "Come on. Naomi is in the pool with my girls and the guys are already drinking too much and laughing too loud." She winks at me. "I'm thinking this was a mistake except I love having everyone here." She leads me into the house, guiding me to the stairs while Keith heads directly for the back where the outdoor area is. "I have a suit for you. Jas mentioned you didn't have one. Let's get you changed."

"She doesn't have to swim, Vi," Keith calls out.

"But I'd like to," I throw back, glaring at him over the railing of the stairs. Keith stomps off and I can't stop my small laugh.

"What's up his ass?"

"Me," I state. I wonder how much I should tell Viola Diamond since she is who she is, and these people do not keep secrets. But I could really use a girlfriend right now, something I've never really had before. "I kissed him in the elevator on Monday." Her eyes pop open wide. "It just kind of happened."

"Um. How does kissing someone just kind of happen?"

"We were arguing as we always do, and I said something, and he smacked my ass and I kissed him."

"Holy shit," she barks out in a cackle, throwing her head back and everything. "That's freaking awesome. Do the other guys know?"

I shake my head, my expression growing severe so she understands the magnitude of this. "No. I don't think Keith told them and I'd like it to stay that way."

"I won't say anything to Jasper. Did he kiss you back?"

Oh yeah, he did. "It doesn't mean anything."

"Why not?" She scrunches up her nose like that doesn't make any sense at all.

"Nothing can happen between us. That's what he said right after it happened and since then, he's been a monk where I'm concerned. He's made our relationship and position very clear. He's right though," I quickly tack on. "Trust me on that."

Viola purses her lips like she's giving this some actual thought. "I hear what you're saying but Keith doesn't just go around kissing girls, you know. He's very specific about the women he fools around with."

"He didn't kiss me. I kissed him. And anyway, I work for him and I'm temporarily living at his place and I can't lose this job."

"Girl, I get you hard on that one." She squeezes my arm. "It wasn't easy managing Jasper's moods when he hired me to be Ady's nanny while they went out on tour. But I needed the job and he needed a nanny, so we tried ignoring the storm brewing between us."

"Yes, but Keith and I are not you and Jasper. Nowhere close. We've known each other like not even two weeks."

"And sometimes all you need is a minute with someone. If there's chemistry, there's chemistry." She points a stern, motherly finger at me. "And you and Keith? You have chemistry."

"Well, chemistry or not, we're pretending it didn't happen. Which is how we both want it to be," I finish, so she knows this genuinely is different from how she and Jasper were. So, she doesn't get it into her adorable head that more is going on than really is. Her and Jasper had already known each other since childhood and Jasper had always had a secret thing for her.

So yeah, different. So, so different.

"Okay. But for the record, I've known Keith a long time and the way he looks at you isn't how he's looked at any other girl. And that includes Amy. You're nothing like her, you know. I mean that. Keith feels something for *you* whether he admits it or not. He just doesn't know how to get out of his own way. Now, let's get you changed up if you want to swim. Then we'll eat."

Ten minutes later, and after some very awkward help from Vi, I'm wearing a bikini that would have fit my little sister if I had had one. It's far too small in the bust—then again, what the fuck isn't. She handed me a T-shirt to throw over, but it doesn't do much to hide what's beneath.

"You look hot, but if you're uncomfortable, just keep the shirt on."

Right. Isn't that what I told Keith I'd do. "No one likes a rogue nipple popping out at the family barbeque."

Marco sees me first just as I step foot onto the patio and whistles out a catcall. "Damn. Check out my sexy beech. Slay it girl." I glare balefully at him and he instantly throws his hands up in surrender, though the shit-eating grin doesn't so much as slip an inch. "Come off it. If I had your body, I'd work that shit all over Sunset Boulevard."

"Are you calling her a prostitute?" Some guy with blond hair and light eyes asks, his brow pinched at Marco until he looks up at me with a dazzling smile. "Don't worry, honey. I'll kick his ass for you. You don't look like a hooker. You look stunning. I'm Ethan, by the way." He waves at me, and I offer a weak half-wave back because I'm too embarrassed to do much else.

"Um. Hi."

"I'm not intentionally calling her a hooker. I'm just saying she looks damn good."

"Both of you watch your mouths," Keith snarls, making Ethan and Marco grin from ear to ear like the Cheshire Cat.

"Yes. And cool it on the swearing. My girls are in the pool and can probably hear you since you're shouting," Jasper gripes, taking a sip of his beer.

"Well, this was fun and all, but I think I'm going to go swim with the ladies," I state, trying to cool the inferno that is my face. "Feels a lot safer and slightly less degrading than discussing my body and whether or not I look like a hooker in front of a group of men," I deadpan, cocking a pointing brow just for Marco.

"She's right. That wasn't the nicest, guys. Objectifying women by their bodies is wrong." Henry winks at me. "Just so you know, when you finally agree to date me, I'd never do that to you. I treat you like the goddess you are and kill anyone who said otherwise."

"Uh huh. Okay then. I'm just gonna..." I point to the pool and head in that direction.

Keith stands almost as if he's electrocuted out of his seat. Almost as if he's terrified I'm going to take off my shirt since he's eyeing the hell out of it. His eyes drink me in, starting at the hem of the clearly offending shirt that hits just above the aqua bottoms I'm wearing and glides up along to my thinly veiled tits, all the way up to my hair which Vi helped put up for me since I can't manage that one on my own.

He licks his lips and then takes a long pull from his beer. "Be careful with your cast," he warns, but something tells me concern for my cast wasn't what was on his mind. I'm tempted to pull the shirt over my head because I can be a total bitch like that, but I really don't want to show off my too-small bikini to everyone here. Just him.

Which again makes me crazy for even thinking that.

"Relax, big guy, I'm not going in past my waist." He still doesn't look happy, but he'll get over it. He has no choice. Bunching the shirt up around my belly button, I descend onto the step before sinking down into the warm water.

I force myself not to look back at him.

And I do my best to block out any noise of traffic coming from over in the lounge area.

This outdoor space is like something out of a magazine, and I take it all in, enjoying the tickle of water as it laps against my lower half and the warm California breeze as it hits my face, rustling the few errant strands that escaped my updo.

Naomi Kent, the popstar and Gus's fiancée, is in the pool. She's with Adalyn, who is Jasper's young, female doppelganger, and baby Cora, who is in a floaty thing with her sprig of blonde hair sticking up straight on top of her head. I make a silly face at her, sticking my tongue out and loving how a smile blindingly illuminates her chubby little face.

"Hi Ady," I offer with a wave and a smile just for her.

She looks at me, whispers, "Hi," in her sweet melodic voice and immediately goes back to her swimming. The first time I met Adalyn, she did a lot of staring at me without a lot of words. She warmed up, but I have to imagine having this many people around is tough for her, so I give her space to do her thing. She's an incredible little girl. Smart, silly, sweet. Really, everything. A couple of years ago the press had a field day over her diagnosis. Like a child being autistic is somehow newsworthy.

It's criminal the things they put them all through, especially her.

"She hates the noisy crowds," Naomi says, echoing my thoughts.

"She's a trooper though. And truth be told, I can't blame her for that."

"That she most definitely is. Still, the first time I met her, she didn't want to say hi to me, so you're already ahead of the game." Naomi's hands are on the baby floaty thing, playing and making faces similar to the ones I just was at Cora who is all giggles and excited splashes. "It's aggravating, right? Dealing with the guys when they're being poopy heads." She sticks out her tongue at the baby and winks at me.

I laugh, instantly relaxing. "Just a bit."

"I went through their initiation once. It gets better. Sort of. I don't know about with Keith. He likes to tease, it seems."

"He doesn't tease me so much anymore. Just picks fights."

"Oh, and you don't? I've heard the two of you together," Viola says, joining us. She hands me a glass of something before she walks down the steps back into the pool, going immediately for her daughters. "It's lemonade and non-alcoholic," she warns me as she stands in between Cora and Adalyn. "But if you'd like something a bit stronger to get through this crowd, we have plenty over at the bar."

I shake my head, taking a sip. "This is perfect. Thank you." I take another sip and then set it down on the edge of the pool.

"If you change your mind, neither of us would blame you. Keith hasn't taken his eyes off you since you came back out. Not once. His intensity is starting to get to me and he's not even looking at me. I swear, it's like Jasper redux."

Naomi laughs. "Lord, I still pant whenever I think about the chemistry Gus and I were throwing back and forth when we first met. I love where we are now and I would *never* go back in time, but sometimes I miss the build-up, you know?"

"Not really," both Vi and I say in unison before our eyes clash with each other and the three of us crack up.

"Jasper and I hate-loved each other," she continues. "We certainly didn't have the easy-going thing you and Gus had. And Keith is acting like a freaking alpha wolf when it comes to her." Vi points at me. "See. He's talking, sipping his damn beer while Q-ing it up at the grill, but he's staring so hard he doesn't even realize I'm catching him in the act of doing it."

Curiosity can be a real nuisance and before I can stop it, I'm glancing over. Straight into his electric blue eyes that are in fact staring straight at me. Into me. All over me. He's now standing beside Jasper, helping him make whatever they're grilling that smells so heavenly.

But yes, he's staring at me—a deep look with no end.

And no, his eyes are not happy.

They're feral. I want to yell, it was one damn kiss at him, but present company aside, I can't. Because I'm struggling too.

I quickly look away.

Keith Dawson is a mindfuck I can't indulge in. Even though I know I kinda started the battle, I'm holding up my white flag, needing to end the war.

I can't keep playing this game with him. The one where I'm consumed with trying to figure him out. The one where I get lost staring into his eyes because it's such a beautiful place to get lost in. I try not to let Viola's words from earlier latch on, but it's hard not to when he does, in fact, look at me differently.

I kissed him and we haven't talked about it. I kissed him and now he pretends like it never happened. So okay. Message received.

Still... I can't find it in me to regret it. And I can't stop myself from wanting to do it again, even when I know I absolutely should not.

16

eith

"If you don't go after her, I will," Henry tells me plain as freaking day, no punches pulled or sarcasm gracing his lips. "She's hot. She's smart. She's feisty. Fuck, a total firecracker. The complete package. And she totally digs me."

I scoff at that last bit if only to deflect. "I think you're wrong on that last one, bro." *Because that hot, smart, feisty girl kissed me. Not you.* But we're certainly not talking about that right now because none of these guys know my sweet darlin' planted a big one on me.

Or that I reciprocated like a man offered a second chance at life.

At breathing.

"You need to quit that. She works for us," I tell Henry since that's my mantra and I'm holding firm to it.

"Yeah, but look at Vi and Jas."

I growl. Because that's all I seem to do this week. I had a feeling he was going to go there. "That was different, and you know it."

"Maybe. Maybe not. She lives with you, so I think that makes her more off-limits for you than me. All I'm saying is if you want her, you should stake your claim before someone better does. Someone like me."

"I didn't think you liked them so curvy. You tend to go for the more petit ones."

He hitches up an unconcerned shoulder. "Maybe I've been missing out. Maybe it's time I try something new." He stabs his thumb into his chest with a smug smirk because he knows me well enough to know he's got me. Even if he's a lying bastard.

Because I seriously want to kill every asshole here. Especially Marco and Ethan, who keep going on and on about her body like it's something to gossip about. It's not. I get that they don't like pussy, but every other dude here does. And the last pussy on earth I want the straight males focused on is hers.

"Knock it off, Okay? I mean it."

"You're dumb. That's all I'm saying. You have a hot woman who you're obviously into living in your house. Every man, straight and gay" —he points at Ethan and Marco— "want her. You want her. You want her so bad you haven't stopped staring. What's your hang-up? Because she works for us? Or is it something—"

I glare at him. I glare fucking hard. "Stop—"

"Gotta jump back into the ocean sometime, brother. And she might just be the perfect fish to help you swim again."

She could be. I haven't known her long, but I know we have something different.

I like her. Hell, how could I not? And yeah, okay, I might really like her.

But that doesn't change our reality. Or at least mine.

We're a ticking time bomb. A game of Russian roulette. We're those angry looking storm clouds you see right before the funnel drops and a tornado wipes out your goddamn town.

We're power and heat and electricity. But all I see when I allow myself to feel any of that energy is destruction. Is chaos. Is loss.

She's sitting in the pool in those tiny panty-like bottoms and a T-shirt that does zero to hide her glorious tits beneath, and I don't like how Henry notices just how incredible she is.

She was right.

She *is* my Pandora's box.

Her evils are all over me, and I want to lick, taste, smell, kiss, touch, and fuck every last one of them. But I want more than that too, and that's why Henry really needs to shut up.

Life rule #1: Under no circumstances can you sleep with your band's stunning, completely untouched new assistant.

Yeah, that's made it to the top of the heap. Because it's so much more than the fact that her life has been rough. So much more than the fact that she's living with me and needs to feel safe. So much more than she works for us.

And Henry knows it despite his goading.

"Since when do you care or notice things like that? Since when do you care about dating or relationships?"

He grins like the devil despite the hard glint to his eyes. "*I* don't. *You* do. I will never want that whereas you're secretly dying for it."

I can't say anything else without giving everything away, so instead I get up and move over to the grill where Jasper is dropping burgers, dogs, and steaks to cook. He even has veggie burgers for Lyric since she's a vegetarian.

"You okay?" he asks because he knows me, and he knows I'm not.

I shake my head while contradicting myself. "I'm fine. Let's just eat and stop focusing on all things me and Maia."

We do eat and we joke and mercifully Maia puts her clothes back on and I try not to watch her all through dinner.

But on the car ride home, I ask something I've been wondering about since she first told me. "Why are you a virgin?"

Her head swivels in my direction, but I can't glance over long enough to meet her eyes. I have no business asking this question, but I have to know the answer all the same.

"That's hardly a question a boss should ask his employee."

No. It's certainly not. "And asking about the women I have sex with is hardly a question an employee should ask her employer. Humor me."

"Why does it matter?"

I don't know. But it does. Everything about her suddenly matters. Even when it shouldn't. "I'd like to know if you're okay with telling me."

"You know everything about me, Keith, and yet I know so little about you."

"You're looking for a little reciprocity?"

"Yeah. Maybe I am. You're getting personal with me. It's only fair."

"Okay. Answer this for me and I'll answer something in return."

Finally, after an eternity of dark silence, she says, "It wasn't some methodical, well-thought-out plan. It just sort of happened that way."

"Explain," I say gruffly, tossing her favorite freaking word back at her.

She huffs and puffs a little, but then she settles down. Then she shifts just a little closer to me. Enough so I can smell the salt from the saltwater pool on her skin. Enough so that I catch the hint of jasmine in her hair.

"In high school, girls in my town got knocked up like that's just what kids did on Friday nights. Many of those girls didn't graduate high school. They didn't go on to become whatever they imagined themselves being when they were seven. They could have, even with a baby. But instead they got pregnant and stayed at home because that's just what people from my town did. And the douchebags who injected their semen inside them didn't care so much that they now had kids. Condoms aren't free. They're expensive and getting birth control where I grew up required parental consent and insurance. So I abstained. I didn't like any of the STI kings who walked the halls of my school anyway."

"And when you went to college?"

She shrugs her bad shoulder. "I don't know. Old habits die hard? College boys liked my tits. They liked my ass. And they wanted to fuck both. But I can't remember any one of them asking me what I was majoring in. Or what I wanted to do as a career after college. Or even what my name was."

She says that last bit with a harsh bite and I get the connotation behind it immediately.

Because I told her point blank I didn't care about the names of the women I fucked. And I didn't. They didn't care about my name either other than the fact that it was tied to someone who is rich and famous and plays drums in a band. In that respect, it's not much better. It might even be worse.

I used them for their bodies. They used me for my celebrity.

But I know Maia. I know her name and I want to know her story. Every facet of it.

"What about after you moved here?"

She huffs once more, so very done with my questions. "More of the same, Keith. Sex wasn't exactly on my mind. Surviving was. Paying off the debts in my name was. I was already at the point where I had held out long enough so why squander something that should still be considered precious on just anyone."

I don't want to be just anyone to her. It's troubling the hell out of me.

Since the second I saw her, I've wanted to be everything to this girl. Her hero. Her savior. Her knight. Her lover. Her friend. And then she went and kissed me and screwed that all up. Because now I don't just want those things. I *crave* them. I *need* them.

But I have no right to them. I haven't gotten close to any woman for a reason.

"I'm glad you're still a virgin. I'm glad you have dreams beyond where you grew up. I'm glad you want more from your life. And I fucking love how you fight for it."

Maia swallows loudly. It's the sort of sound that someone does when they're trying to hold their emotions in. And before I know what I'm doing, I reach out into the darkness of the car and play with a strand of her hair.

Her breath catches deep in her throat but it's dark in the car and it's dark outside and I can't look at her. Looking at her makes me want to kiss her again and I cannot kiss her again.

"I'm not sorry I kissed you," she says. "I know you want me to be. I think you're sorry I did. But I'm not."

I shake my head. Suddenly so inexplicably and wrongfully angry. Because Maia kissed me. Why the fuck did she have to do that?

I want Maia in a way I never even wanted anyone else, and I've only known her two weeks. I loved Amy but I never spent hours awake at night thinking about all the ways I wanted her. I never stared at her because I couldn't stop. I never teased and provoked her because her reactions to me never did to me half of what Maia's do.

And I hate it.

I loathe it. It's so wrong it twists inside me, corrosively burning a hole through me and eating me alive from the inside out. I should have been like that with Amy. Maybe then...

You're gutting me, Maia, and I have no fucking clue what to do about that.

I know you want me just as much as I want you. I do not want to get attached to you. I do not want to get emotionally involved.

Especially with a girl who already has so much power over me. With a girl I'm already going above and beyond for. Helping in any way I can. Putting every ounce of who I am on the line.

Just like I did with Amy.

And look how that turned out.

"I am no different from those boys in college," I bite out. "I want your body in every dirty, depraved way possible. I want to tie you up by your wrists and lick your pussy until it's dripping all over my bed and my face. Down into your tight little asshole. I want your breathy moans and your pleading. I want you to beg for my cock to break open that tight, untouched pussy of yours. Then I want your tears because it hurts so fucking good for you. That's how fucked up I am with you. Is that what you want to hear? Does that sound safe?" Each question bellows louder past my lips. "I want your trust, dammit. I want to be a good guy in your story. And you constantly try to force me over into the darkness."

Without warning, she reaches up, grabs my hand out of her hair, and tugs it onto her lap. And she just holds it. So tight. Squeezing me.

"I trust you," she tells me, and I fucking crack. Wide. Open. My heart is raw and exposed, and I can't stand this. This fucking feeling. It's terrorizing. It's thrusting me to the very brink of my sanity and my wits. She grasps my wrists, holding it firm as I try to flee. "I trust you," she repeats.

"You shouldn't. The things I want to do to you..."

"What would that feel like? Those things?"

"Stop it. Stop being such a naughty, naughty tease."

"No. I want to tease you. I'm hoping you'll slip your hands up my dress if I do."

I lock my jaw, clenching my teeth so hard my head hurts. "What will I find, Maia?"

"Me. Wet. Should I show you with my own fingers first?"

No! "Yes," I hiss, unable to stop it. She releases me and I graze my hand over my aching cock through my jeans while she watches me in the dark light of the car. Then she lifts her dress and her fingers slip beneath her panties into her wet, wet pussy. I can fucking hear how wet she is. Smell how aroused.

She pumps herself a few times, moaning, writhing, arching her back, thrusting her tits and driving me absolutely out of my mind insane.

"Tell me," I demand.

"It feels *so* good. Why don't you try for yourself? Your fingers are thicker than mine. I bet they'll feel even better."

"I'm not gentle, Maia."

"That doesn't scare me, Keith. You don't scare me. I trust you. You were watching me all night."

"I might have been." I'm always watching her. Even when she doesn't know I am.

"You know you were. Explain."

"Maia," I warn, my voice sharp.

"Do you want to touch me, Keith? Now? Here? In the darkness of the car? In the place where my fingers just were? Where we can pretend a little? Tomorrow is tomorrow. I'm not thinking about that now. I just know I want you to touch me."

"Maia!" I scream it this time. I fucking scream her name. My heart is thrashing violently in my chest as blood rushes through my ears and pulses in my cock. Yet I still manage to hear her move even if I can't look over to see her.

Before I know what the hell is happening, she lifts her dress higher. I glance over reflexively and a deep, guttural moan flees my lips on its own accord. White panties. So pure. So perfect. So sexy and enticing and everything I've been jerking off to since I met her.

"Tell me to stop if you don't want to touch me," she whispers, but her voice is pleading with me not to.

I can't.

That's when my fingers flee the wheel, leaving only one hand on it to steer us safely home. I skim the rough texture of the lace over the warm wetness of the heaven beneath. Fuck. She really is so wet. And fuck, she smells *so* good. And much like my Pandora, I cannot remember all the reasons this is the worst idea ever. All the reasons this should never happen.

My desire has a power of its own. An urgency.

"I'm not fucking you tonight," I caution, my voice hoarse. "This is here and it's now and I want it so bad I don't give a fuck about anything else. But I won't do that to you. I have enough sense left in me to know how wrong that would be."

"I know. I just want you to make me come. And tomorrow we can go back to us. We can pretend like I never asked you for this and you never gave it to me. If that's what you want."

It's not at all but it's all I can tolerate with her.

"Are you sure?"

"Yes," she pants. "I'm sure."

I shake my head. "No. Maia."

"Please don't stop. Just... let me have this. I've never had this, and I trust you. I *want* it to be you."

My chest clenches impossibly tight and it's a wonder I haven't killed us ten ways to tomorrow driving us home. My cock jerks in my jeans. Leaks in my briefs. I want her so goddamn much. "I can't do more. I can't," I croak out. *I can't go through it again,* I think but don't say.

"I know. But even tomorrow, when the light of day makes every truth feel harsher, I won't regret it. In the darkness of night, my body wants your hands all over it. And that's enough for me right now."

Jesus.

My fingers nudge her panties to the side, finding her swollen clit, finding her *soaked* for me, and listening as her breath catches. As it shudders along with her body. I slip a finger inside her only to roll my wrist so my thumb can rub her clit.

Her hips thrust up, her back arching as the top of her head hits the spine of the seat, her long hair spilling everywhere behind her. "Holy. Oh my god. It's..."

"Tell me."

"I..." she moans. Low and loud and my cock painfully slams into the zipper of my jeans, anxious and ready and needing her. Only her. Nothing and no one else has made me hard like this. "More. I want more."

That's exactly what I give her. I drive us home, one hand steering us, my eyes straight ahead. But my other hand is fucking her senseless. My mind completely enthralled on every move and sound she makes. I pump two fingers in and out, slowly. Slow enough it forces her to grind harder against me as she searches for what she needs.

As she explores her pleasure on my hand.

And while my fingers may be going slow, my thumb is not. My thumb is rubbing her clit, harder and harder, working her up to a frenzy that is sexy as all hell. The dichotomy between fast and slow is driving her out of her mind with need. She's panting and moaning and gripping the windowsill with her good hand.

I wish it were my hair or my arm she was gripping like that. I wish I could feel her body writhe against mine.

"Keith," she breathes, and I'm dying right now. I'm dying to watch her. Needing to see her. But I can't. I'm driving. I'm not pulling over. I won't do it. But that doesn't mean I don't feel her.

"You're so tight."

"Yes."

"The way you clench around me. The way you grind against me. It's so fucking hot. You're so fucking hot, Maia. Fuck my fingers until you come. Make yourself come on me. I want you to drip all over me."

"I'm close."

She is. I can feel the way her walls start to clench tighter. The way she coats my fingers. The sounds she's making.

"Oh my god, Keith. Don't stop. *Please*. This is... *Oh!*"

I look at her. I have to. She's coming so hard, all over my fingers and my car, and she's so *so* beautiful as she does.

I pull into my driveway just as her body sags back down in the seat. I slide my fingers from her, knowing her eyes are on me as I slip them into my mouth and taste her. Heaven. My Pandora tastes like heaven.

I don't want to go inside with her. I want to shift my seat back all the way, lift her up and drag her onto my lap. I want to kiss her and bury myself inside of her.

She doesn't belong to me, but I want her to be mine.

I put the car in park, turn to her to say... something, but then her lips are on mine.

Sloppy and wet with her tears. She's crying and she's kissing me, and I kiss her back.

Holy hell, do I kiss her back. I cup the back of her head and I hold her to me. My lips moving against hers. Desperate and hungry and anxious. And tender. This was more for me and she needs to understand that. She let me touch her and that is not something I take lightly.

I may be burning with a ferocity for all she's doing to me, but I'm also burning for *her*. And not just because I want her body. But because something inside me needs her there. Needs this wild, out of control, nonsensical connection I feel with her.

That I know she feels with me too.

"Maia," I whisper into her, regret lining my voice. I hate that she's crying. "Did I hurt you, baby?"

"No. That's not why I'm crying."

"Tell me," I beg. I brush my thumb up and down her face, staring into her eyes, desperate to understand what happened. What I did wrong.

"I'm okay. I just... I didn't expect it to be like that." My eyebrows knit together, hoping she'll explain further. "I'm fine. But I need some space tonight." With that, she pulls away from me completely and gets out of the truck. The harsh inner light of the cab flicks on when she opens the door momentarily blinding me, but I don't move. I don't chase after her.

I sit here thinking. Wrecked with anxiety and guilt.

Even after the door shuts and the light is out and she's gone inside.

I'm struck sideways with a bold and unsettling realization. I think I'm starting to fall for Maia Alice Angelo.

17

Keith

"Did you forget something?" an exasperated Jasper asks as he opens the door, a tired and fussing Adalyn in his arms.

"Why is she still awake?" I ask instead of answering him.

"That's a seriously good question. One you should likely ask her since I can't seem to figure it out. The girl won't go down. Vi is nursing Cora and trying to get her to bed. But this one is being a little monster for her daddy." Jasper tickles Adalyn's belly and she peels out a delighted squeal. "I have no idea how Vi is going to manage both when we go on tour."

I smirk. Watching daddy Jasper wasn't as fun when he was a single dad with an infant or when he was dealing with a toddler newly diagnosed with ASD. It was new and strange and a little scary for all of us since we didn't know what to expect or how to help.

But now that Jasper is an old pro and has Vi and baby Cora,

watching him with five-year-old Adalyn who likes to put her father through his paces is amusing as hell.

"Um. Probably like the kick-butt mommy she is." I look to Adalyn, bending so we're eye level and keeping some distance so she doesn't get upset. "Ady, what's up my girl? Aren't you tired?"

"No. Not tired. No sleep." she says, stubbornly shaking her head. She's wearing purple Little Mermaid jammies. Her long reddish-brown hair is a mess and her green eyes are already drooping. But this girl is fighting it. That's for sure.

"Can I put you down?"

She blinks at me as if she has no idea what to do with that question, only to launch her little body away from Jasper and straight into my arms in the next breath. I catch her instinctively, tucking her into my chest and giving her a squeeze because that's what we all do when we hug Adalyn Diamond.

"Keith, I no wanna go to bed. I not tired."

I smile indulgently down at the sweet baby in my arms. "I know it, doll. I know it. How about you show me your room though? I'd love to see the new mermaids Mommy put on your walls. Are Mickey and Minnie in there? I want to say hi."

She wiggles out of my grasp and takes my hand, leading me toward the stairs. I catch the sound of Jasper's relieved sigh as he walks behind me. "Mickey and Minnie are sleeping. Minnie wears a pink dress and Mickey has two buttons."

"Right you are, girl. Show me."

"Mickey and Minnie love Adalyn soooo much," she chimes, her voice high and sweet and practiced as this is her common phrase when it comes to Mickey and Minnie and their undying affection for her.

"Yes, they do. Who else loves you soooo much?" She doesn't answer my question. "Does Keith love you so much?"

"Yes," she says softly, turning over her shoulder to smile at me. "Keith loves Adalyn soooo much."

I blow her a kiss and then lower my voice. "She's still talking about herself in the third person?"

Jasper nods. "Yes. But no longer in the plural and she no longer starts her sentences with say. So I'll take what I can get."

"I need to spend more time with her. I don't see her enough. I'm missing stuff."

"Do I want to know why you're here?" Jasper murmurs, cutting to the chase.

I grimace, throwing him a sideways glance. In truth, I'm not sure why I drove all the way back here. I don't even know what to say. I was just sitting in my truck and I knew Maia was inside and all I wanted to do was go upstairs and crawl in her bed and hold her. Well, I wanted to do more than hold her. But she was upset when she got out of my car and I didn't know why or what to do with that.

Plus, she made it clear she wanted to be alone and not talk about it.

So I left and just drove and found myself here.

"Oh, Ady. Look at the pretty nightlight. It looks like the ocean in here."

"Yeah," Jasper grumbles. "Don't remind me."

I chuckle under my breath and scoop the little miss up into my arms. Dropping her onto her bed, I tuck her in under her Minnie blanket and crawl on beside her. "Silly daddy doesn't like you swimming so much."

"Can you blame me?" he grouses, and no, I can't. Jasper's and Gus's mom drowned in the ocean when they were kids and Adalyn is obsessed with water. All she wants to do is swim, and though she's gotten much better with that, it terrifies him to no end. Justifiably.

"Oh, look…" I point to the end of her large bed. "You're right. Mickey and Minnie are sleeping. Shhh… we don't want to wake them up. They're so tired. Just like you."

Ady curls up into my chest and I inhale the irresistible scent of her hair. I think I needed a little Adalyn time more than I need Jasper's advice. "Mickey, Keith."

"You want your Mickey?"

She doesn't answer, but if she doesn't say no, that's usually a silent affirmative. I grab her huge stuffed Mickey that was chilling at the end of her bed and tuck him in between us. Then I shift a little toward the edge of the bed.

"'Night, pretty doll. Love you." I kiss the top of her head.

"'Night," she breathes, already half-asleep, and I creep out of her bed, slinking to the door where Jasper is lingering.

"How'd you do that?" Jasper asks as we shut the door to her room and head down the hall to his large media room. "I spent over an hour just trying to settle her down. Mickey didn't do anything for me and he's always my go-to guy."

I hitch up a shoulder. "I have five younger sisters and parents who worked long hours. You learn shit. And I'm not you. That makes all the difference with her. She knows she can push you in a way she can't push me."

Jasper points to the large leather sectional and I dutifully take a seat. He grabs two beers out of the drink fridge, popping the top on the expensive import, and then handing one to me. "Talk. What happened in the hour since you left here?"

Everything, I want to say. Everything happened.

That woman flipped my world upside down without even batting an eye or an ounce of remorse. For someone so young and so inexperienced, she's impossibly bold and brazen and I fucking worship that about her. I'd never steal an inch of it from her either, but it breaks my heart that the Amy's of the world don't have that same fire and tenacity.

"We're out here living this life because of me. Because all I could stand after Amy died was playing my drums. It was the only thing to drown out every other sound or thought from my head."

"Are you saying you regret that? Look at us."

I don't regret that. But every time we play live, I still look to the first row where she was always supposed to be.

I take a sip of my beer instead of answering him.

"If we hadn't come, I wouldn't have Adalyn. I wouldn't be with Vi because she'd likely be married to Gus. Miserable, of course." He gives me a cheeky grin. "Gus wouldn't have Naomi. And you wouldn't have met Maia."

"Yeah, the girl who is launching bottle rockets in my head."

"Exactly," Jasper says like I just figured out something monumental. Funny, it doesn't feel that way. "You've got some dark shit stuck in your head. Maybe it's time someone came in and blew all that up. Pushed it out. Forced you to deal with it in a way you never did." He blows out a breath, leaning forward and dropping his elbows to his thighs as he levels me with his discerning gaze. "You never talked about what happened with Amy. You never told us anything about what you went through that night and we didn't push because what could we have said? We were young and rattled. We had no comfort to offer you other than playing music and just being there. You were beyond grieving. You were entrenched in a tragedy that pulled you apart and left your pieces under an ocean of guilt. Maybe Maia is your antidote, but in order to snuff out the disease you have to be sick with it."

"I've been sick with it for ten years."

"Yes, and we still don't know anything about it or how to help you because you won't talk about it. That in itself breeds more toxins. That is never a cure. Why the fuck do you think I write so much, man? The truth is always there, lurking under the surface. Ignoring it doesn't make it go away, it makes it fester."

I don't know how to talk about that night. How to let it go. How to get over all the things I did wrong. All the decisions I wish I could change and can't.

I wake up drenched in a cold sweat from nightmares. My insides quake every time I think or say her name. I don't know how to stop that. He can say that talking helps you heal, but they also say that about time, and in ten years, I haven't healed. Not even a little.

Some wounds might be unrepairable. No matter what you do.

"What was your breaking point with Viola?" I ask instead.

Jasper chuckles under his breath, taking a sip of his beer. "She was. She was absolutely my breaking point. That woman made it so that it got to the point where no matter what I did or how hard I tried to resist her or how much I pretended to hate her; she saw right through. And she found every weak chink in my armor and exploited it. In truth, I was doomed from the start with her."

I sag. Like actually fucking sag. Like a ten-year-old boy who was just told his favorite video game is no longer in production.

"How deep into her are you?"

I take a long pull of my beer, wiping my mouth with the back of my hand and staring down at the dark floors. "Here's the thing about that... it's complicated. How can I ever fully tell if my feelings for her are about her or if they're tied to Amy?"

"Do you think about Amy when you're with her?"

"Sometimes. Not often. Not really in the last week or so. But at first, yeah. At first, I compared them a lot. When I first got a good look at her face, Amy was all I could think about."

"You know, I don't think they look that much alike."

I glance up. "No?"

"No. I mean, sure, the hair color is similar. But lots of girls have light blonde hair, right? Especially in this town."

"I guess," I relent.

"And maybe their noses and high cheekbones are also similar. But would you even notice that if it weren't for the hair?"

I take another sip and sit back, tossing my ankle up onto my opposite knee. "I don't know. That night she hit me, all I saw was Amy. Bleeding. Standing there a mess, and I just..."

I swallow so hard. But it does zilch to clear the emotion that clogs my throat when I think about Amy bleeding. About all the ways I couldn't help her when she truly needed me to. A bone-deep tremor rattles through me as visions assault every ounce of my mind.

"I don't know how to be with someone anymore. Fuck, I haven't wanted to since Amy. It's just not worth it to me, man. None of it is. In truth, the idea of being with someone scares the shit out of me. I loved Amy with everything I had and then..."

Jasper waits me out, sitting patiently, but his eyes are on mine, letting me know he's waiting for me to continue and won't accept anything else.

"I don't want to hurt Maia. I don't want to let her down. She's so young and so inexperienced and has been wronged so much by people who were supposed to love her. Who she should have been able to trust and rely on." Like me, I don't add, but I'm certain he knows I'm thinking it. "My head is a mess. And I don't see this thing between us going any other way than bad. It's wrong. I know it is."

"But you can't resist her, otherwise you wouldn't be here," he surmises, and I hate how Jasper does this. Gus told me all about the day he laid it straight for him with Naomi and even though I showed up on his doorstep tonight, I'm terrified beyond my wits.

What if he says something brilliant? What then?

What if he gives me a green light or makes things sound so perfect in my head?

What if I try to be with Maia only to have it implode, hurting us both?

"Is Amy the last woman you let yourself care for? Before Maia, I mean." And here we go. Jasper psych 101. That's not even a life rule, it's just a universal truth. His comment about me caring for Maia isn't even a lead-in. It's a foregone conclusion because the bastard knows all.

"Yes."

"Why?"

I spring out of my seat, heading for the window and downing the rest of my beer in two large gulps, wishing it were Jack. My gold standard. My savior on so many nights when I thought my necrotic heart would finally find a way to pound its way out of my chest, coated in a blackness and baked in insufferable heartbreak. Loss may be an inevitability for us all, but when the one you love is savagely, wrongfully stolen from you like a thief in the night, leaving your soul decimated and unsalvageable, you don't recover.

You don't.

I've been trying for years.

In order to prevent further destruction, you go to extremes to stop that loss from happening again. In any form. But then something, or someone in this case, comes along and blindsides you. Hits you in the one place you weren't expecting. And that's it. Show's over, folks, you're fucking done for.

Then what do you do?

"Do you think time will help?"

No. "Maybe," I answer.

"Then give yourself time to figure out what's best for both of you. What you can stand to live with and who you can't stand to live without. But I'm going to be honest since bullshit is really more Gus's bag than mine. I think you're perfect for each other. We all do." I spin around and he just rolls his eyes at my murderous expression. "Yeah, brother. We talked about it. Grow up and shit. What did you expect?"

"Um. How about fuck you?"

He laughs. "You're not pissed. You're angry with yourself and searching for your nearest outlet to unleash on. Figure out your shit with Amy. Talk to a therapist, write in a journal, write her letters. I don't know. But it's time to forgive yourself for things that could not be helped or changed. That were *not* your fault. And after you've done all that, don't let Maia get away. Because that blonde sleeping in your guest room is it. She's amazing. She's your girl, Keith. I think you know it too which is why you came back tonight. Don't fuck it up. That's my best piece of advice and I strongly suggest you take it."

Jasper stands up, walks over to me and claps me hard on the shoulder.

"We leave in a little more than two weeks. And she's coming with us one way or another."

And with that, he's gone. Just walks out of here, taking his beer with him.

He has his woman waiting for him. A woman he risked his relationship with his brother for. Am I ready to risk everything for Maia?

Figure my shit out with Amy, he said.

And he's right. Because in all the many years since she died, I haven't done that. I pushed it back into a box and shoved it into the darkest corner of my mind. Maybe Maia isn't my Pandora after all. Maybe she's my salvation. My way forward. My way back.

Maybe.

Or maybe I'm the one about to unleash all my evils on her.

18

Maia

MY EYES BLINK OPEN, staring sightlessly at the ceiling of my bedroom. And just as they did all night long during my restless, sleepless night, visions of what happened in the car come hurtling back to me. I told Keith I wouldn't regret it, and I don't.

But I was right about the harsh light of day thing.

Because even though I don't regret it, I'm not sure it was the wisest choice to let my boss finger fuck me to orgasm in his car. Especially after he told me he had enough sense not to fuck me. That he wouldn't do that to me, whatever that means. *You know what that means.*

Yeah. I do know what that means.

Then again, like the lust-drunk woman I was last night, I told him I was cool with us going back to normal today. Am I? I honestly don't know. I've never had a man do that to me before and the first to do it is someone I'm developing quick and hard feelings for. It's a conundrum.

One I need to navigate past carefully.

After I came upstairs and bawled my eyes out and didn't fall asleep, I made myself a promise. That what happened last night, truly would not happen again. That I would focus on my job and paying off my debts and finding a new place to live. That I would force my heart to shelter in place. To go on complete lockdown where Keith Dawson is concerned.

I think the fact that I live here and spend so much time with him is the main culprit with us. We obviously have a thing going. A chemistry. But hopefully all this heat will fizzle out and die once I leave and we only see each other in a professional capacity.

It has to.

He doesn't want to be with anyone who isn't Amy, and I don't want to risk not only my job but my heart. So there. Decision made. Thank god we didn't have sex. That would have really ruined everything. He was right in that, and I was wrong to push us as far as I did.

Even if I don't regret it.

A loud clang from downstairs startles me upright, my eyebrows pinching in at the unfamiliar sound as I clamor out of bed, hitting my cast on the nightstand and yelping out. I hate this cast. I hate every white inch of it. Two more weeks and I'll be a free woman.

Another heavy banging startles me, and after I use the bathroom, clean up my face, brush my teeth and get dressed, I open my door only to be assaulted with the scent of cooking oil and some kind of sweet batter.

I make my way down the stairs with slow, cautious steps, as jitters creep up my spine.

I'm nervous to face Keith after last night.

It's Saturday and I know Marco is not coming early. Typically, Keith would be swimming but when I looked out the window, not only did I not see him in the pool, but I found dark gloomy clouds and a lot of rain. Which means he's the one making all that noise in the kitchen.

Which means I need to pull my big girl panties up and face him.

"Yeah, I think I got it," I hear Keith say only I don't catch anyone else speaking to him, so I assume he's on the phone. He laughs. "You seriously want that? Fine. I'll take a picture of how it turns out and send it to you but if it ends up on IG, I won't be so thrilled." I hear him moving around the kitchen, the sound of pots and pans shifting on the stove and the aromas of cooking food growing heavier in the air. "I know," he says solemnly. "I know. I'm glad it's you. I don't think I could have done it with anyone else. Truly, I really appreciate it and I owe you one." He laughs again. "Fine. Consider it done. Yeah."

I take another step down the stairs and the board creaks beneath my foot. Shit. He totally heard that and knows I'm eavesdropping. No hiding it now. I suck in a deep breath, holding it steady in my lungs as I descend the rest of the steps and round the corner into the kitchen. Keith is wearing a red apron with a big heart imprinted on it that says no one's cooking is better than mama's. He's in front of his huge eight-burner stove, placing pieces of what look like battered chicken into a pot of bubbling oil. Beside it, he has a waffle iron going with a large bowl of thick, creamy batter beside it.

What the ever-loving fuck is he doing?

"I gotta go, babe." *Babe?* "My houseguest just walked in." He smirks at me, throwing me a wink. *Houseguest*? Wow. I'm not sure which one stings more. The fact that he's clearly talking to a woman he called babe or that he just referred to me to that woman as his houseguest. I mean, I guess I am, but still. "Yeah, we'll talk later. Love you too. Bye now."

He disconnects the call and greets me with a huge warm smile I can't find in me to match. I want to ask a million questions, but I'm not entitled to any of the answers. So instead I force a smile and say, "'Morning. Sorry, I didn't mean to interrupt your call."

"You didn't. That was my sister, Beth, and we were pretty much done talking." His sister. I shouldn't be as relieved to hear that as I am. *Lockdown, remember?*

"And how many sisters do you have again?"

"Five. Five younger sisters. Beth is second behind me. Then

comes Danielle and Gabrielle, they're the twins. Followed by Joy and then Eden is the youngest."

"Damn." I snicker. "I would have gone crazy with an overprotected bear like you as an older brother."

He chuckles. "You have no idea. My parents worked a lot. My dad ran a garage, and my mom was a nurse working graveyard shifts. I helped raise my sisters. And let's just say, I made sure none of the local boys, including my bandmates, went anywhere near my sisters."

"And they still talk to you? Your sisters I mean."

"Yup. We're all still very close. I've been lucky enough to be able to pay for school for all my sisters and help my parents retire. Not sure all that would have been possible without Wild Minds' success."

"That's amazing, Keith. Truly. They must be proud."

"The pride is mutual. Did you sleep well?"

There's a wild gleam to his eyes I can't quite place as he asks that.

He pours a ladle of what can only be waffle batter onto the iron and closes the lid. Then he checks on the chicken that's bubbling and popping in the oil. I can't stop staring at him, utterly perplexed.

"Um. Not great, actually. You?" Because it suddenly dawns on me he's wearing the same outfit he was yesterday. And now that I think about it, I don't remember hearing him come back home after he tore out of here after dropping me off.

He laughs and the sound is a bit manic. "Haven't gone to bed yet."

Okay then. I really don't want to think about where he was all night or what he was doing.

"Hungry? I'm making you breakfast. Chicken and waffles okay? Beth gave me the recipe and told me you'd love it." Before I can formulate a response, he continues. "Sit. Here, have some coffee."

He pours me a cup and walks it around the island to hand it to me, kissing my cheek before he returns to the food. He kissed my cheek. Not my lips. I think that one gesture just said more than anything else. But really, what did I expect? He's trying to bring us back to us, and I need to fall in line with that.

After all, I set those rules.

I take a sip of my coffee and smile at him. Because I can do this. I really can. "The food smells amazing. I can't believe you went to all this trouble." For a peace offering, I don't add. That's what this is, right? A sweet one. A considerate one. One that shows he does, in fact, care about me.

So these other yucky feelings? The ones souring my stomach with churning acid? They can fuck off.

"Especially since you didn't sleep," I tack on.

He grins. He hasn't stopped. It's a little disconcerting after his week of non-stop growling.

"It's nothing. I wanted to make something special for you."

Shut up, Keith. Just stop talking and looking at me and smiling.

Of course, he doesn't. "I was thinking after we eat, and I clean up, we could sack out on the couch and watch one of your movies. It's a shitty day out. Can I fix you a plate?"

"Uh. Sure. Thanks. Can I do anything?"

He shakes his head. "No. You sit there and look beautiful. I've got this."

Pulling out the steaming waffle from the iron, he drops it onto a plate and then adds a piece of chicken directly on top of it. He lathers the whole thing with some kind of maple syrup that's a touch more golden than brown and cuts it all up for me because I can't.

So he's doing it for me. Again. Damn him.

He sets it in front of me with a triumphant smile and hovers while I take the first bite. "You're creeping me out, Keith."

He laughs but doesn't move.

I take a bite and the flavors explode in my mouth. Savory and sweet and crunchy and soft. I can't hold back my moan as I chew and swallow. "Oh my god. This is so good. Thank you. This is truly above and beyond."

He grins, reaching out with his thumb to swipe an errant drop of syrup from the corner of my lips. He pops it into his mouth, sucking it off. I nearly choke on my bite.

"It's the honey in the syrup that's the key, Beth told me. That and my mama's fried chicken recipe."

I point my fork at his apron. "That hers?"

"No," he says as he goes about making himself a plate. "My mom bought it for me when I bought the house a few years back. My sisters bought me the waffle iron and a lot of other random cooking things I have no idea what to do with. They thought it was funny, and until today, I've never worn the apron."

"It suits you."

"You're mocking me again."

I smirk cheekily but I'm actually not mocking him.

I like that he has his family.

I know he talks to his dad every Sunday afternoon. Only to his dad, and they talk for a while. I've heard him on the phone with his mom at random times, and this morning he was chatting and laughing with one of his sisters who gave him the recipe.

I don't like being jealous but I am.

I want a family of my own. I want people I can rely on. Friends who have my back and consider me theirs. People who love me.

I want what he has.

I never realized how lonely I was until I met him. All my time was spent working and not thinking. Surviving the only way I knew how. Now that's all changed and there isn't necessarily beauty in that awareness.

We finish eating and he cleans up because he won't let me help. I sit here useless like tits on a bull, nervous and fidgety. "I'm thinking tomorrow I might start apartment hunting."

He pauses mid-counter swipe. "Why would you do that?" He returns to the counter, now wiping the same spot over and over again.

"Um. Because I can't live here forever? My cast comes off in two weeks. By that point, I should be able to cook my own food and even cut it up. I won't have to have you put a plastic bag over my arm to shower and I'll even be able to put on a regular bra."

"Maia."

"I'm your houseguest, Keith. You said so yourself. I'm not living here forever. It could take me weeks to find a place."

He throws the wipe into the trash with a bit more gusto than required and meets my eyes with a hard glint before he just as quickly looks back down. "I was joking when I said that to Beth. She knows exactly who you are."

And who am I, I want to ask. But I don't. I never had a problem speaking my mind, but after last night, something about that question feels impossible.

"Can you just wait?" he asks, his eyes finally coming back up to mine. It's only now that I note the dark purple stains beneath them. "Wait until we finish the album. Until we get back from tour. You'll have more time to find a decent place in a decent neighborhood and you'll have had a few more weeks to save up."

I know what he's saying makes sense, but I don't like how itchy I'm feeling around him now. Then again, there isn't an ounce of unease coming from him. It's all me feeling like this and that speaks volumes. Can I last another few weeks around this man without doing more damage to myself than I've already done after a couple of stolen kisses and an orgasm?

"Okay, fine. I'll wait until we get back."

He blows out a relieved breath, and I don't understand it. You'd think he'd be jazzed to get rid of me. Are all men this complicated to understand? I somehow doubt it. It's a Keith thing and it's driving me up a cotton-picking wall.

"Good. That's good. Go put on a terrible—" I throw him a menacing glare that only makes him grin harder. "—I meant terrific old movie that I can nap to. I'm gonna grab a quick shower and I'll meet you in the media room."

"Just for that, I'm going to put on a really good one you won't be able to fall asleep while watching."

"Oh yeah?" he calls as he jogs up the steps.

"Two words for you. Marilyn Monroe." I hear him pause and then his head peeks down so he can catch my eye. "Who needs her when I'm living with my very own version. But we'll see if she annoys me half as much as you do. The fact that she can't talk back to me should be in her favor." Another fucking wink, and then he's running up again.

"I officially hate you."

He laughs. Bastard. And I swear I think I catch him mutter something that sounds a lot like 'you weren't saying that last night.'

Double bastard.

But still, my body zaps with relief over how this morning went. The ride is making me dizzy though. The constant up and down of the rollercoaster he and I can't seem to get off. Keith is the first man I've ever had real feelings for, and those feelings are nothing short of complicated and demanding. They require so much energy and effort and time from me.

Maybe he's right about the nap.

Maybe we can both use the breather.

Just focus on you, I remind myself. Hoping my heart hears the words and takes the reprimand more seriously than it has been.

By the time I have *Some Like It Hot* cued up, Keith is sauntering into the media room complete with a fitted white T-shirt, low-slung designer jeans, and damp hair. He looks like a bad boy from a nineteen fifties biker movie and far too tempting.

I look away immediately. "Good timing. I went with *Some Like It Hot* instead of *Gentlemen Prefer Blonds*. It's black and white and less music, which means maybe we'll both nap."

"Sounds perfect." He jumps onto the long sectional but instead of giving us space—*I need space Keith!*—he slides right up beside me, dropping his wet head to my lap.

"What the Christmas goose do you think you're doing?"

He chuckles, the sound vibrating. Right into my upper thighs. Because that's where his freaking head is.

"Christmas goose?"

I shrug.

"I'm getting comfortable. You're comfortable to lie on."

I balk at that. "How would you know. You've never done it before." I try to shove him off, but the determined man does not budge. He's big and muscular and let's be honest here, my attempt is half-assed at best. Have I mentioned how good he smells? Like OMG *so* good. It's his body wash or shampoo or whatever because he's not wearing his cologne right now.

Still, it's criminal and it makes my recently touched lady parts zing with desire.

"I'm doing it now, quit trying to push me off. I'm fucking exhausted and you're comfortable." He wraps his arms around me, adjusting me so he's holding me closer while his head is directly over my pussy now. If my pussy were to speak, it would be whispering directly into his ear.

I rest my casted arm on the dip of his waist and my other hand finds the strands of his hair, unable to resist. I run through the coarse wet strands, loving the texture as it dances along my fingers. He lets out a deep hum of contentment as he sinks deeper into me.

"You feel good," he murmurs, his eyes already heavy. "And whatever you're doing with my hair is heaven."

His eyes close and his breathing evens out within seconds as my fingers continue to glide through his hair. He looks so peaceful. So content as he holds me so damn close.

And just for this moment, just because he's asleep and can't feel my thoughts, I allow them to stray. To imagine. To pretend this could be real. Knowing all the while it's not. That it never will be. But wanting it to be all the same.

19

Maia

"THEY'RE NOT GOING to let me in," I say, staring out the window of the huge black SUV complete with tinted windows and security detail.

"You mean because you're practically naked?"

I ignore Keith's jab completely. Mostly because it's true. The guys finished their album early this morning. They laid down the last track and Lyric said it was brilliant. Now all she has to do is go through it all and perfect it. Album number six. That's a pretty big deal, and these guys have been working tirelessly in the studio over the last few weeks.

Which meant long endless hours for me too.

"Don't listen to him," Henry says, reaching out, squeezing my shoulder. "You look incredible and perfect for where we're going."

I glance in Henry's direction and smile. Henry and I have gotten close. And not the type of close you'd think would happen between a single girl and a single guy. Nope. We're totally and completely friends. His words, not even mine. He told me he didn't have a choice in the matter and that was that.

He friend-zoned me.

I still have no idea what he meant when he said he didn't have a choice, but it really doesn't matter since I love hanging out with him so much.

Keith is another matter entirely.

"No. I just meant because I'm not twenty-one."

"You look twenty-one. Hell, you look twenty-five the way Naomi and I did you all up," Ethan chimes in. "And don't worry, honey, you're with us. That means you get in and no one gets carded."

"If you say so."

"I know so. Besides, it's not like you're drinking so no harm no foul. Relax and have some fun. You look super sexy hot. Own it."

"I've never worn so much makeup and so few clothes in my life."

Ethan and Naomi had way too much fun getting me ready for tonight. I'm wearing an outfit Naomi told me she wore on stage once. It's a black, one-shoulder sequin crop top that has a drape down the back that connects to a matching skirt. The skirt is long in the back, just below my knees, but in the front, it slopes up and has an epic slit that goes practically all the way up. I'm showing some serious leg. And belly. And cleavage.

"That I believe," Ethan snickers. "But if I were straight, I'd fuck you. That's how good you look. So at least you have that going for you. What else matters?"

I roll my eyes at him, turning to the window as we glide up along the sidewalk in front of the club.

"Are you ready?" Keith whispers in my ear, his fingers gently tracing the back hem of my skirt where it meets my skin.

I glance over my shoulder at him and beam a smile. "I'm ready."

That's when the back door to the SUV opens and a zillion flashes of light happen all at once. The main security detail for the band, Marsellus, throws me a rare grin and takes my hand, helping me down, which I appreciate since I'm in heels. "Have fun tonight, Miss Maia. I will be upstairs with you all if you need anything."

"Thank you."

Keith's instantly behind me, his hand now splayed on my lower back, guiding me forward, toward the entrance of the club, his body angled in and around mine like a protective shield as we're assaulted with questions and demands for pictures by the paparazzi lining the street. A soft hypnotic pulse drifts out, coating me in its warm vibration and I smile, finally a bit giddy at my first time in a club.

Henry flanks my other side, holding on gently to my upper arm right above my cast. Out of the corner of my eye, I catch the second SUV pull up and watch as Gus, Naomi, Jasper, Viola, Lyric, and Jameson all step out. Marco took the night to be with his boyfriend since we're leaving for tour on Sunday.

Tomorrow I get my cast off.

Saturday night we have a party we're attending, and then bright and shiny Sunday morning we hit the road.

It's a whirlwind of fantasy and fun.

I love this job. I love the people I'm working with who already treat me like one of their own. Like part of their family. I love making the hotel arrangements and ensuring the guys get what they need. I love running their schedules and their social media which has exploded with fan engagement.

This past month has been a dream come true.

The only problem has been the man on my right. The big one. The one touching the skin of my back. The one sheltering me from the excited press. The one who whispers in my ear, "I want to dance with you tonight."

I've held firm. I haven't kissed him since that night in the car. Since his confession and my passion for him took over. He hasn't tried anything either. Nothing. Zilch.

We went back to being us.

Like the car or the elevator never happened.

He started going out occasionally, leaving me home if I decline joining him or to hang out with Naomi, Viola, and the girls. And every night he went out, I was racked with jealousy. Fighting it in fits and waves while resisting the urge to text or call him.

I'm not his girlfriend. I had no right to my jealousy.

But then he'd come home early, and always make a point to find me to say good night or see how my night was or hang out with me on the couch if I was up watching something.

Whether he had been with any women in the hours he was gone, I don't know.

My gut tells me no. He always appeared exactly how he left, flawless. Unrumpled by the hands and scent of another woman. I tell myself it doesn't matter. I'm on lockdown, after all.

But everything with him matters, and my pep talks are growing more futile as the days spent with him pile up.

Stepping over the threshold of the club, I feel hands slip from my body as I meander farther into the dark room, taking it all in. It's exactly what I expected a club to be. Warm, loud heavy bass music, flashing lights, and gyrating bodies.

"Break her heart and I'll break your face," I hear Henry murmur behind me.

"Huh?" I whip out, spinning around.

Henry glances over to me with a wan expression. Just as quickly he returns to Keith who is shaking his head balefully.

"Nothing," Henry states firmly. "It was nothing. You know. Just guy shit."

"But you just *Some Kind of Wonderful-ed* him. Why?"

Henry rolls his eyes. "I'm pretty sure that's not a saying."

I roll my eyes back. "I just made it one. What gives?"

"You're not supposed to know that line. Watts was a drummer and Keith was obsessed with her from like the time he grew pubes on."

"Dude, it's like you don't even know me," I say to Henry, feigning injury as I hold my hand over my heart. "I've seen practically every film since the invention of film, and that includes silent films."

"We know," Keith growls in deflective annoyance. "You've made me watch them all with you."

"And you love it, so quit your nitching." I return my focus to Henry. "Tell me what you meant by that."

"Nitching? That's not even a word."

I cock a brow at him as he glances uneasily at Keith.

"Bro code, princess," Henry states. "Back out of it. It's between me and your domestic partner. But let's just say the warning has been laid down and it extends to you as well though I would never break your pretty face. For you, I'm speaking metaphorically. For him, I'm not."

"Oh my god!" I exclaim, grabbing on to Keith's shoulder and giving it a good shake. "I just realized the dude in that movie, his name is Keith."

Henry laughs, pointing at me. "Now she's finally getting it. If you're going to Some Kind of Wonderful him, make it count. The only things in his life he cares about are you and his drums." He winks at me before walking off.

"You said the line wrong," I yell after Henry who just throws up a hand as he disappears into the crowd of dancers.

Keith scowls. "Don't even try. It's Henry." He states this like that should be a sufficient enough reason, and I think it is. Henry is kind of an enigma. You wouldn't think his soul goes as deep as it does but yeah...

Still, I want to ask why Keith needs any warnings when it comes to me since I've been persona non grata since the fingering in the car incident.

And because I'm me... "Why does he feel you need a warning. Nothing's happened for weeks. Does he know about the car?"

Keith grunts at the mention of the car, but I need to know. Even though I shouldn't ask. I should just let it ride because I've been doing my job and Keith's been doing his, and things have been really good between us. And when he doesn't answer me, I do let it ride and for once keep my mouth shut. Mama used to tell me not to rock a boat I didn't want to capsize.

She was rarely right about anything, but in this instance, I think she is.

We're ushered into a waiting elevator only to step off once we hit the fifth floor. Up here is a completely different club than the one I caught a glimpse of on the first and second levels. It's not as dark for one, but the deep purple mood lighting casts a sexy, sultry glow over the white furniture. There are about a dozen separate lounge areas surrounding a large open dance floor in the center where a DJ is spinning a mix of techno and pop.

"This is a private, members-only floor," Keith half-shouts into my ear so I can hear him over the music. "If you look around at the other people, you'll understand what I mean."

Surveying the room, it takes me a half-beat (literally) to understand what he means. It's filled with actors and musicians, as well as businessmen and women who look like they're busy running the world while out having a good time. All have entourages. All have lavish bottles of champagne, cognac, and vodka on their tables that they're drinking as if there is no price associated with the expensive liquors.

This is so far removed from my world, from who I am that I hardly know how to process what I'm seeing. And most of the time, I don't view the band in this sphere of wealth either. But in this moment, as we're led over to a large U-shaped sectional that is equally as stacked as the other tables, if not more so, I realize just how wrong I am.

"Come dance with us," Naomi demands, clutching my good hand and tugging me away from Keith. I roll my head over my shoulder and find him with the guys at the table, already pouring himself a drink of his favorite Jack Daniels. He tosses me a wink and a smirk and then proceeds to look away.

"Oh my god," Vi exclaims already shaking her ass all over the dance floor, a bright smile plastered across her face. "I love my girls, but a night out as a grownup is everything."

I laugh. I can only imagine.

"How long are Jasper's and Gus's parents in town?" I shout as I start to move my body to the music.

"Just the weekend, but they offered to babysit the girls so we could have this night out together and I'm very grateful. They've really been making an effort to be involved more."

"Yes," Naomi agrees. "They offered to do the rehearsal dinner for our wedding. I think that really meant a lot to Gus."

"Less than five months to go. Not that I'm counting or anything." Viola beams at Naomi. "I can't believe how quickly it's coming up. I'm so flipping excited."

"Shhh," Naomi hisses with a playful grin. "No one can know anything about it."

Viola laughs, throwing her head back and her arms over her head. "Right. Like the press didn't find out about mine and Jasper's. Good luck with that one."

"I can't wait to see your dress," I tell her.

"I pick it up while you're are away on tour, but when you come back, I'll show it to you. I have no idea how I'm going to hide it from Gus."

"You'll put it in Cora's closet. The guys never go in there."

"Oh!" Naomi chirps with bright eyes. "That's freaking brilliant. Speaking of the guys, has Keith asked you to be his date for it yet?"

Naomi especially has been all over trying to push me together with Keith. Both of them know about the kiss in the elevator, though I didn't not tell them what happened in the car. That's between me and Keith and no one else as far as I'm concerned.

"I won't be living with him by then and I'll be able to drive, so there will be no obligation for him to tote me around anymore."

"That's clearly not what I meant by *date*, Maia. Stop deflecting."

"I'm not. It's true," I bark defensively.

Naomi stares dramatically at me like I'm a fool. "You do know he doesn't drag you around and I can tell you he feels zero obligation when it comes to you. He brings you along, well, for your job yes, but also because he likes having you around. He likes you watching them play in the studio. He likes talking with you every second he can. And when you're both in the same room, his eyes are always on you. Always. He even told Gus he's trying to figure things out with you."

"What does that mean?"

She shrugs up a shoulder. "No idea. But girl, he worships you."

"Yes," Vi agrees with a hearty nod of her head. "Yes! And whenever you enter a room, his face lights up. His face never lights up, Maia. Like ever. If he's not in love with you, which we all know he is, at the very least he's obsessed. You are his sun and he orbits around you because he can't stand not feeling your gravitational pull."

Now it's my turn to roll my eyes dramatically. "You bitches are crazy. And now I sound like Marco. But still, it's true. I know it comes off like a good story, but I've been living with him for a month now and other than that kiss, that *I* planted on him, he's kept a very clear and unmistakable separation between us."

"Well," Naomi coos with a devilish grin. "Tonight is suddenly seeming like the perfect night to change all that." She juts her chin over her shoulder and my head spins so fast I'm like Linda Blair from *The Exorcist* minus the green vomit.

Keith is lounging on the sofa, Gus on his right as the two of them talk. Keith has a glass in his hand that's stretched along the back of the couch, but his eyes are roving over every inch of me until they clash with my eyes. They gleam, sparking with such an intense heat my breath quickens. A slow, sexy smile curls up his face and I watch as he says something to Gus and then rises to his feet. He tosses back the last of his drink, his eyes never wavering from mine as he sets it down and then stalks with purposeful strides over to us.

"Holy hell, I think I need a fire extinguisher. I'm about to combust and the man isn't even making those fuck-me eyes at me."

"I think we need a drink. Like right now." Naomi tugs on Viola and the two of them abandon me here on the dance floor like a lost sheep helplessly watching the wolf come in for the slaughter. Real smooth ladies. And I want to roll my eyes or laugh, but I can't do anything other than stare at Keith the way he's staring at me.

My heart rate kicks up, matching the tempo of the music as he reaches me, slipping his hand around my waist and tugging me into his hard chest without even uttering a word. His palm rests on my back, his fingers splayed down just above the crest of my ass. His other hand comes up, brushing my long hair that I foolishly wore down over my shoulders and down my back.

"Put your arms around my neck," he instructs, taking my good hand and doing it for me.

"I feel foolish doing that with my cast."

"I can't dance with you the way I want to dance with you with that thing between us." He gives me an insistent look and I reluctantly set it on his upper chest. The moment it lands there, Keith draws me in closer until our bodies are pressed together as one. "Much better," he breathes, his breath fanning over my face as I gaze up into his eyes. He starts to dance with me, close and sexy and slow against the fast beat. "You look so beautiful tonight. Did I tell you that earlier?"

I stare silently up at him as words fail me.

"Every man in this club has been staring at you since the second we walked in here."

I grin at his scowl. "I take it you don't like that."

His scowl deepens. "I fucking hate it, Maia. It drives me insane the way every man who looks at you wants you. I hate how Ethan and Naomi dressed you with so much of your creamy skin showing that no one should see—" He stops abruptly, his words cutting off sharply, but I don't need him to finish to know what he was going to say.

"Why do you suddenly care?"

"I've always cared. I've just been better at hiding before."

"What's changed then? The fact that random men are staring at me? The fact that I'm showing off a little skin? The caveman in you doesn't want me but doesn't want anyone else to have me. Is that it?" I spit at him, showing him just how much this pisses me off.

It also confuses me endlessly. For weeks now this thing between us has been bubbling under the surface. But it's been pretended away. Stealthily ignored. I pushed him and pushed him and all it got me was a couple of kisses, an orgasm, and a tormented heart. I want him. I made that pretty damn clear, and in return, he made it pretty damn clear the feelings are not mutual.

So I dealt with it. I focused on work and forced myself to be his goddamn friend. And I was doing so well with that. I mean, it wasn't great. It hurt. But I'm used to hurt, so that wasn't anything new for me.

Now he turns all that around with the flip of a switch and pulls this shit? No. Uh huh.

He doesn't answer. Instead his face dips, his forehead meeting my shoulder as he breathes harshly in and out. His hand slides to my side, gripping my hip as he struggles.

And Lord, is he struggling.

I can feel the way he's fighting himself at every turn.

Only I have no desire to be a casualty in his war.

I don't even see a different outcome for me. At the end of the day, our obstacles are unchanged. It's why I plan to move out right after we get back from the tour. It's time and I've saved enough to be able to do that. I need to take care of myself. To look out for myself.

Keith Dawson is owning more and more of my heart, but unfortunately, I will never own his.

And I can't live like that.

Like this.

Suddenly Henry's threat makes perfect sense.

He saw the way Keith was looking at me tonight. But he also knows him well enough to know that he doesn't get emotionally involved. With anyone. Keith doesn't date and he doesn't do girlfriends. Henry was trying to protect me. I think I love Henry just a bit more in this moment.

I take a small step back and Keith lets me, and I know for certain that what Viola said is wrong. He loves a ghost. Not me. He hates that he wants me, and I hate that I want him. So in that respect, I guess we're even.

"I think I'm going to take a cab home."

He stands up to his full height, his eyes casting about my face, wracked in misery and indecision. "I'll take you."

"No. Stay and have fun with your friends. You deserve it. I need to pack, and I have a million things to get ready before we leave."

"Maia—"

"Please, Keith. I want you to stay, but I need to go."

He runs his hands through his hair before grasping my arm and leading me over to Marsellus. "Can you make sure she gets home okay? I don't want her in a cab. Can one of the guys take her?"

"Of course, sir."

Marsellus speaks into his earpiece and Keith spins back around. His eyes pierce mine like he as a million things on the tip of his tongue that are dying to break free. He'll never say them. I already know that. "I won't be out late."

I shake my head, beyond incensed with this man. "I'm not your mother, your wife, or your girlfriend. Stay out as late as you want."

"So fucking stubborn," I hear him growl under his breath before he marches off but what does he expect from me? I left the ball in his court weeks ago and he did nothing with it. Suddenly because I'm dressed up and catching a few stares, he thinks he can spin this all back around? That I'll be here waiting for him no matter what?

Doesn't he see how wrong that is?

My job is all I have right now, and I won't let his mind games get in the way of that.

I WAKE WITH A SMALL JOLT. A feeling of someone standing there in the darkness. I start to roll over only feel a hand on my shoulder pushing me back onto my side. A scream starts to lurch past my lungs only to be shuddered to a halt when Keith whispers, "Shhh. It's just me. Go back to sleep."

"What time is it?" I rasp out.

"About two."

"What are you doing?"

"Checking on you. Watching you sleep. Thinking."

My eyes open, staring toward the window that is free of curtains but still not offering much in the way of light seeping in. "How long have you been doing that?"

"A while," he admits, and that shouldn't affect me the way it does.

"What is it you're thinking about?"

"How much I want to sleep in here tonight holding you."

Fuck. Just fuck.

Before I can talk myself out of it, I scoot closer to the window side of the bed, giving him the silent invitation. I clench my eyes shut and sink my teeth into my bottom lip as I hear him take off his shoes, shirt, and pants. I'm wearing a T-shirt and boy shorts, but that's it. I don't even have panties on beneath.

Not that it matters.

He said he wants to sleep holding me. That's it. That's all I'll let happen between us anyway.

I feel the blankets pull back and the cool blast of air that accompanies it only to have it quickly replaced with the blissful heat of his chest against my back. His right arm slides under my head along my neck and his other arm drifts around my stomach. He fingers the material of my shirt for a second and then slides me back into him.

Burying his face in my hair, he takes a deep inhale, and I start to tremble.

Something I know he feels as he holds me tighter.

But what he can't feel are the tears I'm fighting with everything inside of me. I've never laid like this with anyone before. Never spooned or been held.

It's everything I ever imagined it would be and then a whole lot more. Or maybe it's just the man doing the spooning and holding.

"I'm sorry, Maia." He plants a kiss on my shoulder, and I just about break. "I'm not trying to play games with you. I care about you so much and I never want to hurt you, though I know I am. I don't mean to be such a mess. I'm working on it. Now go to sleep, sweet darlin'. Tomorrow I'm gonna take you to get that cast off and then out for lunch. Anywhere you want to go, I'll take you."

I can't say anything. If I do, I'll cry for sure, or I'll turn around and kiss him. I'm not sure which, and I can't take the risk of doing either. So I close my eyes and allow myself to seek refuge in his comfort. In his scent and the way he feels against me.

And just as I start to drift, I hear him whisper something into my hair. Something I can't make out. Something feather-light as it floats away, my consciousness along with it.

. . .

Maia

"ONLY RICH PEOPLE would buy shit like this," I grumble under my breath, staring bewilderedly at a canvas that is taller than I am painted entirely in black lacquer. I could have done this with a two-ninety-nine can of spray paint that I purchased from Home Depot. Then again, I'd bet that's what this 'artist' did. "I'm in the wrong profession."

"You don't consider this art?" A voice out of nowhere startles me. I pivot to find a handsome, slightly older man with dark eyes and equally dark hair holding two glasses of champagne. He's polished. I'll say that much. His clothes openly cost a small fortune if the various brand-named logos scattered across them are any indication.

He hands me one of the glasses of champagne, and though I won't drink it, I accept it anyway.

"Um. Is it wrong if I say no?" I shrug a shoulder, resting my injured arm against my chest. My cast came off yesterday morning. I have a brace I'm supposed to wear at night to sleep and as much during the day as I can tolerate. I'm also supposed to start physical therapy on Monday. Only tomorrow we leave for ten days for the guys' tour, so my physical therapy will have to wait till we get back.

It feels both equally amazing and strange to have it off.

"What about it don't you find striking?"

Striking? Is he for real?

"It just seems… I don't know. Basic, I guess. There isn't much to it. Not even any bold brush strokes to suggest and provoke emotion. To me, it appears it was purchased because some big-name artist created it. Only it looks like he or she bought a can of spray paint and had a go with it on a large canvas. Then again, I don't pretend to know a whole lot about art. I was always more into modern or renaissance than contemporary."

"And yet for someone who claims not to know a lot about art, you understand the distinction between modern and contemporary," he challenges with a cock of his perfectly coiffed eyebrow.

"I guess. But I've always found difficulty clumping Andy Warhol and Monet in the same boat. So maybe I'm the problem and not art if you know what I mean."

"I can say you are absolutely not the problem. How much do you think this was purchased for?"

"Twenty grand?" I speculate, over-inflating the number given the caliber of mansion we're in.

"Thirty-two."

Oh fuck.

My face heats like an oven coming up to temperature. "This is your home, isn't it? Your painting?"

"Yup."

"And I just completely insulted your very expensive art. I'm so—"

"Refreshingly honest? Yes, you're most certainly that."

"Yet somehow, in this moment, I feel nothing short of humiliated. Is there a hole somewhere in this place I can crawl in to?" I'm sure there must be. This mansion and the surrounding grounds are larger than the town I grew up in. Seriously.

I still don't understand why we had to come here tonight. Why Keith, Henry and I are here, I correct since Gus is home with Naomi and Jasper is home with Viola and his little ones. And now I just insulted our host.

"How about instead of you crawling into a hole you agree to have dinner with me tomorrow evening."

I blink, slightly stunned.

"I. Um."

"Cannot accept," Keith finishes for me, waltzing up to us with a cocky smirk aimed at the man as he slips his hand possessively around my waist.

I'm still kinda PO'd with Keith. He came into my bed the other night, held me while I slept, but was gone before I woke up. Already doing laps in his pool though it was so early the sun was hardly a thought in the pre-dawn sky.

I know why he did it.

Part of me is even grateful he had the foresight.

But you don't hold someone all night and then duck out on them.

I haven't said much to him since as a result. Not even when I got my cast off or when he took me out for lunch. We're leaving for ten days and getting into a big fight about something that should not happen seems ill-timed and futile. We're tormented with each other, and that can never lead anywhere good.

Going on tour will help.

He'll be preoccupied with shows and I'll be running around doing my job and we'll be in a hotel, separated from each other. And when we come home, I'm moving out.

If I wasn't sure about that before, I'm positive about it now.

"Yes," I tell the man, ignoring Keith. "I'm sorry, but I'll be traveling for work for the next ten days."

The man does not seem fazed by Keith's sudden appearance or his hand on my hip. "When you return, perhaps? That is if the band will allow their beautiful assistant out of their sight."

I blink, slightly stunned. "You knew who I was?"

"Of course." He laughs. "I make it a point to know all my guests. I'm Jonathan Albright."

Now my jaw becomes unhinged and I step forward, but I don't get far as Keith tightens his grip on me. "You're a director. I love your work. You have such a unique style with scene lighting and camera angles."

"Thank you," he says, impressed, his arrogant smile growing. His gaze swiftly shifts to Keith and then back to me with a gleam. "So is that a yes to dinner when you return?"

This guy cannot want to date me. He's at least twenty-five years older than me. Then again, this is Hollywood. "I—"

"It's a hard no, Johnny," Keith cuts in. "Now if you'll excuse us, I need a word with my assistant."

Keith drags me away in the rudest manner possible. "It was nice meeting you," I call out, only I can't even turn to catch the man's eyes because Keith is shoving me along at light speed. Some of the champagne in my hand sloshes, spilling over the side, and he takes the glass from my hand, setting it down on a side table. "Quit it," I bark, smacking at him with my good hand. "That was a seriously shitty thing to do."

"The hell it was. That man is more than twice your age."

Keith looks left and then right down a massive hallway and leads me to a closed door. He opens it, peeks inside and practically shoves me in. It's a bathroom, but it's easily the size of my old apartment. Before I can continue my yelling, Keith picks me up by my hips and sets me down on the spacious marble counter before stepping back and creating space between us.

I fold my arms over my chest and cross my legs, the silky fabric of my borrowed dress slipping up my thighs a bit.

"What do you think you're doing? You had no right barging in like that and dragging me out like I'm some kind of child. I know how to handle myself, Keith."

"I didn't like him talking to you. He goes through women like you wouldn't believe."

"And you don't?"

I get a hard glare for that comment and shrug my shoulder, still pissed off and wanting him to be equally as pissed.

"So what?" I continue. "Even if he does, that's my business."

"You can't go out with him," he growls, pinning me with his cold stare as he takes a large step in my direction, crowding me just a bit.

"I can do whatever I want. Go out with whoever I want."

"No, dammit. You can't."

"Says who?" I snap, shoving at his brick wall of a chest so he'll give me space. Newsflash: it doesn't work. He just comes in closer. Invading my space because clearly he has zero respect for situational boundaries when it comes to me. "You are the most stubborn, bull-headed, pain in my ass—"

"I think you're talking about yourself there, darlin'—"

"—Stupid bastard I've ever met. Tell me why I can't date that man," I demand, so fucking tired of dancing around this.

"Because you belong to me!" he yells, startling me. I frown deep and hard. Even as a warm flutter fills my belly.

"I don't belong to anyone. No one owns me." A warning note

creeps into my hoarse voice as I say it. Those are the exact words Carvalo said to me when my father essentially sold me to him. No. Not fuckin' happening.

"That's not how I meant it. Fuck," he barks, running his hands through his hair. "You're the only woman I can't have and fuck me if that doesn't make me want you more than anything or anyone else."

That should be hot to me, but instead it rubs me all kinds of wrong. "I'm not interested in you wanting me simply because you think you can't have me."

"That's not why I want you, Maia. You know that all too well."

"But you won't do anything about it." Isn't that what he's telling me? "Maybe I should just fuck Henry then," I say, my voice sharp like a razor, hoping I cut into him the way he's cutting into me. Keith growls like a madman, so I must have hit my mark.

"The fuck you should."

"Why not?" I throw back, ready to shake the man. I'm the one risking everything. How does he not see that? My heart, my job, my financial freedom. Everything. What does he have to lose? Nothing. He wants me. I know he does. And not just because I'm forbidden to him. I refuse to believe that bullshit.

"Because you work for him."

I roll my eyes at that. Like hard. "Same as I do for you?"

"Yes." Only he yells it. Screams it. It's an expletive. A four-letter word.

"You can't have it both ways. Either you want me, or you don't. Make up your fucking mind already. I'm sick of you fucking with my head! You slept holding me. You put your fingers inside of me until I came on them. And you haven't said a word about any of it."

He runs a hand through his hair again. Across his stubbled jaw. He even kicks the cabinet I'm sitting on. None of that helps. He's unglued and I think I like him like this. Burning with fury. Desperate with passion. Exploding with barely contained rage.

He's a jealous, possessive man.

And though I may not want to be owned, I sure as hell want to be consumed.

"What do you want me to say, Maia?"

"Maia? I'm no longer your sweet darlin'?" I smirk, taunting him. His eyes rake over me with a predatory gleam and my heart does a crazy flip in my chest. Anticipation buzzes along my skin. "You want me so bad you can't stand it. Admit it. Just please, finally admit it."

He laughs sardonically. "You think you have any clue what's been going through my head? You think you're the only one struggling with this."

"Tell me!"

"I want you so bad I can't fucking think straight. Is that what you want me to say?" In the next second, his mouth slams into mine, forcing me back, my head bumping into the mirror behind me with the brutality of his blazing kiss. My arms fly around his neck, needing to stabilize myself against his assault. I kiss him back, equally as hungry with no desire or way to stop the rising swell of lust as it swarms through me.

My body temperature flames to a pulsing heat.

He breaks the kiss as quickly as he started it, leaving us panting and our eyes glowing as we stare into each other.

"Jesus Christ." He punches the wall. "Fuck! No woman has ever aggravated me more. I don't know whether to spank you or fuck you."

"Both. I'll take both please."

He shakes his head, roaring as his teeth gnash into my bottom lip before sucking it into his mouth to ease the sting. He finds no humor in my poor attempt at a joke. He's a cornered animal, wild and unpredictable and fiercely dangerous. And right now, all I want to do is provoke him, so he'll unleash all that on me.

"I waltz repeatedly right up to the edge, knowing better the entire time. And yet, I can't stop myself from doing it. I want you, Maia. Like I've never wanted anyone else. It's tearing me up inside, but I'm so tired of fighting it. You're a wildfire I'm dangerously close to burning alive in and I can't even find it in me to care anymore."

"Make me burn with you."

He shakes his head, but his eyes are glittering with a barely contained lust. "You're too young. Too untouched."

"Am I so untouched still?"

"Baby, you have no idea what it is to be fully touched by me."

No. But I really want to. And just as he's tired of fighting it, I am too.

He spreads my thighs by stepping in between them. "I've wanted you for what feels like forever now. It's non-stop. It's constant. It's consuming. It's deranged. And yet there is no evading it or making it disappear. Every second I'm with you, I only seem to want you more."

Slipping my dress up, his hands glide along the shimmery fabric until he's exposed my panties. My breath hitches. He stares down at me, breathing hard, a swirling storm of desire in his eyes. I spread my legs a little wider. Knowing this isn't going to end with me simply coming on his fingers.

I plant my hand on his chest, waiting until he meets my eyes again. "I'm not a one-time, screw around with me to get me out of your system, girl. If we do this, if I give you this piece of me, I'm yours. And screw Henry's warning, if you break my heart, I will break yours back."

He swallows thickly and nods. "I think you've always been mine. You're under my skin. Once with you could never be enough." He cups my face roughly, his thumbs grazing my jaw and bottom lip.

"I love this job, Keith. But more importantly, I need it."

He shakes my head violently. "What kind of monster do you take me for? All I've done since I've met you is try to make your world a better place. Try to ease the pain and fear I recognize in your eyes. Not once have I placed any condition on my help. Do you honestly believe that anything that happens or doesn't happen between us would ever impact your job?" He bristles. Pretty hard, actually. "*Never*," he emphasizes. "Never, Maia. This job is yours for however long you want it or don't. I am not a factor in that and will never make myself one. You hear me?"

"Then why aren't you kissing me?"

His expression grows bleak, distraught. Broken. He emits a shaky breath and once again, he's at war with himself. "You need to know this has nothing to do with Amy. My feelings for you are not tied to her. I know you worry about that. I see it in your eyes all the damn time. But when I look at you, I don't see her. When I think about you, I don't think about her. It's only you, Maia. My sweet darlin'. Just you."

Now it's my turn to swallow. Because I believe him. Even though I can also see how much it costs him to say that. That's what's breaking him. He's a festering wound of guilt.

As much as that cost him to say, this could cost me everything to do.

I blow out a silent breath.

His head dips toward mine, resting inches from my lips. "I need you."

An uncontrollable shiver skitters up my spine at the heat and carnality in his gaze. My insides quiver. After one heart-stopping moment, Keith drops his hand to my thigh before slowly sliding it up.

"Can I have you, Maia? Finally? Say yes."

20

Keith

SHE STARES into my eyes for forever. What she sees in mine beyond my desire for her, I'm not sure. I told her I want her. I told her I need her. I told her, her job is secure. I told her it's not about Amy. And yet, she still stares at me.

"Maia?"

She looks terrified as she says, "Yes."

"Are you saying yes to me saying your name or yes to me?"

She grins, but it's shaky. "Both."

"You sure?"

She nods.

"Maia?"

"I'm sure. Yes. I want you. I want this."

"You're scared?"

Her eyes bounce back and forth between mine. "I'm scared."

"Me too. But we can do this together. I *want* to do this together."

"Okay. Together. Now kiss me."

I cup her jaw. "I'm not fucking you in this bathroom," I tell her. "That's not how your first time will go."

"Then what exactly are you planning to do in here?"

I grin wickedly. "I'm going to eat you out and then I'm going to take you home and spend the rest of tonight inside of you."

"Is that what you think is happening tonight?"

I slide her body along the smooth marble until she practically falls off the edge. My eyes locked on hers, I reach up and shred her panties into tatters of satin. It was surprisingly too easy and the way she gasps tells me she knows I'm going to do exactly that tonight.

"Spread your legs wide, darlin'. I want to see every inch of your beautiful pussy. I've tasted it on my fingers, but never from the source. I have a feeling it'll be even sweeter this way."

At first, she refuses. Because this is Maia and Maia never does anything I ask on the first go around. No, my stubborn woman has to fight back at every turn.

I lean in, bringing my mouth directly beside her ear without touching her. "Show me my future paradise and I swear I'll worship her accordingly."

Brazenly, losing any last shred of her resistance or fight, she spreads her legs as wide as they can go on the counter. I glance down. Pink. Swollen. Wet. Paradise indeed. She is goddamn perfection. Saliva pools in my mouth as I kiss the spot just beneath her ear and then drop to my knees.

I glance up at her, my heart thundering in my chest. I've resisted her for so long. Warred with myself. Fought everything inside of me. Because the truth is, I am scared. This woman terrifies me. She leaves me raw. So fucking vulnerable.

But she's mine. I need her.

The fire that lights up all my dark corners.

"You're so beautiful." I kiss the inside of her thigh, loving how just that simple move makes her shudder. "Put your bad arm on my shoulder, baby. I don't want you to use it to steady yourself. But this going to feel really good and you're going to want to grip my hair or the counter while you're fucking my face and we're not going to reinjure your arm tonight."

"You seem very confident that this is going to feel that good."

I grin like a cocky motherfucker. "I am. There are many things I'm really good at, darlin', but eating pussy might be one of my talents."

She huffs out a loud, annoyed breath. Just as I knew she would. "You're such a douche. Pointing out your previous work experience may be super cool during a job interview, but not when you're about to be with a new lover."

Stroking her inner thighs, I tell her a truth I've scarcely allowed myself to believe. "Jealous already? Lucky for you that shit turns me on. But don't fret, darlin'. You're not just my new lover, you're my only lover. The only woman I want. Ever."

"You're such an arrogant—Oh my god," she cries out as I lick her slit from her opening all the way up to her mound where I place a wet open-mouthed kiss.

"You were saying?" I smirk into her.

"Do that again," she pants, her back already arching.

I chuckle, blowing on her sensitive skin. She's so responsive to everything I do. My dick is granite in my pants with the thought of it. Circling her clit with my tongue, I pull it into my mouth before gently sucking on it, loving the hell out of the way her hips buck and her head falls back and her lips part.

So stunning, my girl. And every bit as delicious as I knew she would be.

"Keith," she gasps as I pull back, blowing on her again.

"I could eat you for hours, baby, and never tire of making you come. My Pandora. My beautiful, delicious Pandora." My tongue glides up into her hot channel, flicking back and forth and thrusting in as deep as I can go. Her frantic hand shoots up from my shoulder, grasping my hair and then she whimpers, both in pleasure and pain.

I pull back with an admonishing glare.

"Sorry. I'll be good. Just don't stop."

I kiss her clit again as she relaxes her hand. "If I had known eating you out would make you this agreeable, I'd have done it a month ago."

She laughs, her eyes dancing with lust and... happiness? Adoration? I don't know. Whatever it is, it's magic. It's unleashing something primal in me. It makes me want to pound my chest like a caveman for being the one who put it there.

I want to keep this look on her face always.

My finger slides inside her, curving, angling up as I stroke in and out of her. Watching her as I do. I was robbed of this the first time in the car. Seeing how she looks when I touch her. The way I make her feel. Her cheeks are flushed, and her nipples are hard points under the material of her dress. Her dark eyes are nearly black, her lust-drunk yearning lowering her lids to half-mast and making her look sexy as all hell.

"I can't wait to fuck you. I'm going to drive home with the taste of you on my lips. But when I get you home... I won't be able to hold back."

"Don't hold back," she moans as I zero in on her clit with my tongue, my finger still pumping in and out, my pace increasing as I go. I add another one and she cries out, her inner walls clamping down. "Oh my god. Keith. I... I... I'm going to come."

"Yes, baby. Come. I'm dying to see you. You're so fucking gorgeous."

She detonates, a loud half-scream, half-moan fleeing her lips. I have no doubt everyone at this party can hear her.

Her pussy convulses around my fingers as she rocks hard against my hand and harder against my face. Satisfaction slams into me with the force of a runaway train as I watch her explode with ecstasy, steadying her with my other hand so she doesn't fall off the counter. Or worse, hurt her arm again.

Finally, she sags, falling forward, her body collapsing onto mine to the point where I have to catch her, cradling her chest against mine. She opens her eyes, right into mine, a smile across her face just as a giggle bursts forth. "Hi."

"Hi beautiful," I whisper.

"That was fun."

I laugh, rubbing my nose against hers. "I'm glad. Can I take you home now?"

"Yes. But I think I need a minute before I can walk. My legs are jelly. Is it like this with everyone?"

"You're never going to find out, so why ask?"

She rolls her eyes at me. "You don't own my pussy, Keith. And since this is only our second interlude, I think it's a bit too soon for such bold statements." The brat is smirking at me. She thinks she's got me with that one.

"Strange because I was about to text my lawyer to draft up ownership documents. You should receive them in about ten to fourteen business days."

"Awesome. Plenty of time to go exploring and see if another can do me better."

I smack the inside of her thigh before leaning in and licking the sting away. She yelps and I grin into her flesh, nipping at it before trailing up and lapping her entire swollen and glistening pussy that is still fully on display for me. She gasps, hissing out a noise, and I follow that move up by licking her neck and then her lips. "I licked you so now you're mine. That's how this works."

"How very fourth grade of you. We can discuss this further once I regain control of my faculties and manage to stand on my own strength."

I grin dopily. "I can carry you."

"Noooo," she emphasizes, those pretty sated eyes of hers going wide. "But I do wish we were already home. I don't want the time in between."

I kiss her lips, knowing what she means. We said we were in this together, and yet something about us still feels unsettled. Fleeting, perhaps. Like we know how something this good can't possibly last because it never has before.

Love has not been kind.

For either of us.

Love has been pain. It's been devastating. It's been torment and disappointment. It's been everything that is wrong with love. And when you experience the worst love has to offer, you do everything in your power to stay away from it. You avoid it all costs. Spend years not looking it in the eye or taking it to your bed or into your home. You lock yourself away and make sure your shutters are closed and your barriers are impenetrable.

Until one day, someone comes out of nowhere and blindsides you.

Then all that protection you thought you so deceptively and cleverly had in place disintegrates.

"Tonight is ours, darlin'. Ain't no one coming to steal it from us."

"And what about tomorrow?"

"Tomorrow we leave for tour. And before I go on stage, I'm going to kiss you for luck. You'll watch the show from the wings, and when that's all done, I'm going to kiss you again. I'll sit you on my lap and hug you with my sweaty body while you swat at me because I'm mussin' your pretty all up. When we go out celebrating, you'll be on my arm and when we go back to the hotel after all that's done, you'll be in my bed."

"That sounds pretty perfect."

"*I* won't always be perfect," I warn. "I'll get plenty wrong."

"And I'll keep pushing all your buttons. Fighting you at every turn."

The hazy passion in her eyes and the alluring flush on her cheeks kicks my heart rate up a notch. Two shattered souls that with the right rearranging of our broken pieces have the potential to become whole again. I can find myself in Maia. She grounds me. She connects me.

She sees me, flaws, fucked-upness and all.

It's everything else that I'm battling. Not my feelings for her.

I lean in and kiss her lips. Softly. A gentle coaxing but with enough heat behind it to remind her of what's to come. Standing, I push her back upright and help her off the counter, holding onto her as she adjusts her dress and fluffs out her hair. She meets my eyes in the mirror and winks at me, making my chest clench.

This is where I belong. With her. And I will fight everything, even myself, to keep it that way.

I plant a kiss in the crook of her neck, inhaling her fragrance and groaning. "Goddamn, I'm addicted to you." The urge to fuck her is driving me insane.

A virgin.

That shit's blowing my mind.

And I can't even tell if that's in a good way or not. It's a challenge. Sure as hell, it is. But more than that, I want it to be perfect for her. When a girl waits until they're twenty and picks you to go take their V-card, you better make damn sure it is.

And Maia isn't just any girl.

A swift and uncontained sense of urgency slingshots through me. I take her hand and drag her out of the bathroom, down the hall, and straight through the front door of the mansion.

"In a rush?" she teases.

Life rule #69: Apply numbered since it's smart-mouthed women make me hard while driving me crazy. Or maybe that's not a life rule so much as a simple fact? Whatever. I am not to be trifled with. There is only so much remaining blood flow in my brain, and I will need all of it to get us home safely.

I throw her a cocked eyebrow and a sideways glance, and she quickly shuts up. She can see I am in no fucking around mode.

I bypass the curious valet attendant and find my truck quickly. No one here drives a truck. They all drive flashy sports cars. I help Maia up and in, and once she's settled, I run around to get in. Time to go home. Time to ruin myself in this woman once and for all.

21

M aia

ANTICIPATION BEATS out a heavy staccato through veins, making me edge, needy, nervous. The car ride home wasn't quiet. It wasn't riled with sexual tension either. It was easy. It was conversational. We discussed all the things that would happen on tour. All the roles and responsibilities I would have.

I'm going on tour with a major rock band.

That is no small thing. In fact, it's a huge undertaking. The guys, and me, are flying on a private jet but their gear travels by huge buses like a caravan. Keith explained how this can be especially difficult with his drums and I listened to everything he had to say, mostly because I was still a bit shocked by how easy we just ebb and flow into different forms of us.

I've never known this level of comfort or intimacy with someone.

It's euphoric and panic-inducing all in the same breath.

But now we're home. In his home.

And tonight, I will not be sleeping in my bed.

"Go upstairs, get undressed and wait for me."

That's all he says before walking off toward his music room. Get undressed. Okay, that I can do. But does he mean fully naked? Then I inwardly laugh because I am fully naked beneath this dress. The man shredded my panties like he was tearing a piece of paper.

I take the steps, my heart thrumming like a rabbit as I reach my room. Wait for him. Do I do that in here? In his room?

Dammit, doesn't he know this is my first time? That I have no idea what I'm doing?

And why am I letting him call all the shots?

You know why, my brain chimes in, and I do. Because I want him to.

I like to open my mouth and talk back about everything but when it comes to his hands on my body, I want to feel his power. It makes me feel wanton and desired and fucking protected. It makes me high, which is certainly not something I ever expected, but there it is.

Still, I decide to make him come to me.

I will crawl on my hands and knees to him, obey his every dirty command and love every second of it, but I have limits with that, and my need for control and self-preservation still appreciate knowing they have some skin in this game.

Slipping out of my dress, I stand naked at the foot of the bed and not even two hundred and forty seconds later—I counted—he enters the room, wearing nothing but the dress slacks he was wearing out tonight. His shirt is gone, as are his shoes and socks, and I take a moment to appreciate his chest and abs with my eyes.

So cut and chiseled, I can't wait to run my hands all over him. An opportunity I have not been afforded as of yet. His eyes devour me, burning a path over every place they touch.

"Why are you in here?" he asks softly, sauntering over to me and stopping only a few inches away. I can feel the heat radiating from his chest. His masculine scent permeates the air. It's heady and I take a deep inhale, shameless in my worship of him.

"You didn't tell me where to go after I got undressed. All you said was wait for you."

A slow, sexy smile curls up his lips. One hand comes up, cupping my jaw and tilting my head back. His other finds my bare hip, sliding back until he squeezes my ass cheek. His lips meet mine, just a delicate brush, a light tickle before they trail down across my jaw, moving lower to my neck.

"You're finally admitting I'm in charge."

I roll my eyes, trying for a levity I don't even come close to feeling. "Sure. If you want to believe the illusion I bestow upon you, go for it."

He's not taking the bait. Instead, his eyes are intense and serious as they spear mine. "Tell me you're ready," he hums, returning to my neck. "Tell me yes."

My eyes roll back into my head and all he's doing is kneading my ass and kissing my neck. But it's the way he's kissing it. Hot, open-mouthed kisses along my pulse line. It's so good I can—

Smack!

The hard crack on my ass jolts me back, and I remember he asked me a question. "Yes, I'm ready. And yes, I am telling you yes." Then I smile because that last sentence was a bit redundant, but who cares. The message is obviously received because he swoops me effortlessly up into his arms and marches me down the hall toward his bedroom.

He kisses me, whispering sweet and dirty words in my ear, and I'm already dizzy.

"Open your eyes," he commands. I hadn't even realized I shut them. But when I open, I'm hit with the warm, soft, flickering glow of what can only be candlelight, and I gasp as he sets me down on my feet. My hand comes up to cover my mouth as I take in the scene Keith has arranged for me. His arms wrap around my waist from behind, his chin dropping to my shoulder. "Your first time should be special," is all he says, and I have to swallow repeatedly so I don't cry. As it is, tears are already clinging to my lashes.

"It's beautiful," I manage, but it's so much more than that. I had no idea Keith had all these candles in his house, but wow. Fat pillar candles are on his tall dresser. Small votives line his short one. There are even a few more on his nightstands.

I think I just fell head over heels in love with this man.

He spins me around in his arms and marches me backward toward the bed. His volcanic blue eyes are glowing along with the candles as he rakes over every inch of me. He's seen me, but only in increments. That first day in my bra. Tonight in the bathroom. But never fully on display like this for him.

"God, Maia," he whispers reverently. "How did I get so lucky?"

I keep asking myself the same thing.

His hands cup my face as his mouth crashes down on me, his tongue diving past my parted lips and dancing with mine. The fingers of one hand drag through the long strands of my hair where he grips me by the roots, tilting my head to deepen our connection.

Gone is the gentle, romantic man who lit candles.

The one kissing me now is lit with passion and fueled by carnal desire.

A match to flint there is no stopping the fire between us. Excitement burns through the air and across my body in pulsing waves, smothering the last remnants of my nerves.

My hands become greedy, needing to touch him. To explore every inch of him. I start at his shoulders, dragging down over his large biceps before I find his chest. His heart is racing beneath my palm and something about that seems to spike my own. His abs ripple and tense as my fingers touch him, my nails scraping, toying with the trail of hair just below his navel.

He is cut from stone. A beautiful wall of muscle and flesh.

And mine. This man is so mine, I'm not sure there was any other alternative.

The hand on my cheek slides down my neck, tossing my long hair back over my shoulder, exposing my breast to him. He takes full advantage, cupping it in his large hand and lifting it up, testing its weight as it overflows. His thumb brushes over my painfully hard nipple and I whimper into his mouth as sparks of pleasure zap through me.

"You like that?" he rasps, and I can only nod as he pinches it harder. His other hand scoops up the other breast, squeezing them together with a firm grasp. "You have the most perfect breasts I've ever seen. So gorgeous they've starred in every fantasy I've had about you. And now I get to enjoy them." He sucks one pert nipple into his mouth, twirling his tongue around and around before scraping the tender flesh with his teeth.

"How many fantasies have you had about me?" I pant.

I feel him smile against me, a low chuckle rumbling into me. "How long have you been living here?"

"I've wanted you too. Tons of fantasies all about you."

He groans, rocking his hips, and with each thrust, he hits my aching pussy. My good hand clings to his back, my nails digging in. My other hand flies up to his hair as I unexpectedly cry out.

It's so good it's almost too much.

"Keith," I plead, my voice a high-pitched keen as he continues his exquisite torment on my breasts, driving me up higher and higher as he thrusts and thrusts.

He slips two fingers inside me, growling when he feels how wet I am, and sucks harder on my nipple. The vibrations do me in, and the second his thumb hits my clit, I detonate. Stars flash across my vision as my knees start to buckle beneath me. Keith swoops his hand along my lower back, holding me up without slowing the pace of his fingers until I'm completely boneless.

He emits a husky humming sound, something tinted with his own pleasure and satisfaction.

My caveman likes to make me come it seems.

Keith gently lowers me to the bed, and I fall back, not even able to hold myself upright or play it cool. A breathy laugh flees my lungs. "Okay. You win. You're in control."

He grins triumphantly. "Glad we got that out of the way. There is nothing sexier or more beautiful than when you come, so I plan on doing that a lot."

His lips fuse themselves to mine, kissing and nipping at me and within seconds, I'm craving more of it. Needing to feel him everywhere. I want the pressure of his weight on top of me. His scent and taste on my tongue. His body inside of mine.

He shifts, cool air replacing his body, and I open my eyes find him staring at me while he takes off his pants. Holy hell, in a handbasket, this is actually happening. His cock springs free, long, thick, and hard, and I reach out to touch it before I can stop myself. I give it a firm squeeze and he grunts. It's steel encased in smooth velvet, and I start to pump it.

I look up at him, his gaze burning into mine. "You're going to have to teach me how to pleasure you."

He groans, his head falling back as he bites out a slew of curses before meeting my eyes again. "Darlin', I can already tell you're a natural, but I'll happily teach you anything you want to learn."

Leanding down, he kisses me as I continue to stroke him, but all too soon he pulls away, going to his nightstand drawer and pulling out a condom. He sheaths himself up while I watch, utterly captivated by his raw, delicious masculinity. I'm already so turned on again just by the sight of him putting a condom on his dick that I can feel myself leaking onto his bed.

I have no idea if that's normal or not, but I have a feeling in the next few minutes any extra lubrication will be a blessing. Keith is big. And did I mention thick?

Oh boy.

He prowls on all fours on the bed, moving toward me with hunger in his eyes. My breath comes out in choppy pants as I swivel around to face him, spreading my legs and laying back. He takes his cock in hand, teasing it at my entrance, slipping in the tiniest amount before dragging it back out and toying with my clit.

"Keith, please." I can't take the suspense anymore. He grunts, his face tight with concentration. His tongue moistens his lips as his broad, muscular chest rises and falls with heavy breaths. "Don't make me do it myself."

A gust of air escapes in the form of a strained laugh. "Oh, baby, I'm going to do it. I'm going to fuck you so good. But I don't want to rush it either. I want to do it slow. I want you to remember every second of it so that when it's over, you still feel my cock every time you move."

Lips meets mine in a scorching hot kiss just as his cock presses against my entrance again. He grasps one leg, bending it at the knee and spreading me wider as he tucks it against his chest. My other leg loops around his lean hips, resting on the crest right above his ass.

His teeth drag along my bottom lip as our foreheads meet.

And with his eyes on mine, he thrusts forward.

My head snaps away like a slingshot, my breath lodged in my chest as I bite down on my bottom lip. That feels... not so fun. Like my insides are burning and tearing.

"Breathe, Maia. Take a deep breath in and relax, baby. The hard part is over. After this it will be all pleasure, I promise."

I turn back to him only to discover my hands are planted in his chest, pushing him back. He stares at me warily, concern etched in his tightly drawn brow. He nods his head, a silent encouragement, and instead of screaming at him or strangling him or shoving him off me and running into the bathroom to hide, I do as he says. Trusting him.

But wowzers, my vagina is not happy right now.

"Are you okay?" he asks, his hand stroking my cheek as he searches my face.

Am I? "I think so."

As I take that deep breath and focus on relaxing, the burn starts to lessen. The sting not so pronounced. His lips capture mine as his hand starts to fondle my breasts, toying with my nipples in just such a way that a spark of desire begins to eclipse the discomfort that snuffed it out.

Keith rocks his hips into me, not really sliding in and out, but just gently grinding, allowing me to acclimate to his size. To the feel of him inside me. And when he hits my clit with each forward motion, pleasure takes over.

"So tight," he moans. "Fucking hell you feel so amazing."

"Holy wow. Keith. It's intense as shit. *Jesus*," I hiss.

"Mmmm," he hums into me. "Yes. That's it. Feel how good this can be. The way your tight pussy stretches around my cock. Pretty soon I'll have you begging me for it. Waking me up at three am because you just have to have it right. That. Second." He punctuates each word with a deep, grinding thrust.

A tremor rolls through me, like thunder right before the lightning strike. Electricity is building inside me. Keith picks up his pace, sliding nearly all the way out before pushing back in. With each pull away, I feel empty. With every thrust in, full.

It's everything and yet, I need so much more.

He starts to fuck me like he's possessed. His hips piston faster and faster.

"God, *yes*," I moan, my head falling back as I arch up into him, wanting to feel his chest against mine as he takes me. Both my legs are around his waist now, my bad hand above my head, my other clutching his shoulder blade as I hold on, meeting him thrust for thrust.

He glances down, watching where our bodies are meeting and then back up at me. "Good?" he grinds out, sweat coating his brow.

"Yes. So good."

"Can you take it harder? I want to give it to you harder."

Jesus. "Harder," is all I can manage as the rising swell of an impending orgasm begins to steal my breath. My eyes close as he adjusts me again, lifting one of my legs until my knee is on his shoulder and he bends forward until my thigh is against my chest. "Holy shit," I cry out as he fucks me hard at this new angle, so much deeper than before. His cock hits something inside of me and I can't hold it off any longer.

My orgasm rips through me with a scream. Endorphins slam into me making my head spin and my thoughts scatter. Keith groans, his hips changing speed and momentum as he too follows me over the edge.

He stills in me, keeping his weight up until I drag him down on top of me and then he rolls us so my head is on his chest, right over his pounding heart. Adjusting my hips carefully, he slides me off, holding onto the condom as he does. "Be right back," he whispers into my hair before planting a kiss there. A few seconds later, he returns with a warm wet cloth. "Spread your legs for me."

"Didn't I already do that?" I quip, so tired I do it anyway because I really don't have much left in me.

"You did." He kisses my forehead as he places the cloth between my legs, wiping a few times before holding it against my tender flesh. It feels so good I groan, my eyes closing, heavy and sated. "Being with you was heaven, Maia. It was everything."

"Yeah?" I ask, suddenly feeling a smattering of girlish self-consciousness for the first time.

He smiles down at me with glittering eyes that speak to emotions I can't even think about dreaming up in this moment. But I can't help but smile in return all the same, matching that emotion, no doubt.

"I don't have words for how incredible you are. For how much that meant to me. How much you mean to me."

I think him not having words speaks more than if he did.

"You make me feel very special," I murmur, my eyes closing and staying that way.

"You are special, Maia. Don't ever forget it. Sleep, my sweet darlin'. Sleep."

He kisses my forehead and I feel him move me, tucking me under the covers and crawling in behind me. He wraps me up in his arms and I settle in, hoping, praying, he won't turn into yet another heartache I have to survive.

22

M aia

"You know I grew up in a trailer, right? And not even a doublewide. Like a bargain basement, legit, trailer."

Keith glances over at me as I gnaw on my lip while staring at the large, sleek, private plane we're about to board. I knew we were traveling this way, but I just didn't think... I don't know. It just all seems so surreal.

This last month has been surreal.

I can't even think of another word for it.

It's like Cinderella-type shit, right?

I mean, I get it, I'm just the worker bee, and Keith doesn't actually own this plane himself, his band does, but come the fuck on.

"Viola did too, you know. She grew up in a trailer. Jasper and Gus grew up in a small one-story house. My house was four bedrooms, but it was handed down to my parents by my grandparents and there were eight of us living in it. Henry's story is a bit different, but not money wise. So yeah, I get it. I really do."

I shift my gaze over to him. "Does everyone know? About us, I mean."

"We don't keep secrets from each other. After everything that went down with Gus, Jasper, and Viola, there are no secrets. So if they don't know yet, they will in about two minutes when we board the plane. But all of them already know how I feel about you."

"Oh," is all I can say because he pretty much just admitted he has feelings for me. I mean beyond sex. I'm seriously hoping I didn't misread that because my feelings for him I'm positive go way deeper than his for me and it would really suck if this was just sex to him. "And this won't impact our work?"

He shakes his head, squeezing my hand. "Not even a little."

"Okay. I'm ready. Let's do this."

I shift to get out of the car but before I can go anywhere, Keith grabs my jaw and kisses me. Hard. His tongue tangles with mine until I'm a breathless, flushed mess. "Now you're ready." He winks at me, opening the car door and helping me out.

Damn him. Just damn him.

Keith helps me up the steps into the plane and then takes my hand, intertwining our fingers. I suck in a rush of air, blushing like a fifteen-year-old girl bringing a boy home for the first time. But since I never did that, this clearly my moment.

"You're so pretty when you blush."

"And you're a jerk," I grumble.

He laughs, dragging me onto the plane. All heads come up at once—since we're the last to arrive—and then one by one, they all focus on our joined hands. I might as well be wearing a T-shirt that says I'm with this guy and an arrow pointing in his direction.

Then the moment is over, and they move on.

Like it's no big deal.

Which it isn't, right? They don't care that I'm dating Keith. If that's even what we're doing because it's not like we actually go out on dates. I sigh.

I'm really overthinking something I shouldn't.

"Relax," he whispers to me as if he just overheard my inner turmoil, and I can only pray I didn't say any of that aloud. "Just go with the flow."

I'm not a go-with-the-flow girl, Keith! "I'm fine."

He throws me a sly smirk, leans in and kisses the corner of my mouth. "You sure as hell are."

He starts to drag me back toward where Henry is sitting when Marco practically launches himself at us. "No," he determinedly barks. I jolt back a step, my eyes wide. "You are not sitting with him during takeoff. He's going to want to play Madden or Fortnite against Henry, and that means I won't hear any of the juicy details until I can corner you later. Sorry, but that's just too far away for me to handle without stroking out at thirty-thousand feet."

"Um. Okay." I glance to Keith, and he just shrugs with a 'this is Marco, so you better do as he says' expression.

I'm not exactly given the chance. Marco grabs my elbow right above my brace and drags me over to the front of the plane while Keith heads to the back where the massive television is set up and Henry is already gaming.

Gus and Jasper are sitting in the middle facing each other with heads bent close, talking about who knows what in quiet tones. And it's in this moment I realize just how big this plane is. There is a bedroom in the back. A freaking bedroom. And like two bathrooms, one with a shower, I was told. There's a bar and a small galley kitchen and an office area. Huge.

It's also my first time on a plane. I didn't want to say anything to Keith but it's true. But I've seen enough movies to know this is not your standard plane. Even for a private one.

"I'm freaking out."

Marco rolls his eyes at me. "Stop deflecting. They're rich. They own a plane. Get over it." He points to a two-person bench seat that's facing the front of the plane. We buckle up and the plane starts to move slowly, heading for the runway. "That night you bailed on them at the club the bill was fifteen grand. Jasper didn't even blink an eye when he signed for it. Do you not realize who these guys are? Each concert night of this tour, they're making over six million dollars. That's thirty-six million over the next ten days, and that's just these concerts. You feel me?"

Thirty-six million over ten days?! The plane picks this moment to pick up speed on the runway, tilting up and taking flight. My stomach swooshes up into my chest before it drops down into my feet. "I'm going to be sick."

"No, you're not. You lost your V-card and you're sublimely happy and quite possibly in love with the gorgeous devil. The feeling is obviously mutual since Keith has *never* done this before. So dish it girl. Did he finally drop a scoop of ice cream on your cherry pie, if you know what I'm saying?"

I shake my head at him. "I don't think anyone other than you knows what you're saying. What the fuck do you mean ice cream on top of your pie?"

He sighs in exasperation. "Do I really need to explain the metaphor of *cherry* pie and ice *cream*?"

"I think that's more of a euphemism than a metaphor."

"Christ, Maia. Cut the shit and tell me if he fucked your brains out," he yells over the loud humming sound of the jets.

I smack his arm, glancing over my shoulder at the other guys. "Shhh. Keep your voice down."

"Right," he snorts, sitting back and crossing his legs, getting comfortable for the trip up to Seattle. "Like everyone on here doesn't already know. We knew Keith had a thing for you from like minute one."

I sag into him, resting my head against his butter-yellow shirt. Incidentally, it matches quite nicely against the soft leather of the seats. "Yes. The whole ice cream on my cherry pie." I hiccup out a laugh. "I can't believe I just said that."

"Own it. He certainly is. You're the only one having a small kitten over it."

That's because Keith doesn't get it. Neither does Marco. They don't know what it is to struggle the way I do. To have things you worked so hard to get ripped away from you. To lose everything, and then, when you think it can't get any worse, it does.

"What happens to me when this turns south?" When Keith grows bored or loses interest? When I'm no longer the bright, shiny new toy? When the thrill of what was forbidden is over and he's sated his desire and wants something new?

Because inevitably, that's what will happen.

It always does.

Like Murphy's Law, that's how predictable my life is with this stuff.

He tilts my chin up so I'm forced to meet his dark eyes. "Do you mean with your job or the fact that you're living with him or that you're in love with him?"

I shrug. "All of it," I say, not even bothering to lie about the love part because what's the point in that? He's said it enough times that it's a foregone conclusion. "Not the living part so much because I'm already searching for apartments. I can't stay with him any longer. My arm is on the mend and I won't mooch off him any more than I already have. Especially now that we're sleeping together."

His brows knit together. "Does Keith know you're doing that?"

I nod. "I mentioned it."

He shakes his head, his lips pinching to the side. They smell like raspberry gloss and I love Marco so much.

"Sweets, I can tell you now, the man won't like that. He's insanely protective over you. Be that as it may, your job is your job and who you fuck is who you fuck. The two are not related, even if they are. You technically work for me and the band, and you're doing an *incredible* job. They won't let you go, and neither will I, so put that part aside. There is no reason to think anything will go south just because it has in the past."

"It's hard to imagine otherwise when it's all I've known."

He hums, thinking about that for a moment. "I can understand what you're saying, but for now, focus on the tour. Focus on the fun. This is the dream, babe, and you're living it. You've got a cool job and an awesome boss" —he winks at me— "and you're getting hot and sweaty with a man who not only adores you but looks like a party favor from God. Just relax and enjoy it."

Enjoy it. The dream. He's right about all of it.

And if, *when*, I get my heart broken, well, at least I know how to weather that storm.

"Have you ever been to Seattle?" Keith asks as he tosses his arm around my shoulder in the back of yet another humungo black SUV. We're driving through the gray-skied streets, past such beautiful scenery it's impossible not to be glued to the window.

"Is that meant to be a joke or are you being ironic?" I retort. "I've been to the place I grew up and Los Angeles. Any pit stop on my trek out west was exactly that. I couldn't even tell you one town from the next, but no, I haven't been to Seattle."

"I've been all over the world but I'm not sure how much any of us have seen of it. One city bleeds into the next. One hotel the same as the one before it."

"Strange we've never rented an island," Henry muses and all of us turn in synchrony to him. He grins with a shrug of his shoulders. "What? We've got Ady and now Cora. An island would be fun. Think of Ady in her cute little purple bathing suit splashing in the waves. Might be weird being the only single one of us, but that's life, right?"

"When did you become fucking Viola?" Gus asks, and all of us start cracking up because that is exactly something Viola would suggest.

"Fine," Henry growls. "But my wingmen are dropping like flies." He glares at Keith who just smirks.

"Sorry, not sorry, dude."

I inwardly smile at that. Or outwardly, since I'm rubbish at holding in my emotions.

"It's cool. I'll just hit it up with one of your sisters next time they come for a visit."

"The fuck you will," Keith barks at Henry. "I will kick your ass from here to East Jesus."

I snort out a laugh at that, but Keith throws me a sideways glare.

He points a finger at Henry. "You're not going to touch, Eden."

"How do you know I'm talking about Eden?" Henry challenges with a gleam in his eyes.

Keith growls. "Because you're always talking about Eden. She's the only one you ever mention. That shit is wrong. She's too young for you. Too innocent and—"

"Hypocrite," Henry barks out as a fake cough, and now Jasper, Gus, and I are smiling like fools, trying to contain our laughter.

"She's a—"

"Grown woman, you were about to say," Henry interjects sharply. "I might not have seen her since our tour a few years back, but she was... what? nineteen then?"

"Right. She was *nineteen* then. Not a grown woman. Nineteen is too young, and you shouldn't have been talking about her."

"So now she's more like somewhere in between Maia and Naomi's age."

"No way you can be serious about her when you've decided never to be serious about anyone. She's still in school, bro."

Suddenly all eyes fall on me and the noise in the car tuns to zilch. Because I was in school once and if things had continued on course, I would *still* be in school. Which I guess officially makes me too young for Keith to be serious about. Awesomesauce.

I look to the window, only to feel him squeeze my shoulder. I refuse to acknowledge it. Our mess is what it is and it's too late to backtrack at this point.

I get it, though. That's the point of all this, right? I'm too young so he can't be serious. This can't happen for real.

Got it.

"Oh look," Marco sings out. "We're here. Maia, you hooked us up good, girl. The Fairmont is glorious. Can't wait to see how they've arranged our rooms."

I throw Marco a grateful eye just as the car rolls to a stop and the doors are opened. We're ushered immediately into a private elevator up to a private floor I've requested for the guys and all of our security as well as myself and Marco. But before I can slip my card into my door, Keith wraps his arm around my waist and throws me over his shoulder fireman style. He jogs us down the hall, despite my noisy protests, until I'm forced into his suite where he sets me on my feet and shuts the door behind us.

The suite is beautiful with large windows and gorgeous luxurious furnishings and once again I'm reminded just how far from Kansas, or northwestern Virginia, I've come. I don't get much time to appreciate the digs as Keith gets right up in my face.

"I have five younger sisters, Maia. Five girls I helped raise while my mom worked graveyards as a nurse and my father worked days as a mechanic. That shit between me and Henry over Eden has been going on forever. He saw her a few years back and something shifted in him and it drives me up a wall. He knows it does, so he pushes it. It's not in any way related to me and you."

I want to believe him. I truly do.

"I think what you did for your sisters is incredible. They're lucky." He reads me clearly, but I mean it. I'm not one of those people who hate on others for having more. Everyone should have more, and no one should have less. But at the same time, I had no one to do that for me. "I'm twenty. How many times have you told me I'm too young? Too innocent. Too forbidden."

"You are all those things. Why do you think I tried so hard to stay away from you?"

"Is that supposed to make me feel better?"

He runs a frustrated hand through his hair. "You're different in my head to me than my baby sister is. I don't know how to explain that any other way. Your situation was shitty. I get it. And there is no limit on the amount of anger or bitterness you should feel for that. It's the same for anyone, rich or poor, life is a motherfucker that doesn't stop or care about whether or not you're happy or your life is fair. I get it," he repeats. "But so far, you haven't needed me. Not the way my sisters did. You haven't needed anyone because you've done it all on your own. You're the strongest woman I know."

He has no idea. I'm strong because I had no choice. I had to be.

I needed so many heroes over the years that I dreamt up all kinds of fairy tales. Hell, Disney is not nearly as creative as I was. But they've been never real. They've always been pretend. Maybe that's why I love old movies so much. The happily ever after was guaranteed. And god, who doesn't need that?

"You have no idea what I needed," I tell him, resentment clouding my tone because I will not be told his sisters needed someone more than I did.

He walked into my life and tossed all my crap out the window like the trash it was and replaced the refuse with promises of better. And I believed him. I fell for it all. All of him.

It makes me feel stupid and restless.

"You're right. I shouldn't have said that." He scrubs his hands up and down his face before grabbing my shoulders and staring straight into my eyes. "You're twenty, but are you, Maia? Are you really? How long have you been taking care of yourself? How long have you been the adult in your world? You're twenty, but you're an old soul and it's not the fucking same. Please see that. Please know that. I not only want you. I fucking *need* you. Don't get your head full of shit that's between me and Henry."

I can try. But it's difficult not to.

I was never so insecure about myself and my situation until he came along, and I don't like the feel of it on my skin or in my head.

"I'll see you at soundcheck." I walk out of his room and he lets me go. And part of me thinks, it's too early for this. But then I remember this is fleeting. And he does nothing to prove me wrong.

23

Keith

If Fuck-Up were a name, its middle name would be Keith. Or maybe that name would be Keith Fuck-Up. It seriously doesn't matter the order because the sentiment is unchanged. I fucked up. Big time. Because that's all I seem to do.

I fly out my suite door and sprint down the hall seconds after her.

Her hand touches her keycard to the door, and I snatch it from her hand, opening the door for her and leading her inside. She starts to argue, as she always does, but I have ground to make up for and I can't do that and make soundcheck if I let her mouth start in on me now.

I peel off her T-shirt, followed quickly by her bra. Then I take off my shirt.

She's yelling, even swatting a bit, but I can't focus on that.

I'm a man on a mission.

Her leggings follow, my hands sliding them along with her

panties down over her hips and legs until they hit the floor. I get a smack to the face followed by another to my chest before she takes my nipple and twists it hard between her fingers.

"Brat, that hurt."

"It was supposed to, you asshole."

I pick her up the way I did earlier and toss her on the bed with a heavy bounce, her tits doing the same and it makes my dick jerk in my pants.

"Stop looking for reasons to push me away," I tell her, crawling over to her, hovering above her while she stares daggers into my eyes. She's so hot when she's mad, it's almost impossible to get these words out. "I want you. I don't know how many ways I have to keep telling you the same damn thing, but if I have to do it a hundred times a day, I will. I. Want. You. Too young. Too innocent. Too forbidden. Doesn't matter. It's you. All of you. Do you hear me?"

She swallows hard, some of her ire slipping. "I think I'm still scared." She whispers those words and they're so feather-light I have to strain to hear them.

I sink down onto her, pressing her into the mattress with my weight because I need to hold her. Scared I can work with. Her walking out on me, I can't.

"What are you scared of, baby? I'm not going anywhere."

"I'm not very good at trusting. I have no faith." She clears her throat and boldly meets my gaze. "Love cannot live without trust."

I press my forehead to hers and smile.

"Are you Psyche and me Eros?"

She gasps, her eyes growing wide.

"You told me Greek mythology was your lady porn. I did my research."

"You did?" Her eyes glitter as she cups my jaw, her fingers gliding along my stubbled face.

"It's a pretty amazing love story."

"It is," she sighs wistfully. "And like Psyche, I have difficulty trusting in the man who sleeps beside me in the darkness."

"I have trouble trusting too. Like Eros after Psyche didn't trust in him first. So we'll work on that one together, remember? And we'll talk. And fight because that's what we do with each other, and I'll be honest, it turns me on." I smirk, glancing down at my rock-hard cock that's pressed into her belly and then back up at her. "But we're not going to walk away from each other, okay? No more of that shit."

"Okay," she relents, some dawn breaking through her storm clouds. "Now kiss me because you just rocked my world with my lady porn and we only have an hour before your soundcheck. We are not missing that."

"Yes, ma'am. Just as soon as you spread those beautiful legs of yours."

She lets out a breathy laugh. "I said kiss me."

"And I plan on it." I give her an impish smirk, drifting down her body and taking one perfect nipple into my mouth.

"Keith," she gasps out. "I meant my lips."

Christ, she's so damn adorable. "You mean these lips?" I stroke her wet folds with my middle finger before dipping it inside her. She emits a shaky breath with a moan on the end. "I'm getting there, darlin'. I don't want to neglect my favorite girls on the way."

"I guess I can't argue that. Proceed."

I chuckle, grazing my teeth along the sensitive flesh. "Thanks for granting me permission." I remove my finger from inside her, squeezing her amazing tits and taking the wetness on my finger and rolling it around her nipple. I meet her eyes. "Taste yourself," I command, lifting her full breast up so she can lick at her own nipple. Her tongue juts out, flicking the tight bud and I just about lose my mind. "You like that?"

"Mmmm. But do you know what I really want to do right now?"

Fuck.

"What?"

"I want you to dip your cock into my pussy and then let me suck it after."

Motherfucker.

"You do, huh?"

She nods her head, her eyes filled with filthy delights I'm only too happy to deliver.

"You're a dirty little goddess, aren't you?"

She shoves my head down toward her pussy. "I've had a lot of time over the years to think about all the things I want to do." She props herself up on her elbows, watching me as my tongue comes out for a taste. "And Keith? There are a lot of really dirty, *dirty* things I want to do."

And I'm in love. That's not even my dick talking.

Well, maybe it is. Just a little.

But I think this is the moment of falling. I don't even care if that makes me a sick, depraved bastard. This girl is absolutely perfect for me. In the history of the world, there will be no other to match her.

I want to rock her imagination's world. I want to give her everything she will never experience with another lover. I want her every fantasy to start and end with me.

My tongue slides inside of her while I watch those pretty tits she's now playing with rise as her back arches. "Yes," she groans. "I love that. God, Keith. I *love* that."

"Life rule #101: Always give your woman what she wants and always leave her satisfied."

She laughs. "I like that one. Some of your others I can live without, but that's a keeper."

I lean in and suck her clit. Hard. She shudders and shakes beneath me. "What do you mean, some of my others you can live without."

Her hand grips to roots of my hair as I repeat the motion and the second I slip my fingers back into her, she comes so hard, she screams out her release.

Just as her body begins to sag, I get up on my knees and thrust into her tight, wet heat. And fuck is she tight like this. And holy hell is she warm and wet and... I clench my teeth so I don't come on the spot. I pump into her a few times before I pull out and scoot up her body. She's a wild, stunning mess of lust but she manages to open her eyes and when she sees I'm giving her exactly what she asked for, she greedily opens her mouth for me.

She eagerly takes my cock down her throat in one long pull and white spots flicker before my eyes. "Jesus, Maia. *Fuck!*" Her small hand comes up, gripping me at the base as she slips back, pumping me a few times and then diving back down like she can't get enough. "Flatten your tongue. Yes. Perfect."

My eyes spring open, needing to watch her swallow me down. A hand wraps around her throat, just resting there, feeling her muscles work.

"Have you ever done this before?"

She shakes her head against me, murmuring something that sounds like, uh uh and I think I'm going to pass out from how good those vibrations feel. "Well darlin', like at everything else you attempt, you're a natural. You have no idea how incredible this feels."

She hums in pleasure, the sound shooting up my cock and tightening my balls. If I don't pull out of her mouth now, I'm going to come. I start to pull back, but she grabs my ass, holding me there.

I chuckle on a shaky moan. "Maia, I'm about to come, and I really want to fuck you before we have to go to soundcheck. Please, baby."

She releases me with a wet pop, wiping away the excess moisture from her mouth with the back of her hand. Leaning down, I capture her lips, twisting our tongues together while I devour her. Hands rake through my hair, holding me close. I want to spend all day inside of her. But time is of the essence.

"On your knees and turn around facing the headboard," I order, and for once, she obeys without protest. "Fold your arms and rest them on top of it." The second she does, I grasp her hips and tug them back in my direction, running my hand over the creamy soft skin of her perfect ass. I lean in, brushing my lips by her ear. "Bad girls get punished, Maia. Only good girls get rewarded." My hand comes down with a heavy *smack*. She bucks forward, but I hold her tight, not letting her get away. "That's for thinking you were supposed to come in here instead of directly to my room." I smack her other ass cheek, equally as hard. This time she whimpers, her breath a heavy pant. Her skin reddens before my eyes and I soothe her flesh with a gentle caress. "That's for walking out on me before we were done talking." I smack her again. "That's for hitting me after I followed you in here." I smack her two more times, loving how her back bows and her ass pushes back into me, seeking more.

I slip two fingers into her and she crumples forward with a long, low moan.

"You're soaked, darlin'. My naughty girl likes her punishment a little too much."

"Yes," she cries as I find her clit, rubbing it with my thumb while I continue to pump in and out of her.

"Are you going to keep being bad?"

"Yes," she rasps, her tone harsh and impatient. "Now fuck me before I make you tie me up and spank me some more."

Christ, I'm so screwed with this woman.

I leave her quickly to find a condom and once I'm covered, I slam into her before setting a relentless pace. Nothing gentle this time. No easy going. I fuck her with wild, powerful strokes. With one hand on her hip, guiding her movements, my other wraps into her hair, holding it in my fist and yanking her head back. My lips connect with hers in a hungry kiss, my pace never slowing for a second. My tongue licks hers possessively, unwilling to pull away from her mouth.

I tell her a hundred dirty things. Everything that floats through my head leaves my lips traveling straight into hers. I tell her all the things I want to do to her. All the things I *will* do to her. And all she can do is hold on as I take her over and over and over. Her cries become louder. Her movements more erratic and when she explodes, clamping down on my cock like a vise, I lose the last shred of my control, growling out my release on an orgasm that feels like it's never-ending.

We collapse in a sweaty heap onto the bed, my mind hazy and drunk.

"That was the best orgasm of my life," I mumble, wondering if my words are even coherent.

"For me as well. Too bad we can't enjoy it and do it again. We have twenty minutes before we have to be downstairs to get to the stadium."

"Well that sucks." I laugh, taking her hand and kissing the inside of her wrist. "At least we can grab a quick shower first. Come on."

She rises up, moving directly for the bathroom, and for a minute, I just watch her.

I think I love you, Maia. No more falling. It's all there. And I'm not sure what to do about that.

Especially as those thoughts are complemented with yet another surge of guilt.

Maia whips her blonde hair and my chest squeezes impossibly tight.

I want to deserve you. I want to be everything I promised you I would be.

"You comin'?" she calls out with an amused grin.

I nod. But this feeling, it isn't going away. It's time for another phone call. Another talk. I just hope it helps me get over this hurdle and make me the man she deserves.

24

Maia

"This tour is not really a tour," Marco tells me as we go through the final checklist for the concert that's already underway with the opening act on stage. The guys are in the greenroom, hanging out and laughing. This is old hat to them, but completely new for me. Keith's drums were a nightmare during soundcheck, but everything seems to be in order now.

"What do you mean by that?" I ask, tilting my head and pinching my brows in.

"It's a collection of six shows, each in different cities and each with a different opening act. If this were a tour, we'd likely have one or two consistent opening acts as part of the ticket and we'd often play more than one night at a particular location depending on the draw that city provides."

"Okay. Why the different opening acts this time? No one would sign on for just the six shows?"

"That was Keith's idea, actually. Local bands in each city had to submit a demo and then the guys picked two out of all the applicants to open for them in each location."

My eyes pop open like someone just electrocuted me. Keith never mentioned anything about that and in truth, I didn't exactly give the opening acts a whole lot of consideration. I was too busy making sure that the greenrooms were stacked with the guys' favorite drinks and snacks. Making sure that groupies were not allowed passes—seriously not complaining on that one. That security knows their schedule.

The list goes on. So yeah, no, I didn't think about the opening acts.

"That's seriously cool. Someone should have told me! I would have blasted that all over their social media. It's fantastic PR both for the up-and-coming bands as well as our guys."

Marco nods with enthusiasm, laughing as I run for the door with my work phone in hand. He chases after me, and once I reach the edge of the stage, I video the band currently playing and then post it all over our social media, explaining what Wild Minds is doing for local bands and asking their fans to show support. Then I tag both opening acts.

"Done." I practically sag in relief. "Dammit, Marco. Next time keep me in the loop."

"The guys don't care about it being good PR for themselves."

I roll my eyes dismissively. "Yeah, but you and I do and it's not only about them. It's about these other bands too."

"Fine. We'll do this in each city. They consider it their way of paying it forward, so I'm sure they'll like you doing that. Some of them are pretty good. I think Lyric and Turn Records even signed a few. Anyway, as I was saying" —he drags me back away from the stage to a quiet room— "this isn't a tour per se. But we're mirroring this again every six months, only in different cities. I'm working on getting them to extend this to Europe or Asia for a few weeks before Adalyn starts kindergarten, because Lord knows, Jasper will never go on tour again once his baby girl is in school like that."

I laugh at the pinched expression on Marco's face, despite his indulgent tone. No one questions Jasper and his decision making. Not the band. Not Marco. No one.

Especially when it comes to his girls.

All the guys are equally as protective of them.

A few nights before we left, Jasper called, stating that Ady was asking for Keith to put her down to bed. Keith didn't hesitate before flying out the door to go and do that.

I might have swooned just a little. Or maybe a lot. What is it about a strong man who adores a little girl? I think my reaction to it is even stronger since I never had anything close to that with my own father.

"Well everything is all set for them for tonight and then again for when we reach San Francisco, though we have a break in between shows." That's so the caravan of equipment and roadies can reach San Francisco since it has to drive there. That and I think the guys like a break in between. "I feel like Ringling Brothers when they would storm into a small town on the train and set up their mobile city. Did you know they had tens of thousands of employees for everything? It was incredible how they had it managed down to such an exact science. Unpacking all the people, animals, and gear. Setting up the tents and the various attractions only to turn around and dismantle it a few days or a week later and move on to the next place. It was so much more than just the attractions though. It was food tents and medical tents and everything else the workers needed to live from place to place."

"Do you live on Wikipedia?"

"Um, no. I just find history fascinating."

"Did you know that I was front row for Nirvana's first concert and the invention of the mosh pit began? I also have a signed guitar by Kirk Cobain, but that is seriously not even close to the coolest piece of memorabilia I have stashed in my safe room."

I snort out a laugh. "You have a safe room?"

"Sweets, I was raised by a devout Catholic mother who on her deathbed still prayed for my heathen gay soul, a violent father who served time for robbing banks, and an ex-lover who thought fucking random dudes was like sport fishing—the more fish you reel in the merrier. Yeah, I've got a safe room. And that's not even close to my top level of crazy."

I reach out and hug him. "You're my people."

"How do you have such a big heart?"

"What?" I laugh into him, still hugging him.

"Your childhood might in fact be worse than Vi's and that's saying some serious shit. I still don't know how you both love with such openness."

I pull away, shrugging up a shoulder. "Because if I end up like them, they win. My parents and my past do not dictate who I am or how I live my life. I do."

"For someone so young, you are incredibly wise."

Suddenly a voice crackles through our earpieces. "Five minutes."

A swell of excitement surges through me, bursting forth with a smile to match. "EEEK. Showtime."

Before Marco and I can even make for the door, it flies open and I'm instantly swept off my feet. Again. A hand smacks harshly against my ass cheek, one, then the other. Again. And just like earlier, I moan into his back. "My naughty girl, you like the punishment too much."

He wants me naughty. I can destroy him.

"You just have to make it rougher. So I learn my lesson, that is."

I smirk into his back as he growls out more swears than I've ever heard in my life.

He shifts me until his mouth presses into my temple. "You want me hard while I'm playing tonight? You want my mind on your pussy instead of my drums?"

His hand cups me through the fabric of my skinny jeans.

My mind goes fuzzy with that move. "Is that a legitimate question?"

I get another series of smacks before I'm forced to slide down his body. We're on the periphery of the stage. It's all blackness, but it's far from silent. The crowd is going insane, impatiently cheering for their rock gods. It's an incredible, heady vibe. The kind that seeps into every cell inside your body and ignites it.

The vibrations rush through me like a drug and my resulting smile is unstoppable. “I’m so excited I can hardly take it. I’m going to stand here all night and watch you.”

He leans in to whisper into my ear. “You’re falling hard for me, darlin’. Ain’t nothin’ you can do about it. I guess it sucks to be you.” He shrugs at me, planting a kiss on my lips, and then he runs out onto the stage.

“You’re a jerk,” I yell out after him, even though I shouldn’t. “Ugh!” I bellow just as the sticks in his hand start out a heavy beat that signals their first song of the night. Purple and blue stage lights flash across his face, and I catch him winking at me. I flip him off and he blows me a kiss. “Smug bastard,” I grumble just as Henry, Gus, and then finally Jasper find their way past me. “Kill it out there tonight, guys.”

Henry too plants a kiss on my cheek as he passes and both Gus and Jasper throw me dazzling smiles. They live for this. You can just tell. The adrenaline rush. The endorphins. The high of playing to a live audience. The fans feel it too. Feed off it.

“Damn, this is going to be such a good show,” Marco marvels directly beside me, and I turn to him, bouncing up and down on the toes of my shoes.

The guys break out into a song from the last album and the night takes off from there. They play for a solid two hours, only taking a break here or there as Jasper talks to the audience and the guys catch their breaths with a few sips of water. I’ve been a fan of them for what feels like forever. I sat up in the nosebleed seats just to watch them live.

They’re my band and now they’re my bosses and friends and my… *boyfriend?* I guess that’s what he is, though calling Keith a boy feels almost ridiculous. All I know is that I never want this feeling to go away. Ever.

“Did you go to college?” I ask Marco during a small lull in the action. It’s nearing the end of the night. The boys are drenched in sweat, but their enthusiasm and energy level hasn’t waned.

“Yes. I was a business major and right after, I moved out to California and got a job as a gofer for a record label exec. Worst and best job I ever had. Then I became a PA, like you, for a few bands and eventually managed one before I got introduced to the guys. We clicked instantly and it's been this way since."

I glance in his direction, staring into his dark eyes that pick up flecks of the multicolored stage lights making them look like fireworks against a black sky. "I'm starting to rethink everything I thought I wanted. I love what I'm doing. It makes me really happy. I always thought I wanted to be a school counselor because their work is so important. But now, I'm not so sure anymore."

"This work is not all glamor and rainbows. It's taking and eating a lot of shit. From the bands, from the record companies, from the vendors and everyone else who wants a piece of the action. It's cutthroat and catty, and at times, can be very fake. I'm not saying this to dissuade you, I'm just saying that you're lucky with who you work for now, but if you continue in this business, it can break your soul sometimes. My best advice is to finish college and study stuff you find interesting. The rest will fall into place."

I turn back to watching the band, thinking about that. Fall semester starts in a week and I didn't register for it because of money and my arm and this new job and this tour that is not really a tour. It just felt like a little too much to take on. But I think Marco is right. And I think I won't let any more life excuses prevent me from finishing my degree.

And just as the words float through my head, I feel my phone vibrate in my back pocket. Slipping it out, I see my father's number. I stare dumbstruck as it continues to vibrate in my hand, his name glowing in the darkness.

"Everything okay?" Marco asks, and I nod even though that's a lie. I don't pick up. I just dismiss the call and slip it back into my pocket, trying to ignore the vitriol cooking up to a mad boil in my brain. A minute later I feel it vibrate again, only this time it's indicating he left a voice message.

What could he possibly want with me now?

The moment the guys leave the stage, sweaty and exhausted, I'm scooped up once again, tossed like a doll over Keith's shoulder. "Ass-hat," I bark. "I broke my arm, not my leg."

"But your ass looks so much better next to my face. Less having to look down."

He tosses me onto the sofa in the greenroom. I fall back into the cushions, watching as the guys grab bottles of alcohol and strip out of sweaty shirts. They toast each other, laughing and smiling, giving hugs as they complement one another.

Keith points at me as he lifts his signature bottle of Jack Daniels to his lips, downing a swig. "I'm taking you somewhere tonight."

I snort. "Is that caveman speak for we're going on a date? Because I thought you didn't do those." I grin cheekily at him.

"I don't." He grins back. "That's not what this is."

"I thought you spoke Keith by this point," Gus bursts out, dropping into the seat beside me and tossing his sweaty, gross arm over my shoulder. I attempt to shrug him off, but he just wiggles in closer. I never had big brothers, but I imagine their level of annoying broaches close to that.

"You stink." I scrunch up my nose at him.

He ignores me completely. "Keith is a drummer, which inherently means he lacks couth and finesse. He's more, I bang hard on drums with sticks, if you know what I mean. Especially when it comes to women. Not to mention he's ridiculously out of practice."

"Are you getting to a point, asshole?" Jasper laughs.

Gus flips him off. "What Keith is poorly explaining is that he's planned a night out for just the two of you. We helped so if you don't like it, don't say anything. It'll not just break his heart, but ours as well."

"I didn't realize this was dating by committee," I jest, cocking an eyebrow at Keith who is smirking like the smirking bastard he is while he continues to sip at his Jack. "Can I have some?"

"When you turn twenty-one," he deadpans.

"You have no idea how old I am in trailer girl years. We make dog years look like a sad joke." The sad part of that is it's true. We age at a rate no girl should age at. I stand if for no other reason than to escape a sweaty Gus. "I'm going to change for my non-date." I walk backward toward the door. "You guys were bullshit hot tonight. Beasts of the stage. Legends of music. True Apollos."

"Huh?" Henry lets out a bemused laugh as he sips on some tequila.

"He was noted to be the Greek god of music amongst other things. In any event, my job here tonight is done as is yours. Enjoy the rest of your evening, gentlemen."

"Wear something warm," Keith calls out, and I shut the door behind me, needing to flee fast and furious. My hand covers my mouth and I let out a stupid giggle. A girlish squeal. It makes me so disappointed in myself and yet so goddamn happy. He planned a night for us. He asked for input on it.

It sucks that he was right. I am falling so hard for him.

Hook. Line. Sinker. Drop the damn mic, I'm his.

I'm not sure there was ever a choice in the matter. I'll always want him. I can already feel it. He's my penguin. Our souls are inextricably connected.

I think part of me knew it that first night.

I can try to hold off. But there is only so long that'll last. He's wearing down my resistance like a well-oiled machine. A marching army whose singular intent is to conquer and claim.

All I can do now is hold on for the ride and allow it to take me wherever it wants. Regardless of future outcomes.

25

Maia

THE KNOCK COMES on my door nearly an hour later. It's midnight. Did I mention that? It's freaking late and I'm freaking exhausted. But I'm also really jazzed. I figure I can sleep in tomorrow since we're not scheduled to leave for San Francisco until two.

Sucking in a deep breath and tamping down my giddy nerves, I swing the door open to find Keith wearing dark jeans and a navy sweater that makes his eyes glow the most extraordinary color. Almost as if they're trying to compete with the bold blue of the fabric.

"Hey," he says, taking me in. His eyes do a slow sweep of me and when they meet mine again, the heat in them is unmistakable. "You look beautiful. Good enough to eat, in fact. Maybe we should rethink this going out thing." I'm in skinny jeans, a white long sleeve tee and a wraparound pink sweater because that's all I brought that's somewhat warm. My wardrobe was limited before the accident and considering it's been hotter than Hades in LA this last month, I haven't exactly been shopping for fall/winter gear.

"Nope. It's the middle of the night. You told me I'm going on a non-date and I'm ready."

"Then let's go. But first." He steps forward and wraps his fist around the braid draped over my shoulder. He kisses me. Nothing hot or heavy or even all that passionate. Just a kiss that still somehow manages to make my knees weak because it feels like it means something more. "Now we're ready."

"Where are we going anyway?" I ask as I grab my purse and make sure the door to my room is shut. I'm not sure whether or not I'll be sleeping in there tonight. My guess is no, but one never knows with us.

"You'll see."

Twenty minutes later, Keith takes my hand, helping me out of the large SUV as I look at the scene around us. The wind kicks up, brushing cool salty air across my face. "Are you trying to get us jacked?" We're at a marina lined with boats of every shape and size, bobbing gently in the water. But it's also completely deserted save for us.

Keith doesn't say anything as he takes my hand, intertwining our fingers and leading me down one of the longer docks to the very end where a huge sailboat is waiting. Schooner? Is that what they call these? I don't know. I'm hardly up on my nautical terms since I've never actually been anywhere near a boat before.

"Are we stealing a boat," I hiss, looking around. Seriously, it's dead freaking quiet and dark as a mofo. Only the lights of the city behind us provide any sort of illumination.

"Yeah," Keith deadpans. "That a problem for you?"

The words are no sooner out of his mouth then someone steps up onto the deck of the ship and says, "Good evening." And like the hand of the great and powerful Wizard of Oz is in charge, a string of gold Christmas lights that line the sails and mast switch on creating the most magnificent and magical glow. "Welcome aboard the Persephone. Please mind your step as you climb on."

I glance to Keith, my eyes wide, my jaw agape, my heart thundering so loud I'm sure he can hear it. "A boat?"

Keith nods.

"We're going sailing in the middle of the night on a ship named Persephone?"

He nods again, this time a bit nervous, and before I can do something crazy like tackle him to the dock and kiss every inch of this romantic, thoughtful, incredible man, I cautiously step onto the boat. The man reaches out, offering me some assistance and I take it gratefully.

"I'm Charlie. You must be Maia. It's a pleasure to meet you. Please, make yourself comfortable. Everything has been arranged and we'll be underway shortly."

I swallow past the frog of emotion lodged in my throat and say, "Thank you."

He guides me to the front of the ship where a sitting area is set up with the most perfect picnic. Candles flicker in hurricane jars showing off a spread of cheese, crackers, fruit, chocolates, and coffee, and I'm done. I just start crying.

Strong arms wrap around my waist, Keith's mouth dipping to my ear. "Do you like it?"

I shake my head because I can't speak. I'm too busy crying.

"No? Maybe we should go then." I smack his hand, and he chuckles. "Wanna go on a boat ride with me, Psyche, my goddess?"

"I'm no longer Pandora?" I manage after a few attempts at clearing my throat.

"Let's see how this boat ride turns out and I'll let you know."

I laugh, and it releases the weight of the world from my chest. He spins me around in his arms and levels me with a searing kiss. One that knocks me back a step, especially as the boat begins to move. His hands cup my face and he holds me so close, breathing me in and kissing me. Our foreheads meet, his nose brushing against mine.

"Are you hungry?"

I swallow and nod against him. He presses his wet lips to mine one last time and then he takes my hand, leading me over and helping me to sit down so I'm facing the front of the boat and have the most perfect view of a glowing Seattle.

He drops a blanket over my legs and pours me a cup of coffee, handing the steaming mug to me. I take it, thankful for its warmth on the chilly night.

Keith settles in beside me, tugging on me until I'm resting on his chest. The air is cold, especially out here on the water in the dead of night. But I don't mind it enough for it to detract from the splendor.

"How did you arrange this?" I ask as we set out a little deeper into the dark waters, the twinkling lights of the city growing fainter.

"Will it sound terrible if I tell you there is very little money can't buy?"

I smile, knowing he can't see it. "Terrible? No. And since you did this for me and I'm having the best time ever, I'm not complaining about whatever small fortune you spent on this."

"For once."

"For once," I concede.

"You like it?"

"At the risk of using a particular four-letter word, yes, I *like* it." He squeezes my side and I burst into giggles. "Quit that. You'll make me spill my coffee."

He wraps his arms tighter around me, holding me as the boat glides effortlessly through the water. With the city asleep and us watching from afar, it makes me feel like we're in our own private world. We fall silent, letting our own introspection take over.

But I can feel Keith stirring behind me. I can feel something brewing in his mind.

I'm just not sure I want to know what it is.

It can't be good if he's not saying it, can it? He and I talk. We freaking share and even overshare. We don't do the hold back our thoughts and feelings well. But in this moment, I don't mind that he's holding his thoughts close. I'm doing the same.

I have a lot on my mind and not all of it is Keith or this tour.

My father's call tonight has been weighing on me. It's something he hasn't done, well, ever. Certainly not since I left after screaming at him for putting me in debt and under the thumb of a notorious mob boss. I told him I never wanted to see or hear from him again, and now, today, he calls. All his voice message said was that he wanted to talk. About what, I have no clue. Cryptic bastard knows how to build up my curiosity.

The only thing I can come up with is that he's looking for money.

I set my now empty mug of coffee down, and pop a chocolate into my mouth and nuzzle in deeper into Keith who seems only too happy to have me do that. His lips drop to the crook of my neck and for the longest of moments, he just breathes in and out, the weight of what's troubling him building momentum.

Then suddenly it hits me. Like a fucking kamikaze.

Amy.

And though I don't want to ruin this magical, most romantic night in the world, I want to know about her. Not only do I sort of deserve to know since I resemble her, but the more time I spend with Keith, the more I want him to let me into places he doesn't let anyone in.

Not even the guys.

Sucking in a deep breath, I prepare myself to be ripped apart once more. Because let's face it, hearing about a woman he loved who is now dead is going to brutally suck. Because—

"I haven't talked about it since that night," he says out of nowhere, like he was freaking reading my mind. Again.

I still.

"Did I say something out loud?"

"No. But I know you, Maia. I know your body language. I can practically hear your thoughts as you plaster them all over yourself so well. And, well, it was on my mind too."

"Oh." I lick my suddenly dry lips. I barely move. Hell, I'm terrified to breathe. "You don't have to tell me now. I'm sorry if I ruined this perfectly romantic and wonderful boat ride."

He chuckles into me, kissing my skin. "You didn't ruin anything. And in truth, I should tell you already. I should talk about it. That's what people tell you to do, right? Talk about it. It's been a decade and I couldn't even say her name until you came along. Until I crashed into this beautiful blonde woman who resembles a girl I once loved. A girl who died."

My eyes pinch shut, my teeth sinking into my bottom lip. How easy he says he loved her. How deep that love must have gone. I ache for him and that loss. I ache for the girl who died. And I ache for myself knowing I'll never hold his heart the way she did.

"Amy moved to our town sophomore year of high school. I didn't notice her so much at first. She was quiet and stayed to herself. Junior year we started talking at a party and I asked her out. And for the first four months we were together, everything was perfect. She was still quiet. Reserved. Sweet as the day is long. She certainly never talked back to me or pushed me to the brink of my sanity."

He tugs on my braid a bit, so I know he's talking about me now, as if I had any other illusions. But still, I appreciate him making the point of how different we are.

"How long were you two together?"

"Eight months when she died."

I swallow a lump of sadness with that. I can't comprehend that level of grief.

He wraps my hair around his hand a little tighter. "About four months into dating, I started to notice some things she had been really good at hiding from me. Things like how she wouldn't eat or sometimes when she did, she'd go to the bathroom immediately after and throw up. Things like how she would cut herself in places she didn't think I'd find. Things like how sometimes she couldn't get out of bed or she'd stare off into space for long periods of time, lost in her head. She cried a lot. And shut down whenever I tried to talk to her about any of it.

"She was in therapy and on a lot of different medications. And some days, weeks, were better than others. She never wanted me to bother with any of it. Told me that's what her parents and doctors were for. But when you love someone the way I loved her; all you want to do is fix them. Is make them better and happy. And no matter what I did, how hard I tried, I couldn't do that with Amy."

"She was sick," I whisper.

"Yes," he answers even though it was a statement and not a question. "Amy was very sick. Had been since she was a little girl. Then one night I dropped her off at home after a party. It had been a good night. I was always stressed, you see. Always tense and on edge around her because I never knew what was going on in her head. Which way her mood would swing. In truth, she scared me. But that night, she was great, and I was so happy. I kept thinking maybe she was starting to get better. But as I drove away after dropping her off, something was troubling me, and I couldn't figure it out. It was just a bubble of panic in my gut and no matter how hard I tried; I couldn't talk myself out of it.

"I was halfway home before I turned around and raced back to her house. She always slept with the window open, so I lifted up the screen and climbed into her room. I called her name, but she didn't answer. All the lights were on in her room, but she wasn't there."

His body starts to tremble against mine and I wrap my arms around my chest, holding onto his that are surrounding me. Tears streak my face and I'm so angry with myself for doing this to him. To us. To this night that was so perfect.

"Then I heard a gasping sound coming from the bathroom."

"Keith. You don't—"

"I found her in the bathroom. In the bathtub. Blood everywhere. That gasp must have been her last breath of life because by the time I pulled her out of the tub, she was gone. I knew it even as I tried to do CPR as best I could. I screamed for her parents who took forever to come and when they did, they were groggy and disoriented. Amy had slipped sleeping pills into their dinner it turns out because she didn't want them to wake up and find her too soon."

Oh God. A sob sticks in the back of my throat and I try so hard to push it back down.

"Keith..."

"She was happy and fun that night at the party because she had a plan and was ready. But I wasn't ready, and neither were her parents. And no matter how hard I fought to make her better, to make her happy, I never did, and she died."

I suck in a ragged breath, aching to spin around in his arms and hold him. But I know he'd hate that. He's telling me this because he doesn't have to look at me while he does.

"You couldn't have saved her, Keith. Not if she was that determined."

"If I hadn't fought my instincts and gone back sooner, I might have been able to save her that night. She could have gone to the hospital and gotten the help she needed."

"I'm so sorry," I whisper on a half-sob, no longer able to hold it in. Christ, how much guilt has this man been living with over something he could not have prevented?

"You've given me so much, Maia. You've changed everything for me in the best possible way. I wasn't living beyond the band and the guys, and now I am. I'm crazy about you. Please don't doubt that for a second. You are not Amy. You're my Maia. My Pandora and my Psyche. My fucking sweet darlin' who I cannot get enough of. I just need a bit more time, okay? Can you be patient? I haven't dealt with any of this for ten years and now suddenly I am and it's hard. Sometimes so much harder than I thought it would be. But I'm trying and I want you with me while I do."

This time I do spin around in his arms, pushing him down until he's on his back and I'm crawling over him. I press my forehead to his and stare into his dark eyes. "I'm with you," I tell him, even though it scares me to.

Some secrets are more like confessions than kept truths, but their release doesn't always set you free. And that's what this was. This was his confession that he's kept bottled up for ten years and is still tormented with.

His guilt that he couldn't save her.

That he couldn't make her happy, and she took her own life after spending an evening with him.

The fact that he found her the way he did and tried to save her, knowing it was too late.

The agony over the fact he didn't listen to his gut earlier and find her faster.

He offers up a wan smile that doesn't reach his eyes, and suddenly I'm so scared this man is going to not just break my heart but shatter it for good. I may be his Maia and Pandora and Psyche and whatever other names he throws at me.

But I'm not his Amy.

And something tells me that makes all the difference.

26

Keith

Dawn can be a real motherfucker after nights filled with the highest of highs and the lowest of lows. My eyes crack open only to discover that dawn is long since gone and now we're likely rounding on mid to late morning.

Visions of my nightmare ratchet through my head and I close my eyes again, trying to clear my thoughts. I knew this would happen once I started talking about it. I was warned, after all. Doesn't make it any easier to swallow. It's a miracle I didn't wake Maia up. Even I felt my unrest, but the second I woke up, I scrambled out of bed and made the call.

I spent an hour on the phone with her just talking. Just telling her everything that happened in the dream. The dream that is the mirror image of a reality I don't know if I want to forget or torment myself with.

"Grief comes in stages, Keith," she told me. "You've been

trapped between pain and guilt and anger and bargaining for a very long time. Add to that what very likely sounds like some PTSD and you're going to have nightmares. You're going to experience this on a very visceral level. But if you can push through and find your way to accept what happened that night and your roll in it, to forgive yourself once and for all for things you could not and cannot change, you will come out on the other side stronger than ever. It will come in waves, some bigger and more powerful than others. Just keep doing what you're doing, and we'll get you there. We will."

I have no choice but to believe her. I just don't want to hurt Maia in the meantime.

The sweet naked body beside me stirs and I smile at the groan she emits, likely from coming to the same realization I just did. I slip my hand beneath her belly and slide her along the cool white hotel room sheets until she's flush against me.

She quirks one eye open before it narrows. "I haven't had enough sleep since you convinced me to let you take me to your bed."

I chuckle. "It didn't exactly take a lot of persuasion on my part."

She scowls the most adorable scowl. "That's unfortunately true. I can't even argue it since I'm essentially a harlot who swept in and stole your virtue. Oh wait, maybe I have that the other way around."

My face dives into her hair that still smells of the fresh air we were immersed in last night and her shampoo. No perfume for this one and I'd wager it's because it's an unnecessary expense in her mind. Same with makeup that she rarely wears unless someone does it up for her.

What would I give to make it so she never has a worry again?

I wonder if my sweet Maia knows she talks in her sleep.

Her sleeping words as I crawled back into bed last night aren't settling in me like the lead weight I expected they would. Instead my chest feels lighter than it ever has, and I have to question if it's from her confession or mine. I want to ask if she meant it just so I can hear her say it again, but until I'm ready to rap a sonnet in her honor, I need to keep my mouth shut.

The thing is, I want to tell her I feel the same way. Because I think I do.

Only she has no idea she told me she loved me because she was asleep while she did it.

I've only told one woman I loved her, and she went and killed herself after spending the evening with me and telling me she loved me too. I'll never know if Amy was anticipating I'd be the one to find her body or not. She knew I was set to come back early the next morning to take her to breakfast.

A breakfast that never happened.

It took me hours in the shower to clean all her blood off my skin and out from under my nails. For weeks I swore I could still smell it. That's when I stopped being me and turned into this guy. The one who smiles and laughs and teases with the best of them because he's dead on the inside and is terrified of people knowing.

But are you still dead inside?

Maia squirms in my arms, her tits rubbing across my chest as she rolls over to face the window, sliding her pert little ass against my very happy to see her morning wood. I reach down and squeeze one cheek. "Do I get to take this?"

"My ass?" she squawks.

"Your ass."

"I. Um. I don't know." She laughs on a shaky breath. "I've never really thought about that before. The whole vaginal penetration and breaking of the hymen thing always sort of stole the show."

"We'll work up to it then."

"Maybe with some toys first?"

A growl rips from my throat as my cock jerks right into the object of my immediate fantasy. "You want toys, Maia? I can definitely get us some fucking toys."

"I've always been curious about them."

"What else are you curious about?"

"Lots of things. I'm inexperienced, remember."

"I'm happy to teach you and show you whatever you want to know, darlin'. It would be my pleasure and then some. Literally."

"I had a feeling you'd say that." She giggles, wiggling against me again, and my heart jerks in my chest at her smile.

Did you mean it, Maia? Do you really love me?

"Tell me something no one knows about you," I ask, changing our mood instantly from fun and sexy to serious and possibly sad. The serious is because that's just how Maia seems to roll when it comes to things no one knows about her. The sad because that's just how *I* seem to roll lately.

But for some reason, our words last night have set me off on a collision course with needing more from her. More in every way, and though I feel like I already know so much that there is to know about Maia Angelo, I know I'm missing a shit ton more. My fingers glide gently along the curve of her ribs down the dip of her waist and back up the rise of her hips.

She is so sexy I don't know how to fathom it.

Or where to start with my hands.

"I used to wish upon the first star I saw every evening. It wasn't until I left for college that I stopped."

I smile at the way her hope never seemed to fizzle, even when her life was real shit. Many would have given up a million times over. Accepted what was being dealt because it's easier than fighting. But not Maia Alice Angelo. My lips press into the soft skin just beneath her jaw. "What did you wish for?"

"Lots of different things," she says in a tone that tells me she doesn't want to answer.

"Why did you stop?"

"I don't know. I got my first big wish which was to get into college and leave. After that I felt a bit greedy wishing for more. Once I had to leave school and came out to California, you couldn't exactly see the stars in the night sky so well and by that point, I was too angry to wish for much."

Oh Maia. I kiss her again, holding her a little tighter against me.

"You next."

"Something no one knows about me?" She nods her head. "Okay.

Let me think." There's likely a lot people don't know about me. Even the guys. "I love what I do, but I hate being famous."

She laughs. "I already knew that."

"You did?"

She nods her head, laughing harder. "Everyone knows that, Keith. You drive a Ford truck. You wear jeans and T-shirts unless you're forced to go somewhere nice and every time you slip on nice pants or nice shoes, you grimace at them. You force a smile whenever someone tries to take your picture. You live in a house that is so anti-Hollywood and you don't have an ounce of entitled in you. All you guys are like that actually. You and Jasper the most though."

I run a hand back through my hair that's messily flopping down on my face. "Maybe that was too easy then. Alright, I have one that will knock your socks off, but it's true so you can't judge."

"Oh. Now we're getting somewhere."

"The best quick snap decision I ever made was to lie to the nurse in the hospital and tell them I was your fiancé so I could stay with you."

She sucks in a rush of air, as I knew she would.

"You're not serious? That was your best decision?"

"And the smartest was when I forced you to move in with me and become the band's PA."

"You don't mean that."

I brush her hair back from her face, staring down at her from above. "I do. Look at all the amazing sex I'm getting out of that deal." She smacks me, and I laugh, planting a trail of kisses along her skin from the tip of her shoulder up to the base of her ear. "All joking aside, I mean it. I'm so happy you're living with me and working for us. Best thing I ever did."

"And no one else knows this?"

I grin, running my nose up her ear and whispering, "Now you do. But don't tell anyone, okay? It's our secret."

She sighs, reaching back and running her hands along my stubbled jaw and into my hair. Her dark eyes are calm and peaceful, content even, as I angle over her, propped up by my elbow. It's not a look you see on her face often. She typically has an arsenal of unrest built up inside of her.

But not right now.

Right now, she's so beautifully happy here in my arms with my sweet words floating in her brain. The sight of her like this seems to lighten me further. More of my own darkness dissipating, being burned off with the morning sun.

Maybe there's hope for us after all? Maybe we can make this insanity work?

Leaning down, I kiss her, my lips spreading hers and my tongue diving in, needing the contact of her warm, sweet mouth. Needing her touch and taste and heat. Just needing *her*.

My fingers graze down her face, along her neck and over her collarbone. As I'm about to cup one supple breast and make her moan my name, there's a knock on my door. "You've got one-hour asshole," Henry barks. "And next time pick up your phones, so we know you're not dead."

"I guess it's later than we thought." Maia giggles, rolling back over to face me.

I lift the sheets and stare down at the glory hidden beneath and groan.

"I want too many hours naked in a bed with you."

"How about we start that plan in San Fran. We've got all night, right? You don't play until tomorrow."

"Darlin' there is no amount of time that will satisfy my desire for you." I plant a kiss on her lips and then get out of bed because if I continue kissing her the way I want to; we'll miss that flight for sure.

She rolls over, taking the sheet with her and sitting facing the window with her back to me. Picking up her phone from the nightstand where it was plugged in, I hear her exhale a heavy sigh.

"What? What is it?" I ask, while quickly finish packing up the last of my things and grabbing what I'll need for a shower.

Her head rolls over her shoulder, catching my eye briefly before turning back to her phone. "My father," she says, the ire in her voice unmistakable. "He called last night during the show, leaving a voice message saying he wants to talk. He called again this morning."

"Did he leave another message?"

She shakes her head but otherwise doesn't answer.

"Are you going to call him back?"

Another heavy sigh. "I don't know. I don't think so. The only time he's ever acknowledged my existence was when I inherited that twenty grand. He was pissed I used it for college and didn't give it to him. We had a conversation before I left for LA and let's just say it didn't go well. Lots of angry words were shared by both of us."

I walk over to her, sitting beside her and putting my arm around her shoulder, drawing her head to my chest. "Can I do something?"

"No. He's my mess and for now, I plan on ignoring him. He's taken enough from me. I don't want to talk to him, and I have nothing left to say. And the absolute last thing I want is for you and the guys to get tangled up with him."

I kiss the top of her head. "I'm here for you. For whatever you need."

"What I need is some coffee, breakfast, and a shower. Not necessarily in that order."

My fingers glide along the smooth skin of her back, silk, satin, sin, and heaven all wrapped up into one. "Come shower with me. Then I'll feed you and give you caffeine."

Her hand meets my arm, her dark eyes glittering up at me against the shining sun. It never ceases to amaze me how the slightest touch from her leaves me breathless. I get the feeling it's been her entire life since she's felt any semblance of hope. Is it too much to ask that that's something I can give her?

I love that you love me, Maia.

"I can't say no to any of those things. Then you're going to whisk me off to yet another city I've never been to before on your private jet. I feel like I'm in some Hallmark movie or a fantastically smutty romance novel. I can't decide which one I prefer."

"If we're polling opinions, I'm going with option B. I don't think Hallmark is known for kinking it up too often."

She rolls her eyes at me, standing up and walking completely naked into the bathroom. Too bad we're once again on a time constraint. I wasn't lying when I said I want too many hours with her naked. No, my biggest problem isn't all the things I want to do with her. Or to her.

My biggest problem is trying to fight through a past that still haunts me.

One that still sits on my soul, coating it in darkness. Still clings to me like an extra layer of skin I can't shed.

In ten years, there have been very few nights where I don't close my eyes and picture Amy dead in my arms or alive with her last smile for me.

I'm scared of loving Maia the way I want to. I'm scared of the things I come with, the sick poison that lives in my head and heart. She deserves better than that. And right now, she deserves better than me.

So I'm trying. For the first fucking time, I'm trying. For her. For me. For us.

All I can hope is that she doesn't give up on me too soon. Is hope she believes me when I tell her I'm trying. I just need a little more time, Maia. I can do this. I know I can.

27

Maia

"WHAT WOULD you be doing right now if I wasn't dragging you all around?"

"Probably sleeping. You know, because I can't remember the last time I got more than four consecutive hours of that," Keith deadpans, and I smirk coyly at him.

"That's because you keep pressing your dick into me, Keith. What's a girl to do? Ignore it?"

He laughs, picking up a chicken wing and practically inhaling the whole thing in one bite. Such a caveman. "Did you have any boyfriends growing up?" he asks, and even though I should be surprised by his asking me this, I'm not. He's been asking non-stop questions since we left Seattle and that was almost a week ago now. I can't imagine he has anything left to ask me, but clearly I'm wrong.

I shake my head. "Not really. I dated a guy in college for a couple of weeks. He was cute, a football player. A senior to my freshman."

"And where is he now?"

I can't stop my grin at the jealous gleam in his eyes and the sharp lock of his jaw. "New Orleans. Playing for your team as your QB."

Keith's eyes bug out of his head. "You're telling me your first official boyfriend was Jake Nethers?" That locked jaw pops open when I nod, trying and fighting to hide my shit-eating smile behind a chicken wing. "And you didn't fuck him?"

I roll my eyes. "I think you already know I didn't. That's why we didn't last all that long. He tried the first night we met and when he found out I was a virgin, he tried even harder in the following weeks. I was only too aware that was all he wanted with me, and I just... I don't know. I didn't want him to have it. He screwed every girl on campus."

"It makes me want to intercept the football, score a pick-six, and spike it in the endzone right in his face."

"That's very mature of you."

"I know. You're very lucky to be with someone like me. You should feel really good about yourself for not giving him your beautiful V-card. Can you imagine the lack of orgasms you would have had? It's a good thing you held onto it and let me have it. I shudder for you just contemplating the alternative."

"Very gracious of you."

"You have sauce all over your face." He reaches across the table in the flash of an eye and licks all over my cheeks and lips. I swat at him, pushing him off and wiping my face with a napkin. "Life Rule #286: Once a man licks something, it's his. That means no one else can ever kiss your face again."

"You already licked me in that bathroom at the mansion to claim me. You seriously didn't have to do it again. And you do know that's not a life rule, right?"

"Oh, I remember licking you in that bathroom," he chides with an impish smirk that makes me blush instantly. "I'm just re-staking my claim. You know, in case anyone isn't already aware you're mine. It was just you and me that first time in the bathroom, so no one else saw me lick you."

"You're cute when you're jealous, so I'll let it slide. For now. But stop licking my face and claiming it as yours. It's gross."

"Sweet darlin', let this be known now. I am possessive. I am jealous. I am determined. And because I am crazy about you, all of those things are magnified by a thousand. Let it slide. Get used to it. However you need to manage it, it's there, and it's the truth. I never want another man to touch you now that I have. And that will never change."

My heart pounds faster than a hummingbird's wings.

It's when he says things like this that I do my best to push everything else that is hanging over our heads away.

I cling to his words. To his looks. To his freaking caveman antics. They're my life's blood. My stupid, girlish lifelines. And I hate them as much as I hate how desperate I am for more of them.

The worst part? I get off on it. I thrive on his reactions. On his crazy, nonsensical jealousy and the way he worships me not just with his words but with his eyes and body. It makes my panties wet when he marks me because I'm his and he needs to keep me that way.

He makes me feel fucking wanted and no one has ever done that and meant it on a real level before.

Never.

I almost wish he weren't this guy. This rich, rock star who has been on more than one 'Most Eligible Bachelor' list. Our playing field is so far from even. He could find a million other women who will fall at his feet and not snark back.

But he'll never find another you.

I smile at that. It's true. And it's me who he wants.

That's what I cling to. Not the ugly heartbreak of his past that still sits firmly between us.

We finish lunch up and head for one of the Smithsonian museums. I could spend weeks here exploring all the history of DC but unfortunately, we have only today, and I couldn't pass up this place even though it was a tough call to make.

We enter the National Museum of American History, and Keith instantly takes my hand, intertwining our fingers. He brings it up to his lips, absently kissing my knuckles as we stroll. That simple innocuous move shouldn't do to my insides what it's doing.

I had no idea it was possible to be this in love with someone.

And by all rights, that should scare me the way it did when this all first began. But I'm too swept up to imagine ever hitting the ground. Even when I know it's lurking right beneath me.

My eyes wander, reading signs and unsure where to start first. "Good afternoon," a woman with a tidy gray bun and a warm smile greets us. "My name is Joselyn. I'll be your guide for today." I glance over to Keith who just shrugs with a smug smirk on his lips.

"You deserve the full experience," is his only explanation, and by the time I take two steps following after Joselyn, another voice whispers in my ear.

"He just wants to see Prince's yellow Cloud electric guitar." Henry. I pivot in his direction and he laughs at my expression. "What? You're not the only one who gets off on this shit. We rented the place out."

"You can do that?" I gasp out incredulously. I hadn't realized that there were no other tourists lurking about until he said that.

"We can do anything we want. We're playing in their city tonight. It was barely a phone call," Gus says with a wink.

"I feel like I should have been the one to do that," I grouse.

"But then it wouldn't have been a surprise," Keith states, squeezing my hand tighter.

"She wore a raspberry beret. The kind you find in a second-hand store," Henry sings.

"Um, you do realize that Washington's uniform is here. Dorothy's ruby slippers. The freaking desk the Declaration of Independence was written on. Edison's lightbulb."

Henry nudges into me. "And you're not a history professor because..." He leaves that hanging, and it suddenly strikes me funny. Vi is an elementary school special education teacher. A substitute at this point since she's mostly home with the girls, but that's what she was doing before she was hired as Adalyn's nanny prior to her and Jasper getting together.

Is that something I could do?

Teach history? World history since the history of the world is so fascinating. I read tons of historical non-fiction any chance I get. It's like crack being funneled to me through an IV. But do I want to teach it? Ugh! So much to figure out. So many things to try out once I go back to school. I wish it were tomorrow.

I wish it could be sooner than I know it will be.

"Lincoln's top hat is here as well as Graham Bell's large telephone," Jasper tacks on, catching my eye. "I've been to DC at least a dozen times and never once ventured out into the museums. I'm so bummed Vi and the girls couldn't be here for this. They'd love it."

Gus slaps him on the back. "It's like Henry's island, bro. We'll do this up right when the girls are bigger. When Naomi and I have brats of our own."

I step back a little, watching these guys examine the plaques and read the signs and stare in awe at the exhibits. I do too. I mean, this is *history*. It's so gorgeous to witness. To read about. To try and fathom. I want to go to the Holocaust museum. That will break me wide open, but as a human, it is something we should all witness. I want to go to the botanical gardens and the art museum. I want to go to the African American History museum because, again, it's something every human should experience.

But I also want to travel the world and experience it as well.

Keith turns back to me after all five of us listen to Joselyn explain the first Apple Mac computer. He's all smiles. Like a triumphant king. He did this for me. He set up that cruise in Seattle just for me. A late dinner date in San Francisco and a stroll through Central Park in New York.

And now here are we are in DC in a museum he rented out so I could take in all the fucking history without people dripping all over the band as they tend to do when we're out in public.

I love you, I think, but don't dare blurt out. Instead, I bite the inside of my cheek to stop the words before they tumble from my lips. They've been hovering there for a while now and if they choose this moment to finally break free, it'll ruin everything. I mean, goddammit, how can they not?

"You okay? You're making a face."

I blush like mad. "A face? No, I'm not making a face."

He gives me an amused smirk. "You are, actually. Like you're thinking something but don't want to say it. What's up?"

Damn him being able to read me so well. I look away before he can see all.

"I'm just really happy. You make me so, so happy and I think... wooh," I blow out. *Hold it in, girl!* "Nothing. It's nothing. You've just done so much for me this past week and it's been nothing short of incredible." I chance a glance back over at him and now his eyes are wide. Stunned, sure, but maybe a little wary too, so I rush on. "I'm not telling you this expecting you to tell me I make you happy back. I'm not. It's just that, yeah, it's like you said back in Seattle before you went on stage." *Shut up! Shut up!* "You're just you and then you did this and I..." I sag on an exaggerated sigh. "Thank you. That's all I'm very poorly trying to say."

His face lights up, just lights up, but he remains silent even as my rant dies out and I'm left standing here blushing. Now I know how Julia Roberts felt in *Notting Hill* when she told Hugh Grant that she's just a girl standing in front of a boy asking him to love her. Dammit. Why does love have to be like this? All complicated and shit.

The other guys are here and they're all over it but it's not the same. Keith knows it, and so do I. He rented out the fucking National American History Museum.

He did this for me.

Because I told him I wanted to go here.

"One day, when you guys tour the world again, will you show me all the history?"

His lips meet mine. Hard. Rough. Reckless. They don't know what to do with me. But something about this kiss feels different. A bit more passionate. A touch more demanding. He might not be able to tell me he loves me with his words, but this kiss is certainly doing it for him.

His actions too, and that's what I love most.

His tongue sweeps out as he deepens our connection, one hand in my hair, the other on my lower back, pressing me deeper into him like he can't get close enough. "Maia," he hums into me, gripping the roots of my hair in a tight fist of desperation.

A sudden shrill whistle pierces the air.

"Either get a room or catch up but quit it with all the PDA," Gus calls out. "It's disgusting."

Henry makes an exaggerated vomiting noise, and Keith and I pull away with a laugh. He throws Gus the middle finger. "You're a dozen times worse with Naomi."

"Actually, I think Jasper and Vi are the worst," Henry chimes in as the guys continue on through the museum.

Keith's forehead drops to mine, his hand cupping my face. He hasn't said anything to me since I dropped the crazy verbal diarrhea of happiness on his head. He just continues to stare into my eyes, and I can't take it anymore.

I toss him a wink and pull back, moving to catch up with the others.

We finish the rest of the tour, which is incredible. I could have lingered all day, but we have to get moving for soundcheck. The guys play tonight at FedEx field and as we walk through the underground part of the stadium on our way up to the field, Jasper tells me all about the last time they were here. When the media was all over the band, but in particular, him, Gus, and Viola.

"It was such a nightmare," he explains, a strange, almost pained expression crossing his features before it just as quickly turns impish. "It was also one of the best parts of the trip as it's when Vi and I finally got together."

"In secret," Gus retorts with a sly grin. "They kept it a secret for nearly two weeks after that."

Jasper laughs, and it's so difficult to imagine how all that drama turned out the way it did. That they came out stronger than they were before. I don't have siblings and my only living relative is a blood-sucking vampire, so for me, it would be nearly impossible to comprehend this level of love and devotion if I weren't witnessing it on a daily basis.

We reach the center of the field where the stage is set up for tonight. Marco has been here all day trying to put out one fire after another and when he greets me on the side of the stage, he looks worn. "It's a shame it's such a beautiful afternoon and my job isn't nearly finished."

"Huh?" I laugh, tilting my chin in his direction.

"Today has sucked warty cock and all I want to do is eat a bacon cheeseburger in my room with the shades closed. But I can't."

I reach out, squeezing his shoulders just as the guys start in with the sound crew and the event director. "Sorry. I would have stayed to help."

He shakes his head. "No. Keith would have cut a bitch. And that bitch would have been me. How was the museum?"

"It was fantastic. Oh my gosh, there was this—" My words are cut off by the ringing of my phone. The event director throws me an icy glare and I quickly pull out my phone, answering it without even looking as I skedaddle off to the side and down the stage back onto the covered field. "Hello?"

"I was wondering when you were going to pick up." My eyes slam shut, cinching tight at the sound of my father's voice. Shit. I could have gone forever without speaking to him again.

"What do you want? Why do you keep calling and texting?"

"Where are you? What's all that noise in the background?"

"I'm at work," I tell him without elaborating on just what that works is. "You know, so I can pay off all the debt you put me in."

"And if you had given me the money your mother left you then there wouldn't have been a problem in the first place."

I shake my head, my fist squeezing the phone so tight I'm shocked it's not cracking. "Except you racked up more than double what mom left me. Add to that a fucking crazy drug dealing bookie. The only reason you're not in jail or dead is because of me." I blow out a harsh, aggravated breath. We've had this conversation so many times it makes my head spin.

I didn't report him to law enforcement after I found out he opened the cards in my name. I should have. I regret it now, but it's too late as I've been paying down the debt for more than a year at this point. And when Carvalo said if I didn't pay off the debt somehow, either with my body or money, that he'd kill my father and likely me too, I believed him.

The problem was, I was a scared kid. Angry as hell, yes, but my father was my father at the end of the day. Despite the way he treated me, I didn't know how to do the things I should have done. I enabled him. I realize that now. And look where it's gotten me. I had to freeze my credit so he couldn't do anything else, and as far as I know, Carvalo isn't bothering with him anymore.

"What do you want?" I bark out. "I don't want to talk to you. I made that clear when I left. I'm done with you."

"Carvalo has been coming around asking about you. He came to pay you a friendly visit, and you were no longer living in your apartment or working at the restaurant or law office."

I stagger a few steps over, reaching for the thick padded wall that separates the field from the seats. "Why was he looking for me?"

"I didn't ask, but I'm sure it's important for him to try to find you."

"He's getting his money. What more does he want?!" I scream, wanting to chuck my phone with all my might so I don't have to listen to this. So I don't have to think about a man like Carvalo coming to look for me. He doesn't know about Keith or the band, and I'm so grateful for that. God, I can't imagine placing this on them.

All my evils.

I was never the goddess Psyche. I was always Pandora.

"I'm just the messenger. So where are you anyway? You said you were at work. Where is that exactly?"

My blood freezes over instantly. My father's trying to help Carvalo find me. He may even be listening in as we speak. Jesus.

I disconnect the call, blocking my father's number for good. I check my phone and find that the location settings are still set to private. It's a relief, but a small one.

For now, I'm safe. I just don't know how long I can go before he finds me. And them.

28

Keith

Sweat drips down my back as my muscles bunch and twist with each strike of my sticks. Jasper's voice comes through my earpiece, but I don't really need to hear him to hit my beat perfectly. Gus walks in my direction, his face flushed, and his hair wet with his own sweat, but it's his infectious smile that pulls my own to my lips.

We haven't played live in a few years before this mini-tour.

I think all that happened on the last one took some of the sweetness out of it, but when our last album came out, we knew we couldn't put it off any longer. I don't think any of us are regretting that decision now. There is just something so profound about playing to a live audience. It's truly why we started in this game beyond our love of making music.

But tonight, everything feels different.

Every beat, every rhythm I've played has echoed three words that haven't stopped repeating through my mind since Seattle. Maia loves me.

And today, at the museum, I think she nearly said it. I think that's what that whole crazy rant and her mentioning what I said before I went on stage in Seattle was all about. I told her that night that she was falling hard for me and today, she confirmed it.

It's had me riding a high like none other. Even if I couldn't come right out and tell her I was there with her. The words were there. Right on my tongue. But no matter how I tried, I couldn't push them out.

I know I'm not betraying Amy or her memory. I know that by loving Maia I'm not forgetting Amy or replacing her or what we had. But still... I can't stop this fucking grief, and I'd give anything to at this point. My eyes glide over to the front row, my heart aching because Amy is not sitting there.

Amy is not alive.

Could I have saved her? If I had just gotten there a little earlier? If I had just listened to my instincts? That's why I brought Maia to the hospital. That's why I stayed with her. That's why I dragged her ass back to my house and kept her there with me.

Instinct.

She looked up at me with those big brown eyes, scared and bleeding, and something inside of me shifted. The world just moved differently. Had an alternate beat—one I had to listen to and follow.

I think of Maia and am unable to picture my world without her in it. And that shit right there? That shit knocks me sideways like no other.

Because I've lost someone I loved. In the most gruesome of ways.

And I will not, cannot, go through that again.

"You guys have been such an incredible audience tonight," Jasper says as the song comes to a close. The crowd erupts in thunderous cheers and applause. "I mean it. This is why we love playing here, DC. You guys just know how to do it."

I rotate my wrists, releasing some built-up tension. Playing the drums is a hell of a lot more demanding than playing the guitar or bass all night. It's a non-stop workout that requires a strong back, abdominals, and arm muscles. It's why I swim as many laps as I do and lift weights and run on my treadmill. No way I can keep this up without being in peak physical shape.

"This is our last song of the night and we want to thank you for coming out." Jasper turns to me and in his eyes, I can see he's about to switch things up. He doesn't do this often in the middle of a tour or concert. The sound and lighting people like to have a strict set list. "Hey Keith?" he calls out, and I can't stop my laugh. Gus and Henry are the same.

"What's up, brother?" I reply, and for some reason, whenever I speak, I always get an extra loud burst of whistles or cheers. Maybe because no one expects much from the drummer other than, well, playing the drums.

"How do you feel about playing something new for the fine people here tonight?"

I pick back up my sticks and straighten my spine. I have a feeling where he's going with this. "What'd you have in mind?"

Yup. That's the devil's grin on his face now. "Switch."

I shake my head at him but start to tap out the opening beat for it all the same. Instead of growing more urgent, the crowd quiets down, anxious to hear a song no one has heard before. Gus throws me a withering glance before he follows in with Jasper. If I didn't know Jasper wrote this song for me before, Gus's expression now just confirmed it.

Time is a capsule unexplored.
Time is a lie with no detour.
But if time is a lie then you saw my truth.
A switch of fate no one can undo.
So brighten my sky, my darkest day.
Loves a game I no longer know how to play.
Switch. Switch. Switch it for me.
Lost in that memory rushing me out to sea.
Switch. Switch. Switch it that way.
That high I feel in your eyes is here to stay.

Switch. Switch. Switch till it stops bleedin'.

Finding you could be all I needed.

I listen to the lyrics. All of them. Similar to the way I did that first day when Maia and I were heading to the studio to lay it down. Is this what he's telling me? That Maia is my switch? That finding her was all I needed?

We only have one more show after tonight and my plan is to have it all straight in my head by the time we reach home.

Because I don't want Maia to move out.

I don't want her to go apartment shopping the way she says she's planning to. I want her in my bed every night for all the nights there are to come. I don't even care if it's too soon. Everything with Maia has been too soon and too rushed, and it doesn't fucking matter.

I just need to not feel like shit every time I think about that, and it's proving a little harder than I thought it would. I didn't think the guilt would still hold on to me this tight after this long.

Still, I wanted Maia to know how special she is to me.

Making her happy is a drug I've become addicted to. She's my unicorn. The proof that even the slightest rain can turn into a hurricane. Because I sure as shit never saw her coming. This crazy, wild girl has become every obsession I never knew was possible to have.

We end up playing "Time Surrender" as an encore, one of our biggest hits, and when we walk off the stage, all smiles and laughs, all I can think about burying myself deep inside of Maia. All I can think about is watching her as I do.

"DON'T LOOK TOO EXCITED," Marco admonishes, wagging a finger in our direction. "You boys have a lounge appearance you're scheduled to make."

Shit. I forgot all about that. Some radio station set it up and that's just how this business goes. This is the part we hate. Because there is no unwind when you're not only on the clock but under public scrutiny with multiple cameras homed in on your face. It's great to meet the fans directly and that's what a lot of tonight will be, but still.

"Where's Maia?" I ask, looking around for her. She's either been on the side of the stage watching us every night or in here waiting on me.

"She said she wasn't feeling great, so I sent her back to the hotel," Marco explains, and my stomach drops. I should have said something today when she was telling me how happy I make her. Why didn't I say it back? She's had nothing good in her life, no love from anyone, and she opened her heart up to me.

And what did I do?

I didn't fucking say anything!

"Is she okay?" Henry asks, concerned.

Marco shrugs. "I guess so. She looked a bit pale and said she had a headache. Probably just all this travel is catching up to her."

She was unusually quiet and withdrawn after the soundcheck, and I know it's because of me. I know I must have hurt her. She said she was fine when I asked, but how can she be?

"Can I bail on this tonight?" I ask Marco even though I already know his answer.

"Nice try. She's probably sleeping anyway, and you guys made a commitment for all of you to be there."

I sigh but nod in defeat.

I check my phone and find she messaged me earlier while I was on stage.

Maia: Going back to the hotel. I have a nasty headache. Kiss me when you come in.

Maybe she really does have a headache and I'm reading too much into this?

Me: Wish you were with me tonight. Hope you're feeling better. Get some rest, my sweet darlin'.

She doesn't respond, and I take that to mean she's already asleep. Wasn't I the one lamenting earlier today about how we haven't gotten much sleep this week? Still, my chest sits uneasy as I showered and head over to the large downtown DC bar.

The radio station has completely taken over the space. The only people permitted inside are winners of contests done through the radio satiation as well as specific elite fans of the opening acts. We also gave away a hundred lottery tickets to fans of ours, so the place is pretty packed.

Before we even make it to the second floor, we take about fifty selfies and posed pictures as well as sign all the autographs the people in attendance want. I don't mind this part. I never have and I know the guys feel the same. No matter how long we've been at this game, it's still a trip that people not only want to meet us but give a shit about our name scrawled on something.

"Come have a drink," Gus demands, slapping his hand on my shoulder and leading me over to the bar. "We'll have two shots of good whiskey," he tells the bartender who smiles at us seductively. And if this were a couple of months ago, I'd act on it.

She lines up four shots instead of two, leaving us with a wink as we eye our drinks suspiciously.

"Do you think she drugged them?" Gus questions with a sickened look. After what he went through with that, I don't blame him for wondering.

"No. I think she's hoping to fuck us tonight. Both of us if I had to guess." I lift the first glass and hold it up in salute. He clicks his in return and we down the amber liquid that hasn't burned the back of my throat since the night I found Amy dead in her bathtub. "I'm a fucking mess," I murmur under my breath.

Gus nods as if he already knows this because that's kinda how Gus and I roll.

"We're all a mess, dude. We never have our shit together. When I met Naomi, I was still in love with Vi, asking Naomi to sing a duet I wrote for Vi. Think of that shit. Yet, when I met Naomi, everything just... shifted. Like she was always there, just waiting for me to discover her. We crawl at their feet, unable to rise up on solid legs. I mean, sometimes we play it tight, right? But in the end, they own us, and they know it. Still, I wouldn't change it." He points a finger at me. "And I'm guessing you wouldn't either. So what has you all in a twist?"

I glare at him and he shakes his head.

"You can't let ghosts from the past rule your life in the present."

"I don't know how to stop it."

"But you're working on that, right? I mean, you're dealing with it?"

"Yeah. I am. And I feel good about it, though it's slower going than I thought it would by this point. She's worth it though."

"She is," he agrees. "She could be your Naomi and Viola if you let her."

"I think she is," I tell him.

"Then why do you look like I just doused you in gasoline and lit a match?"

"Because I don't know how to let go of that night. Of the things I didn't do. Of the fact that she's dead."

He eyes me for a moment, thinking. "You might never. But that doesn't mean you put your life or hers on hold. That doesn't mean you clump being with Maia together with what happened with Amy."

I hear his words. I know what he's saying. And the biggest part of me wants to say, yes, totally and smile my way through this. But I just can't.

"I'm trying." I clap him on the shoulder and leave the bar. Just like that. I don't even give a shit in this moment.

I just need Maia in my arms while I think.

I just need to think. That's all. In ten fucking years, I haven't done that. I just pushed and brushed it away. Pretended and ignored. And it's catching up with me. Hard. No matter how many times I call Beth. No matter how long our 'therapy' sessions go on for.

And Maia is paying the price.

I make it back to the hotel in record time and into my dark hotel suite, hoping to find her here instead of in her room. She never canceled her rooms for this trip despite my urging her to. She was worried she might need them at certain points and other than that first day in Seattle, I'm pleased to say she hasn't.

Now as I walk through the dark living room, I wonder if tonight was one of those nights for her. But when I turn the corner into the bedroom I catch sight of her beautiful body sleeping face down in my bed. I breathe out the breath I didn't realize I was holding.

"I love you," I whisper.

She doesn't move and I don't know if I'm disappointed by that or not. I continue to watch her, but her breathing is as slow and even as it always is when she's in a deep sleep.

"I'm a fucking mess, Maia. I am. I want to be the man you deserve so much but my mind just keeps dragging back to..." I trail off. She knows where it keeps dragging. "By the time we get home, everything will be different. I promise. Just a little more time, darlin'." I'm doing everything I need to be doing. Everything Beth tells me to. All the therapy I should have done ten years ago.

I feel so certain in this that I take off my clothes and slip into bed behind her. My hands wrap around her, dragging her back until she's flush with me.

"Keith?" she stirs.

I grin into her hair. "Who else were you expecting?"

"Hades," she retorts, and now my grin turns into a smile.

"I'm not stealing you away, Persephone. But if it takes a small trick or two to keep you, I'll resort to just about anything." I roll her in my arms and meet her eyes in the dusky darkness. "How's your headache?" I kiss her forehead.

"Better."

I trail my fingers along her face, staring down at her in awe. And just like that first time I looked into her eyes, my world shifts once more. "I missed you tonight."

Without waiting for her reply, I fuse our lips, parting them and instantly sweeping my tongue with hers. I roll on top of her, cupping her face as I deepen our connection. She moans into me as I lower myself onto her, rolling my hips up into her the way I know she likes.

In a flurry of movement, I remove the thin tee and boy shorts she was wearing, not removing my lips from hers. I can't get enough of the way she tastes. Of the way she smells. Of the way she feels. There is no limit with her. No end.

I had no idea I was capable of being like this with someone, but with Maia, I'm not sure I ever had a choice.

Then I'm inside of her, intertwining our hands and raising them above her head. I stare into her eyes as I move in and out of her, slowly, watching as she feels me fill her up and then slip out of her.

It hits me like a bolt of lightning. She's the first woman I've looked in the eyes while being inside of them since Amy. And something about that realization makes me smile. Makes me think I've got this.

I can love you, Maia. I can.

Sweat collects along my hairline and in between my shoulder blades as her legs wrap around my back and she angles her body up, deepening the way I take her. Over and over, her hands now clenching mine the closer she gets. Harder and harder, she begs me for more.

It's all I want to give her.

My forehead drops, pressing to hers, but our eyes never close. Our gazes never wander. Our hearts beat as one. It's in this moment the difference between making love and fucking truly hits home.

Because that's what I'm doing.

I'm making love to Maia.

She's given me her heart. All of it. So selflessly. So beautifully. Just like her.

I am wild for her.

Captured and enraptured and desperate.

Like Hades was when he tricked Persephone into eating those pomegranate seeds. He would do anything to keep the woman he loved with him, to not lose her, and I am no different. I want to do the same. I want to trick her. To keep her. To own whatever piece of her she'll allow me to have.

To never lose her

Life rule #43: Don't fuck up when fucking up is not an option. You just might lose everything if you do.

29

Maia

"Bug, you need to go to bed for Mommy," Jasper pleads, staring at Adalyn's bright green eyes on his iPhone through FaceTime. "You're so tired. I can see it. And tomorrow Daddy is coming home. We can play all afternoon."

We're in the greenroom, the last show just finished up and you'd think all the guys would want to do is go out and celebrate. But it's a weird vibe tonight. They played an incredible show. I mean, I think it was their best yet. So much energy. The fans were beyond anything they've been thus far on this trip. And now the guys are sweaty, but instead of exalted as they typically are after a show, they're a bit on the unsettled side.

I'm thinking they just want to get home.

"No, Daddy. No. I no wanna to go to bed right now."

Jasper puffs out a breath. I can feel his frustration from here. He hates not being there with his girls. He hates leaving it all for Viola to do.

"Ady, baby doll," Gus jumps in with his signature smile for his little lady, as he calls her. "You gotta go to sleep or tomorrow you won't be able to come over to play with me and Aunt Naomi at the beach."

"Love you, Gus," she says, and I can't stop the smile that cracks on my lips. Neither can Marco and Henry. Adalyn Diamond really is so flipping cute.

"Love you too, doll. Always. But you gotta go to bed. You gotta snuggle Mickey and Minnie for me."

"Can you be a good girl for Mommy?" Jasper cuts in, and I catch Viola's blonde head kissing Adalyn's cheek as she picks her up.

"You wanna snuggle with Daddy?" Viola asks. "I'll bring the phone into bed with you and you can snuggle with Mickey and Daddy."

"Want hugs and snuggles," Adalyn states on a big yawn, and I think I see Jasper's heart both breaking and melting at the same time.

As if proving my point, he rolls his head over his shoulder and finds Marco. "Next time they come with us or I can't do it."

Marco doesn't reply because he knows that's between Jasper and Vi. The tour dates are already set in another six months and tickets have been purchased. The shows won't be canceled. Jasper just has to find a way.

"Where's Keith?" I whisper to Marco while Jasper and Gus sit there on the phone, giving Adalyn air squeezes and kisses through the phone, coaching her to bed. I mean, just watching them has my ovaries sighing with longing. I wish the world could see this side of the band. These hot, sexy, tatted-up rock stars as they lose their mind over the five-year-old little girl. Forget all the other stuff, this is what makes them sexy. Their love and commitment turns me on more than anything else.

"You need to sleep just like Cora is."

Adalyn adamantly shakes her head. "Cora is a baby. I a big girl."

Oh boy.

"I don't know," Marco states, resting his head on my shoulder. He's also feeling the weight, and this is nothing near what their last tour was. That was five months. This was ten days. "He was here a few minutes ago and then it was like he disappeared."

It's true. He came in sweaty and charged with the rest of the guys, but he wasn't smiling the way they were. He grabbed his bottle of Jack Daniels and said he'd be right back. Then Viola called with Adalyn and we all got distracted.

"I'm gonna go look for him." I kiss Marco's head and stand. I don't say goodbye to the guys as they're all still working on Adalyn and I don't want to interrupt. Even Henry's now getting in on the action, strumming a song on Gus's acoustic for Adalyn while Jasper sings it to her. Damn these men.

I meander my way through the tunnels of the arena and stop when I nearly bump into Marsellus. "He's on the stage," he tells me without my even having to ask.

My brows pinch in. "Is he okay?"

Marsellus nods and then shrugs a huge shoulder. "He's just playing guitar and drinking. Seemed fine and the stadium is now empty. The crews aren't set to break down everything until tomorrow morning since we're done with the tour."

"Okay. Thanks." I pat his arm as I continue on, heading for the stage. A bubble of unrest starts to grow in me until it becomes a pang of nausea when I see him. He is just sitting on the stage, his legs dangling off the end, a guitar resting on his thighs that he's strumming away on. It's not a song I know. Not one of Wild Minds'. He takes breaks every couple of seconds to sip on his Jack Daniels.

I can feel the turbulence in his mind from here.

For the longest time, I can't propel myself forward. I can't make myself move from this spot as the silent voyeur.

It feels wrong.

Like I'm intruding on him while he's trying to work through whatever it is he's trying to work through.

But I don't know how to leave either.

Keith made love to me in DC that night. That's what happened. I felt it in his touch. Saw it in his eyes. And then we flew out here and it was non-stop movement since. Radio interviews and a photoshoot and a meet and greet with fans and sound checks and a hundred other things. We didn't have any time to ourselves and when we did, we slept.

And tomorrow we're set to return home. Back to California. Back to me looking for a new place to live even though the thought of not living with him after the month in his house and the ten days on the road with him is crushing. I want to be with Keith more than I want my next breath… and despite how close we've gotten and how much we care for each other, right now, watching him, it doesn't feel like enough.

I don't want bits and pieces of him, I want all of him.

Maybe that's unfair to ask and expect after such a short amount of time together, but I don't think so. I think I deserve that in return when that's exactly what I'm giving out. I'm just not sure that's possible for him.

Something inside of me starts to crack. Starts to crumble.

It's my tough-girl shell. The one I started building when I was just a kid. It saw me through more times than I can count. The one I never wanted to break because I needed it so much.

Movement behind me startles me and I turn to find Gus there with a sheepish expression on his face. "Sorry," he whispers. "I didn't mean to startle you."

I shake my head, letting him know I'm okay. Well, at least from that.

"I didn't even know he plays guitar," I say instead of anything else, turning my focus back to Keith.

"He doesn't often. But yeah, he can. Just like we can play each other's instruments if we had to."

"You can play the drums?"

Gus laughs. "Not well. Bass, yeah. Piano, a bit. Drums, well, let's just say I'm not so great with those."

I grin, thankful that I can still manage it when everything inside of me feels so heavy and dejected. "He's battling a lot of demons."

"Yeah. He is. He's battling that he loves you more than he ever loved her."

"What?" I spin around to face him.

Gus smiles but it's filled with such sadness it quickly slips into a frown. Not a look you see on Gus Diamond often. "He loved Amy. We were all there while they were together, and we were all there after she died. But the last couple of months of her life, she didn't give him much. She couldn't. I think she tried in her limited way and I think Keith hung on because he loved her and didn't know what else to do. He wanted to be her hero. But the truth is there was no saving that girl. That's what he hates. That's what haunts him. Because deep down, he thinks he could have. He blames himself for something there is no blame for. His heart is too big, and when she died, a huge piece of him died right along with her."

Gus reaches out, putting his arm around my shoulder, tucking me into his side. Maybe he can read that I need the comfort or maybe the memories are more than he can bear.

"He lived like that for ten years, Maia. No woman got close. He could barely look at them. No one got in and he never spoke about any of it let alone said Amy's name. Until you came along. You relit his torch, and now he's trying to reconcile all these disjointed pieces he's never allowed himself to acknowledge. He's fighting his guilt and his love for you, and sometimes that takes a man a while to wrap his head around and his heart to fully accept."

I swallow thickly, fighting the lump of emotion clogging my throat, making it nearly impossible to breathe past. "How do you know all this?"

Gus rests his head on top of mine the way I imagine a brother doing with a little sister. "Because I know him. Because I've known him since I was a kid. Because he's my brother and I love him. But most of all, because I've never seen him this way with anyone before. Including Amy. That's what he's battling with. His guilt over that. Not his love or affection for you. If he didn't love you as much as he does, none of this would be as hard for him as it is."

Gus squeezes my shoulder and then walks off. Leaving me here alone to think about all he just said.

The thing is… I believe him.

Sucking in a deep fortifying breath, I let all of that settle in on me. And then I walk out into the dark quiet night, right onto the stage. A place I actually haven't stepped foot on now that I think about it. In all these shows, I haven't come out here, and as I do, I look out to the seats and a rush of nervous adrenaline hits me.

Out of the corner of my eye, I watch as Keith peeks up, finding me though his playing doesn't falter for even a beat.

"I have no idea how you guys come out here and play and talk. No one is even in the stands, but still, this is terrifying. I think I might have stage fright. Who knew?"

"Come here," is his only reply, and the somber edge to his voice has me complying instantly. I sit beside him, matching his position with my legs hanging off the edge that I scissor back and forth, trying to work out some of this excess tumult that's humming through my veins.

Keith swings the guitar up and over his head, bringing it down around me. The strap sits on my shoulder and he takes my hands, positioning them.

"Does this hurt your fingers or arm?" he asks, running his hands over my bad arm.

I shake my head because even if it is a little uncomfortable, I don't want him to stop what he's doing.

He shifts, sliding in behind me with his thighs spread around me, his chest against my back and his hands on mine as he guides my motions. I can smell the Jack Daniels and the sweat from the show clinging to his skin. He smells like hard work and too much pain, and I'm intimately familiar with both of those things. I sink back into him, letting him show me how to play the guitar.

"Here," he whispers in my ear. "Like this." His hands start to move, start to play whatever song he was just strumming. He holds my hands, moving them this way and that, plucking at the strings.

After a minute or so, as the sound comes out all wrong, I let my hands fall away from the instrument, dropping them down beside me.

The vibrations from the guitar funnel through me and my eyes close as my head falls back against him, meeting the crook of his shoulder.

He doesn't sing any words—sometimes there just aren't any words to be sung—but I don't care. The feeling of him playing music against me while holding me on an empty stage is something I never want to forget.

He's poetry and heartache. Beautiful and broken.

And he's leading me down the rabbit hole with him.

No matter how this turns out between us, this is the moment everything changes.

This is a love song and a goodbye song. A hope that tomorrow will be a little brighter, a touch easier. And just like with this song, sometimes there aren't any words to be said.

30

Keith

Time seems to stand still, suspended above my head like an angry cloud as I stare up into the starless night through the windshield. It's going to storm tomorrow. I can feel it in my bones. If it storms, I won't have football practice. That means I can sit inside all day and jam with the guys. She'll come for that. She always does.

She loves to watch us play.

"Keith," she whispers, and I smile, turning to her in the passenger seat. She's so pretty when she smiles it makes my chest flutter.

I haven't seen her smiles in so long. Not the real ones anyway, which is what this is.

Her smiles haven't touched her eyes in months. Maybe longer. I don't even know anymore. But tonight feels different—it fills me with a burgeoning hope.

She had fun at the party. She laughed and danced with her friends.

Maybe she's finally starting to get better?

I reach out and touch her face, the bones sharp yet fragile beneath my fingers. The hollow dip of her cheek is more pronounced than it was even a few weeks ago. I frown a little at that before I can stop it, a swell of anxiety filling up my gut.

She catches my expression and pulls away, staring straight ahead and out the car window. I take her hand instead, bringing it up to my lips, and press a kiss into her palm. I need to fix the mood I just soured and any time I open my mouth lately, I practically cringe, petrified I'm going to make things worse not better.

"Tonight was fun."

She nods, turning back to me, and her face has more of that glow it had before I touched her cheek. "It was. I'm so glad I came out with you."

"School starts in a week. Senior year."

"And you're leaving for California when that's all done."

I chuckle at her excited yet insistent tone. "If the Crimson Tide and my father don't get their hands on me first."

She shakes her head, her smile light and playful. "No way. You're meant for the stage, Keith Dawson. Bright lights and drumsticks."

"And you'll be there front row."

"No matter what, I'm forever and always your biggest fan."

I stare into her eyes and kiss her palm again. Knowing she loves it when I do that.

"You should get in before your mama comes out here and tans my hide for keeping you out late," I tell her though I hate the idea of her going inside and our perfect night ending.

White teeth sparkle as her smile widens, her pale blue eyes glittering against the sliver of moonlight that somehow manages to seep into the car. "She's asleep. Both of my parents are."

I laugh, bouncing my eyebrows suggestively. "Are you inviting me in then with you, babe?"

Her smile falters. "Not tonight."

There's something in her voice that tears at me a little, and I can't understand what it is. Did I say something wrong? She hasn't let me touch her in so long, and all I want to do is touch her. Show her how much I love her. Always.

None of that other stuff matters to me because I'm here with her to the end.

"Goodnight, Keith. I love you."

31

I open my mouth to say it back, staring into her eyes that are suddenly brown and not blue. Amy has blue eyes. Not brown.

"I love you," she repeats, and my voice lodges in my throat. I tell her I love her back. That's what I did. Why can't I say it?

Then she's gone. Like floating mist, coating me in its sickly dew, stinking of death and blood. No. *NO!* I run through the room and all the lights are on. My eyes blink against the harshness as I call out her name. "Maia!"

Then my stomach plummets.

No. Amy. It's supposed to be Amy. Not Maia.

But something inside me knows this time is different.

This time it's Maia.

I sprint for the bathroom, only I'm hardly moving. My legs are slow, heavy, some unseen force holding me in place, and I can't get to her. Panic tainted adrenaline coasts through my veins, making my heart race like it never has before.

I need to get to her. Not again. Please, not again. Not Maia too!

A gasp. Was that me? No. I know it wasn't.

"Maia!" I scream, already knowing she won't answer me. I reach the bathroom door, slamming it open against the wall with a loud *smack. Smack. Smack.*

What is that?

Blood. There's so much blood. It's everywhere. All over her bathroom sink. All over the floor. Dripping down the side of the tub. The water is red. It's so red, and I fall to my knees, a savage wail ripping past my tormented lungs out into the night.

"Keith."

"Not tonight. Not you."

"Keith!" Another *smack,* and I bolt upright, sweat clinging to my face and body, my breathing ragged and harsh without showing any signs of slowing. Where am I? I look around, seeing nothing but a sea of white. Not red.

It was a dream.

Motherfucker, that felt so real. So. Fucking. Real.

So real that the visions of it are still stuck in my head, behind my eyes. They're all I can see. All I can feel.

But it wasn't Amy, I was seeing dead in that tub, it was Maia. It wasn't Amy's last gasp I heard; it was Maia's. It wasn't Amy who told me she loved me. It. Was. Maia.

"Keith. Slow your breathing. You're hyperventilating. It was a dream. It was just a dream. You're okay." She presses her hands to my face, trying to calm me, and I swat them away.

I'm not okay. I am anything but okay in this moment.

"Your blood," I rasp past my ravaged lungs. It was everywhere. Her blood. Maia's blood. *No*. I can't… I can't breathe. Why can't I breathe? I stagger out of bed, my eyes wild as I stare down at my hands void of blood, and then the scene around me. It's the hotel suite in Dallas. It's Maia standing on the opposite side of the bed, her expression distraught, her eyes, dark and wide, her body clutching the sheet over her bare chest.

She looks just as shaken as I feel.

I can practically still feel her blood on my hands.

"Keith. Are you okay?"

My body convulses. Retches. Sick. Nothing comes up.

I can't find the light amongst this darkness. I want to laugh at that question. I'm so not okay there isn't even an intelligible response. "I have to go."

I can't fucking breathe!

"Not you too! Not your blood too."

"What?" she gasps. She doesn't understand. "Wait. Talk to me. You were having a nightmare."

"No. I can't look at you. I can't fucking look at you!" I bellow.

I can't do it. Doesn't she get it? I can't fucking look at her right now because two seconds ago she was dead in a motherfucking bathtub. She was gasping out her last breath. She was covered in blood I could not stop.

And I was too late.

I'm always too late and I can never save her.

"I can't do it anymore!" I cry. I watch as she flinches. I watch as she takes a scared step back.

What the fuck am I doing?

I don't even know. I have no control right now. None. "I'm sorry. I have to go. I can't be here with you right now."

I scrub my hands up and down my face, but it does nothing to clear this. I somehow find my pants and the first shirt I come across, but I still can't look at her. I don't want to see the fear in her eyes. I don't want to see the blood on her body.

I don't want to lose you, Maia, and now that's all I can think about.

The door slams behind me before I even realize I've opened it and am standing in the hallway. I glance left and right, but it's so dark and long and desolate. I hear the latch of the door behind me start to move. I still can't look at her right now. I can't look into her brown eyes after what I just saw. After what I just experienced.

My phone. How am I clutching my phone?

Somehow, I am, and I dial Beth's number. She's a psychologist. A doctor. The doors begin to close on the elevator, and I don't remember pressing the button or stepping on.

"Keith?" Beth answers into the phone, her voice dripping with sleep and worry. "Are you okay?"

"No, I'm not," I tell her just as the doors begin to close and Maia's face falls into my line of sight just before they seal shut. But her expression? It was stricken. It was heartbroken. I ran out on her when we promised we would never run out on each other. I have no idea what I even said to her. I sag back against the wall behind me. "I think I told her I can't look at her."

Shit. Her eyes. Her haunted, beautiful eyes as they met mine that last second before the doors closed.

"I'm not understanding."

"I'm going to lose her, Beth. How do I not lose her when I'm losing myself?"

I hear her moving around in the background. I hear her telling Jacob, her husband who is on the phone. Then I hear her say, "You're not losing yourself, Keith. You're in the process of finding yourself. It's an ugly thing to do. Most often, we don't like what we find when we search."

"I saw her tonight, Beth. I had the worst nightmare I've ever had. Maia was Amy and she was dead. It was her fucking blood everywhere. Her body lifeless in the tub."

I sink down to the floor of the elevator, my heart barely beating yet not able to stop pounding in my chest.

"She's going to leave me and I don't blame her for it."

"Keith, tell me about Maia in the bathtub."

I shake my head. I shake it so hard.

"It was her. She was bleeding. I heard her gasp. I heard myself scream."

"And when you woke up, who was there?"

My eyes cinch so tight I can't imagine light ever finding its way back in. "She was. Maia"

"And tomorrow? Who will be there?"

"Maia."

"Is Maia, Amy?"

"No," I respond automatically as the elevator hits the first floor and I burst forth, taking to the streets, not caring where my path leads me. "She's not. Why didn't Amy have Maia's heart? Have her strength? Why was Amy's world so hard for her?"

"I can't answer that and likely, Amy couldn't either. She suffered. You both did, but her more than you. Imagine how hard and painful her world was. No one could help her. No one could reach her. But you did. You made her time so much better. You couldn't save her, but you made what time she had the best of it. And no matter what, her taking her life was not. Your. Fault. Nothing that happened that night was your fault. You tried to save her the best you could when she was impossible to save. Tell me that."

"Beth..."

"Tell me, Keith," she demands in a tone not to be ignored.

"I did everything I could to save her when she could not be saved." I collapse to the ground. I don't even know where I am. The air is mild, and the ground is hard and my heart *hurts*. "I couldn't save her."

"No. You could not."

My eyes blink open. Staring. Unseeing. But seeing everything I never saw before.

"You do not need to save Maia. She is not Amy. She will not be in that bathtub. You're not going to lose her the way you lost Amy. You need to find faith in that, Keith."

I nod. I know this. Maia is not Amy, and Amy was not Maia. "The dream felt so real."

"And you might have others. Grief is a multifaceted thing. It is not stationary. It moves. It flows. But you have all the tools you need to combat it. You're ready. You deserve love. You deserve Maia."

I do. I deserve love and I deserve Maia.

"You need to talk to her about your dream. About what happened. About all the work we've been doing these weeks because if she's not a part of it, then she can't help you the way you need her to."

"I ran out on her," I manage on a strained whisper. How will she ever forgive me after that? After the things I said to her?

"Then you might have to chase after her, so she knows you'll never run from her again."

32

Maia

My mind races, flying through ugly thoughts and even uglier directions. The things he said. I don't know how to make sense of the things he said. He was panicked. He wasn't himself. He had just woken from a nightmare.

I know all of this.

But for some reason, I find no solace in that.

It's impossible to be there for someone when they won't open up to you. He told me what happened to Amy and that he needed time to work everything through but that was the last we spoke about it. He ran out of here and called someone immediately to talk to them.

Someone who isn't me.

How can one man give so much and so little at the same time?

What if your past is just too much to overcome, no matter how hard you try? No matter who loves you in the present? I don't know what to do. I don't know how to reach him. I don't know what to say or how to comfort him.

I just know that I love him and I'm afraid of losing him.

I also appreciate that I might have already.

I can't lie on this bed any longer waiting for him to return, so I finish packing up the remainder of my stuff and then take a shower. I get myself dressed and ready though it's little more than three a.m. and our flight doesn't leave until ten.

Then I sit. And then I stand. And then I pace.

I hold my phone like it's a lifeline and I debate texting and calling him so many times I'm shocked my phone doesn't reach out and bitch slap me. It's been more than an hour since he left and I… I don't know what to do.

"Tell me what to do," I demand of my phone who just stares blankly back at me. It's like it's mocking me now and I think I'm going just a touch crazy. And when my phone lights up like a lighthouse in the stormy night sky, I jump only to realize it's not Keith calling me.

It's a number I don't recognize from an area code I wish I didn't.

I don't want to answer but I'm so flipping angry and frustrated and scared and upset because it's not Keith calling that maybe taking out my ire on my father isn't the worst of ideas. "Didn't I tell you never to call me again," I spew into the phone as I answer, only to be greeted with silence on the other end. I pull the phone away and stare at it. Yup, whoever called is still on the line. Suddenly I'm considering that this may not be my father calling from a different number. And at this hour. "Hello?"

"Um. Yes. Hello. Is this Maia Angelo?"

Oops. Not my father. "Yes. Sorry, I thought you were someone else."

"Maia, this is Travis Gold. I'm not sure if you remember me or not. We lived in the same park growing up."

I blink into the darkness of the room. "You were three trailers down and across the way. You graduated the year I entered high school."

"Yes," he says, sounding so relieved that I remember him when all

I can think is, why is he calling me at three-thirty in the morning. "I apologize for calling you at this hour. Maia," he says my name in such a way that has me sitting down, my hand over my heart that's suddenly pounding in my chest. "I'm not sure if you're aware of this, but I am the deputy police detective for Brookside. I don't know how to do this other than to just say it. Maia, I'm sorry to inform you that your father is dead."

I feel like I should gasp. Cover my mouth in shocked horror. That's what they always do in my films. Old and new, that's what they do. But I'm not doing that. I'm not in shocked horror. Strangely I feel numb.

"What happened?"

He clears his throat. "Your father was shot and then his trailer that was set on fire. Your neighbors called it in immediately, and the fire was put out before the entire trailer burned."

"I'm sorry, did you say he was *shot*?"

"Yes."

"When?"

"The night before last. We had some difficulty obtaining your phone number."

"Do you know who did it?"

"Giovanni Carvalo was arrested almost immediately after, but I cannot speak to the specifics of an open investigation."

Carvalo?!

I fall back onto the bed, throwing my arm over my forehead, my mind spinning. "You're telling me Giovanni *Carvalo* is in custody and my father is dead?"

"Yes, Maia. That's exactly what I'm telling you. I'm so sorry for your loss. There's a lot to explain, none of which I can do over the phone." He clears his throat again. "We're actually going to need you to fly here if you're able. Part of this case has fallen under the jurisdiction of the FBI—"

"The FBI?" I bark incredulously.

"Yes. The FBI." I stare sightlessly up at the ceiling, unable to wrap my head around what he's telling me.

"My father?" Really? The FBI?

"Are you able to come home?"

Home? Is that a joke? I have no home. At least that's how it feels right now.

"The FBI would like to meet with you and ask some questions. I'm sure you'd also like to start making arrangements for your father."

Ummm... yeah, not so much. Not sure if that makes me a bad person or not, but no, I honestly don't want to make arrangements for my father. And truth be told, I don't want to meet with the FBI either. I swore I would never step foot back in Brookside. That my father was no longer my father. That I put that life behind me even if I was stuck paying down those debts.

Carvalo is in jail. My father is dead. Shot.

"Maia?" he says, pulling me out of my thoughts.

"Yes." I pull my phone away and see it's still so early it's almost comical. "I'll catch the first flight up and be there as soon as I can be. I'm in Texas at the moment and I have no idea how long it will take me."

"That's fine. The FBI as well as our local department are still investigating."

"But Carvalo is in prison?" I press.

"He's in our local jail. He's been remanded without bail. Is this a good number to text you where to go or would you prefer I email you?"

"No. This number is perfect. I'll be there as soon as I can."

I disconnect the call and just... let the revaluation sink inwardly for a few moments. I don't know how to react to this. How to feel. I don't feel much of anything still and I can't decide if I'm grateful for that or not. This day is already so fucked up, and it isn't even dawn yet.

I dial Keith before I can think twice about it, and his phone instantly goes to voicemail.

"Dammit Keith. I need you right now. How do I leave when you're scaring the shit out of me? When I don't even know where you are, and your phone is off. And what does it mean for us if I leave before you come back?"

If he's coming back.

I inwardly shake myself at that. No. He'll come back. He just might not want to look at me when he does. I wonder if that was it. His breaking point. If him running like that when we said no running is our end.

I puff out a breath as an errant tear streaks down my face. I quickly brush it away, forcing myself to push through this. Now is not the time to fall apart. Still, my heart festers like a diseased wound. For him and for me.

Maybe going to Brookside is what I need. A little distance. A little space to think.

I've been so consumed with him and this tour for the last ten days. Hell, for the month prior to that too. He's taken up so much space in my life, in my head, in my heart.

I'm starting to think that's a dangerous thing to have allowed him to do.

I call him again and when his voicemail instantly asks me to leave a message, I do. "Hi. It's me. I have no idea where you are and I'm worried. I need to talk to you. About what happened earlier. About a call I got after. I need to go and you're not here and I don't know... I love you. I'm just going to say it so you know. I won't be here when you return but it's not—" The phone gives me an annoyingly loud beep in my ear, signaling the end of my allotted message.

Fine. I said what I needed to say. What he does with it is up to him.

I pull myself up and off the bed. I'm glad I showered. I'm glad I'm dressed. I don't know if I'm glad my father is dead. It makes me feel like shit to feel some relief in his death, but it's there. He was a horrible man who never loved me. Who made sure I knew that too.

"I'm an E True Hollywood Story cliché!"

I grab the handle of my suitcase and leave Keith's suite behind. I may or may not bury my face in his pillow, inhaling his scent one last time but I'm in a zero-judgment zone, so I don't even second guess it or give it an afterthought.

My knuckles rap on Henry's door three times before he opens it up. His light hair is mussed, and his eyes are dark with sleep. He's also not wearing any clothing. Like not even boxers. I immediately spin around so I can't look any longer at his... whoa! I wasn't expecting...

"You're naked!" *And huge!*

"Shit," he hisses, and then I hear a bunch of noise and even an ow or two, and then he's back. "I'm dressed." I turn back around, only his version of dressed means boxer briefs. I'll take what I can get. "What's up? What are you doing here at this hour?"

That's when I break down into tears. For the first time since Keith woke from his nightmare. Since I got that call. My face falls into Henry's shoulder and I let go. I shake and sob into him, not even caring if my tears are drenching him and possibly mixing with snot.

I'm a mess.

I'm scared.

I'm so heartbroken I don't even know what to do.

Now I have to go home and deal with the FBI and my father being dead. I'm alone in this. As always, but after finally feeling like I had someone helping to hold my burden up, his absence feels especially crushing.

"What's going on?" Henry soothes, running his hand down my hair.

"Keith woke up from a terrible nightmare. I think he was having a panic attack. He kept talking about my blood and that he couldn't look at me. He left, Henry. He just got dressed, grabbed his phone, got in the elevator, and left. I have no idea where he is now. I tried to call him, but his phone went straight to voicemail. Then, a kid I grew up with who is now a detective calls to tell me my father was murdered by the asshole criminal I've spent the last year plus paying off. I have to go home to speak to the FBI."

"Are you kidding me with this?" His arms wrap tightly around my back, rubbing up and down to comfort me further, and I'm so grateful for him right now.

"Do I sound like I am?" I half-sob, only to sniffle in and shudder. "Sorry. I'm just… I'm worried about him. I have to go to the airport. I have to go, and I can't find him, Henry. Can you find him and make sure he gets home okay? I don't think he wants to see me anymore. He said that. He can't look at me. Being with me is obviously too much for him and…" I can't do this anymore. "I need to take care of myself."

"Maia," Henry garbles out, his voice stricken. "Give me ten minutes, and I'll come with you. You shouldn't be alone."

Except being alone is all I've ever been.

"No. Thank you. I need to do this myself. Just find him for me, okay? I'll… I don't know. I'll send for my things. I'm not even sure. I'll be in touch." I pull away and plant a chaste kiss on his cheek. Then I turn and leave. I ignore his yelling protests because I know if I listen, I'll easily cave. And I can't cave right now. I can't.

Keith doesn't even have his phone on because he doesn't want to talk to me.

"I can't look at you. I can't fucking look at you!" That was shortly followed up by, *"I can't do it anymore!"* Got it. Message received.

Part of me knew it would end like this anyway.

"Airport please," I tell the cab driver as I slip inside. If Carvalo is in jail, then I don't have to pay him. If that portion of my debt is gone then I can manage the rest. I just hope the guys let me continue to work for them, even if it means I'll still have to see Keith. He told me my job was not related to anything that happens or doesn't happen between us, and since I need this job as much as I do, I'm going to trust in that.

At least until I can find something else.

My hand and arm are all better now. My options wide open.

"What airline, miss?" the driver asks as more tears fall down my cheeks.

"Whichever one will get me out of here the fastest," I tell him, closing my eyes and letting the car drive me away, knowing that I left my heart behind in that hotel suite.

It's funny or maybe not… I thought I understood what it felt like to get your heart trampled on and your soul decimated by someone you love. I was wrong. This feels nothing like that. This feels like devastation. So much more than heartbreak. This level of pain makes me wonder if I'll ever be right again.

33

Keith

"ARE YOU OKAY?" Henry asks as I step off the elevator, heading for my hotel suite. It's somewhere near five in the morning, I think. After talking to Beth, I turned off my phone and sat on a bench and watched the impending sunrise begin to lighten the sky. Just thinking. Just figuring everything out for myself. I couldn't return until I was in the right headspace. Until I could fix everything I did and said and be ready to fully, truly commit to Maia.

Now all I can think about is getting to her.

"Huh?" I ask, wondering why Henry is sitting outside my door in nothing but a pair of shorts.

"Are. You. Okay?" he repeats sharply, enunciating each word as he rises off the floor.

Am I? "Yeah. I think I am." Or at least I will be. Once I get my girl back in my arms and tell her everything.

His fist lands in my face. Right between my cheekbone and my left eye. I stagger back, smacking into the opposite wall behind me. Blinding white-hot pain shoots through my entire face to the point where I swear my eye is about to burst.

"What the fuck?" I bellow, covering my face with my hand and already feeling how hot and tender the skin is beneath my touch.

"I warned you, motherfucker," he barks, standing over me since now since my knees are bent and my body is sagging against the wall, his eyes cold and menacing. "I warned you if you broke her heart, I'd break your face. And now you know I meant it."

Break her heart? No. Did I do that? "Where is she?" I push out, forcing myself back up to my feet and ignoring the throbbing of my eye and cheek.

"Gone. You, stupid piece of shit. Gone. She cried on my shoulder and told me what you said to her. She didn't deserve that, Keith. None of that."

"I know. I... I didn't know what I was saying!" I yell, and not even defensively. Because he's right and I was wrong. I freaked and I said shit and I ran. I just assumed she'd know. That she'd see how panicked I was and... understand.

She understands so much about me without my even having to say anything. Always has.

But it seems I overestimated that in the worst possible way.

Jesus. Poor Maia. What did I do to her?

"Well, you did it this time," Henry says as if answering my unspoken thoughts. "Did you know her father was murdered by the guy she's been paying off?"

The fuck? "What? When?"

He throws his hands up, looking like he wants to hit me again. "Must have happened after you ran out on her. She's on her way back to Virginia to meet with the FBI and guess who's not with her holding her goddamn hand and supporting her?"

Me. I'm not with her because I wasn't here. Because she had to deal with my breakdown, with me yelling horrible things I didn't mean at her, and then she got a call like that.

I deserved that punch and then a whole lot more.

"You should have cleared your head from Amy before you even touched Maia. Isn't that what we told you to do? Isn't that what you said you were going to do?"

I nod, staring down at the carpet of the hallway because he's right. I should have done exactly that. I told the guys I would. I tried to resist her and failed miserably because I just couldn't stay away from her. I loved Maia hard, but also not the way I should have. I didn't give myself over to her the way she did with me.

Something I intend to remedy.

I look up and meet Henry's furious green eyes. "I love her, man. I love Maia more than I love anyone or anything. I fucked up, but I'm going to fix it."

"Then you better get your ass on a plane and I mean right now."

Get my ass on a plane. I can do that. Easy shit right there.

I reach out and hug my friend, my brother. "Thanks, Henry. For loving her. For loving me. For punching some sense into me. That was your one freebie, asshole. Don't try it again." I slap him on the back and then I spin right around and head for the elevator. "Grab my shit and bring it home for me, would ya?" I call out as I step back onto the elevator. "I won't be home again until Maia is with me," I murmur to myself as the doors close.

I hop in the first cab I come across and speed off into the growing dawn.

If you've never been to the airport in the Dallas-Fort Worth area, let me tell you, it's fucking huge. And when the taxi driver asks me which airline, I have no clue. I don't know who flies up to that part of the country. I'd take the jet, but it's already set and scheduled to take everyone back to California today and no way I can ask them to reroute that for me.

I tell the cab driver to drop me at American Airlines, since that's the first one I see, and then I practically sprint inside, rushing up to the counter. There's a decent line in the economy area but first class is empty so that's where I go.

But as I approach, I catch the woman eyeing me like she's a hot beat from calling security. It's only now I realize the mess I must be. I woke up after the nightmare of my life, threw on some random clothes and rushed out into the middle of the night. Add to that, I very likely have a nice new shiner curtsey of Henry.

"May I help you?" she asks like that's the absolute last thing she wants to do.

"Yes, I need a one-way ticket to..." Shit. What's the damn name of her town? "Brookside, Virginia."

She purses her lips and types a bunch of crap into her computer and then spews out the most convoluted travel itinerary imaginable.

"You're telling me it will take me three planes to get there?"

"Yes, sir. I am. The best way to get there is to fly into Charlotte then catch a connection to Roanoke regional airport and then we can get you into one of the smaller, local airports or you can rent a car in Roanoke and drive."

"And that won't get me into Brookside until twelve hours from now?" I ask, beyond incredulous.

"That's correct. Would you like me to book these flights for you?" She smiles that customer service smile that doesn't reach her eyes. No, those are filled with a silent plea for me to say no thanks, I've changed my mind.

"What about a private plane? Can I rent a private plane?"

SHE STARES AT ME DISMISSIVELY, tilting her head and everything. Likely because I look like a bum who got dragged out of bed and proceeded to get the shit kicked out of him.

I PULL out my wallet and drop my black Amex on the counter. "How about now? Can we see about that private plane now?"

She glances down at the card. At the name printed on the card. And then back up at me, recognition now brightening her features.

"We don't do private planes here through American Airlines, Mr. Dawson, but um..." She starts blushing like... well, like Maia after I say something dirty to her. "Let me just make a couple of phone calls for you. I'd be happy to assist you with whatever your travel needs are."

"Thank you so much..." I lean forward, checking out her name tag. "Carla. I truly appreciate any help you can give me."

More blushing and a little simper, and then she gets to work on renting me a private plane. I don't even pay attention when she tells me how much it's going to cost.

I don't care.

I'm jumping out of my skin to get to Maia and any time in between then and now is too long.

I slip my phone out for the first time since I ran out of the hotel and find a missed call and a voice message from Maia. With trembling fingers, I hit play, bringing the phone up to my ear. Her sweet voice comes through and I just about die hearing how sad she sounds.

"Hi. It's me. I have no idea where you are and I'm worried. I need to talk to you. About what happened earlier. About a call I got after. I need to go and you're not here and I don't know... I love you. I'm just going to say it so you know. I won't be here when you return but it's not—"

My eyes shut as my breath stalls in my chest.

She said it.

Consciously said it. Even after the way I treated her, she still said it. I dial her number immediately, but it goes to voicemail. She's likely on the airplane now, flying up to Virginia. Alone.

"Excuse me, Carla?" She pauses what she's doing and meets my eyes. "Will you do me a huge favor?"

34

Maia

THE PLANE FINALLY STOPS, having pulled up to the gate after what feels like the longest flight of my life. Then again, this is my first time flying coach. My first time flying commercial. My first time sitting in the middle seat in between two people, one who smelled like an ashtray coated in body odor and the other who kept taking over the armrest while invading my side of the damn line!

All this was super fun considering I got a shitty night's sleep, had the man I love walk out the door on me, and found out my father was murdered. And to add insult to injury, our plane sat on the runway for like an extra forty minutes for no reason I could discern.

I think it's safe to say I'm officially in a crap mood.

The thought of getting on another plane to fly into a regional airport only to then drive several hours has me near the breaking point of tears. I have no way of getting in touch with these FBI people, only the local police.

At this rate, I won't be anywhere near Brookside before dark.

And then what?

Where do I go?

We weren't exactly bathed in hotels or even motels when I left town. I'm alone. I have no idea where I should go. And ALL I want to do is curl up under the covers and have a good old-fashioned breakdown for the ages.

But that's not an option, which means I need to get my shit together and find a way through.

Like I always do.

Like I always have.

Some of my best attributes are my resiliency and ability to adapt. "I've got this," I mumble under my breath.

"What was that?" The guy next to me asks, an unlit cigarette already dangling from his lips.

"Nothing. But why aren't they opening the doors to let us out?"

Just as the words pass my lips, the flight attendant gets on the loudspeaker. "Attention ladies and gentlemen. We want to thank you all again for flying with us. We apologize for the delay, but everything seems to be in order now and we will open the doors momentarily."

"About time," the guy grouses, checking his watch. "I've got a connection to make."

Me too, I think, but don't say. I've got three hours before that plane takes off. Then a four-hour drive.

I shuffle my way off the plane, turning my phone back on only to find a text from Henry, asking if I'm okay and if there's anything he can do. One from Marco saying that Henry updated them and for me to take as much time as I need and for me to promise to call when I get where I need to be so he knows I'm safe. Even Jasper and Gus chimed in on our group chat.

But nothing from Keith.

I told him I loved him, albeit in a voice message, but still. I said the words.

And nothing.

I can't focus on that right now. If I do, the pain will rip me apart and I'll break down for sure.

I make my way off the plane and through the gate over to the bathroom. The line takes forever, as it always freaking does for the ladies' room, and when I catch sight of my reflection in the mirror as I'm washing my hands, I nearly gasp aloud.

I'm a disaster.

Dark circles under haunted dark eyes. Broken frown. Matted, unkempt hair.

I shouldn't care, but I do. I don't want to stroll back into my hometown looking like this. I want my chin up and my eyes bright and my heart strong.

I don't feel any of that seeing myself like this.

I quickly apply some Chapstick, since that's all I've got in my purse, and run some water through my hair before throwing it up into a ponytail, doing my best to tame it into submission.

"You look lovely, deary," the elderly woman at the sink beside me says, smiling kindly at my reflection in the mirror.

"Thank you. Now I just have to get my insides to match my outsides," I jest only we both know I'm not joking.

Her expression grows somber and serious. "You look like you can use some friendly words of wisdom."

"Boy, can I ever."

"The best piece of advice my grandmother ever gave was for me to direct anyone who dared to make me feel less than I am to go fuck themselves. That goes for both lover and beast, if you know what I'm saying."

I choke on my own saliva. "Uh."

She grins cheekily. "Clearly you're not accustomed to old Jewish women, but yes, those were her words—well, in Yiddish—but the sentiment is the same, and that woman lived through the Holocaust."

"Thank you," I manage once I regain control of my voice and my breathing. "I will absolutely remember that."

She pats my arm. "Good. Because that's how we stay strong. If it's the lover, he or she should never be the one you have to tell that to. If it's the beast, those words are the difference between it owning your life and your choices and you owning them."

In the blink of an eye, she's gone, well, walking slowly with a haunch out of the bathroom, but in a way that suggests she didn't just rock my world while becoming my hero.

Because she's right.

In so many ways.

And I know exactly who deserves to hear those words from me. Because I will no longer allow the beast to own me.

Steeling my spine, I tug my suitcase behind me as I leave the bathroom, checking the signs for the way to my next terminal. "I've got a much better way to get you where you need to go, sweet darlin'," a smooth whiskey baritone with a hint of a southern accent says directly behind me.

So close his breath brushes the exposed skin of my neck leaving chills in its wake.

"Oh yeah?" I question, my eyes closing as my bottom lip starts to tremble. "And what makes you think I want anything you've got to offer me?"

Strong arms wrap around my waist, drawing me into his even stronger chest, and I don't have anything left in me to fight where he's concerned.

He's here.

He found me.

Considering I didn't even know what flight I was getting on until I got to the airport, he had to do a bit of sleuthing to get here.

His lips meet my neck and for a moment, he just breathes me in. My heart races in my chest and the urge to cry grows so strong now I have to bite my lip to stop it. "Don't do this unless you mean it," I beg. I can't do it anymore. I tried, but my feelings run too deep to play games. To only get half of his love and heart because the rest belongs to someone else.

He spins me around in his arms and crushes his lips to mine. Right here in the middle of the airport with hundreds of people walking around us. With kids screaming and adults talking on their phones.

Keith Dawson is kissing me like he means it.

His hands cup my face, his forehead pressing to mine. "I'm so sorry about this morning, Maia. Sorry for whatever it is I said to you and the way I ran out on you when I swore we wouldn't do that. I'm sorry I wasn't there when you got that call and had to go through all that alone. I never wanted to hurt you, and that's what I'm sorry for the most. I had the worst nightmare I've ever had. It shook me to the marrow of my bones, and I couldn't look at you because the dream was about you. I've been talking to Beth—"

"Your sister?"

He nods against me, pecking my lips. "Yeah. She's a psychologist. I knew I needed help. That I couldn't do it all on my own. But I didn't want to start therapy with someone I didn't know. Someone who didn't know me or what happened. It's probably not the best way to do it, using family, but she's helped me so much these past few weeks. Then I had that dream this morning. And as terrifying as it was, it was also my breaking point. I need you and I can't lose you and I very nearly did anyway. My worst nightmare realized."

I lean in and kiss him again. "You didn't lose me. I knew what happened. I was hurt and scared, but I understood. Well, as best I could."

He shakes his head. "That's not good enough for you. I asked you to be patient with me when we were back in Seattle. But I don't want you to be patient anymore."

"No?" I ask, my voice wobbly as the first of the tears start to fall.

"No. Because I love you, Maia Alice Angelo," he whispers into my lips, his hands cupping my cheeks and wiping my tears. "I think I fell in love with you that first night you crashed into my car. The second you opened those big beautiful brown eyes of yours and looked right into mine. Since that moment, I've been hooked on you. Just you. Only you. I just got stuck for a bit, but I'm not stuck anymore. I want this with you. All of it. Because you have all of me."

"I do?"

He smiles, the blue in his eyes the lightest I've seen it since I met him. Well, except for that shiner. I reach up, my fingers skimming along the swollen, purple tissue.

"Yeah, darlin'." He takes my hand from his face and places it over his heart. "This only beats for you. You and no one else. And for the first time, I'm okay with that. I waited ten years for you to come along and give me this second chance at my life. Now all I want to do is spend it with you."

"I love you too," I tell him, and the most stunning smile erupts across his face, his eyes dancing over me. Strong lips rain down on mine, kissing me hungrily. Like any air or space between us is just too much for him to bear. He kisses me until I'm breathless. Until my knees are weak and my heart is weightless in my chest.

Then he intertwines our fingers with one hand, takes my suitcase in the other, and leads me in the complete opposite direction of my next flight.

"Where are we going?"

"You would not believe the shit it was going to take for me to get to you. I had missed the flight you came in on, so it was going to take me two layovers and then a long ass drive." He shrugs, giving me a sideways glance and a smirk to match the cockiness I see in his eyes. "So I rented a plane."

I roll my eyes at him. "Why am I not surprised. How much did that set you back?"

"Whatever it was, it was worth it. You were about to wait three more hours in this airport to take your puddle jumper into a regional airport and then drive for hours. Nope. Not happening, darlin'. We're going to land where they set us down and get ourselves a place to stay for the night. After that, we'll rent a car and drive wherever the hell we have to drive together. After all that is done, I'm taking you back home, and by home, in case this isn't clear, is my house in California."

"We're going to talk about that, Keith."

He winks at me. "Oh goodie. I feel a fight brewing. Have I ever told you how hot you look when we fight?"

"We will fight about it. Just not today. I'm too drained to fight."

He releases my hand and throws his arm over my shoulder, tugging me into his side. He kisses my temple. "I'm sorry. A lot of that is on me. I'm also sorry about your father."

"I need to get more information, but is it wrong if I'm not? He called me the other day when we were in DC. I spoke to him. Carvalo had come out to California to look for me. I have no idea why, but it was pretty clear on the phone my father was helping him do it. Tomorrow, before we meet with the FBI, I want to go to the jail and talk to Carvalo."

Keith shakes his head. "Can you even do that?"

"I don't see why not."

"I don't want you anywhere near him."

"He's in jail, Keith. He can't do much. But I need to tell him that regardless of what happens with him, I'm done. I will not pay him another cent. And I need to look him in the eyes when I do that."

35

M

aia

When we pull up to the local jail. It's not much of a building. Not like what I imagine the big state prison is like. Other than the curled barbed wire sitting atop the wrought-iron fence, you'd never know this place houses criminals. I realize I have no idea what I'm doing. "What am I doing?"

Keith puts the rental in park and clasps my hand. "You're taking back your life from those who tried to own it and use it against you."

I nod. That sounds pretty good. The taking back my life part, not the second half.

"I don't even know if I can see him."

Keith hitches up an unconcerned shoulder. "Only one way to find out. Whether you can or not, you're done with him. This is your past and from here on out, it's nothing but future for your darlin'."

I like the sound of that too, so I lean across the console and kiss him.

The courage of my convictions is sitting square on my shoulders and I will not go in there afraid. I have my mini panic attack in the car instead. Keith stares at me with a bit of a grin and slightly wide eyes as I scream and pull on my hair.

When I finally stop, his grin widens. "I must really love you. That was something to witness."

"You're mocking me?"

He smiles from ear to ear. "I'm mocking you. But I also punctuated that with I love you, so I think that absolves me for my sin."

"Whatever. I can't focus on you. Let's do this before I either change my mind or throw up."

We don't get very far before we're stopped by a guard who asks our names and requests our IDs. "I'm sorry, sir, but you're not on the approved list. You'll have to wait out here," the guard explains to Keith.

I blink, stupefied. "Does that mean *I'm* on the approved list?"

"Yes, ma'am. You're able to go in."

I can feel Keith's troubled gaze touching my face but before I can talk myself out of it, I take a step forward only to have Keith stop me. I turn back to him, meeting his eyes with a forced smile. "I can do it."

He nods slowly on a heavy swallow. This is hard for him. My caveman doesn't like this one bit. I stand on my toes and give him a chaste kiss, hoping that helps him.

It doesn't do much, but he does let me go.

And as I enter the jail, go through the metal detector and let them search my purse, my breath is stuck somewhere between my heart and my head, unable to be expelled.

"You'll have ten minutes. Visiting hours are almost over for the day."

I can't speak, so I just follow after the man leading me into a long row of booths separated with thick glass. They even have those phones you use in movies. For some reason that makes me want to laugh. It also relaxes me some as I sit in my instructed seat and wait for Giovanni Carvalo to come.

Not even two minutes later, the door opens and Giovanni, dressed in the orange jumpsuit I expected walks in and smiles the biggest goddamn smug smile I've ever seen on anyone. He picks up the phone, dark eyes piercing and assessing. "You came. I knew you would."

For some reason, him expecting me aggravates me more than it should.

"Why did you want to see me? Why did you come out to California?"

I don't ask why he killed my father. It's honestly not really important, and I doubt he'll tell me anything of worth considering our conversation is no doubt being recorded.

"I wanted to see you. Did you truly believe I would let you continue to pay such a small sum indefinitely with all that you owed? I only allowed it because I admired your fire. You were not afraid to speak to me the way so many others are. But I was also ready to collect what was originally owed to me. I was tired of waiting. I won't be in here long," he says confidently. "Soon enough you will pay me the *full* price of the contract." His dark eyes take in as much of me as they can.

Such a sick, twisted man. I could look at him and tell him all the different things I'm thinking. Things like I would rather have died then become one of his harem. Things like it wasn't my debt and I didn't owe him shit. Things like he agreed to the term of our arrangement.

But instead, I look at the man in prison orange, stuck behind glass, walls, and bars, and lean forward as close as I can go without touching the nasty glass. "By killing my father, you nullified the terms of the contract." His eyes go wide as I expected they would. "You told me if I didn't pay then you'd kill him. That it was the money, my body —which I had refused to give you—or my father's life. Well, you killed him, which means the contract is now paid in full. I don't care if you ever get out of here. But if you do and try to come after me, I will unleash the full wrath of that fire you liked so much. And let me tell you, I'll make sure you burn."

With that, I set the phone back in its place. I get up and I walk out, not even bothering to look back to see if he's watching me or trying to yell for me.

The moment I reach the outside and the gate closes, I blow out the breath I didn't realize I was holding. Keith wraps his arms around me, folding me into his side as we head back to the car. Time to go meet with the FBI.

"How was it?"

"Fun. Seriously, I had a fantastic time. If I was ever considering committing a major crime before, I've since changed my mind."

"Good to know. Bailing you out would be bad for my image."

I smack his chest and he kisses my cheek. "Nearly done. Nearly done."

The police station in the town I grew up in is small and old. Like everything else here. Bleach and two-day-old coffee permeate the air. The combination making my already nervous stomach roll and twist in protest. There are two agents with the FBI waiting on me, and thankfully they don't waste any time with pleasantries as they guide us into a room.

"Ms. Angelo, I'm Agent Nobel and this is Agent Thomas." He points to the guy beside him. "We're grateful you were able to make the trip in."

"I'll be honest with you, I'm surprised you're here," I tell them.

Agent Nobel sits up a little straighter. "I can't go into all the specifics, but we've had an agent inside Carvalo's organization for about eight months now. We were building quite the case against him. We knew of your situation. We knew about the deal he made with your father. And when he went to California to look for you himself, we thought you might be a weakness for him. That's when we dug deeper into your father. Carvalo's activity with him had been increasing, especially since Carvalo seemed adamant in finding you and had yet to be successful since you moved from your apartment and left your previous jobs. Our undercover agent approached your father a week before his death, and your father readily agreed to help us in exchange for immunity. Your father had been involved in selling drugs as well as acting as a physical presence for Carvalo."

I stare at the agents, floored by this. "My father was selling drugs?" They both nod, eyes trained on me. "And by physical presence you mean..."

"A button. An enforcer. Someone who was sent in when a customer wasn't paying up or acting the way Carvalo wanted them to."

I think I'm going to be sick.

"Did he kill people?"

"Not that we're aware of."

Keith takes my hand under the table, holding it tightly. It grounds me when I feel anything but.

"And the debt my father accrued in my name?"

"Was only the tip of your father's connection with him. Your father was working for him to maintain his rather large addiction to pills. Oxycodone, in particular. We believe Carvalo discovered your father was up charging his customers for pills because he was skimming such a large quantity off the top for his own personal use. Carvalo shot your father during what your neighbors describe as a heated argument, and then he proceeded to set fire to the trailer to cover any evidence. He's being held without bail and given the strength of our case, he won't be on the streets again."

"He disagrees with that. He told me he would be out soon."

"He doesn't know we're involved yet. He still believes these are local and state charges only because at this time they are. We are set to drop federal charges tomorrow."

"How do you know it was him who did all this?"

"Your neighbors called it in while the fight was still going on. More calls came in after the sound of gunfire. There is video of Carvalo fleeing the scene and then the inside of the trailer on fire seconds after."

I sag back in my chair, my mind reeling as I try to think all this through. "So what do you need from me?"

"We'd like you to explain the exact nature of your dealings with Giovanni Carvalo. We'd like any physical evidence you have, things like voice messages, texts, letters, etc. And if necessary, testify against him."

I spend the next two hours detailing everything I know for the FBI. Giving them everything I have, which really isn't much. I think I have one or two texts from him with mild threats about payment. Most of our interactions were in person, so therefore it's simply going based on my word.

They promise to be in touch when, if, they need anything else from me. Then Keith and I leave. It feels strangely too simple given the conversation we just had.

The weight of a thousand suns is suddenly off my shoulders. I already told Keith I don't want to see the trailer I grew up in. The place where my father was murdered. It's a crime scene anyway, but even if there was something that survived the fire, it doesn't belong to me.

The FBI still has my father's body as they're conducting an autopsy. I was told once they release it, I can make final arrangements. But for now, I don't have to think about it. I'm still not sure how to process everything that happened.

How my father died. The things he was doing.

As far as I'm concerned, I've been an orphan for a very long time. I just want to get the hell out of here. Keith does too, I think. It's been a very long couple of days.

And even though I'm with Keith, I still feel lost. Disorganized. Like I don't have a place I truly belong and it's unsettling. Do I go home with him? Just like that? Is that even the right move for me to make? I don't know.

"I don't know what I'm doing."

"You don't have to."

I shake my head no, because he's wrong on that. I do have to know. I need certainty. I need tangible hard facts. I need reality, not the fairy tale where I fall in love with a rich rock star. It feels real and it doesn't and I...

"I love you, Maia. I can tell you don't have faith in much right now, but I hope you have faith in that. In us."

I glance over to him, staring contemplatively at his profile as he drives us the hell out of here. "I love you too." I guess that's something to build on.

"Move in with me," he asks, reaching over and toying with my fingers. "Or better yet, just don't move out."

I pivot to face him.

"What?" he asks, fighting the grin curling up his lips and failing. "Why is your face scrunched up in disgust like that?"

"Now?" I bark incredulously. "You ask me this now? After I left a jail and just spent two hours speaking to the damn FBI about a mob boss I was entangled with and my father's murder?"

"Right. Bad timing?"

I snort out a laugh. "Ya think?"

He shakes his head, undeterred. "You're stalling. It has nothing to do with the timing."

I bluster out a breath. "We just got together. Don't you think that's moving a bit fast?"

"No. We've been living together for six weeks already."

"Keith."

"Maia," he parrots, mocking my tone. "I don't want you to come over to my place and I go over to yours. I don't want to lug shit back and forth. I want to wake up with you in the morning and make you breakfast. I want you to come with me when I go to the studio and I want to be able to go to my music room and play while you're doing your work in the office next door. Then, when we're done with our work, I want dinner in front of a crappy old movie—"

"A what?" I interrupt sharply.

He smirks. "An epic cinematic classic. Isn't that what I said?"

"Um. No."

His fingers caress the bones of my hand, his eyes on the road when I know they want to be on mine. Still, his smile is spreading by the minute. His conviction making me love him that much more.

"I want you to beat me at chess, even when I cheat. I want to kiss you whenever I feel like it. Whenever I walk into a room and see you there. I want your girly crap all over *our* bathroom and your sexy panties in *our* dryer. Every time we go out, I want you on my arm while I tell the world you're mine because you can never ever be anyone else's. I want to buy you a million things you'll yell at me for because you don't like me makin' a fuss over you when that's *all* I want to do. And then, after I've done all those things—all those things that you secretly love though you're outwardly yelling at me for—then I want to spend the whole night, every night, making love to you. I don't want to date you, Maia. I want a life with you. What do you say?"

36

Maia
Four months later

"I'M GOING to be honest with you, I'm totally freaking out right now."

My eyes are glued to the front of the room where Blind Tears, where freaking Gabriel Rose, is singing a special song he wrote just for Gus and Naomi. I mean, what the fuck? How is this reality? How am I here, watching Blind Tears play at a wedding?

"Naomi's dad before he died was very close with Gabriel. Lyric and Naomi practically grew up together."

All I can do is shake my head in disbelief.

"Why do you react like this for every other musician you meet, but you never did with me?"

I grin as I let Keith start to lead me again on the dance floor of the huge mansion Gus rented out for his wedding. "Why do you keep asking me that?"

"Maia—"

"What can I say? You're just not as cool as Gabriel Rose is. You're all, I bang sticks on a drum and think I'm hot shit," I say, trying to imitate his caveman voice.

I get a smack on the ass for that and it makes me laugh.

He wouldn't continuously ask that question if he didn't like punishing me for my answers. And I wouldn't continue to indulge him if I didn't like his punishments. It's what you call a win-win in the relationship world.

A world I'm learning all about.

I told Keith no to moving in with him for real. Of course, I did. Because that's how Keith and I work. I tell him no and he fights me and eventually I relent because I don't really want to say no. I always want to say yes to him.

We returned to California and I never left. I moved into his room and took over the empty closet in there since he had two walk-in closets and that was that.

Well, sort of.

I was actually more shaken up than I thought I would be over what went down with my father and Carvalo and the FBI. Giovanni Carvalo took a plea deal. He was looking at life in prison with some pretty strong evidence against him. He settled for twenty-five to life, but only after he gave the FBI what they were looking for.

I don't have to testify. I don't have to see him again.

He's in prison. That's all I care about.

My debt with him is done.

I had my father buried beside my mother and anything that was left of the trailer, taken care of. I didn't have a funeral for him. I just couldn't do it. I couldn't stand there and think of anything good to say about him. I couldn't mourn his loss and part of me is troubled by that.

But the other part of me accepts that sometimes the family you're born into isn't the family you're meant to end up with.

The family you find, the family you create for yourself, is where you'll find a love that never ends.

And for the first time in my life, I feel like I've done exactly that.

With a little something extra.

Which brings me back to Keith and this wedding reception.

Keith continues to sway us on the dance floor as he holds me close, his hands pressed into my back, his face stuck in my neck where he continues to breathe me in like I am his air and suffuse him with life. "I love you," he whispers.

"How much?" I ask in return as my heart starts to flutter and my belly churns, my nerves a hot riot.

I feel his smile against me when he says, "More than anything."

Lord, I hope so.

I pull back and meet his blue eyes, my hands gliding up and into the back of his hair. "I did a thing."

"What thing?"

"I enrolled at UCLA starting in the fall."

His face lights up. Poor bastard. He has no idea what's headed his way.

"That's incredible. I'm so happy for you. Did you decide on a major?"

I did. I'm excited about it too. "I'm not sure I'm going to be able to start in the fall though. I might have to put it off another semester." His eyebrows pinch in at my cryptic words and solemn expression. "Keith..." Deep breath. "I'm pregnant."

He studies me for the longest of moments. His eyes bouncing back and forth between mine as if he's trying to see through my words and into my soul. "How? When?"

I inhale a sharp breath, releasing it slowly. "I missed my period last week and didn't think too much about it. I've been irregular before. That's the when. The how is we're not exactly all that careful."

He can't argue that. We aren't. Sometimes he wakes me up in the middle of the night and things happen. Or he pounces when we're on the couch watching something. It happens a lot in a lot of random places. He usually pulls out.

Not always though.

We've been tested, but I didn't do well on the pill when I started it and I was in between appointments, looking to find a better alternative. Oops.

"You took a test?"

I nod. "I took a test this morning."

"And it was positive?"

I frown. Obviously, it was positive since I just told him I was pregnant. "Yeah."

"Like, you're one hundred percent sure?"

"Keith! Yes. I mean, I need to see my doctor at some point, but yeah. I'm fucking pregnant asshole. This is not how you're supposed to respond when the woman you claim to love tells you she's knocked up with your spawn."

The biggest, most breathtaking smile breaks free, igniting his entire face in a dazzling radiance. "How do you want me to respond? Like this?" He drops to his knees, wraps his hands around my back and plants the sweetest most tender kiss on my lower belly. Then he looks up at me. "How's that? Does that work?"

I shake my head, my teeth sinking into my bottom lip.

"No? Not good enough?"

That's not at all what I meant. What he just did was absolutely perfect. Because I'll be honest, I'm scared out of my mind. I'm twenty. Which is insanely young to have a baby. Keith and I haven't even been together all that long. We're just getting settled together. We're just finding our rhythm.

And now there's a new life coming into the mix.

But somehow, when I look into his eyes, all my fears and worries and uncertainty dissolve into nothing.

He stands up, cupping my face in his hands and kisses me like he's never kissed me before.

Not ever.

This is a kiss swimming in pure unrestrained joy. I can feel it pouring off him in waves. He's radiating with it. A stunning pulsing vibration that's engulfing his entire body and seeping effortlessly into mine.

"A baby," he hums reverently, almost as if he's testing the word on his tongue. "It'll play drums for sure. Oh, if it's a girl, can we name her Watts?"

I laugh as the first of my tears helplessly falls. "You're not mad?"

"Mad?" He half-laughs, his tone delightfully incredulous. "How can I be mad? First of all, I got you pregnant, so getting mad at something I was intimately a part of is just ludicrous. Second of all—"

"Oh my god," Viola gasps, interrupting Keith as we simultaneously turn in her direction. "She said yes? I thought you weren't going to ask her until tonight."

"Huh?" I push out, a crease forming between my eyebrows. "Ask me what?"

Keith groans with a mirthless half-laugh, his head dropping back for a second. "For Christ's sake, Vi. I haven't asked yet. That's not what this was because yeah, I was gonna wait until tonight."

Vi's smile plummets, her eyes stunned wide. She covers her mouth with her hand as her cheeks turn bright pink.

Jasper is cracking up, trying so hard to hide it and failing.

"Shit. I just totally ruined everything." Vi drops her head onto Jasper's chest. "Holy crap, I can't believe I did that. Forget I said anything," she cries, her voice now muffled by Jasper's tuxedo jacket as she buries her face in him as deep as she can go. "Keith. I... you were on your knees and then she was crying, and you were kissing her and..."

Jasper kisses the top of Vi's head, encircling his arms around his wife. "Come on, dream girl. I think we need to leave Keith and Maia alone. I'm guessing you could use another glass of champagne about now. Or maybe something stronger."

"I'm so sorry," Vi calls out, twisting in Jasper's chest to meet Keith's eyes. She looks stricken.

I turn back to Keith, tilting my head in question. "Were you going to ask me to marry you?"

He meets my eyes, his tone steady and his gaze firm, giving nothing away. "Yeah. I was."

"Keith! We've only been together like a hot second. I'm only twenty. Don't you think that's jumping the gun just a bit?"

He drops back down onto one knee, planting another kiss right over my lower belly while pulling a small black box from his pocket.

His eyes lock on mine. "No. I don't think I'm jumping the gun at all. Life rule #1: When you meet the one you're meant to spend the rest of your life with, you do the smart thing and put a ring on it. You don't wait around for the perfect time because there is no such thing. I want to marry you, Maia, because I love you. I want to marry you because there is no other woman in the world for me than you. And there never will be, my sweet darlin'. Marry me?"

"Life rule #1?"

"You're always life rule #1."

He opens the box, revealing a large round diamond on a platinum band. It's simple and stunning and so perfect.

"I... um... yes!" I laugh. "Yes, I'll marry you."

In the next second, Keith lifts me up into his arms and opens my mouth with his, slipping his tongue inside so he can taste me. "I'm your baby daddy," he whispers into me, setting me back on my feet and dropping his forehead to mine.

I burst out laughing. "You most definitely are my baby daddy."

"And you're going to be my wife."

"No longer your Pandora."

He shakes his head, his lips pressing into mine because he can't stop kissing me. He can't stop touching me. He can't stop smiling. "Maia, my goddess, we're our own love story. No myth, we're the real thing. And whatever our future story is meant to be, we'll write it together."

EPILOGUE

Henry - Three years earlier
- unedited and subject to change

BLUE. If I had to guess, that would be the color I would pick. They're not iridescent enough to be green and so far from dark there is no way those beautiful irises are brown. The heavy house bass coats me in its never-ending torrent of sound, quickening my pulse and heating my blood.

Silently, I live for this.

The freedom of the room. The darkness of the shrouding anonymity. The static zing of sexual energy as it swells without restraint, filling the warm sticky air with a spicy flavor and erotic texture. Down here is my escape. And not once have my bandmates, my lifelong best friends, ever questioned my flying solo down here. They might not understand it, but they do understand my need for it.

Even if they don't, and never will, know the reason behind it.

But this woman... the one I'm staring at... the one I've been staring at since I step into this enormous, gyrating body-filled room five minutes ago and instantly spotted her... she ignites my blood. Makes me hard.

And best of all... she's alone.

Like me.

Gorgeous. That's not even a question. But she's more than that.

She has an aura.

Something unique, exotic, and captivating as hell. I can't even place what it is about her, but I haven't been able to look away for a second.

I waited. I watched. She's a slave to the music as it flows through her bones, calling her muscles into action. Arms above her head, hips swiveling, eyes now closed. She's not here for the men who have come up to her, demanding her attention and body.

And there have been plenty.

They see what I see. However, where they all failed, I already know I'll succeed.

She's here for me tonight whether she knows it or not.

I don't question my motives as I slide through the menage of bodies.

I don't hesitate as I lower my mouth to her ear and whisper, "Want to dance with a stranger in the dark?"

Her eyes flash open, ready to explain in explicit detail all the ways I can fuck off since my hands are now on her waist and my face is right before hers. Instead, her pithy retort dies on her tongue, her eyes filling with recognition as those deep blues cast about my face.

"How did you know?" she replies playfully, her body inadvertently drawing closer.

The high of the show we played tonight hasn't abated. It still hums along my skin and spears my lips with its smile. And right now, I'm thankful for that. Otherwise, the smile she's reflecting—the one I've seen on a thousand other women when they look into my eyes and see a world-famous rock star—would seriously turn me off.

Still, the disappointment that she clearly recognizes me doesn't stop me from snaking my arms deeper around her back, guiding her gorgeous body into mine. Something foreign and heavy floods my chest when she's finally seated against me, staring up into my eyes. I lick my suddenly dry lips, trying to ignore whatever this is, desperate for this brand-new sensation to remain unnamed.

I start to move us, grinding into her in sync with the beat of the music.

She sucks in a gasp of air, those heavy-lidded eyes growing wide with shock. Her head frantically snaps about, her eyes scanning like she's afraid we're going to be caught by someone.

"Do you have a boyfriend?" I ask, because I don't do that. I don't share. Never and not even close.

"N-no," she stutters and then shivers, reacting to the glide my hands up her back and into her long, brown mane of hair. "It's just that... I never thought... you... this. You're touching me and looking at me and..." A self-deprecating laugh chokes past her full lips. "Never mind. I'm gonna shut up now."

"Do you wish I wasn't touching you?" My fingers descend, dragging down her neck and along the smooth, exposed skin of her arms that feels almost electric beneath my touch. "Looking at you?" My face drifts closer, our eyes locked and only inches away. My breath catches in a way it never has before. *Goddamn...*

She licks her lips, her eyes bouncing back and forth between mine. Like she's trying to read me. See what my intentions are with her. I don't hide my want and when she realizes it, her eyes come to life with a heat that makes my cock twitch.

"I like you touching me. I love the way you're looking at me. I don't want you to stop. I guess I just assumed you'd be upstairs. Not down here with everyone else. With me."

She's referring to the private floor, and all I can do is shake my head. The women on the private floor do nothing for me. They're all the same. Not an ounce of real outside or in between any of them. They're agenda driven. They see money and fame and zero in.

I can't stand any of them. Not even for a night.

"Are you down here alone?" she pushes, peeking around me once more.

"Looking for someone else?"

Her eyes snap back to mine. "Not when you're the one I've always wanted. I'm just making sure we won't be interrupted by anyone we wouldn't want to find us."

"We won't be."

"Well then," she murmurs, her smile growing. "In that case, sure. I'd love a dance in the dark with a stranger like you." She snakes her arms around my neck, her fingers boldly coiling into the strands at my nape. Yet her eyes are guarded, her movements hesitant, almost as if she's waiting for me to push her away. "Is it off-putting if I say I've always dreamt of this but never in a million years imaged it would happen?"

"With me?"

"Yes," she laughs the word like I'm crazy for asking. "With you, Henry Gauthier. Though I think you already knew that."

"You're beautiful. Any man would be lucky to dance with you. Many before me have tried."

Her arms fly up above her head, her head tilting back as her eyes fall closed, moving with me to the heavy house beat. I lied just now when I told her she's beautiful. She's so much more than that. And looking at her like this, in my arms, she's robbing me of my ability to breathe. The temptation to throw caution to the wind and kiss her here, run my hands all over her body, reach up under her short dress and make her come with hundreds of people around us is so compelling I have to bite my lip to staunch the tenacious need.

"Other men have tried. But I haven't wanted any of them."

"Why's that?"

An impish grin curls up the corners of her lips. "Because they're not you, are they?"

Her body plunges backward, forcing me to dip her, trusting I won't drop her. Fingertips scrape the floor before she rights herself, her eyes glowing, her cheeks bright, and her lips parted with her breathy laugh.

"That was fun. Do you have moves, Henry? So far I'm doing all the leading."

"*I* approached *you*."

"That doesn't make you special."

Fuck. I like this one.

The nerves she had when I first approached her are gone. Now she's a siren. A sexy, confident force of nature. Wild, sinful trouble I want to drown myself in.

"It makes me the one you said yes to."

But the more I study her face, the more something familiar niggles at the darkest recesses of my mind. I can't place it. I feel like I know her somehow, yet I'm nearly positive I've never met this woman before.

Or maybe it's just that I'm more drawn to her than any woman I've encountered lately.

She hikes up on her toes, her body seductively pressing into mine. The scent of her skin and hair hit me hard. Something light and soft and irresistible. Something that makes me want to lick every fucking inch of her.

"What exactly do you think I'm saying yes to?" she whispers in my ear.

"Me. Now. Here. Tonight."

Her breath hitches as my tongue sneaks out, swiping at the line of her jaw. My hand glides up her thigh, my thumb dipping into the softness of her inner thigh. Those pretty blues grow impossibly dark with a hunger that matches my own.

"Tell me no right now or this is happening."

"I want this to happen. Now. Here. Tonight."

"That's all it will be," I warn.

"I know." I don't miss the touch of sadness in her tone. The hint of longing. But her gaze is unwavering as it holds mine.

"You sure?" I ask, studying her.

"Yes. I understand why it's only tonight, and even though one night isn't my style; I've wanted you for too long to ever say no."

Taking her hand, I intertwine our fingers, dragging her through the crowded club to the dark alcove I already scoped out. I never kiss women in public. Sure as hell never touch them in a way I wouldn't be okay with being photographed.

I spin her behind the black curtain that separates the main part of the club from an emergency exit, press her into the wall, cup her face in my hands, and crash my lips to hers. She responds instantly, her hands gripping my triceps, hauling me infinitely closer. Demanding full contact. Our lips move frantically, our tongues seeking, playing, dancing.

She tastes so fucking good; I can't help but angle my mouth, deepening the connection and groaning into her.

She's small. Petite with similar curves, just the way I like 'em.

My hands roam from her face, capturing her breasts over the thin material of her dress before quickly tugging it down. She gasps and as my lips flees hers, stealing one taut nipple in my mouth and sucking it in. Her hands fist my hair, her neck arching against the wall as I devour her breasts while skimming a hand up her inner thigh.

"Yes," she hisses on a throaty moan, half her sounds being absorbed into the chaos of the club just steps away. Normally, I feed off of this. Allow the impersonal nature of it to be my guiding force. But something about this woman makes me want to hear all her sounds. See every sweet inch of her flesh. Watch every ounce of pleasure I'm about to give her.

"What is it about you?" I murmur into her, knowing she can't hear me. The question is for myself because from the second I saw her, instinctively, I knew it was something. Some bewitching magic she exudes that floated through the club and snaked directly into me. It's holding on tight. Making me greedy and ravenous. Making me want to break all my rules and keep her just a bit longer.

My fingers find the smooth satin of her panties, gliding back and forth over the thin strip covering her pussy, gathering moisture. She's so wet and she feels and tastes so good my head is spinning.

I release her nipple, working my way back up her neck with deep, open-mouthed kisses until I find her lips again. Pushing aside the satin, I explore her, rubbing her clit and toying with her opening. She bucks against me, grinding, searching for more. Her breathy pants and delirious moans float into my mouth, forcing themselves inside me as I strain to hear each and every note she produces.

"Trouble," I growl into her, gnashing me teeth into her bottom lip and biting down just enough to let her know I mean it. "You're fucking trouble."

"Good. I never wanted to be easy for you. I always wanted to twist you up as badly as you always have me."

I shake my head at that, not quite understanding her meaning. More hints of recognition spark to life but are just as quickly snuffed as I push two fingers inside her. She rips at my shirt. Trying desperately to undo it. I use my other hand to stop her.

I can't go upstairs after this missing buttons.

"I want to see you. I want to touch you," she begs.

"Not here. Not enough time."

She thunders in frustration, digging her nails into the back of my head and dragging them down my neck, marking me no doubt. "I hate you," she seethes, emotion clouding her voice as I continue to work her.

For some inexplicable reason, I understand her sentiment. I hate her too. I hate all that she's doing to my insides. All that I've never had to fight before that I'm suddenly fighting here, now, with her. I'm a hot second from saying, let's go to my hotel room instead.

But I can't. Not with a girl like this.

The kind of girl who wants me for more than I can give her.

I'd blame it on the Rockstar. On the lifestyle. Only that couldn't be farther from the truth or reality of it. And where there will never be a future for any woman in my life, it's best to not to live beyond the present.

"Let's see how much you hate me. Unzip me."

She shoves me back, my hand slipping out from between her legs, and just when I think she's about to end it, her blue eyes hold mine as she goes for my zipper. My fingers find my mouth, craving a taste of her. I haven't gone down on a girl in forever, and right now, I'm burning up with the desire of it. With the desire for her.

"You feel it too, don't you?" she asks, toying with me. Like she knows just the idea of *feeling* something with her will piss me off. Newsflash: Already there.

I nod my head in agreement, words clogging up the back of my throat.

She smiles at that like an evil temptress.

With my dick in my hand, I roll the condom on, lining myself up to her opening. She hitches her leg up and over my hip before leaning back into the wall, helping our angle. My thumb coasts along her bottom lip. "You're so beautiful," I tell her.

"I bet you say that to all the girls," she muses, a light smile on her lips, her eyes dark with lust.

I blink at her, momentarily stunned. "Actually, I don't. I never say that." Then I slide inside her, burying myself to the hilt. Her back arches and she lets out a loud cry. My mouth takes her, stifling the sound. "People will hear and think I'm killing you."

She laughs. "I think you just did. Jesus. Size thirteen shoe really does correlate."

I hold myself still. Giving her a second to get used to me, sure, but how does she know my shoe size? That's hardly common knowledge. Only the guys and—

"Move. Please, I need you to move."

I do. I clear all thoughts from my head and start to pound into her. One hand on her hip, the other tangled in her long, thick, brown hair as I take her over and over again. Her hands are all over me. In my hair. Digging down my shirt. Scraping along the fabric over my chest, abs and arms. Her eyes are closed, her head is back, her mouth is open, and I'm looking at her. I'm watching her.

Yet another thing I never do. What the motherfuck is going on?

"Harder. Yes. Holy hell, Henry, just like that."

Her eyes flash open, locking on mine. That in combination with my name on her lips does something to me. It drives me into her harder. Deeper. I press against her and I consume her mouth. Our bodies move in sync, our rhythm increasing and holy hell it's perfect. Just so Ungodly perfect. I feel her body start to convulse around me, her moans turning into cries as she writhes in pleasure, coming without restraint. I follow her over the edge, the air sucked from my lungs as I grunt and groan and growl, losing my mind as flashes of light dance behind my eyes.

My forehead lands against hers, our breathing ragged.

She laughs as she lowers her body back to the ground. I only now realize I had lifted her up. "Well, that was unexpected."

It absolutely was. In the best of ways. I stare down at her through a fan of lashes, wanting to lick at her smile. Maybe I can stretch this a bit longer? Break my rules just this once? All I know is the idea of walking away from her and never seeing her again feels—

"I certainly didn't think that would happen when I came here tonight to meet up with you guys."

That pulls me up short. "You came here tonight to meet up with us?"

Her eyebrows furrow as she adjusts her clothes, putting everything back in place. "Of course, I was. Why else would I be here?"

Dread pools low in my gut as horrible pieces of the puzzle start coming together. I tie off the condom, sticking it my pocket and tucking my dick back inside my pants, zipping up. "What's your name?"

"My name?" she parrots, pain flashing across her face quickly followed by anger. "You don't know who I am? Are you fucking kidding me?" She stares at me, waiting for me to laugh or tell her I'm joking. She puffs out an incredulous burst of air. "You really didn't know who I was, did you?" She scrubs her hands up and down her face. "I can't believe this. I thought..." A humorless laugh barks past her lips. "How stupid. I thought after all these years you finally wanted me back," she murmurs that last part, more to herself than to me, but I hear it all the same.

"I'm sorry..."

Her hands fall and her eyes—narrowed slits of fury—ensnare mine. "Eden Dawson. You know, your *bandmate's*, your *best friend's* little sister. You remember me now, right?" she spits, vitriol dripping from each syllable. "You've only known me my entire fucking life."

"Eden." I choke on her name. Keith's baby sister. How could I have...

Guilt and remorse clog my throat. I reach for her and she shoves me away.

"Don't touch me. You're such a piece of shit. How could you not have known?!"

"God, Eden. I'm so, so sorry. I didn't realize. I haven't seen you in a few years and you look so different. Nothing like Keith or your other sisters. I swear to God, I didn't know. I would never have touched you if—"

She smacks my face. Hard. Flashes of pain prickle across my cheek, a trail of burning heat closely follows. I stare into her blue eyes, not even the slightest bit stunned. I deserve so much worse than that. She's right. I am a piece of shit. The absolute worst sort.

Because I didn't recognize her. In fairness, I made a point never to notice Eden Dawson or any of Keith's sisters. The last time I saw her, she was sixteen and looked like she was twelve. She was not this woman standing before me.

Christ. Her brother will murder me where I stand. Deservedly so.

"Just go."

I shake my head, trying to touch her again only to drop my hand at the last second. I don't deserve her touch or forgiveness. Still... "I can't. Eden—"

"Don't say my name. You bastard, just go. Now I really do hate you."

I stand immobile.

"Go," she screams, shoving at me with all her might. This time I listen. With my heart in my throat and my stomach churning with every nasty emotion I can throw at it, I walk away. I just fucked my best friend's baby sister in the middle of a club like any other meaningless woman. Only she's not meaningless and not because she's Keith's sister.

She was more before I even knew her name. Knew who she was.

For that reason alone, I should be relieved she slapped me while spitting venom in my face. I should be...

Something inside of me stirs uncomfortably.

I need to fix this.

Need to see her again.

Only...I have no idea how I'm going to do that. Not when her brother will kill me if he ever finds out what I just did to his baby sister.

THE END

Want more of Henry and Eden's STEAMY forbidden romance? Download Promise to Love You now! You'll get plenty more of all the Wild Love characters including more of Keith and Maia's story!

Thank you so much for taking the time to read Love to Tempt You. Keep reading for my end of book note! And if you haven't read this series from the beginning, you can start with Jasper and Viola's story, Love to Hate Her

ALSO BY J. SAMAN

Wild Love Series:

Love to Hate Her

Hate to Love Him

Crazy to Love You

Love to Tempt You

Reckless to Love You (prequel)

The Edge Series:

The Edge of Temptation

The Edge of Forever

The Edge of Reason

Start Again Series:

Start Again

Start Over

Start With Me

Las Vegas Sin Series:

Touching Sin

Catching Sin

Darkest Sin

Standalones:

Just One Kiss

Love Rewritten

Beautiful Potential

Forward - FREE

END OF BOOK NOTE

If you've read me before this is the *unedited* part where I break down the story a bit. Or at least my thinking on it. When I started this series with Love to Hate Her, I knew I was going to write Gus's story because come on, I had to.

But a reader/blogger had asked if I was going to write Keith's and Henry's stories as well. My immediate reaction was no. And not because I didn't want them to have one, but because I had other things in mind I wanted to work on. Let's say you, the readers, quickly changed my mind and here we are.

So Keith, I knew he was going to be different. An alpha with a heart of gold. But also a man who struggles because of it. I know I say this about all my heroes, but I fell so fucking hard for this man. I just couldn't get enough of him. We all need a Keith in our lives.

Amy… I did not simply write her for drama or shock value. When I was in high school, I lost a friend to suicide. It was unexpected and heartbreaking and though my experience was very different from Keith's, my friend's death has clung to me all these years later.

With suicide, we focus on the victim. On what they're going through because it's heartbreaking and tragic. Depression, hopelessness, they're diseases, often without any cure. But as someone who cared deeply for someone who took their own life, I know what the aftermath looks like too. Losing someone you love is devastating regardless of the reason they're gone. But suicide does a little something extra to people. It leaves a different imprint. Trust me, I've unfortunately lost other people to other things as well. You wear the grief of suicide differently.

So that's Keith. And that's his story. And because he was so tormented, I gave him Maia. Maia who has a fire and spirit like no other female heroine I've written before. Did she make some mistakes? Don't we all. But her grit and determination are what I loved most about her. It's why I couldn't really break them apart in the end. Their journey was too hard won, especially for Keith.

I labored over her father and Carvalo. I debated having more drama with that, but in the end, I just didn't think it was necessary. Keith and Maia's journey was the story. Her father and Carvalo were background music and that's where I wanted them to stay.

Okay, enough rambling. I want to thank my amazing betas Danielle and Patricia who helped to make this story as incredible as it is (at least I think it is). Thank you to my husband, my girls, and my family. You are my eternal support system and I love you fiercely and endlessly. And to you, the readers. You are who I do this for. You are my reason for it all.

XO

Julie (J. Saman)

Milton Keynes UK
Ingram Content Group UK Ltd.
UKHW010057060224
437294UK00008B/443